Relic

Relic

The Quest for the Golden Shrine

Tom Egeland
Translated by Tara Chace

JOHN MURRAY

First published in Great Britain in 2010 by John Murray (Publishers)
An Hachette UK Company

First published in paperback in 2011

2

This translation has been published with the financial support of NORLA

A CIP catalogue record for this title is available from the British Library

ISBN 978-0-7195-2173-7
Ebook ISBN 978-1-84854-392-8

Typeset in Monotype Sabon by Servis Filmsetting Ltd,
Stockport, Cheshire

Printed and bound by Clays Ltd, St Ives plc

John Murray policy is to use papers that are natural, renewable and recyclable
products and made from wood grown in sustainable forests. The logging and
manufacturing processes are expected to conform to the environmental regulations
of the country of origin.

John Murray (Publishers)
338 Euston Road
London NW1 3BH

www.johnmurray.co.uk

Contents

'These are the secret words, which the living Jesus spoke
and which Didymus Judas Thomas wrote down.
Jesus said: He who shall find the interpretation of these
   words
shall not taste of death. He who seeks, let him not cease
seeking until he finds; and when he finds
he will be troubled, and when he is troubled
he will be amazed, and he will reign over the All.'

FROM THE GOSPEL OF THOMAS, THE 'FIFTH GOSPEL',
WHICH WAS OMITTED FROM THE NEW TESTAMENT.
THE MANUSCRIPT WAS DISCOVERED IN EGYPT IN 1945.

Oslo

Værne Monastery
(Johannite Monastery, ca.1188–1532)

Oxford

London

Paris

Rennes-le-
Château

Rome

Messina

Gozo

—MALTA

Tripoli

Black Sea

CRETE

RHODES

CYPRUS

Acre
*(Crusader
fortress, fell
in 1291)*

Jerusalem

Qumran
*(Dead Sea
scrolls
1947–62)*

Masada
(Jewish fortress)

Nag Hammadi
(Gospel of Thomas 1945)

The rain started in the afternoon the day Grethe died.

I can just make out a bit of the fjord, glistening and cold like a river, through the beads of water and naked branches. For hours at a time I sit here watching the droplets trickle down the windowpane, thinking and writing. The squalls form a sinuous lattice over the fogged-up windowpane.

I have pushed my desk right up to the window; this way I can write and look out at the same time. Clumps of rotten kelp throb in the low tide. The waves lap idly against the smooth, rocky shoreline. A tern screeches half-heartedly, weary of life.

I can see the gnarled branches of the oak out in the yard, wet and black with a few leaves still clinging to them as if they haven't quite realised that autumn will be coming for them soon.

It was summer when my father passed away. He was thirty-one years, four months, two weeks and three days old. I heard the scream.

Most people think it was an accident.

For a while after his death, my mother sealed herself in a silent cocoon of grief. Then, in a metamorphosis that still stings to this day, she started drinking and neglecting me. People talked. Our little side street had eyes and ears. People gave me sympathetic looks at the grocery store. The neighbourhood kids made up awful songs about her; they would draw pictures of her naked in chalk on the asphalt playground at school.

Some memories stick with you.

*

Why am I not surprised that they were here while I was away? They searched room by room and removed any trace of her. It's as if she had never existed.

But they weren't infallible. They forgot to take the four silk ropes dangling limply from the bedposts.

I'm going to write in my journal about everything that happened to me this summer.

If it weren't for the scabs and burning itch, I might have thought this past summer had been one great, lucid delusion – that I had spent it in my room at the clinic, in a straitjacket, doped up on Valium. Maybe I'll never understand any of what happened. It doesn't matter. What little I have understood, or not understood, will do me for a long time.

My journal is a thick, leather-bound book with my name printed in gold at the bottom right-hand corner of the front cover: Bjørn Beltø.

There are two kinds of archaeology: historical and psychological – excavations of the mind.

My pen scratches against the paper as I calmly weave the gossamer of my memories.

PART I

The Archaeologist

I
The Mystery

1

I'M SQUATTING IN the middle of a checkerboard pattern made of large squares of earth, all exactly the same size, searching for the past. The sun is beating down on the back of my neck. My palms are covered with blisters that sting like crazy. I'm dirty and sweaty. I stink. My T-shirt is clinging to my back like a sticky, old bandage.

The wind and digging have stirred up fine grains of sand that are lingering over the field as a greyish-brown dome of dust. The sand is stinging my eyes. The cloud of dust has parched my mouth and powdered my face. My skin feels dry and cracked. I groan to myself. I cannot believe I used to dream of a life like this. I mean, sure, we all need to make a living . . .

I sneeze.

'Bless you!' a voice calls out. Startled, I look around, but everyone is absorbed in their work.

It turns out the past isn't that easy to find. Several shovel-depths below the topsoil, I'm using my fingers to sift through the raw earth in the dustpan between my grimy shoes. We've excavated our way down to a culture layer that is eight hundred years old. The loamy soil is giving off a rich scent. In one of my old textbooks, *Archaeological Analysis of the Ancient*, Professor Graham Llyleworth writes, 'The dark

3

humus of the earth teems with silent messages from the past.' Will you get a load of that? Professor Llyleworth is one of the world's foremost archaeologists, but he's a little full of his own poetic abilities. His idiosyncrasies require a little forbearance.

At the moment the professor is sitting in the shade under a sheet that's been stretched between four poles. He's reading and sucking on a cigar that he hasn't lit. He looks like an insufferable intellectual, full of a sort of grey-haired, pompous decorum that he hasn't done a thing to deserve. He's probably dreaming about one of the girls digging near by with her rear end sticking up in the air. Now and then he glances down at us with eyes that say, *Ah, yes, I was once the one squatting down there sweating, but that was long ago.*

I scowl up at him through the thick lenses of my glasses and my clip-on shades. Our eyes meet and he looks at me for a second or two and then yawns. A breeze makes the sheet flap. It's been many years since anyone with dirt under his, or her, fingernails has dared to disagree with the professor on anything.

'*Mr Beltoooh?*' he says with exaggerated politeness. I have yet to meet anyone who wasn't Norwegian who could actually pronounce my name; that 'ø' on the end gets them every time. He beckons me over to him the way slave-drivers beckoned their slaves in previous centuries. I pull myself up out of the metre-deep pit and brush the dirt off my jeans.

The professor clears his throat. 'Nothing yet?' he asks in English.

I indicate with a gesture that I haven't found anything yet and then snap to mock-attention, which he completely misses, unfortunately.

'Nothing, sir!' I bark out.

With an expression that only just conceals his disdain, he glances at me and says, 'Everything OK? You look pale today.' Then he chuckles to himself, waiting for a response that I don't have the least intention of giving him.

Lots of people consider Professor Llyleworth malevolent and domineering, but he is neither. He is merely condescending by nature. The professor's view of the surrounding world as one populated by pathetic wretches clutching at his trouser turn-ups was formed early in his life and is now a permanent fixture, sealed in hardened, steel-reinforced concrete. When he smiles, it is with an aloof and patronising indifference. When he listens, it is out of forced politeness (which his mother must have beaten into him with canings and threats). When he says something, you can have faith that he is speaking on behalf of Our Lord.

Llyleworth flicks away a dandelion seed the breeze had deposited upon his grey tailored suit. He sets his cigar down on the field table under the awning where he is keeping track in indelible ink of each pit that has been excavated and emptied. Impassively, he takes the cap off his pen and writes an X through square 003/157 on the site plan.

Then he waves me away with a tired gesture.

At university archaeology students learn that each of us can move up to one cubic metre of dirt a day, and the back dirt pile by the large screen proves that we've had a productive morning. Ina, the student who is doing the water screening on all the dirt we haul over there in dustpans and wheelbarrows, hasn't found anything other than a couple of loom weights and a comb that the excavation teams overlooked. She's standing in a mud puddle wearing tight shorts, a white T-shirt and rubber boots that are way too big for her, holding a green garden hose with a leaky nozzle.

She's pretty sexy. I glance over at her for the two hundred and twelfth time this morning, but she never looks my way.

*

My muscles are aching. I collapse into my camping chair, which, thanks to a bird cherry, is sheltered from the August sun. This is my corner, my safe spot. I can keep an eye on the excavation site from here. I like to keep an eye on things. When you keep an eye on things, you're in control.

Every evening after the sorting and cataloguing, I sign the bottom of the inventory sheet. Professor Llyleworth thinks I'm overly suspicious because I insist on cross-checking the artefacts in the cardboard boxes with his list. So far I haven't caught him in a single inaccuracy, but I don't trust him. I'm here to inspect things, and we both know that.

The professor turns around, as if by chance, to check up on me. I give him a cheerful Boy Scout salute: two fingers to my forehead. He doesn't return the gesture.

I'm happiest in the shade. Because of a defect in my irises, bright light shatters into a burst of splinters in the back of my head. The sun is a disc of concentrated pain for me, so I squint a lot. Some kid once told me, 'Whoa, you've got permanent red-eye, like someone took your picture with a flash.'

With my back to the tool shed, I gaze out over the excavation site. The coordinate system's white strings form a grid of the squares that are being excavated, one by one. Ian and Uri are standing over by the dumpy level and theodolite debating something, looking out over the grid and gesturing with their arms along the axes of the coordinate system. I smile for a second, wondering whether we're digging in the wrong place. If we were, the professor would blow his stupid whistle and yell, 'Stop! This isn't right.' But I can tell from their facial expressions that they're just being impatient.

There are thirty-seven of us archaeologists working on this project. The professor's field supervisors (Ian, Theodore and Pete from Oxford University; Moshe and David from the Hebrew University in Jerusalem; and Uri from the Schimmer

Institute) are each leading their own excavation team of Norwegian graduate students.

Ian, Theo and Pete developed a sophisticated software program for archaeological excavations based on infrared satellite imaging and ground-penetrating sonar.

Moshe has doctorates in theology and physics and was part of the team of scientists who examined the Shroud of Turin in 1995.

David is an expert in interpreting New Testament manuscripts.

Uri is a specialist in the history of the Knights Hospitaller.

And I'm here to keep an eye on things.

2

I used to spend every summer at my grandmother's country house south-east of Oslo on the fjord. A Swiss chalet-style house from the mid-1800s surrounded by fruit trees, berries and flowers. Sun-warmed slate flagstones and over-grown bushes. Flies, carefree bumblebees and butterflies. The scent of tar and seaweed in the air. The boats gliding along, mid-fjord. At the mouth of the fjord, between the village of Larkollen and Bolærne Island – which were both so far away they looked as if they were floating – I could just make out a sliver of open ocean, and over the horizon I pictured America.

About a kilometre from the summer house, along the old highway between Fuglevik and Moss, was Værne Monastery, with its six acres of woods and fields and its history stretching right back to Snorri Sturluson's sagas of the old Norse kings. King Sverre Sigurdsson gave Værne Monastery to the Knights Hospitaller at the end of the twelfth century. The Knights Hospitaller brought our remote corner of civilisation a touch of world history, the Crusades and Christian military orders. The monks' time at Værne Monastery didn't end until 1532.

A lifetime is made up of a series of coincidences. Case in point: Professor Llyleworth's excavation is taking place in one of Værne Monastery's fields.

The professor claims that our objective is to find a Viking-era ring fortress, perhaps two hundred metres in diameter, surrounded by a circular rampart and wooden palisades. Apparently he had come across a map in a Viking grave in York. It's unbelievable, and I don't believe him.

Professor Llyleworth is looking for something. I don't know what. Treasure is way too mundane. A grave with a Viking ship? Remnants of St Olav's Reliquary? Maybe coins from Khwarezm, the empire east of the Aral Sea? Rolls of calfskin rejected by Snorri Sturluson's medieval publisher? A sacrificial vessel made of silver? A magical rune stone? I can only guess. And dedicate myself wholeheartedly to my duties as guard dog.

The professor is going to write yet another textbook based on this dig. Some foundation in England is paying for the whole thing. The landowner received a small fortune for letting us turn his field upside down.

This is going to be some textbook.

I still haven't figured out how, or why, Professor Llyleworth was allowed to release his archaeological storm troopers on Norwegian soil. I'm sure it's the same old story: he must have friends in high places.

It's usually hard for foreigners to get permission to conduct archaeological digs in Norway, but Professor Llyleworth encountered no opposition. Quite the contrary – the Royal Norwegian Office of Cultural Heritage couldn't wait to issue his permit. The University of Oslo eagerly helped select its most qualified graduate students for his excavation teams and arranged work permits for his foreign assistants. They gently cajoled any local officials who might have had qualms. They crossed all their t's and dotted their i's. I was asked to serve as the 'inspector', the Norwegian government's on-site representative, purely a formality. It was almost as if they regretted having me here, but rules are rules. You know how it is. I'm not sure why they selected me, a near-sighted assistant professor of archaeology they found in the office of the Oslo Historical Museum's Antiquities Collection on Frederik Street. I suppose because I could be spared for a few months.

There's a grandfather clock ticking away in the sitting room at my grandmother's country house. I've loved that clock ever since I was little. It's never worked right. It'll start chiming at the oddest hours. Eight minutes to noon! Nine-o-three in the afternoon! Three twenty-eight! Then the gears and springs in its inner workings will smugly click and whir and the clock will shout, 'It doesn't matter to me!'

I mean, who's to say all those other clocks in the world are right or that you can capture time with precision mechanics and hands? I'm a person who tends to mull things over. I suppose it comes with my job. When you dig up a five-hundred-year-old female skeleton that won't let go of the child she's embracing, that moment sticks with you.

The breeze brings in the salty scent of the sea. The sun has cooled. I detest the sun. Very few of us think of the sun as a continual thermonuclear fusion reaction, but I do. And I can't tell you how glad I am that it will all be over in ten million years.

The shout sounds both excited and astonished. Professor Llyleworth stands up under his awning, vigilant but motionless, like a lethargic old guard dog who's thinking about barking.

Archaeologists rarely cry out when they find something. We find things all the time. Every cry strips away a bit of our dignity. Most of the coin fragments and loom weights we unearth ultimately wind up in a light brown box in a dark warehouse, properly conserved, catalogued and prepared for posterity. You are lucky if just once in your career you find something that can be displayed in a glass case. Most archaeologists in Norway, if they look deep enough within themselves, will admit that the last truly amazing archaeological find in the country was the Viking ship found at Oseberg in 1904.

The cry had come from Irene, a graduate student in the Department of Classical Archaeology, a gifted, soft-spoken girl. I could easily have fallen in love with her.

Irene is on Moshe's excavation team. Yesterday morning she uncovered the remnants of a foundation wall, an octagon. The sight of it filled me with a vague, distant memory that I couldn't quite place.

I've never seen Professor Llyleworth so worked up. Every few minutes he's over there, peeking down into her pit.

Irene stands up and climbs up on to the edge. Enthusiastically she waves the professor over.

Several of us have already started running towards her.

The professor blows his whistle: *Pfff-rrr-eeet!*

A magic flute – everyone jerks to a stop, as when an old eight-millimetre movie gets stuck in the projector.

Then obediently they all stand still.

But his magic flute has no effect on me. I approach Irene's

pit at a jog. The professor is coming from the opposite direction. He attempts to stop me with a glare and another whistle blow: *Pfff-rrr-eeet!!!* But he can't. I get there first.

It's a reliquary.

An oblong shrine, thirty or forty centimetres long. The outer layer of reddish brown wood has decomposed.

The professor stops so close to the edge that for a second I hope he will tumble into the pit in his grey suit, the ultimate humiliation. But I'm not that lucky.

The short run has left him out of breath. He smiles, his mouth open, his eyes wide. He looks as if he's having an orgasm.

I follow his eyes, down to the reliquary.

In one long, fluid motion, the professor squats, supports himself on his left hand and hops down into the pit.

A murmur spreads through the crowd.

With his fingertips – those soft fingertips that were created for delicately balancing canapés, holding champagne flutes and cigars, and stroking the silky breasts of shy ladies from Kensington – he starts scooping the dirt away from the reliquary.

In the textbook he authored, *Methods of Modern Archaeology*, Professor Llyleworth writes that exhaustively recording each find is the key to correct interpretation and understanding. 'Patience and thoroughness are an archaeologist's most important virtues,' he states in *Virtues of Archaeology*, an archaeology student's professional bible. So he ought to know he's being too eager now. We're in no hurry here. When something's been lying in the ground for hundreds or thousands of years, we should take a few extra hours to be accurate and careful. We should sketch the reliquary *in situ*, from both a bird's-eye perspective and a lateral view, and photograph it. We need to measure the length, height and width of the find. Only after every conceivable detail has been recorded can we painstakingly coax it out using a pointed trowel and teaspoon, brush away the dirt and sand, and conserve the wood. If there's anything made of metal, it needs to be treated with sesquicarbonate. The professor knows all this.

But he doesn't seem to care.

I leap down next to him. Everyone else is staring at us as if the professor had just announced that he was planning to dig all the way through the Earth's crust to the mantle.

With his bare hands.

Before lunch.

I clear my throat solemnly, with exaggerated clarity, and tell him that he's moving too fast. He ignores me. He has erected a shield between himself and the rest of the world. Even when I assume an official, authoritative tone and order him to stop in the name of the government of the Kingdom of Norway he continues frenetically clawing at the dirt. To him I might as well be representing the Wizard of Oz.

Once he has exposed most of the reliquary, he grabs it in both hands and tugs it free. A bit of the wood falls off.

Several of us cry out in anger, bafflement – this simply is not done! I tell him as much. Each and every archaeological find must be treated with the utmost care.

My words make no impression on him.

He's holding the reliquary in front of him. He stands there agog, staring, breathing hard.

'Shouldn't we,' I suggest icily, my arms folded across my chest, 'record the find?'

His royal highness gazes at the reliquary in awe. He smiles incredulously. Then in his most stiff-upper-lipped Oxford English he absent-mindedly says, 'This. Is. Fucking. Unbelievable.'

'Please give me the reliquary,' I say.

He looks at me blankly.

I clear my throat. 'Professor Llyleworth! Surely you realise that I'm going to have to report this incident to the Institute.' My voice has assumed a cool, formal tone that I don't really recognise. 'The Antiquities Collection and the Royal Norwegian Office of Cultural Heritage will hardly look kindly on your methods.'

Without a word he scrambles up out of the pit and hurries over to the field tent. A cloud of dust swirls, surrounding his suit. The rest of us have ceased to exist.

I don't give up that easily. I run after him.

From inside the tent, behind the taut canvas wall, I hear Professor Llyleworth's overexcited voice. I lift the tent flap aside. I can't see because of the dim light and my clip-on sunglasses, but I can gradually make out the professor's broad back. He's still breathing heavily. 'Yes, yes, yes!' he shouts into his mobile phone. 'Michael, listen to me, it's the shrine!'

More than anything, I'm astonished that he's lit his cigar. He knows full well that tobacco smoke can interfere with the carbon 14 dating.

His voice is tinged with hysterical laughter: 'Good old Charles was right, Michael. It's unbelievable! It's fucking unbelievable.'

The reliquary is on the folding card table next to him. I step into the tent. Just then Ian materialises from the darkness, like an evil spirit guarding a pharaoh's tomb. He grabs me by the upper arms and pushes me heavy-handedly backwards out of the tent.

'For crying out loud . . .' I stammer, my voice quavering with anger and indignation.

Ian glares at me and goes back in. If he could have slammed a door, he would have. But the tent flap just flops loosely shut behind him.

And then the professor emerges. He has wrapped the

reliquary in a piece of cloth. His smoking cigar juts out of the corner of his mouth.

'Please give me the shrine,' I say, just to have said it, but they neither hear nor care.

Professor Llyleworth's car is a lithe, gleaming thoroughbred. A burgundy-red Jaguar XJ6. Two hundred horsepower. Zero to sixty in nine seconds. Leather upholstery. Wood steering wheel. Air conditioning. It may possibly even have a trace of a soul and some nascent self-awareness deep within its engine block, under all the chrome and the metallic finish.

Ian slides in behind the wheel, leans across to open the door for the professor, who climbs in and lays the shrine in his lap.

We stand there staring in our grimy T-shirts and jeans, leaning on our shovels and measuring rods, our mouths hanging open, with sand in our hair and streaks of dirt under our eyes, but they don't see us. We've done our part. We no longer exist.

The Jaguar rolls down the gravel road. As it bumps its way on to the main road, it emits a purr that envelops it in a cloud of dust.

And then it's gone.

In the quiet that falls over us, disturbed only by the wind in the trees and the hushed murmurs of the students, I appreciate two things. One is that I've been tricked. I don't really know how or why, but the certainty of it makes me clench my teeth so hard that my eyes fill with tears. The other is a realisation: I've always been the dutiful, conscientious one – the indispensable, hidden cog that never fails the machine. The Norwegian government's antiquities officials entrusted me with the job of inspector, and I failed.

But I'll be damned if I'm going to let Professor Graham Llyleworth run off with the find. This isn't just between

Llyleworth and the Antiquities Collection or the Royal Norwegian Office of Cultural Heritage or the prosecutor's office.

This is between Llyleworth and me.

I don't have a Jaguar. My car is more like an inflatable beach toy that a child played with and then forgot at the beach. It's pink, a Citroën 2CV. In the summer I roll open the soft top. I call her Bolla. To the extent that a person and a machine can be, we're on the same wavelength.

The seat groans as I fling myself behind the wheel. I have to lift the door a little to get it to latch. The gearshift looks like an umbrella handle that some hysterical old woman accidentally stuck through the dashboard. I put Bolla into first gear, press down on the accelerator and trundle off after the professor.

As car chases go, this one is ludicrous. Bolla goes from zero to sixty in a generation, but I'll get there sooner or later, probably just a little later. I'm in no hurry. First I'm going to pop into the Antiquities Collection and report this to Professor Arntzen. Then I'll go to the police. And then I'll alert customs at the airport and tell them what happened. And the ferry terminals – a Jaguar XJ6 can't get lost in the crowd.

One of the reasons I roll the roof open in the summer is that I love to feel the wind rushing through my crew cut. It makes me dream of a carefree life, driving a roadster up the Pacific Coast Highway, a life as a tanned surfer dude surrounded by bikini-clad girls, Coca-Cola, and pop music.

At school they used to call me Polar Bear. Maybe that's because my first name, Bjørn, means 'bear' in Norwegian. But probably it's because I'm an albino.

4

When Professor Trygve Arntzen asked me in May whether I wanted to serve as the inspector for the Værne Monastery dig later in the summer, I looked at the offer a little bit as a challenge, but mostly as a welcome opportunity to get out of the office. You don't need to be psychotic to occasionally get the sense that four walls, a floor and a ceiling have closed in an inch or two.

Professor Arntzen is my mother's husband. I prefer not to use the word stepfather.

The endless parade of students over the years has rendered the professor blind to the uniqueness of the individual. His students have all merged into a faceless crowd, and the professor has developed an impatient irritation towards this sea of academic uniformity. An inheritance from his father left him quite well off and a tad arrogant. Very few of his students like him. His subordinates talk about him behind his back. I don't have any trouble understanding where they're coming from, actually. I've never liked him. We all have our reasons.

I reach Oslo in the middle of the afternoon rush. Summer is on the wane, but the air is still oppressive and humid.

I drum my fingers against the steering wheel. I wonder where all the other drivers are going and who they are and why they need to be here. Damn them. I look at my watch and wipe the sweat off my forehead. I want the road to myself. We all want that. Each of us contributes to the collective madness of traffic; we just won't admit it to ourselves. Admitting you have a problem is the first step towards recovery.

Professor Arntzen's door is closed. Someone has prised six of the letters off the sign on his door, and with childish fascination I'm standing here reading PRO ES OR YGV AR ZEN. It looks like some kind of Tibetan mantra.

I'm about to knock on the door when I hear voices inside his office, so I wait. I shuffle over to the hallway window, whose sill is covered with a fine layer of dust. Down on the street below cars are queuing up at the traffic lights. Pedestrians are moving slowly in the heat. The employees' car park behind the museum is practically empty.

I can't have been paying attention when I parked Bolla, which isn't like me. But from up here I see it. This is what it must be like for God: able to keep an eye on everything, all the time. Between the professor's charcoal-grey Mercedes 190 and a little Saab 900 Turbo there's a burgundy Jaguar XJ6.

Cautiously I place my ear against the door.

'. . . precautions,' says a voice. Professor Arntzen.

He's speaking English instead of Norwegian. His voice is deferential. It takes a powerful person to make the professor deferential.

I think I know who it is.

A voice mumbles something I don't catch. It's Ian.

'When's he coming?' Arntzen says.

'Early tomorrow,' a deep voice answers. Professor Llyleworth.

I knew it!

Arntzen: 'He's coming in person?'

Llyleworth: 'Of course. But he's at home. The plane's in Toulouse for repairs. Otherwise he'd be here tonight.'

Ian (chuckling): 'He's pretty excited, and impatient, too.'

Llyleworth: 'Certainly understandable.'

Arntzen: 'Is he planning on taking it out of the country himself?'

Llyleworth: 'Obviously. Via London. Tomorrow.'

Ian: 'I still think we ought to bring it with us to the hotel, just until he arrives. I don't like the thought of leaving it here.'

Llyleworth: 'No, no, no, think strategically. We're the ones the police are going to search if that albino causes any trouble.'

Arntzen: 'Bjørn? ... (laughter) ... Relax! I'll handle Bjørn.'

Ian: 'But shouldn't we . . .'

Llyleworth: 'The shrine will be safest here with the professor. After all.'

Arntzen: 'No one will think to look here. I guarantee it.'

Llyleworth: 'Yes, it's best this way.'

Ian: 'If you insist.'

Llyleworth: 'Definitely.'

(Pause.)

Arntzen: 'So he was right all along. He was right.'

Llyleworth: 'Who was?'

Arntzen: 'DeWitt.'

Llyleworth (pauses before responding): 'Good old Charles.'

Arntzen: 'He was right all along. How ironic, huh?'

Llyleworth: 'If only he were here now. Ah well, we finally found it.'

There's something final in Llyleworth's tone, as if he's done with the conversation.

I pull away from the door. I quickly tiptoe down the corridor.

On the blue background on my office door sign, white plastic letters spell out the words ASSISTANT PROFESSOR BJØRN BELTØ. The letters are all slightly crooked, like teeth in need of orthodontia.

I let myself in and drag the rickety, green desk chair over to the window. I can keep an eye on the Jaguar from here.

Not much is happening. Traffic is creeping along in a slow stream. An ambulance is winding and blaring its way down the congested street.

A few minutes later I spot Ian and Professor Llyleworth down in the car park.

Ian has a bouncy gait. Gravity doesn't seem to have the same effect on him as on the rest of us.

Llyleworth moves full speed ahead, like a supertanker.

Neither of them has anything in their hands.

Professor Arntzen emerges a few minutes later. He's carrying his coat over his left arm. He has an umbrella in his right hand. He doesn't have the shrine with him either.

On the bottommost step he stops and glances up at the sky the way he always does. The professor's life is composed of rituals.

Next to the Mercedes, he stops to look for his car keys. He's always misplacing his keys. Before he finds them, he glances up at my window. I freeze. The reflections on the glass make me invisible.

A half-hour later I call Professor Arntzen at home. Luckily he answers and not my mother. He must have been sitting by the phone, waiting.

'Sigurd?' he says.

'It's Bjørn,' I say.

'Bjørn? Oh, hi.'

'I need to talk to you.'

'Are you calling from Værne?'

'We found something,' I say.

Silence. Finally the professor says, 'Really?'

'A reliquary.'

'You don't say?' Silence. 'Really?' Each word drags, as if dipped in tar.

'Which Professor Llyleworth has run off with.'

'Run . . . off . . . with?' The professor is a terrible actor. He doesn't even sound surprised.

'I thought maybe he might contact you,' I continue.

More silence.

'Me?' he says. Then he tries to take control of the conversation: 'Did you see what kind of reliquary it was?'

'Wood.'

'Old?'

'In a layer dating from the 1100s. Possibly older.'

He takes in a quick breath.

'I didn't get to examine it,' I continue. 'But we have to file a complaint.'

'A complaint?'

'Don't you hear what I'm saying? He ran off with the reliquary. It's not just a matter for us and the Royal Norwegian Office of Cultural Heritage any more. I have to call the police.'

'No, no, don't do anything rash. Calm down. I'm in complete control. Just forget it happened.'

'They ran off with the reliquary. Do you hear me? And the fieldwork was disgraceful. I'm going to file a report! Llyleworth might as well have been using a backhoe and dynamite to do the excavating.'

'Have you . . . done anything?'

'No, not yet.'

'Good. Leave it to me.'

'What are you going to do?'

'Calm down, Bjørn. I'll sort it all out. Don't give it another thought.'

'But . . .'

'I'm going to make a few calls. Relax. It'll all be fine. Call me tomorrow.'

Maybe it's not such a big deal, the reliquary. If it's been lying around underground for eight hundred years, surely it'll hardly affect the welfare of humanity if it gets smuggled out of the country. It would just be as if we never found it.

Maybe Professor Llyleworth has big plans. Maybe he's going to sell it to an Arabian sheikh for a fortune or present it to the British Museum, which can then chalk up yet another academic victory by hoarding someone else's rightful cultural heritage.

With all-too-eager assistance from Professor Arntzen.

I don't get it. It's none of my business, but I'm furious. I was the inspector. They tricked me. They put me on the project because they thought I'd be easy to fool. Bjørn, the near-sighted albino.

5

Behind the rambling old house I grew up in there was a stretch of overgrown fields we called the Paddock. In the winter I would make a ski jump on its slopes. During the spring thaw I would have cross-country bike races down the muddy footpath. In the summer I would climb up into the trees and sit up there, inconspicuous as a squirrel, spying on the teenagers who came to drink beer, smoke marijuana and have sex in the tall grass. I was eleven and already a dedicated spy.

On Norwegian Constitution Day, 17 May, in 1977, a young girl was beaten up and raped behind a rowan bush in the Paddock. It happened in the middle of the day. In the distance you could hear people celebrating the national holiday – marching bands performing in the parade, people cheering, firecrackers going off. The week after that another girl was raped. There were some articles in the papers. One afternoon two days later someone set the dry grass on fire. It wasn't that unusual. The kids in the neighbourhood used to have bonfires there, but this time there was no group of kids standing by ready to douse the flames. The fire razed the Paddock and parts of the neighbouring woods. The blaze left a charred, burned-out wasteland, completely unsuitable for raping anyone else. People presumed there was some connection.

We talked about it at school for weeks. The police investigated. We came up with nicknames for whoever started the fire. The Mad Pyromaniac. The King of Flames. The Avenger.

To this day no one knows I was the one who did it.

There are plenty of places Professor Arntzen could have hidden the shrine, but I eliminate most of them. I know how he thinks.

He could have taken the shrine down to the university repository. He could have locked it in one of the fireproof steel storage lockers there, but he didn't. We all have access to the repository. He doesn't want to share the shrine with anyone.

One of life's paradoxes is that sometimes we can't see what's right before our eyes. That's how the professor thinks. The best way to hide something is to act as if you have nothing to hide. If you want to hide a book, put it on the bookshelf.

He hid the shrine in his office in a locked drawer or cabinet behind some boxes or binders. I can jut picture it. My intuition is usually dead on. I can visualise things as clearly as if they were on a movie screen. It's a skill I inherited from my grandmother.

The professor will have locked his office door, but that doesn't matter. When he was away leading a 1996 dig in Telemark in south-east Norway, he gave me a key and forgot about it – as he did so many other things.

His office is twice as big as mine and way more ostentatious. His desk towers in the middle of the room atop an imitation Persian carpet, home to his computer, phone and a paper-clip holder that my half-brother made in woodwork class. His desk chair has a high back and hydraulic shock absorbers. Over by a wall there's a sitting area where he takes coffee with his guests. A bookshelf tilts outward slightly from the south wall, weighed down with knowledge.

I sit down in the chair, which accepts my weight with a pleasant softness. The strong scent of Llyleworth's cigar lingers.

I close my eyes and turn my mind inward, focusing my intuition. I sit like that for a few minutes, then I open my eyes again.

They fall on the filing cabinet.

It's a grey aluminium filing cabinet, three drawers high with a lock at the top right. I walk over to it and give the top drawer a tug.

Locked, of course.

I could break open the lock, but I don't think that will be necessary.

I find the key under the paper clips in the home-made holder on his desk. The professor keeps spare keys all over the place. Spare house keys and keys to his Mercedes hang from a spring on his desk lamp.

I unlock the cabinet and pull open the top drawer. The green hanging folders are full of documents, letters and contracts. In the middle drawer I find clippings from international journals, filed alphabetically by topic.

The shrine is at the very back of the bottom drawer behind the hanging file folders, wrapped in a piece of cloth inside a plastic bag from LORENTZEN YACHTING SUPPLIES, which in turn is in a grey-striped shopping bag under a stack of books.

With the bag under my arm I tidy up after myself. I shut the drawers and lock the filing cabinet, put the key back under the paper clips, and push the desk chair back in. I take one last look – *Is everything where it should be? I didn't forget anything?* – before I slip out, locking the door behind me. The corridor is dark and seemingly endless. I look both ways before I start walking.

Well, well, Mr Beltø, what were you just doing in the professor's office? And what have you got there?

My footsteps echo, my heartbeat, too. I look back.

Mr Beltø? Where are you going with that artefact? Did you steal that from the professor?

I gasp for air, trying to walk as fast as I can without actually running.

You there – stop! Stop right where you are!

I made it! The voices are reverberating in my head. I push open the door to my office and scurry inside. I lean against the inside of the door and exhale.

I carefully lift the shrine out of the shopping bag and remove the plastic bag and the piece of cloth. My hands are shaking.

The shrine is surprisingly heavy. Two brittle bands hold the reddish, rotting wood together. The wood is disintegrating. The cracks reveal what's inside. Another shrine.

I'm no metallurgist, but that doesn't matter. I don't need to take the shrine down to the lab to determine what the inner shrine is made of: gold.

It shimmers, warm and golden, even through the centuries.

I sense something inevitable.

I gaze down at the street through the grimy windowpane while I wait for my heart to stop racing.

Two years ago I spent six months in a psych clinic. I was lucky and got a spot in the same ward where I had previously had group therapy sessions. Time had stood still there. The pattern in the linoleum was the same as before. The walls were still a sallow green and bare. The sounds and smells were the same. Martin was still sitting in his rocking chair knitting. He'd been knitting that same scarf for eighteen years. He stored his shockingly long creation in a tall wicker basket with a lid. Martin nodded at me as if I'd just stepped out for a second to grab a coffee. We'd never spoken to each other, and yet he recognised me and, I suppose, considered me a kind of friend.

Even my mother didn't know I'd been admitted. She worries too much, so I told her I was on a dig in Egypt.

Before I went in, I put a stack of six pre-addressed envelopes into an A4-size Jiffy bag and then sent the whole thing to the main post office in Cairo with a plea for help enclosed. I don't speak Arabic, so I enclosed a twenty-dollar bill, the universal language. A friendly worker there must have understood what I was getting at. He stamped the letters and mailed them to my mother with a Cairo, Egypt, postmark. How cool is that? Like in a detective novel. Of course, I'd meant for him to send one letter a month. I had thought that was obvious. I'd even written the names of the months on the top right. But he had mailed all the letters at one time, that dimwit. Six months of made-up news – amazing archaeological finds, romances with Egyptian belly dancers, stormy desert expeditions on wind-battered camels – all compressed into one week. It says something about my imaginative abilities and my mother's naivety that I managed to explain the whole thing away. She can't have been completely sober.

Therapy helped me get back on my feet. A hospital has its routines, and for me they were pegs to hang my existence on.

There was nothing exotic about my condition, no amusing Napoleonic delusions, no voices in my head, just a life in raven-black darkness.

I'm better now.

7

Frightened, I speed through Oslo's streets, an outlaw fleeing into the sunset. *Delta Foxtrot 30, the suspect is driving a Citroën 2CV and must be apprehended immediately.* For a while a Toyota fills my rear-view mirror. When it finally turns on to a side street, I give a sigh of relief. *The suspect stole a valuable golden shrine and may be dangerous in stressful situations.* I pass St Hanshaugen Park and get stuck behind a shuttle bus that's driving suspiciously slowly. I check the rear-view mirror constantly while vigilantly keeping my eye on the shadowy figures within the shuttle. You never know. I make it to the motorway unscathed. No shots have been fired, yet.

Eventually the high-rise flat complex I live in comes into view. The buildings aren't particularly attractive, but the sight fills me with warmth the way home always does.

I grew up in a big, old, rambling, white gingerbread house with a garden full of apple trees on a side street in a suburb that had a tram line, a fire station and happy people.

My mother and father had a glassed-in balcony outside their bedroom which I could climb out on to through a little window in my own bedroom. I often did that when I couldn't sleep. They would pull a tulle curtain across the half-open sliding door to the balcony, and I would peer in through it. My night-time spy missions filled me with a sweet, unfamiliar tingling sensation and the joy of being invisible.

One night they danced naked in the jumble of shadows in their bedroom, soft bodies on fire, soothing hands and lips. I stood motionless, not understanding, intoxicated by the magic of the moment. Suddenly my mother turned her face and looked right at me. She smiled, but she can't have seen my face through the folds of the curtain because she just leaned back and drowned my father with her sighs and caresses.

Freud would have loved me, don't you think?

My father's compost heap was out in the garden, between two weathered apple trees. The compost emitted an earthy smell that was somehow both repulsive and appealing at the same time. At my father's burial, at the edge of the grave, that same smell hit me like a handful of dirt and sand. My senses filled with the scent that came welling up from the darkness of the grave. I understood that the smell of compost contained both death and the promise of new life. I couldn't articulate the feeling in words back then, but the recollection still brings tears to my eyes.

I've always been sensitive to smells. That's why I used to avoid our cellar, which smelled of mildew and decay and something indeterminate and musty. Under the rotting trapdoor to the cellar, hidden in the jungle behind the house, spiders would spin their cobwebs in peace. Their webs hung like sticky curtains over the stone steps. Whenever my father waded through the nettles and unlocked the padlock and opened the trapdoor, millions of bugs would chime in with their silent screams, scurrying for shelter from the shattering light, while the nasty, invisible clouds of cellar stench floated out into the air. Dad didn't seem to notice, but I knew what was hiding in the dank, putrid darkness: ghosts, vampires, werewolves, one-eyed murderers, all the monsters that fill a little boy's imagination once you leave Dr Seuss and Winnie-the-Pooh behind in the sunlight.

I can still recall the scents of my childhood: trampled dirt on a rainy day, strawberry ice cream, sun-warmed fibreglass boats, raw spring soil, my mother's perfume and my father's aftershave, mundane things that in their triviality form a treasure trove of memories.

At least I'm not a dog.

Roger, my downstairs neighbour, is a friend of the night. He detests the light, just like me. His eyes are dark and full of ennui. He has shoulder-length, black hair and wears an inverted cross hanging on a silver chain around his neck. Roger plays bass guitar in a rock band called Beelzebub's Delight.

I ring his doorbell and wait. It takes him a while. Even though his flat is only fifty square metres, it always seems as if he's been interrupted deep down in the castle catacombs and has to rush up the long, torchlit spiral staircase to answer the door.

Roger's a good boy, at least deep down inside. Like me, he keeps everything negative bottled up, where it festers until the abscess bursts and infects his brain. You can see it in his eyes.

I have no idea why, but Roger likes me.

'Jeez!' he exclaims good-naturedly when he finally opens the door to peer out.

'Did I wake you up?' I ask.

'Um . . . no big deal, I've had plenty of sleep. So you're home already, huh?'

'It's just that I missed you so much.' I grin.

'Man, you look like a fucking sewer rat.'

I catch a glimpse of myself in the mirror in his hall. I should've changed my clothes and cleaned myself up a little. I hold up the bag containing the shrine. 'Can I leave something with you for safe keeping?'

'What is it?' This comes out muffled, sounding sort of like 'Wazzi?'

'A bag.'

He rolls his eyes. 'I'm not fucking blind. What's in it?' he asks, and then laughs. 'Heroin?'

'Just some old stuff. From the olden days.'

To Roger 'the olden days' means a prehistoric era populated with pterodactyls, Victrolas and men in powdered wigs. In other words some time around 1975.

'Hey, we recorded a demo,' he says proudly. 'Wanna hear it?'

Truth be told, I'd rather not, but I don't have the heart to tell him that. I follow him into the living room. The curtains are drawn. In the gleam of the red light bulbs, the living room resembles a darkroom, or a brothel. There's a silver candelabrum with seven black candles sitting on a round mahogany table, an enormous rug featuring a hexagram surrounded by a circle, and posters depicting Satan and some horrible scenes from hell hang on the walls over the flea-market sofa and the thirty-year-old teak table. Roger has his own unique way of making things feel homey.

A black stereo system, centred on the one long wall, towers like an icon that Roger prays to at set times, with a programmable CD player, automatic digital PLL tuner, amplifier with bass booster and super surround system, equaliser, double cassette player with high-speed dubbing, a woofer and four mountainous speakers.

Roger waves his remote, and the stereo system flashes to life in a colourful, soundless display of fireworks of coloured diodes and quivering needles. A tray in the CD player slides

29

out as if it were a genie in an Arabian fairy tale awaiting commands. He presses PLAY.

And then the world explodes.

Later that night, in the shower, I let the icy water wash away the dust and sweat and cool the sunburned strip of skin on the back of my neck. The soap stings in my blisters.

Sometimes a shower becomes a kind of ritual. After a long day, you want to wash away everything unpleasant and difficult. I'm tired, but I don't think I'll dream.

8

My mother is the kind of person who always sounds chipper and alert even when you call her at 3.30 in the morning.

It's 3.30 in the morning.

I've dialled my mother's number. The professor answers. His voice is cloaked with sleep, husky, crabby – that's the kind of person he is.

'It's Bjørn.'

'What?' he snaps. He didn't hear me.

'Let me talk to Mum.'

He thinks I'm my half-brother, Steffen, who's never home at night, who always manages to find a girl who can't bear to be alone in her bed.

With a grunt, the professor passes the heavy marble receiver to my mother. The sheets rustle as my mother and the professor sit up in bed.

'Steffen? Is something wrong?'

My mother's voice, cheerful as ever. It sounds as if she was sitting there awake, eagerly waiting for someone to call, in her red ball gown with her nail polish slowly drying, wearing mascara and with her hair freshly blow dried, with some embroidery in her lap and a little glass within reach.

'It's just me,' I say.

'Little Bear? Little Bjørn? Honey, Bjørn, is that you?' A hint of panic. 'What is it? Did something happen?'

'I . . . I'm sorry I woke you.'

'What happened?'

'Mum . . . It's nothing. I . . .'

She breathes heavily into the receiver. My mother always pictures the worst: car accidents, fires, armed psychopaths. She thinks I'm calling from the ICU at Ullevål Hospital, that they're about to wheel me into the operating room at any minute, that my doctors are letting me make one quick phone call in case the operation is unsuccessful, which is quite likely.

'Ugh, Mum, I don't know why I called.'

I can picture them: my mother, anxious and alert in her stylish nightgown, the professor, a little grouchy in his striped pyjamas, his grimy face sprinkled with grey stubble. They're there in their bed, half lying, half sitting, their backs resting against a soft heap of pillows in silk pillowcases with hand-embroidered monograms. A lamp glows on the bedside table, its shade decorated with tassels.

'Little Bjørn, tell me what's wrong.'

She's still convinced that something awful has happened.

'It's nothing, Mum.'

'Are you at home?'

I know what she's thinking: maybe I'm lying in my own vomit, maybe in some filthy homeless shelter. Maybe I took fifty Rohypnol and thirty Valium with a litre of denatured alcohol and am sitting here fingering a Bic lighter.

'Yes, Mum. I'm at home.'

I shouldn't have called. It was a kind of compulsive behaviour. I'm not always myself. When I wake up at night, the dark thoughts grate on my nerves like a toothache or a sore throat. Everything is worse at night, but I don't need to bother my mother, not at 3.30. I could've taken a Valium, but I dialled my mother's number instead. As if there's ever been any comfort in that.

'I was just lying here, thinking, and then I wanted to hear your voice. That's all.'

'Are you sure, Little Bjørn?'

I sense a hint of irritation behind her words. It is the middle of the night after all. They were sleeping. I could have waited until morning if I had just wanted to hear her voice.

'I'm sorry I woke you,' I say.

She's at a loss. I don't usually call in the middle of the night. Something must have happened, something I don't want to tell her.

'Little Bjørn, do you want me to come over?'

'I just want to . . . chat for a minute.'

I can hear her breathing again; the heavy, rapid breathing fills the receiver, like an obscene call from a stranger.

'Now?' she asks, drawing it out a bit. This allusion to the time is the closest my mother comes to criticising me.

'I was lying here awake, thinking about tomorrow. That's why I wanted to talk to you.'

I wait for the realisation to hit her like an icy polar wind.

'Because it's Tuesday?' she asks.

She doesn't get it or she's playing dumb.

The professor grunts in the background.

I know almost nothing about my mother's childhood. She has never wanted to talk about it. Although it's not hard to understand why Dad fell for her. She wasn't like the other girls in high school. There was something sincere and mystical about her. He hit on my mother the whole time they were in school. Eventually she gave in. You can see the bulge in her belly in her graduation photos.

My mother still looks like a teenager sometimes if the

lighting is dim. She's beautiful and appealing like a fairy queen dancing in the moonlight.

Sometimes I wonder what her childhood did to my mother. Before the war my grandparents used to live up in northern Norway, in a house with lace curtains and oilcloth and walls that the north-west wind swept right through. The house wasn't big. I saw a picture of it. It was out on a point. It had a kitchen, where they peed in the slop sink at night, a living room, and a bedroom in the loft, and an outhouse. It was always clean and tidy. Then the Germans burned it down. My grandparents managed to save a photo album and some clothes. My grandmother lived in northern Sweden while my grandfather was building a new house on the point by the fjord, but it was never the same again. Then they had my mother, but it didn't help. The war had done something to my grandfather. They went to stay with my grandmother's brother in Oslo, but no one had any use for a neurotic fisherman or a woman who could clean a fish in seven seconds, cure infections with herbs and otherwise communicate with dead people after the sun went down.

Every milestone in their life had a catch.

They found my grandfather floating in the harbour when my mother was four years old. There was a superficial police investigation and then the case was dropped. My grandmother got a job as a housekeeper for a wealthy family in Oslo's Grefsen neighbourhood. She met her obligations with stoic dejection. Only those who looked her in the eye discovered the resilient dignity that dwelled in her.

She never found a new husband. She worshipped those five pictures of my grandfather like icons. She kept a shirt in the wardrobe that she hadn't had a chance to wash before he died. It was stained and reeked of sweat and fish entrails. That shirt was how she held on to him.

*

33

My mother was not that devoted.

When my father died, she wiped him out of her memory, erased him from existence, finito, the end. She took down all his pictures, burned his letters, gave away his clothes. He became a mythical figure, one we never spoke of, someone who'd never existed. All reminders of my father were systematically purged from that old Victorian house.

In the end, I was all that was left.

The first night my mother let the professor spend the night at the house – it was a Friday, and it was late – I shut myself in my room, to block out the laughter and clinking. I pretended I was asleep when my mother peeked in on me to say goodnight.

Late that night, when the stairs creaked, I crept out on to the balcony. So my eye could gleam through the crack in the curtains as my mother and the professor tiptoed into the bedroom, locked the door and tossed their clothes on to the floor.

My father was standing there in a corner, perfectly still, invisible.

They'd been drinking. The professor was being playful and my mother was trying to keep him quiet.

My heart struggled like a caged animal, full of fear and secret anticipation.

For weeks after that I punished her with my silence.

Later on there were other games . . .

Six months after my father died, my mother married the professor, my father's colleague and best friend. Forgive me if my smile seems a little forced.

The year my half-brother was born, my mother and the professor sold the Victorian house. I didn't move with them. When I told my mother I wanted to get a place of my own, it was as if she breathed a sigh of relief – as when you look back at all the ground you've covered after a long hike – and started over again.

9

My mother and the professor live in a whitewashed brick house in Oslo's Bogstad neighbourhood, and since the really fancy houses up on nearby Mount Holmenkollen all have spectacular views they like to say they live in Lower Holmenkollen. The house has two and a half storeys and looks as if it were planned and built during one hell of a three-week-long drinking binge. Consequently, of course, the architect has won several awards for it. The whole thing is a jumble of nooks and corners and spiral staircases and built-in corner cabinets where my mother can casually stash her arsenal of half-empty bottles. The sloping garden leading down to the street is full of yellow-flowered cinquefoils, alpenrose rhododendron and Lili Marlene roses, but all you smell is the bracing odour of herbicide and bark mulch. The lawn in front of the house is terraced. Behind the house, on specially imported Scottish slate flagstones, there's a hammock with pillows you could drown in, a massive barbecue hand forged by one of the professor's friends, and a fountain depicting a hermaphroditic angel that spits and pisses and otherwise grins up at the sky. A gardener comes and tends the garden every Friday. A girl from a cleaning service comes the same day. That's a busy day for my mother.

When she opens the door and sees me standing out on the front step, safe and sound and handsome (albeit pale), she claps her hands. I give her a hug, which I don't usually do owing to affectionate gesture rationing. Plus I can't stand the smell of the mouthwash that's supposed to camouflage

35

the alcohol on her breath. I didn't stop by because I wanted to, but to reassure her and remind her what day it is.

The kitchen is light and spacious. The pinewood floor came from a farm in Hadeland. She has made coffee and the professor has left the newspaper scattered all over the table.

'Were you planning on gutting some fish?' I joke, gesturing to the newspaper.

She smiles nonchalantly as if to emphasise that, sure, she's a housewife, but she has people to do the dirty work. She turns on the little portable radio on the windowsill. My mother is addicted to her favourite radio programme, which is on every morning at nine. She has many addictions.

'You've always let other people clean your fish for you,' I say. It's a reference to something that happened a long time ago. She should remember, and feel ashamed.

'Hey, you know Trygve just called,' she says.

She waits for my response, but it doesn't come.

'He's really mad. He wants you to call him. What are you up to, Little Bjørn?'

'Up to? Me?' I say in my best Little Lord Fauntleroy voice.

'Well, anyway, you should call him back.'

'Later.'

'It's very important.'

'I know what it's about.'

'He's furious.'

'I'll call him later,' I lie.

'Oh, hey, we're going to have steak tonight. They had this amazingly tender beef at the butcher's yesterday.'

I stick my finger in my mouth and make a disgusted sound.

'Silly boy! Won't you join us? I'll make you some potatoes au gratin and broccoli.'

'I have a busy day.'

'It's been such a long time. Please? For me?'

36

'I just stopped by to apologise.'

'Nonsense.'

'I wasn't quite myself.'

'What's bothering you?'

'Nothing, not a thing.'

I have a cup of tea with her. We chat about this and that, which is her speciality. My insinuations become increasingly less and less veiled, but she doesn't make the connection. Not even when I tell her I'm going to visit the grave.

My father died twenty years ago today. I'm sure it will occur to her some time over the course of the day.

It wasn't just my father that died that summer. A whole life was lost for my mother. Her existence has been reduced to making life comfortable for the professor and my half-brother. She's turned into a bustling, industrious house-keeper. She makes sure the girls from the cleaning service dust in between the black keys on the grand piano in the music room. The butcher and the fishmonger call her when they get something really good and expensive in. She's the professor's rock, his loving wife, his stunning hostess, his eternally youthful and willing lover. She's my half-brother's cheerful mother, who's always there for him, who slips him some extra cash when he goes out on the town, and who cleans up after him when he staggers back into the house in the early hours of the morning, dead drunk and vomiting.

Every now and then a little of that consideration is directed at me. I'm her guilty conscience, and I'm good at my role.

10

'And you're still a vegetarian, right?' Caspar Scott asks.

He's an unusually handsome man. Truth be told, my own reflection gives me a constant and, considered objectively, very deserved sense of inferiority, but Caspar's appearance is so dazzling that it makes him almost feminine. The women in the cafeteria at the Royal Norwegian Office of Cultural Heritage eye him with affection and longing. He doesn't seem to notice, but I know he's storing up all the attention in a big tank, keeping it in reserve for darker days.

We were friends at university. We also shared a tent for months while working on digs in various parts of the country. When I called him, we had a few awkward moments before we warmed up to each other again and found our old stride.

Now we're sitting in the cafeteria, trying to pretend that nothing has changed. It smells like coffee and pastries and fried hamburgers with onion.

Caspar was born to be an archaeologist. Maybe that's an odd thing to say, but he has a knack for putting a small object, which seems meaningless on its own, into a bigger context. When we were excavating the Larøy field, a few modest remnants of keys and a needle case on a belt told him that we'd finally found the chieftain Hallstein's lost farm. Another time we came across a tiny little silver dagger in a Viking grave that we couldn't make sense of (a toy? jewellery? a symbolic weapon?), until Caspar matter-of-factly explained that they had used it to clean their ears.

Caspar can read the countryside the way the rest of us read a book. He has an astonishing capacity to distinguish the natural formations in the terrain from overgrown man-made ones. He was in charge of the two research groups that discovered the almost eleven-thousand-year-old remnants of late glacial settlements in Rogaland and Finnmark. The finds demonstrated that reindeer hunters from the North Sea area or prehistoric hunter-gatherers from the Kola Peninsula may have been the first ones to make it to the ice-free Norwegian coast.

But Caspar tired of life in the field and the long weeks and months away from Kristin. He grew weary of the scorching sun and the sudden cloudbursts that transformed our work-sites into mud pits, so he became a bureaucrat. He's been working in the Royal Norwegian Office of Cultural Heritage's Archaeology Division for the last several years.

I'm ashamed to realise that that is the reason, the only reason, I've got in touch with him now.

I ask him to tell me about the preparations for this dig.

He takes a sip of coffee and makes a face. 'Funny you should ask,' he says. 'I've always wondered what the real story was.'

I pull my teabag out of the steaming water and look at him expectantly.

'It all started with a couple of phone calls to Director-General Loland,' he says. 'First from Arntzen, then from Director Viestad.'

'They both called?'

'That's what I'm saying. On behalf of a British foundation called SIS, the Society of International Sciences, a non-profit research institution in London. SIS believed there were remnants of a ring fortress at Værne Monastery. I mean, hon-estly, can you believe that? A ring fortress! I've never heard the slightest hint that anyone ever built a fortification like that at Værne Monastery. And then they wanted to know how we'd feel about letting Professor Graham Llyleworth lead the excavation.'

'And naturally you thought that would be fine?'

'Fine? Well, no. You know me, right? The whole thing just didn't add up.'

'I can certainly appreciate that.'

'Yeah. I mean, a ring fortress? There? You can rest assured that I had some questions for them. Why in the world would there be a ring fortress there? And why should a British foun-dation be interested in a Norwegian ring fortress? Who was

39

going to pay for the whole thing? What was the big hurry? What were they going to do if they found the fortress?'

'Maybe take it with them?'

Caspar laughs. 'That would be just like Graham Llyleworth.'

'And as time went on, did it start to make more sense?'

'Not at all. I couldn't get a single answer out of them, just raised eyebrows and sighs because I was being so difficult. The Royal Norwegian Office of Cultural Heritage thinks Llyleworth is some kind of fucking god, and the younger set all think he invented archaeology. OK, I'll concede, he's made some incredible finds and written some important text-books. But, I mean, should we let Graham Llyleworth, that conceited cultural imperialist, just waltz in here with his staff of underlings and his backhoes to do what they will? Well, at any rate, I just shook my head and tried to put the whole busi-ness out of my mind, right up until the formal application came in a few weeks later.'

'Application? I never saw it.'

'A real piece of work. Maps and official seals and fancy signatures. There was quite a commotion in the department when it arrived. It didn't take more than about ten minutes before I was summoned to Sigurd Loland's office. Why was I being so negative? Didn't I see the benefits to international archaeological cooperation? You know how Sigurd gets all worked up about things? I reminded him he was the one with final say. But, oh, it was somehow monumentally important to him that everyone be on board with the whole thing and that I be the one to sign the approval form. Don't ask me why.'

'Maybe because you were the most critical?'

'Hm, that hadn't occurred to me, but if they did want to obscure something, I suppose that would be a smart move.'

'Do you remember any names?'

'Professor Llyleworth was the lead archaeologist, but his funding was coming from SIS in London. The society's chairman of the board was listed as the owner of the project. I think they had a budget of five or six million kroner. To find a ring fortress! In a Norwegian cornfield. For crying out loud.'

'Do you have any idea how I was chosen?'

'As inspector? Don't ask me. We didn't have anyone to spare. I stood my ground on that one. I think Arntzen was the one who picked you.'

'But why me specifically?'

'Because you're good?'

First I laugh, then I tell Caspar about the dig and about the surprising find. I tell him about how Professors Llyleworth and Arntzen acted and about my suspicions, but I don't tell him that I have the shrine.

When I finish, Caspar chuckles and shakes his head. 'What a mess. I had a feeling something fishy was going on.'

A young woman walking past our table – I remember her vaguely from a dig a few years ago – smiles at me in recognition and coos 'Early lunch today?' at Caspar.

He leans over to me and lowers his voice: 'You know what? I'm going to poke around a little and see what I can find out. Why don't you come over and have dinner with Kristin and me tonight? Then we'll look at this together. It'll be a little more discreet than here. Besides, it's been ages. Kristin would love to see you again.'

'I'd love to,' I say. Just the thought of Kristin sets my pulse racing.

'And Bjørn, if I were you, I'd go and have a little chat with Grethe. She knows everything there is to know about those guys.'

'Grethe?'

'Grethe. Don't tell me you've forgotten Grethe?'

I blush. I haven't forgotten Grethe.

11

In front of my building there's a man sitting hunched behind the steering wheel of a freshly washed red Range Rover with diplomatic plates. When he spots me, he quickly looks away. Most people stare at me.

I let myself into my flat. The answering machine is blinking, which is unusual.

The first message is from my mother. She called to remind me that I'm invited to dinner tonight. We both know that I said no. The second message is from an older woman, who politely and apologetically tells the answering machine that she dialled a wrong number. The third is silent. I just hear somebody breathing.

I immediately have the sense that I'm not alone, which happens to me sometimes. It feels as if someone has been here. I tiptoe into the living room. The sun is shining through the curtains. I open the door to the bedroom, where my queen-size waterbed sneers at me like an unfulfilled promise. The bathroom is dark. The office, which for a more patriarchally minded man of my age would have served as a child's bedroom, is overflowing with documents and artefacts I've borrowed.

I'm alone. I still can't shake the feeling that someone else has been here. I open a bottle of beer, ice cold after weeks in the fridge. I drink it while I make yet another round of the flat.

It's not until my fourth round that I see it: someone has moved my computer. Not by much, just a few centimetres, but enough that I finally notice because the dust line doesn't match up. I sit down heavily in my desk chair and turn on the machine. Nothing happens. No beeping or whirring. That irritating ta-da sound that I've been trying to get rid of ever since I bought the computer has finally been silenced.

I soon realise why.

The front is loose. I prise the panel off with my fingertips and peer into the jumble of electronics that make up the organs, lifelines and brain of the machine. I'm no computer expert, but I can tell that someone has removed my hard drive.

A wave of fury washes over me. They invaded my private space. They just made themselves right at home, as if I'd given them the key to my life.

Then I calm down. I still have the upper hand. They didn't get what they were looking for. Filled with reckless zeal, I call the police to report the break-in and then I call Professor Arntzen at the office.

He's out of breath. 'Where's the shrine?' he yells when he realises who's calling.

'The shrine?' I ask, pretending not to have any idea what he's talking about.

'Don't act like you . . .' he starts.

Someone grabs the phone away from him.

'Where's the goddam shrine?' Llyleworth's voice quivers.

'What makes you guys think I have the shrine?'

'Cut the bullshit! Where is it?'

'I'll save you a bunch of time and just tell you right now that there's nothing on my hard drive besides lectures, a few half-finished poems and some awesome computer games.'

'Where's the shrine?'

I hang up, get myself another beer, and wonder what's going to happen next.

The phone rings. I mostly feel like letting it ring. I don't want to talk to anyone. The phone doesn't stop ringing. Finally its persistence prevails.

It's an Englishman. *Dr Rutherford from London*, director of the prestigious Royal British Institute of Archaeology. He offers me money for *the artefact*, which he understands is in my possession.

'The find is Norwegian property,' I protest.

'Fifty thousand pounds,' he parries.

Fifty thousand pounds is a lot of money. It doesn't even occur to me to consider accepting the offer. My stubbornness has never been grounded in common sense.

'I don't have it any more,' I lie.

'You don't?'

I tell him it was stolen. The shrine was just stolen from my flat today; there was a break-in.

Dr Rutherford almost slips up. He's about to say that the shrine wasn't in the flat, that they didn't find it, but he checks himself. I can hear in his voice that I've planted some doubt: What if the burglars he hired actually did steal the shrine? To pull one over on him? As if to assure himself, he asks: 'Are you sure, Mr Beltø?' 'Yes, I'm *quite sure*.' He hesitates. My lie has left him uncertain.

'Would you be interested in a trade?' he asks.

'What do you have that I would be interested in?'

'I can tell you what happened when your father died.'

Time screeches to a halt. Kaleidoscopic images bubble to the surface: the mountain, the rope, the loose rocks at the base of the cliff, the blood. I find myself in a vacuum where time has been standing still for twenty years.

I stare vacantly ahead. It wasn't until many years after my father's death that I realised how little I'd known him. He's a fleeting image in my memory, a contemplative man who rarely touched me or let me into his world. My father kept the doors to his life shut and his curtains drawn. I saw rage flare up in his eyes a couple of times, but mostly he was a man who came home from the office, or a dig, to disappear down into the room in the basement where he was writing an academic treatise that he preferred not to talk about and which I never saw.

When I picture my father, it's through a child's eyes.

My mother never wants to talk about him. And the professor gets so flustered, as if he can't bear the thought that his beloved little wife once loved someone else, deeply and passionately. He has to live with the fact that he was number two in line at the cake plate.

But one thought never ceases to amaze me: My mother has been the professor's wife for twice as long as she was my father's.

I miss my father, but every once in a while I wonder whether a son can look at his father without at some point thinking about the pouch hanging between his father's legs where he once wriggled as an eager little sperm, about the organ dangling between his father's legs that swells up, filling his mother with objectionable carnal pleasure. Sometimes I'm not quite right in the head. Could someone pass me the little plastic cup with the pink pills?

Maybe I see myself in my father. That makes sense. I never looked up to him. Sometimes that bugs me. When I read about fathers moulding their sons, I wonder what part of my father lives on in me. My depression? The fact that I became an archaeologist, like him? A coincidence, it was the attraction of an interpretive science, a field that suits my introverted, inquisitive temperament. Whenever I dared to venture into his study, he would glance up from his papers or artefacts, smile blankly, and show me a loom weight or an arrowhead that he seemed to know everything about. I didn't know the difference between an educated guess and empirical interpretation, but I understood that my father could look back through time.

His sudden interest in rock climbing was completely out of

character. He was a cautious person. Just like me. Sort of anxiety prone. Trygve Arntzen was the one who lured my father up on to all those cliff faces. Suspicious, if you ask me. Maybe that's why I've never been able to forgive Professor Arntzen for not being able to prevent the fall, if he even tried. After all, he was conspicuously quick to volunteer to take over my dad's used widow.

I've been stuck here, perplexed, swirling around in this little eddy in time, with the phone to my ear. Dr Rutherford asks, 'Are you still there?'

'What do you know about my father?' I quickly ask.

'We can come back to that. Once we have the shrine.'

'What do you mean something happened when he died?'

'Again – once we have the shrine . . .'

'We'll see.' I clear my throat, promise to consider the offer, hesitantly thank him for his time and hang up.

I rush out into the hallway, down the stairs and out on to the street. The red Range Rover is gone. It doesn't matter. The driver looked big and strong. Maybe he was waiting for his girlfriend.

I don't know who *Dr Rutherford, Director of the Royal British Institute of Archaeology*, is. Or how easy he thinks I am to fool. But I do know two things:

There's no such thing as the Royal British Institute of Archaeology.

And I thought I was the only one in the whole world who suspected that my father's death wasn't an accident.

12

My father is buried at Grefsen Cemetery, with a simple head-stone under an old birch tree. My mother pays the annual maintenance fee.

I squat down in front of the granite headstone. My father's name is carved into the red stone, no dates, nothing that anchors my father in time, just his name: *Birger Beltø*. My mother and I wanted it that way.

I brought a pot of yellow lilies in a brown paper bag. I plant them in front of the headstone to brighten things up for Dad, wherever he is.

In the woods between my grandmother's country house and Værne Monastery there's an old graveyard underneath the enormous oak trees. I've always wondered who's down there, resting under the heavy iron plate that time erased the text from long ago. My mother said that at one time they had owned Værne Monastery, which is why they were allowed to put the graveyard in the woods. I remember thinking: while the rest of us are relegated to the cemeteries.

Two men are sitting on the hood of a red Range Rover in the car park. I had noticed this car in my rear-view mirror when I drove over to my mother's house this morning. When they see me, one of them hops down and comes towards me. He looks like King Kong. I manage to get into Bolla and shut the door before he reaches me. He pounds on the window. His fingers are thick and hairy and he's wearing a signet ring from a foreign school. In his free hand he's carrying a mobile phone. I start Bolla and begin backing out of the parking spot. He grabs the door handle. Maybe he's considering holding the car back by force. I wouldn't be surprised if he was able to do it, too.

Luckily he lets go. In the mirror I see him running back to his own car.

Bolla was not made to get away from other cars, so I don't even try. I calmly drive up to Kjelsås Street. When the next red bus comes, I turn in behind it. This makes us into a little procession. The bus. Bolla. And the Range Rover.

To dissuade cut-through traffic, the city of Oslo has created a number of artificial dead ends between Kjelsås and Lofthus, installing bus-only gates, which the bus drivers open by radio signal. Our procession steadily approaches one of these bus gates. As the bus driver uses his remote to open the gate and drive through, I hug his bumper and follow him. Just on the other side, I stop, blocking the Range Rover's access. I watch smugly as the gate swings shut between the Range Rover and myself.

II

The Relic

1

'WELL, WELL, LITTLE Bjørn, is it really you?'

She's grown old. I've always thought of her as a real adult (I suppose perhaps *mature* is the word I'm looking for), but she carries her years with a sophisticated, youthful dignity. When I met her she used to wear her silvery blonde hair pulled back casually and would walk around in tight, knit skirts and black lace stockings. Now I can see that the years have taken their toll on her. Her eyes squint at me vivaciously from her slender face, where age spots and wrinkles have painted a map of her decline. Her hands are frail, trembling, like the claws of a baby sparrow. I catch glimpses of her scalp through her shiny white hair. She shakes her head. 'It's been a while . . .' she says, wondering why I'm here, expectant. Her voice is frail, tender. I was in love with her at one time.

Her smile is the same, her eyes are the same, but she's very pale. She steps to the side to let me in.

Her flat is how I remember it: enormous, crammed full of furniture, dark and filled with strong scents, room after room after room. Doors outlined by thick frames, the ceilings done in swoops of stucco. She's recreated the highlights of the Bible in bric-a-brac figurines on her cabinets and narrow shelves: Moses at Mount Sinai, Mary and the baby Jesus in the stall, the Sermon on the Mount, the crucifixion. Fuzzy teddy bears and dolls with lifeless porcelain faces sit in small wicker chairs and woven raffia doll carriages. Maybe this is how Grethe Lid Wøien holds on to the childhood she refuses to talk about. I don't think she has any family. At least none she acknowledges having. I've never heard her talk about anyone who's close to her. Grethe has filled all that empty space with her studies. And with men. There are books everywhere. She's shut herself in here in her flat, on this exclusive street in Oslo's Frogner neighbourhood, to cultivate her loneliness.

She follows me into the study. On the way we walk past her bedroom. The door is half open. I catch a glimpse of her unmade bed. Other people's beds embarrass me so I look away shyly.

She's not the same. She's become an old woman. There's something used up, shocking about her gait.

A cat leaps off a chair and disappears under the grand piano. I have never liked cats and they don't like me either.

She nods towards the velvet sofa. 'I should've offered you something to drink,' she says, collapsing into a chair.

Something is wrong. I sense it, but I still can't make myself ask.

She looks at me and smiles wryly. An enormous wall clock chimes twice.

'I need some help,' I say, suppressing a sneeze. The sofa is covered with cat hair, which makes my nose tickle.

'I thought as much. You've never been one to make a nuisance of yourself with unnecessary visits.'

I can't tell whether she means that as a mild rebuke, a simple observation or a reference to the evening twelve years ago when I plucked up my courage and told her that I loved her. I was twenty. She was well over fifty. I've always been an independent thinker.

'Do you think I've grown old?' she asks.

I've never lied to her. So I don't say anything. Age is just a point in a chronology. The mathematician Kathleen Ollerenshaw was eighty-six when she solved the age-old mathematical riddle of the 'magic square'. No matter how you add up the numbers, the answer is 30:

0	14	3	13
7	9	4	10
12	2	15	1
11	5	8	6

During my silence, Grethe sighs sadly. 'I'm sick,' she says, bluntly. 'Cancer. For two years now. I'm grateful for each day.'

I take her hand in mine. It's like holding the cold hand of a sleeping child.

'My doctor says I'm a tough old coot,' she says.

'Are you in pain?'

She raises her shoulders in a gesture that could mean either yes or no. Then she says, 'Mostly mentally.'

I squeeze her hand.

'So, what can I do for you?' she asks, suddenly all business, pulling her hand back. Her tone has a touch of the authority she wielded in her work as a professor. She retired seven years ago. We still talk about her.

'If you're sick, I don't want to . . .'

'Nonsense.'

'I just thought . . .'

'Little Bjørn.' She's giving me that look of hers.

I don't know where to start.

She helps me out: 'I hear you're working on the Værne Monastery dig.' That's how she always was at the university, too. She knew everything.

'We found something,' I say. Then I get stuck again and find myself searching for the right words. Finally I blurt out: 'I'm just trying to figure out what could have happened!' Then I realise that probably doesn't make any sense.

'What did you find?' she asks.

'A reliquary . . . a shrine.'

'Yes . . .?'

'Made of gold.'

She shakes her head. 'Really?'

'Professor Llyleworth ran off with it.'

She doesn't say anything. She should have started laughing and shaken her head, but she doesn't say anything. She starts coughing, cautiously at first, then loud and rattling. It sounds as if her lungs are flopping back and forth inside her chest. She covers her mouth with both hands. When the attack subsides, she sits there gasping for air. She doesn't look at me, which is good. This way she doesn't have to see the look in my eyes.

She clears her throat several times. She discreetly pulls out a handkerchief and spits.

'Pardon me,' she whispers.

I stare for a long time at the cat curled up asleep under the piano. Back when I was Grethe's star student and admirer, the one who always had some important reason to stop by her home, she had a cat named Lucifer, but this can hardly be the same one. Although it looks exactly the same.

'Is the relic authentic? Is it old?' she asks.

'It certainly appears to be.'

'No one salted the dig?'

I shake my head. Salting is a game that really amuses us archaeologists. We plant modern items in the wrong culture layers – a TV remote among the treasures of a prehistoric king, a safety pin among the potsherds and arrowheads.

'Grethe, the shrine is old, and besides,' I chuckle, 'we're

talking about a dig led by Graham Llyleworth. No one would dare to pollute his site.'

Grethe chuckles too.

'And he knew what we were looking for,' I continue. 'He knew the shrine would be there somewhere. He knew we were going to find it. He knew.'

She contemplates my claim for a while.

'And you think he might want to steal this shrine? To sell it to the highest bidder?' she asks in a voice hoarse with phlegm.

'That thought has occurred to me, but it's not quite that simple.'

'It's not?'

'The Antiquities Collection is in on it.'

She stares at me expectantly, guardedly, waiting for me to continue.

'Probably the Royal Norwegian Office of Cultural Heritage as well,' I add.

Her eyes narrow. I'm sure she's thinking that poor Little Bjørn must be off his rocker.

'I mean everything I'm saying, Grethe.'

'Sure, sure.'

'And I'm not crazy.'

She smiles at me. 'So tell me, what are they up to?'

'I don't know, Grethe. I just don't know . . .'

'Well then, why . . .'

'Maybe it's some kind of commissioned theft?' I blurt out a little too eagerly.

She looks puzzled. 'But why?'

'I don't know. Could Llyleworth be part of some kind of international art ring?'

She smiles coldly. 'Graham? He's way too self-centred to be a part of anything, and certainly not an art ring!' Her outburst is bitter and fraught with emotion.

'You know him?'

'I've . . . run into him.'

'Oh? On a dig?'

'There too. And at Oxford. Twenty-five years ago. Why are you so suspicious?'

'He was planning to smuggle the shrine out of the country.'

'Oh, he would never do that. He probably just . . .'

'Grethe! I know what he was planning to do.'

'How can you be so sure?'

Automatically I lower my voice: 'Because I overheard him.' I give the words time to sink in. 'I overheard him conspiring with Professor Arntzen.'

She shakes her head with a resigned smirk. 'That's just so typically Graham. And I see that you've been up to your old Hardy boys tricks again.'

'I'm just trying to understand.'

'Understand what?'

'How could he know that the shrine would be there, in the ruins of an eight-hundred-year-old octagon, in the middle of a Norwegian grain field?'

Grethe's eyes are suddenly unfathomable. For a while I swim around in them.

'My Lord,' she says, mostly to herself.

'What's wrong?'

'An octagon?'

'Yeah, so? We've excavated portions of it already.'

'I didn't think it was real.'

'You knew about it?'

She has another coughing fit. I lean over and pat her on the back. It takes several minutes before she catches her breath again.

'How are you doing?' I ask. 'Should I call your doctor's office? Do you want me to leave?'

'Tell me about the octagon.'

'I don't know much. I've never heard anything about an octagon at Værne Monastery,' I say.

'Maybe not in Norwegian sources, but it's been discussed in the international literature about the Knights Hospitaller and early Christian myths.'

Hm, I must have missed that lecture.

I ask: 'Do you think Professor Llyleworth would be familiar with the octagon?'

'I should think so.' She says it coyly, understatedly.

'Why didn't he say anything about it? Why did he keep it a secret?'

'Well, it was hardly a secret. I mean, did you ever ask?'

'He said we were looking for a ring fortress. He never said anything about an octagon.'

She nods wearily, as if the conversation is boring her. She folds her hands in her lap. 'And what does Professor Arntzen have to say about all this?'

I look away.

'Little Bjørn?'

'I haven't discussed it with him.'

'Why not?'

'He's one of them.'

'One . . . of . . . them?' she repeats sceptically.

I grin sheepishly because I hear how paranoid I must sound.

I take her hand cautiously in mine. 'Grethe, what's going on?'

'You're asking me?'

'Professor Arntzen and Professor Graham fucking Llyleworth? Grave robbers? Common grave robbers?'

She closes her eyes with a dreamy smile.

'Why are you smiling?' I ask.

'It's not that surprising, not really.'

'It's not?'

'Your dad and Graham studied together at Oxford, you know, in the seventies. With me. Graham and Birger were best friends.'

I lean back on the sofa. A swallow is teetering on a wire outside the window. It sits there for a while before flying off on its way.

'Hasn't your stepfather told you this?' she asks. 'Or Llyleworth?'

'They must've forgotten to mention it. I mean, I knew my dad was at Oxford but not that Llyleworth was there.'

'Your father was the one who introduced Llyleworth and Arntzen to each other.'

'So my dad and Llyleworth were classmates?'

'They co-authored an academic treatise that caused a bit of a stir.'

My mind shuts down.

'Do you have a copy?' I ask.

She points to the bookcase.

I get up slowly and move towards the bookcase, where I run my index finger along the spines.

'Third shelf down,' she says. 'Next to the atlas. Black, hardcover.'

I pull out the book. It's thick. The pages have started to yellow and crack.

I read *Comparative Socio-Archaeological Analysis of Inter-Continental Treasures and Myths* on the dust jacket. 'By Birger Beltø, Charles DeWitt and Graham Llyleworth, University of Oxford, 1973.'

'What's it about?'

'They found commonalities between a number of religious myths and archaeological finds.'

I wonder why the professor and my mother hid the copies my father must surely have left behind.

I flip through the pages at random. On page 2 I read a dedication that someone has crossed out with a felt-tip pen. I hold the paper up to the light. 'The authors wish to express their greatest respect and gratitude to their academic advisers, Michael MacMullin and Grethe Lid Wøien.'

I cast an astonished glance at Grethe. She winks at me.

On page 54 I read a few paragraphs from the chapter on the discovery of the Dead Sea Scrolls in Qumran. On page 466 – this is no piddling text dashed off in a hurry – I come across a ten-page-long footnote drawing parallels between the Hon treasure, which was found in Øvre Eiker in 1834, and artefacts from the Ajía Fotiá graves on Crete. I look up Værne Monastery in the index, but don't find any references. Until I move my index finger to *Varna, 296–301*.

The chapter is called 'The Octagon of Varna: The Myth of the Shrine of Sacred Secrets'.

As I turn to the chapter a bookmark falls out, a business card. It's old fashioned, dignified: 'Charles DeWitt – London Geographical Association'. Reflexively I stuff the card into my pocket as I skim through the chapter.

I'm a fast reader. It takes me only a couple of minutes to scan through the text, which is about the myth of an eight-sided temple – an octagon – that the Knights Hospitaller erected around a reliquary that was said to contain, if I've understood the text correctly, a message of a divine nature. Perhaps from the time of Jesus. Perhaps from the time of the Crusades. The whole thing isn't that easy to understand. I may have misunderstood. I was reading very quickly.

'Can I borrow this?' I ask, holding up the book. 'I'd like to read it more carefully.'

'Sure, of course,' she says enthusiastically, as if she would like nothing better in this world than for me to take it home with me.

'So, tell me what you know about this,' I say.

She winks contentedly and clears her throat. In her frail, quavering voice Grethe tells me about the Crusader who brought a relic to the Knights Hospitaller in Jerusalem in 1186. This relic later came to be known as the Shrine of Sacred Secrets. Pope Clement III commanded the Knights Hospitaller not just to guard the shrine, but to hide it far from thieves and Crusaders and knights, from bishops and popes and royalty. When Saladin captured Jerusalem the following year and the Knights Hospitaller fled, all traces of the shrine disappeared. They only had one lead to go on, all the adventurers and fortune hunters who have searched for the treasure over the centuries: the sacred shrine was in an octagon, an eight-sided temple.

'At Værne Monastery?' I ask snidely.

She's leaning back in her chair, watching me. There's something ever so slightly patronising about her expression. 'Why not at Værne Monastery?'

I can't help but laugh.

She pats me on the knee. 'Little Bjørn, I know what you're thinking. You've always been so impatient, so sceptical, so quick to draw conclusions. What did I used to tell you at university? Didn't I teach you to combine scepticism with imagination, understanding with wonder, doubt with openness? You should listen to the myths, the sagas, the fairy tales and the religions, not because they tell you the truth, Little Bjørn, but because they have grown out of another truth.'

The intensity in her voice and eyes scares me. It's as if she wants to give me the key to eternal life before she vanishes in a puff of smoke and sparks. Neither of these things happens. She leans over and takes a sweet from the bowl on the coffee table. She puts the piece of hard confectionery into her mouth. I hear how it rattles back and forth across her teeth.

She shakes her head. 'Værne Monastery wasn't such a dumb hiding place. The monastery is as far from the Holy

Land as anywhere could possibly be. Norway was definitely an outpost of the civilised world. And the historians have never really been able to explain why the Knights Hospitaller built a monastery in Norway at the end of the twelfth century.' She shakes her head thoughtfully. 'If you really did find the octagon, Little Bjørn, and you really did find a shrine . . .' She leaves the sentence hanging.

'What's in the shrine?' I ask.

'Well, that's really the question, now, isn't it? What's in the shrine?'

'You don't know?'

'No, goodness me,' she says, 'I have no idea. There are lots of rumours. There are those who still contend that the Merovingian dynasty were hiding a treasure of untold riches, gold and jewels that the Church and the royal family had amassed over the centuries.'

'Oh, please!' I interrupt, with a deep, exaggerated sigh. 'Hidden treasure? Have you ever heard of anyone who's found a treasure like that?'

'Maybe it's still out there waiting to be found?'

'Indiana Jones romanticism.'

'Little Bjørn,' she says, pursing her lips together in a way that tells me what she's going to say next, 'I'm referring to rumours that have been circulating among academics for decades. I'm not vouching for them, but I'm also not willing to just perfunctorily brush them aside like a certain young gentleman I know.'

'So what did they say, these . . . rumours?' I spit the word out like a rotten cherry.

'There's a map and a genealogy. The texts are in code. I don't know all the historical details. The tale originates in a village in southern France called Rennes-le-Château, where a young priest found some parchment scrolls late in the nine-teenth century that they say made him rich, unbelievably rich.

No one knows exactly what he found when he went to restore the old church he'd been put in charge of. It's said the parchments contained some big, mind-boggling secret.'

'Which was?'

'If I knew that, Little Bjørn, it would hardly be a secret, now, would it? Some speculated it had to do with religious myths, that he'd found the Arc of the Covenant, which wasn't so outrageous since the church building was erected over the ruins of an old Christian church from the sixth century. Others thought he had found original texts for the Bible. Still others thought it had to do with genealogies, bloodlines. And some thought he had basically found maps leading the way to a medieval treasure trove.'

'And what does all that have to do with Værne Monastery?'

'How should I know? I suppose maybe the treasure, if there is one, is hidden on the monastery grounds? Or the shrine you found contains clues that lead the way to something else?'

'Grethe . . .' I sigh, giving her my best Bambi look.

Then suddenly she exclaims, 'Q!'

'What did you say?'

'The Q manuscript,' Grethe says.

I cock my head, not understanding.

She continues: 'I'm not sure. It's a guess. For all these years I've been wondering what could have been such an important discovery. And now that I'm putting all these little fragments of information together, the puzzle pieces are falling into place. Maybe.'

'The Q manuscript?' I ask.

'Q for "Quelle". Which means "source". In German.'

'Quelle?'

'You've really never heard of it?'

'Nope, don't think so. What the heck is it?'

'Ostensibly a Greek original manuscript.'

'Containing . . .?'

'Containing everything Jesus said.'

'Jesus? Really?'

'His teachings in the form of quotations. The text that Matthew and Luke are supposed to have used as the basis for their gospels, in addition to the Gospel of Mark.'

'I didn't know there was such a thing as the Q manuscript.'

'There may not be. It's a theory.'

'Why would it end up at Værne Monastery?'

'Ask your stepfather.'

'He would know about this?'

'More than I do, anyway,' she eventually says.

'But how—'

'Little Bjørn,' she interrupts, breaking out into good-natured laughter. Then she looks at me thoughtfully. 'Do you want to go to London?'

'London?'

'For me.'

I hesitate.

She adds: 'I'm paying.'

'Why?'

'To clear up an old mystery.'

I don't say anything and neither does Grethe. She stands up, a bit wobbly, and shuffles out of the living room into her bedroom. When she returns, she hands me an envelope. I open it and count out thirty thousand Norwegian crowns.

'Whoa!'

'That should be enough?' she asks.

'It's way too much.'

'Don't say that. You may need to do more travelling . . .'

'You're crazy to keep this much money lying around at home.'

'You don't think I would just hand my money over to a bank, do you?'

I smile blankly, confused. 'What is this all about?'

'Your job is to find that out.'

'Grethe.' I try to catch her eyes, but she looks away. 'Why do you want to get messed up in all of this?'

She looks straight ahead for a moment, then finally looks me in the eye. 'I could have been a part of the whole thing.'

'A part of what?'

'Of what you're scratching the surface of.'

'But?'

'But something happened . . .'

Her eyes well up and she bites her lower lip. It takes a little while for her to regain her composure over the flood of emotion.

I know I'm not going to get anything else out of her, but I suppose her motives aren't important. Not now. Sooner or later I'll get to the bottom of them.

'Will you go?' she asks.

'Of course.'

'The Society of International Sciences, SIS. In London, Whitehall. Ask for the chairman. Michael MacMullin. He has the answers.'

'To what?'

'To everything!'

We look at each other.

She grabs my arm hard. 'Be careful.'

'Careful?' I repeat, not masking my concern.

'MacMullin,' she says, 'is a man with many friends.'

It sounds like a veiled threat.

'Friends,' I repeat. 'Friends like Charles DeWitt?'

The twitch in her face is almost imperceptible. 'Charles?' Her voice is hollow. 'Charles DeWitt? What do you know about him?'

'Nothing.'

For a while she's lost, off in a world I have no access to.

Then she says: 'Well, at least you don't need to fear him.' Her voice is tinged with a distant tenderness.

'What do you know about the accident?' I ask.

'It was a trivial matter,' she says. 'A scratch on his arm. The wound became gangrenous.'

I have no idea what she's talking about.

'He fell . . .' I say

She looks at me, her brow furrowed, then she understands. 'Oh, your father?' Only the look in her eyes reveals her under-lying agitation. 'There's nothing to know,' she says, tersely.

I don't move. 'But Grethe—'

'Nothing!' she barks. The effort triggers a coughing fit. A long moment passes before she manages to get control of herself again. 'Nothing,' she repeats softly, more gently now. 'Nothing you need to know.'

2

It takes twelve minutes for me to drive up to Domus Theologica, which sounds like some kind of Mediterranean shopping mall, but which is really just the self-important name they've given the building that houses the University of Oslo's Department of Theology up on Blindern Street. I know an assistant professor of Hebrew scriptures. I think that may come in handy.

Gert Vikerslåtten is almost six foot seven and thin as an awl, so that it seems as if he has to concentrate to keep his balance, not unlike a stork. He has blotchy skin and a beard that looks as if it's attached too tightly behind the ears and under his chin. Everything about him – his fingers, arms, nose, teeth – is a little too long and awkward.

We spend a few minutes reminiscing about our student days. We talk about our mutual acquaintances, our hopeless teachers, the girls we dreamt about, but never got. Like me, Gert is single. Like me, he hides his small neuroses beneath a patina of academic arrogance.

He asks why I've come. I tell him that I'm looking for someone who can tell me about something called the Q manuscript.

His eyes light up. His Adam's apple starts bobbing up and down. Nothing pleases an expert more than a chance to show off his knowledge.

'Q? Aw yeah, baby. That's a manuscript that doesn't exist.'

'But it must have existed at some point in time?' I ask.

'Well, that's what a lot of people think anyway.'

'And do you agree with them?'

'Definitely.' He flings out his long arms, making me afraid that he'll punch through the walls of the cramped office.

'Even if no one has ever seen so much as a fragment?'

'Q is like a black hole,' he says, forming a circle with his thumb and index finger. 'Even with the strongest telescopes, you can't see it, but you know it's there from the way the other heavenly bodies move.'

'The way you would know there's a magnet under a piece of paper covered with metal filings,' I elaborate. He nods and I continue: 'All I know about Q is that it's written in Greek. And that it supposedly contains many of Jesus' teaching, in the form of quotations, the way they were later recounted by Luke and Matthew. And that it's considered to be a source document for the Bible.'

'Well, then you know the gist.'

'But explain to me – why does it matter if it existed or not?'

'Insight, understanding.' He shrugs. 'I mean, when you

look at it that way it doesn't matter that you archaeologists found the Gokstad ship either, but it's still really cool you did.'

'But in practical terms would finding the Q manuscript make any actual difference?'

'Of course it would.'

'Well, why would it? In what way?'

'Because the Q manuscript could change how we understand and interpret the texts of the Bible. I mean, I'm sure you appreciate how much Christianity directly affects our everyday lives even to this day, as a bearer of culture, and in our laws and rules, our view of humanity. Everything is interrelated.'

'I understand all that. Are you saying that the Q manuscript would change any of that?'

'The Q manuscript could help us understand more about how the New Testament came to be, and in doing so, help us interpret its texts. The early Christian theologian Origen maintained that the words of the Bible should not be interpreted literally – as many people do today – but as allegories or signs of something else, something bigger. The Bible is to be interpreted as a whole. When the Bible tells of a mountain from which one can see the whole world, that's not meant literally! Even though some people insist on interpreting every word literally.'

'How old is the Q manuscript?'

'Almost two thousand years. We think the Q manuscript was written just before Paul wrote and dated the very first of his epistles, in other words as early as twenty years after Jesus was crucified.'

'And who wrote it?'

'We don't know.' He leans in and lowers his voice: 'The interesting thing about the timeline is that that's twenty years before Markus wrote his gospel.' He raises his eyebrows suggestively. He expectantly awaits my reaction, but it doesn't come. I don't understand why he thinks these dates are so interesting. His eyebrows sink back into place, crestfallen.

'As you know,' he continues with exaggerated clarity, bordering on condescension, 'the Gospel of Mark is considered the oldest of the gospels, in other words the first, even though it comes second in the New Testament. It was probably written forty years after the crucifixion, around AD 70.'

'So in a sense the Q manuscript would be more authentic than the later gospels?'

'More authentic?'

'Because it was written closer to when the events occurred?'

'Well . . .' Gert drags it out, grimacing in a way that exposes his oblong teeth and pink gums. 'Ranking the authenticity of old manuscripts, biblical or otherwise, is rather pointless two thousand years after the fact. It's also a matter of belief. But it's obvious that the farther you get from the sources and the events, the more there's a risk that the accounts will be increasingly imprecise and inaccurate.'

'So in a way the old evangelists were like journalists,' I say.

'Well, hardly journalists. More like community activists, preachers, missionaries . . .'

'Exactly! Journalists.' I laugh. 'And the evangelists had access to the Q manuscript?'

'It's quite likely. We think the Q manuscript was circulating among the earliest Christian communities in the first century,' Gert says, and then his lips curl as if he's tickled by the thought of something he shouldn't say. 'What's controversial about the manuscript is that some scholars think some Christian communities didn't consider Jesus a deity but a wise philosopher, someone who wanted to teach people how they should live to be contented Jews. If you take the gospels and Paul out of the New Testament, you're left with a document about reformed Judaism.'

'There must be lots of people who think that?'

'But you have to remember that the Q manuscript, if the manuscript is ever found, would be incredibly authoritative because it was written right after Jesus' lifetime and by eye-witnesses, not by evangelists, who lived much later. You could sort of say that the Q manuscript was a journalistic account – to a greater extent than the coloured, adapted gospels. The Q manuscript portrayed Jesus as an apoca-lyptic rebel and citizen, a contemporary revolutionary. It didn't say anything about whether he was the Son of God or not.'

'So what does the Q manuscript prove?'

'The Q manuscript can't really prove anything at all. But you have to read manuscripts from that period with a basic understanding of the times, of the prevailing societal circumstances.'

'I guess I just thought that theologians would blindly trust everything that's in the Bible.'

'Ha! Theology is a science, not a faith. As early as the 1700s, critical theologians were questioning the dogmas. Professor Herman Samuel Reimarus reduced Jesus to a Jewish political figure. In 1906, Albert Schweitzer followed up with an impressive academic treatise that asked funda-mental questions about prevailing theological views. These theologians drew a distinction between the historical Jesus and the teachings of Jesus. This critical branch of theology has continued to develop until the present day. By combining historical, sociological, anthropological, political and theo-logical approaches, a new picture of Jesus emerges.'

'What sort of picture?'

'Jesus was born in a turbulent era. His teachings were used and abused. Many of the first Christian communities did not emphasise Jesus' death or resurrection at all. They viewed him as a natural charismatic leader like Lenin or Che Guevara. Meanwhile other early Christian communities emphasised just the crucifixion and ascension and pretty much forgot about the historical Jesus altogether.'

'So the Q manuscript doesn't have anything to say about a divine Jesus?'

'No siree. Not a whisper. It doesn't even seem like the manuscript's authors were aware of the circumstances surrounding Jesus' death. And if they were, they completely disregarded the crucifixion, not to mention the resurrection. So you see? Even if the Q manuscript confirms much of what Luke and Matthew wrote, finding the actual Q manuscript would also affect and change our understanding of Jesus. The manuscript's authors never viewed Jesus as God's son, but as an itinerant wise man and agitator, a rebel. The evangelists were the ones who added the dogma about Jesus' resurrection later, which transformed him into a god. Sure, there are some who think that the disciples stole Jesus' body after the crucifixion and made up the whole resurrection. They didn't want to admit defeat – that their saviour just up and died without any sign of the kingdom of God showing up. Even Jesus believed for a long time that the kingdom of God would come during his lifetime.'

'I still don't get why you guys are convinced that the Q manuscript existed?'

Gert runs his fingers over his cheeks, down over his chin, and tugs at his priestly beard. 'Imagine if both of us were to translate the same English text into Norwegian. Our two versions would be similar. But they wouldn't be identical. That's what Matthew and Luke's gospels are like in many ways. Researchers have concluded that a good two hundred and thirty-five verses in Luke and Matthew are so similar that they must be based on the same source. Even if the two gospels were written independently, many of Jesus' words are identical, word for word.'

'So what?'

'So the historical Jesus spoke Aramaic, which had supplanted Hebrew as the language of everyday use in Palestine for four hundred years. He didn't speak Greek, as he does in these manuscripts. Which means the evangelists must have had an original Greek manuscript to refer to and quote from. The Q manuscript! *Quelle*. The source.'

'Well, couldn't Luke and Matthew have just plagiarised each other?'

Gert grins. 'Ha! If only it were that simple. No way. They were writing at different times, in different places, for very different audiences. They contain too many serious differences for Luke and Matthew to have read each other. If they had, they would have harmonised their stories to fit each other, corrected and adapted them. But anyway, we can prove that they both relied on the same source material.'

'The things we know,' I say laconically.

'Or think we know,' Gert says, balancing his chair on its back legs. It occurs to me that the consequences would be far reaching if he tips over. 'Scholars are sure that Mark wrote his gospel first. And that Luke and Matthew wrote their gospels based on Mark and the Q manuscript, but with their own additions. For example, about ninety per cent of Mark's topics also show up in Matthew.'

'How long have theologians known about the Q manuscript?'

'Biblical scholars determined as early as the 1800s that Luke and Matthew must have had a common source. I mean, in addition to Mark. But the source wasn't given a name until 1890.'

'When someone named it the Q manuscript?'

Gert nods. 'Not everyone subscribes to the Q manuscript

theory with equal enthusiasm, which makes sense. It's hard for most people to get all worked up about something that exists only in theory.'

He stands up. It's as if he's envisioning a lecture hall full of enthralled young coeds who want nothing more than some late-night private lessons in theology and applied physiology from Gert, after a nice meal and a bottle of wine.

He says: 'Something exciting happened in 1945. A couple of Egyptian brothers found a big, sealed jar in the dirt at the foot of some cliffs near Nag Hammadi.'

'And out came a genie who granted them three wishes?' I laugh. 'Booze, women and a brand, spanking new camel?'

Gert winks knowingly. 'Almost. Actually the brothers were terrified to open the jar precisely because it might contain a genie. An evil genie. As jars in Egypt have a nasty tendency to do. As any well-trained archaeologist will tell you.'

We chuckle. Gert has a cheerful, bubbly laugh.

'But the brothers' desire for money won out in the end,' he continues. 'I mean, maybe there weren't any genies in the jar. Maybe it was teeming with gold and diamonds. So they decided to risk it and they smashed it.'

'No genie?' I say.

'Not even a little guardian angel.'

'So what *did* they find?'

'Thirteen books. Thirteen codices bound in gazelle leather.'

I shake my head, imagining their disappointment.

Gert slaps his hands on his desk. 'It was a sensational find. Both for archaeologists and theologians. That was the Nag Hammadi library. Among other things the manuscripts contained the complete Gospel of Thomas.'

I squint off into space, trying to place the Gospel of Thomas. To be honest I've never really read the Bible that thoroughly, but I thought I could at least name all the gospels.

'The Gospel of Thomas was never included in the Bible,' Gert explains.

'Wow, it's not everyone who gets their manuscript rejected by God,' I say. 'And were you academics aware of the Gospel of Thomas?'

'Yes, at least to some extent. But nobody had ever seen a complete version, not until 1945. A fragment of the Gospel of Thomas, written in Greek, had previously been found in Oxyrhynchus in Egypt. But the Nag Hammadi version was complete. And not just that – the manuscripts also included what's called the Gospel of Philip and copies of conversations between Jesus and the disciples. It was almost its own complete "new testament", but very different from the one we're familiar with. And, pay attention now, because this is important. And interesting. It was all written in Coptic!'

'No, get out! Coptic?' I exclaim, but my outburst is completely tongue in cheek. And Gert doesn't buy it for a second.

'Coptic,' he repeats, his enthusiasm undiminished, and explains. 'That would be the Egyptian language that was in use until around the end of the Roman Empire.'

'I think I'm following you,' I mumble, even though that might be a bit of an exaggeration.

Gert smiles sympathetically. It must be the same smile he bestows on hesitant freshmen with braids and tight T-shirts. 'Using this text, scholars were able to reconstruct the Gospel of Thomas in its original language, Greek. Unlike the gospels that were included in the Bible, but like the Q manuscript, the Gospel of Thomas contains little or nothing about Jesus' birth, life or death. It contains his words. A hundred and fourteen quotations that all start with "And Jesus said . . ." Many of the quotes in the Gospel of Thomas are astonishingly

71

similar to the ones in Matthew and Luke. It's obvious to academics that Thomas relied on the same source document as Matthew and Luke. Are you still with me?'

'Just barely.'

'Thus, indirectly, the Gospel of Thomas confirms that Matthew and Luke, along with Thomas, must have had a common source document. A corpus that they copied from and touched up as necessary to convince their readers of their version of Jesus' life and teachings. What's interesting is that the author of the Q manuscript, and probably also his contemporaries, interpreted Jesus' words in a totally different way from the authors and readers of the Bible.'

'Rather a delicate issue, in other words.'

Gert bites his lower lip and nods. 'You can say that again! In 1989 a group started reconstructing the Q manuscript by comparing Matthew and Luke's biblical texts with the Thomas manuscript. Just this project, on its own, sparked a controversial and heated discussion about the origins of Christianity.'

I look at Gert, and he looks at me. I suppose he's wondering what this is all leading up to.

I ask: 'What would happen if someone found the Q manuscript?'

He shakes his head absent-mindedly. 'I don't even dare to think about it. It would definitely overshadow the discoveries of the Dead Sea Scrolls and Tutankhamen. We would simply need to rewrite the history of religion.'

I can't help but wonder if the Q manuscript is what's hiding in the golden shrine that's encased in rotting woodwork, wrapped in plastic, inside a paper sack in Roger's flat.

If I were playing the lead in a movie, I'm sure I would have ripped away the wood and prised open the shrine to satisfy my (and the audience's) curiosity by now. But I'm an intelligent person – a serious, cautious academic. A shrine which is that old and which has been lying in the ground for so many years can't just be opened like any old tin can. It needs to be opened with the utmost deliberation and care, by people who know what they're doing. The way you would open an oyster to find a pearl – without harming the oyster. If I set out on a hasty, excited hunt for the contents, I risk causing a catastrophe. In the best-case scenario, I would damage the contents and without even being able to understand what I've found, because my ancient Greek, Hebrew, Aramaic and Coptic are pretty rusty. In the worst-case scenario, everything would be ruined. Old vellum and papyrus can turn to dust overnight.

But I know this: the shrine must be protected.

3

Some women have a charm that goes straight to my pituitary.

She's tall, with reddish hair, green eyes, narrow lips, a smattering of freckles. Her skirt flutters around those long legs, a wide silver belt is cinched tight around her waist. Behind the cotton blouse I sense the weight of her breasts.

I was in love with her for two years. I hope she doesn't know that, but I suspect she does. And there she stands in the doorway in front of me with that same crooked smile that once bewitched me. Her name is Kristin. She's Caspar's wife. If you didn't know Kristin, you'd guess she's a textile artist or a nude model or maybe a trapeze artist in a travelling circus, but Kristin is an economist, a department head at Statistics Norway. When we were at the University of Oslo together, Kristin and Caspar lived with a bunch of other people in a rented house on Maridal Street, an enormous place. There was always jazz and blues-rock playing. The weekends were one long, non-stop party.

Group living wasn't for me: the lack of personal space, the nagging, the mound of boots and shoes by the front door, other people's wet undergarments hanging on the clotheslines in the laundry room, the arguments, the long afternoons in the common rooms, with sunlight pouring in the windows, other people always knowing what you're up to, hearing you when you go to the bathroom, wanting to discuss a book or movie with you, or play cards, or tell you to go to hell when you want to bum a cigarette off them, keeping track of when it's your turn to do the dishes, the illegible signatures on the sign-up sheet for the washing machine, the household meetings, the sense of community, the solidarity, the friction, the sexual tension, the voting on things, the self-recriminations. It's not for me.

One weekend when I crashed in their bedroom, Caspar and Kristin made love silently on their mattress on the floor next to me. It was early in the morning. The room was filled with soft light. I pretended I was asleep. They pretended they thought I was asleep. I remember her suppressed whimpers, the rhythmic rocking of their bodies, Caspar breathing hard through his nose, the sounds, the scents. In the morning we all pretended nothing had happened.

They were anarchists. I never understood what they were rebelling against. Their dedication to the cause has cooled; now they're social democrats. The only thing that distinguishes Kristin and Caspar from the masses is the one odd peculiarity left over from their leftist communal living days: they don't have a television set. They don't want one. It's a matter of principle. And, well, you just have to admire them for that.

'Bjørn!' Kristin cries effusively, pulling me inside while beaming and inspecting me from head to toe. 'You haven't changed at all,' she says. We hug. For a long time. I don't think Kristin has changed much either. And I remember, suddenly, why I was in love with her.

Caspar has covered the entire dining table with copies of papers related to the Værne Monastery dig: stacks of letters, documents, tables, forms, maps – all sprinkled with the kind of mess of stamps and file numbers that any bureaucracy uses to justify its own existence. There are applications and response letters, descriptions and clarifications, in an exhilarating blend of Norwegian and English.

'I felt like a traitor making all these copies,' Caspar says nervously, and I can't tell whether he's joking. I don't think he is. He's become so upstanding over the years. Government jobs have that effect on their loyal servants. They feel that they are one with the system, as if the system is them, which isn't that far from the truth.

Kristin flits around us like an industrious fairy. She lights a thousand little tea lights, which make the flat look like a secluded hillside monastery in ancient Greece. She pours tea into enormous ceramic mugs. She's constantly glancing over at me. Furtive, tense looks that suggest she's waiting for me to say the magic word, but I wasn't planning on doing that. She has baked biscuits and little heart-shaped waffles to go with the tea. Deep down inside Kristin, behind the department head, behind the sexy feminist, behind the economist, behind the revolutionary, behind the beautiful, worldly façade, lives a loving woman who wishes us all well.

I pull out a random page signed by Caspar Scott. Below the Royal Norwegian Office of Cultural Heritage's logo and the lion on Norway's national coat of arms, I read:

Pursuant to the Cultural Heritage Act of 9 June 1978, including amendments, the most recent being from 3 July 1992, the Society of International Sciences (SIS), c/o chairman Michael MacMullin (hereinafter referred to as the 'Developer'), is hereby granted permission to commence an archaeological excavation, under the field management of Professor Graham Llyleworth, in the area specified (NGO/map reference 1306/123/003). These plans fall under the authority of the Office of Cultural Heritage and the Developer undertakes to comply with instructions from this office's designated on-site archaeological representative (inspector). The search for a fortress structure falls under the purview of the Royal Norwegian Office of Cultural Heritage (vide regulations for the division of labour specialities), but because the work has a broader purpose, jurisdiction will be delegated to the local regional archaeological museum (c/o the University of Oslo's Antiquities Collection).

Caspar used to write poetry. In 1986, one of his poems even appeared in the Saturday edition of *Dagbladet*. He had long dreamt of becoming an author, and maybe he could have done it, too. Strange the toll a government job takes on a person's way with words.

There are other papers – specifying the objectives of the dig, where any potential finds will be stored and possibly displayed, requirements for publication. I read that Professor Graham Llyleworth – 'renowned professor of archaeology, author of numerous textbooks and scientific articles published in revered academic journals worldwide' – was the specialist entrusted with ultimate responsibility for the dig. I read about the probability of finding a ring fortress with accompanying barracks. I read the endorsement by Professor Arntzen, who vouched for everything, including my suitability as inspector, and note the official seal and illegible signature of the chair of the department, director Frank Viestad.

I put all the copies on the table and say: 'It's a sham, a cover-up.'

'For what?' Kristin asks.

I know Caspar well enough to know that he's told her everything, and I know Kristin well enough to know that she's dying of curiosity.

'Well, they knew they weren't going to find a ring fortress,' I say.

'Because they weren't looking for a ring fortress,' Caspar adds.

'Precisely! They were looking for something much bigger.'

Kristin glances from me to Caspar, shooting him a concerned *do-you-think-it's-his-nerves* look.

'Bigger than a ring fortress?' Caspar asks.

I wink at Kristin with my most in-control *healthy-as-can-be* smile. 'More important than a ring fortress,' I say to Caspar.

Kristin reaches for a biscuit, and the way her blouse clings distracts me because her nipples are clearly delineated through the material. Caspar follows my eyes and I blush deeply.

'Why are these Englishmen even in the picture?' Kristin asks, and then quickly adds: 'Bjørn, you're all flushed. Are you too hot?'

'They obviously knew,' Caspar says, 'the shrine was there – Llyleworth, MacMullin, SIS. Why else would they have applied for permission to dig up the field?'

'Exactly! They knew full well that the shrine . . .' I start to say before his words trigger the alarm bells. I flip back to the letter I was just reading. There's that name again, in black and white: Michael MacMullin. It's the three 'M's that finally trigger the recollection. MacMullin is the man Grethe asked me to look up in London, the academic adviser that Llyleworth, DeWitt and my father thanked in their book. The world is full of coincidences.

I repeatedly hammer my index finger against the sheet of

paper. 'Hey, do you know who this guy is, Michael MacMullin?'

'The chairman of SIS?' Caspar says, bewildered.

'And my father and Graham Llyleworth's adviser at Oxford back in 1973.' I tell Caspar and Kristin about the treatise and the dedication.

'Really?' Caspar blurts out. 'Wait, I have something else about that guy. Look what I found when I was nosing around in our archives today.' He opens a briefcase and pulls out a copy of the *Journal of Norwegian Archaeology*, volume 4, from 1982. He flips to page 16, to an article about a multi-disciplinary symposium on collaborative international research. The symposium was hosted by the Norwegian Institute of Archaeology, but it was financed by SIS. Caspar has highlighted three names in yellow: presenters Graham Llyleworth and Trygve Arntzen and keynote speaker Michael MacMullin.

'They go back a long way,' Caspar says.

'Something happened at Oxford in 1973,' I say reflectively.

'Llyleworth and your dad must have stumbled across something sensational. Along with this DeWitt guy, whoever he is. A discovery that led them to Værne Monastery,' Caspar says, lost in thought.

'Twenty-five years later.'

'Well, it certainly must have been more than some arrow-head,' Kristin says. Even after ten years of marriage to Caspar, she still has a somewhat simplified view of just what archaeologists do.

'Have you heard the myth of the octagon?' I ask Caspar.

He searches his memory. 'Something about the Knights Hospitaller? Who hid a shrine in an octagonal temple? I read something about that somewhere.'

It doesn't take much to scratch through the veneer of my

self-esteem. Even Caspar's familiar with the myth of the octagon. This realisation depresses me. I was the inspector on the dig. I should have understood the magnitude of the whole thing the second Irene exposed the foundation wall, but I'd never heard of the octagon before.

'We found the shrine in an octagon,' I say.

'You're kidding, right?' Caspar says, looking me right in the eye. 'An octagon? At Værne Monastery?' He sits there shaking his head and staring off into space.

'Then maybe you're familiar with the rumour associated with Rennes-le-Château, too?' I ask.

He furrows his brow. 'Honestly, I'm not sure. Was that the place where they found some old parchments when they were renovating the church?'

I sigh. 'Why am I the only one who missed all the exciting lectures?'

Caspar laughs. 'Maybe because you were so busy chasing after the female professors?'

My cheeks flush a deep red. Kristin flashes Caspar a chastising look. Although, of course, I deserve that one.

'And what do you know about SIS?' I ask, trying to hide my blushing face behind my hand.

'Not much. I started looking into it while we were processing the application. It's a foundation based in London. They have ties to the Royal Geographical Society and the National Geographic Society and the like, and universities and research institutions all over the world. They finance interesting projects anywhere on the planet. For the greater good.'

'The greater good? Ha!' Kristin scoffs. 'There are no fairy godmothers in the world of academic research.'

I tell them about the Q manuscript. And about the Gospel of Thomas.

After that we mostly talk about the old days, about ourselves. My theories may be a little much even for archaeology buffs. I leave when Kristin starts making dinner. Liver in a tarragon cream sauce. Thanks, but no thanks.

4

The policeman is tall, lanky and filled with barely restrained suspicion. He has sallow skin and slightly bulging eyes, as if he had been pulled up from the depths and on to land a little too quickly. A rockfish. When he looks at me, I feel that his eyes don't miss much, not even when they're closed. His lips are stiff, authoritative, but every time he says something it's in the squeaky voice of a eunuch, which explains why he's working as an investigator and not out on the street with all those scary bad guys. He brought a big, black attaché case and an eager officer who's spent the last two minutes brushing my door with a make-up brush.

When I reported the break-in, I took the liberty of insinuating that I represent the University of Oslo and that the break-in might be connected to a crime involving a cultural artefact that the newspapers would surely take an interest in. That kind of thing usually helps. I hadn't even had a chance to hang up my windbreaker before they buzzed me from downstairs. As if they'd been sitting in their car waiting for me.

Evasively, because this policeman is the type who would hastily interpret my hypotheses as paranoid conspiracy theories, I explain that the burglars may have thought the hard drive on my computer contained information about the discovery of a gold shrine that's more than eight hundred years old.

The policeman whistles. Eight hundred years sounds old, and to him everything that's old is valuable, at least if it's really old, like eight hundred years, not to mention made out of gold.

'Wow, you don't say,' he says. It doesn't sound as if he

thinks I'm telling the truth. 'Can you tell me more about this shrine?'

Vaguely, because I don't want to reveal too much but I still want him to believe me, I tell him about the excavation in Østfold. He listens attentively. He takes out a form that he fills out with a ballpoint pen. He's thorough. His penmanship would still earn him praise from his teachers. He runs through his points one by one, asking precise questions. Every time he glances up at me, I feel as if I'm a multiple-choice exam that's full of errors.

'And what is your role at Værne Monastery?' he asks.

'I'm the inspector. The excavation is being led by a British professor of archaeology. I'm there representing the Norwegian antiquities officials. You know, formalities are important,' I add in an attempt to win him over to my side. And just then it occurs to me that I didn't tell him that the excavation is happening at Værne Monastery.

'Does anyone other than you have a key to your flat?' the officer with the make-up brush asks.

'My mother,' I say, and think: *And my stepfather.*

'The door didn't show any signs of forced entry,' he says.

'This shrine,' the boss squeaks, 'is it valuable per se?'

'Very.'

'Where is it now?'

I hesitate. Because he's a policeman, there's a mental reflex to tell the truth, but I restrain myself.

'In the university vault,' I lie.

'Really?' He juts out his lower jaw and sucks air in between his teeth and upper lip with a gurgly sound. Then he exhales, and it must be my imagination that makes his breath smell like seaweed.

'Now, explain to me,' he says, 'why you think that this golden shrine was the reason someone broke into your private flat.'

He's a good policeman, which can spell trouble. Good policemen ask hard questions, especially when you have something to hide. I've been regretting the fact that I called the police for quite a while now. As if they could do anything one way or the other. Aside from taking the joy out of my life. And pestering me with horrible questions. And making sure the shrine winds up in the hands of those who deserve it the least.

I say that the break-in is a mystery to me and ask them whether they want a cup of coffee. They don't.

'Is there anyone else that knows about the find?' he asks.

'Not that I know of. We found the shrine yesterday.'

'And it was locked in the university vault right away?'

I nod so imperceptibly that it can hardly be considered a lie.

'By you?' he asks.

Something is puzzling me. I reported a break-in. Here in my flat. But the shrine is the only thing he's interested in.

'No,' I say, 'not by me.'

'By who?'

'Does that matter? The break-in happened here, not at the vault. The shrine is safe.'

'*The shrine is safe*,' he repeats, imitating me, my voice, my intonation, so well that I think this man could have been an actor if law enforcement hadn't slapped its handcuffs on him first. Contemplatively, absent-mindedly, Mr Squeaky Voice presses the top of his retractable pen against his chin, clicking the tip of the pen in then out. 'If I understand you correctly, then, you think the break-in has something to do with this golden shrine?'

'There are forces that will go to great lengths to steal it.'

'What forces?'

'I don't know. International black marketeers? Art collectors? Corrupt academics?'

'But surely there's no danger of this as long as the shrine is being kept safe in the university vault, right?' He looks at me as if he's issuing a challenge.

'Well, there really isn't any other logical reason to steal my hard drive,' I respond.

'Because you saved information about the shrine on your drive?'

'No, but they must have thought I had. I don't see any other explanation.'

He clicks his pen faster. 'What do you mean?'

I say: 'They must have thought I had information about the shrine on my computer. And they must have thought that the files were well hidden. So that they would need time to find them. I can't see any other reason for stealing my hard drive.'

'Why did they only steal the hard drive?'

'Shouldn't you be asking the thieves that?'

'But what do you think?'

'Maybe they were hoping I wouldn't notice it was gone?'

'Did you have anything else on the drive that might have interested criminals?'

'My poems?'

'Or pictures of cute, naked little children on a beach?' His voice is cloyingly saccharine. He's one of those people who always thinks the worst of those of us who look different. Goddam rockfish! I have the urge to dump all the water out of the algae-green aquarium he undoubtedly spends his long, lonely nights in.

'I thought I called you guys about a break-in,' I say cynically. 'I had no idea I was being investigated for child pornography.'

'The police have received a report about you,' he says, letting his fish-eyes rest lethargically on my face to observe my reaction.

At first I'm paralysed. Then I shake my head in disbelief. 'Someone reported me? Me?'

'As I said.'

'For paedophilia? Or possession of Internet pornography?'

'No, you've misunderstood,' he says. 'For stealing the golden shrine.'

The doorbell rings. Urgently. As if someone is trying to press their thumb and the button through the wall. We quickly exchange glances. I go and open the door.

Professor Graham Llyleworth is standing in the hallway along with my old buddy King Kong.

At first they say nothing. They just stare at me in fury.

'You prick! Where is it?' Professor Llyleworth bursts out.

It's not a question. It's an order.

'Come in, come in. Please, don't stand out here in the cold.'

Thrown by my faked kindness, they step into my flat. First Llyleworth, then even more hesitantly King Kong, as if he's waiting for Llyleworth's next order, which will probably be to break my fingers and pull out the nails, one by one, until I give them the shrine.

Then they catch sight of the two policemen.

'The Rozzers,' I say cheerfully in Norwegian, and then realise that Llyleworth speaks only English. So I translate it for him: '*The Rozzers.*' That's me, Bjørn the simultaneous interpreter.

The policemen eye the two newcomers with indifference. Until I tell them who Llyleworth is.

'Ah, so you're Professor Graham Llyleworth,' Mr Squeaky Voice says in stellar English, holding out his hand. 'A pleasure to meet you.'

'The pleasure's *all mine*,' Llyleworth says, shaking his hand.

I try not to stare, but I don't know whether I'm succeeding.

'Have you got anywhere with him?' Professor Llyleworth asks.

The policeman looks from the professor to me and then back again.

'He claims the shrine is in a vault at the university.'

Professor Llyleworth wrinkles his brow. 'Oh, he does, now, does he?'

'Hey, what's going on here?' I ask, even though I can guess the answer.

'You stole the shrine,' the professor says.

'Now look here,' I say, addressing the policeman, 'they were planning to take it out of the country. Without permission. They were planning to steal it!'

There is a brief silence.

'As far as I understand,' the policeman says slowly, 'Professor Llyleworth is in charge of the excavation at Værne Monastery?'

'Yes.'

'So wouldn't it be odd for him to plan on stealing what he finds?'

'But that's exactly what he . . .'

'Wait!' The policeman pulls out one of the documents I had seen a copy of at Caspar's place. 'Here's the permit from the Office of Cultural Heritage . . .'

'You don't understand,' I interrupt. 'We were looking for a ring fortress. Read the application. They applied for permission to find a ring fortress. They never said anything about intending to find a golden shrine.'

The policeman shakes his head. 'So archaeologists know in advance what they're looking for and what they're going to find?'

'No, not like that. But the shrine was what the professor

was actually looking for. All along. The golden shrine! The ring fortress was a sham. He wanted to find the shrine and take it out of the country. Don't you get it? The ring fortress is a cover-up!'

The policeman doesn't say anything. Llyleworth tries not to protest.

The silence is effective. I can hear the hysterical ring to my own words.

'Gentlemen,' Llyleworth says in his most courteous and professorial voice, 'excuse me. Could I have a word with you?'

He leads the two policemen into the kitchen. Through the glass door I watch Llyleworth hand them his business card. The card is tiny, but his long string of academic titles carries a lot of weight in the policemen's paws.

Llyleworth explains something. The policemen listen reverently. Mr Squeaky Voice looks at me with those fish-eyes of his. His mouth opens and closes noiselessly.

After a bit they come back out. Llyleworth beckons to King Kong, who slinks over to him as if Llyleworth had lured him over with a bunch of bananas.

'I would have insisted they ransack the house,' the professor tells me, 'but you're hardly careless enough to keep the shrine here in the flat.'

'You only know that because your boys would have found it when they searched the place,' I say.

'So you admit that the shrine is in your possession?' the policeman asks.

'I don't admit anything,' I say.

'We'll be in touch,' Llyleworth says – I don't know whether his words are directed at me or the police officers – and leaves with King Kong in tow.

'Well, well, well,' Mr Squeaky Voice says, putting his form in his briefcase.

'What did the professor say?' I ask.

He just looks at me. As if I'm some poor slob with problems. Which, actually, I kind of am.

Then they walk over to the front door.

'Beltø,' he says, and clears his throat, 'the police have every reason to believe that the shrine is in your custody.'

'Is that a question? Or an accusation?'

'I would advise you to cooperate with us.'

'I'll do whatever it takes to save the golden shrine from crooks,' I say.

He ponders my response for a few seconds.

'What happens now?' I ask.

'Owing to the special nature of this case, I need to consult with my superiors before we proceed with the investigation and consider charges.'

'And, um, what about the break-in?'

'If there even was a break-in.'

'So we're going to drop it owing to lack of evidence?' I suggest.

'You'll be hearing from us.' It sounds like a standard response the cadets practise in front of a mirror in some class-room at the Police Academy, a lie so broad and transparent that it can hardly be considered a lie, but rather more of a pat expression along the lines of 'I'll give you a call' or 'let's do lunch'.

I open the door for them and stand there in the doorway until the lift is on its way down. From the balcony I follow them with my eyes as they walk towards their car. Thunderous bass rhythms pour out of Roger's flat below me. A crime requires a law to be broken, a victim. In this case there is neither.

I'm trapped in a web of contradictions. I'm trying to prevent a crime that, from both a criminal and a practical perspective, has not been committed yet, a crime that doesn't have any victim, a crime which, strictly speaking, has not had an impact on anyone at all. The only thing that warrants my intervention is the Cultural Heritage Act, a technicality, a collection of inert paragraphs. No one owns the golden shrine. It has been lying in the ground for eight hundred years, like an undiscovered diamond deep within a crack in the rock, like a hidden vein of gold. The shrine could have lain there for another eight hundred years if Professor Llyleworth hadn't known where to dig.

So ironically I suppose I'm the one who's breaking the law.

5

The evening is light and calm and filled with a silent happiness. Clouds of tiny gnats hang over the cotoneaster hedge. The sprinklers are spraying a little mist. I park Bolla on top of a chalk hopscotch grid, in the shade of a big tree. Through the open sunroof I breathe in the scents of freshly mown grass, barbecuing and twilight.

I stroll up a narrow side road and open a wrought-iron gate whose hinges need oiling. The gravel crunches under my feet. I make my way up the slate steps. The doorbell chimes *ding-dong* with a deep, dignified ring, as if in a medieval cathedral. It takes a minute for him to open the door. I glance at the time, almost seven. I'm sure he must have to walk through several grand ballrooms to get to the door.

He's wearing a bathrobe with a monogram on the chest pocket. His grey hair is wet and freshly combed. He's holding a brandy glass in his hand. He doesn't say a word. He looks at me in astonishment.

He knows. I can see it in his eyes. He knows about the shrine and everything that's happened.

Eventually he stammers, 'Bjørn?' As if he's just placed who I am.

'Yes, sir, at your service.'

For some reason or other I feel like a tardy errand boy or a disobedient servant. I say: 'I need to talk to you.'

He lets me in. His breath smells like Martell cognac. He closes the door behind me. And locks it.

I've never met institute director Frank Viestad's wife before, but I've spoken to her on the phone many times. She always sounds as if she's on the verge of hysteria even when she's just calling about dinner. Now she's standing in the middle of the runner in the hallway, anxious, her arms crossed in front of her. She's twenty-five years younger than him and still a beautiful woman. It never ceases to amaze me that gifted, attractive students fall for their greying professors. Of course, I'm really not one to judge.

What does she do with all the time she spends in this white house with the big garden? Our eyes meet for a second or two and that's all the time I need to penetrate into her world of remorse and boredom and embitterment. I smile at her politely as Viestad leads me past. She smiles back. It's a smile that could easily make me believe she likes me.

The walls are hung with lithographs by Kaare Espolin Johnson and flamboyant watercolours with illegible signatures. We walk past a little sitting room that Viestad usually refers to as the library. A chandelier tinkles softly.

His home office is exactly how I pictured it: overcrowded bookshelves, mahogany desk, brown cardboard boxes and transparent plastic bags full of artefacts, a globe ... and, there, where a beat-up old black Remington typewriter must have sat at one time, he's made room for a stylish iMac.

'My cave,' he says shyly.

Through the window he has a view of the apple orchard and the neighbour's place. His neighbour seems like the kind of guy who's probably named Preben and doesn't give a damn about the asthmatics of the world or greenhouse gases as he dumps his leaves on to a burning pile of garden waste.

Director Viestad pulls over a high-backed chair with arms carved to look like dragons, which I sit on. He sits down behind his desk.

'I'm sure you know why I'm here,' I say.

I can tell from his face that I'm right. Director Viestad has never been a very good actor. On the other hand, he's a good and popular department chair. He's organised, conscientious, loyal, and he respects the students.

'Where did you hide the shrine, Bjørn?'

'What do you know about it?'

'Virtually nothing.'

I cock my head to the side, keeping my eyes on him.

'That's the truth. Nothing,' he repeats.

'Then why are you asking me about it?'

'You stole it from your father's office.'

He has always called Professor Arntzen my father, even though I have asked him not to.

'That is a very subjective question, who stole it,' I say.

He leans his head back. 'Bjørn, you have to give it back.'

'Plus, he's not my father.'

His eyes suddenly look tired. 'Cognac?' he asks.

'I'm driving.'

He gets a bottle of apple cider and a glass, pours some for me and returns to his seat. Viestad leans back and massages his temples with his fingertips. He raises his cognac glass in my direction. We say 'cheers'.

He says: 'When I was new to the university, I quickly learned that there was no use in fighting some things, tilting at windmills, you know, academic powers that be, truths, scientific dogmas. I didn't have to understand. I didn't have to like it. But I realised that some things are bigger than myself. Some things are bigger than you suspect.'

I'm not sure where he's going with this.

'Do you believe in God?' he asks.

'No.'

My response catches him off guard. 'Anyway. Surely you can understand that Christians believe in God without grasping His omnipotence.'

The conversation has taken a turn that confuses me. I ask: 'Are you trying to tell me that this has something to do with the Shrine of Sacred Secrets? Or the Q manuscript?'

The effect of the question on him is like an electric shock to his brain. He sits straight up in his chair. 'Listen to me,' he says. 'This story isn't as simple as you think. Have you ever put together one of those Ravensburger puzzles with five thousand pieces? With a picture of a forest or a castle or blue sky? Right now you know enough to put three pieces together, but there are still 4,997 pieces left before you see the whole thing, before you can really see it.'

I stare at him. Sometimes my gleaming red eyes have a mildly hypnotic effect. So that people say more than they had planned to.

He continues: 'Yes, the old myth about the relic is a part of the whole. And, yes, the octagon is a part of the whole.'

'What whole?'

'I don't know.'

'They broke into my flat. You knew that, right?'

'No, I didn't. But the shrine is important to them, you have to understand. More important than you suspect.'

'I'm just wondering why.'

'That I can't tell you.'

'Because you don't know? Or because you don't want to?'

'Both, Bjørn. What little I do know, I've taken an oath not to reveal.'

I know him well enough to know that he would take an oath very seriously.

Outside, somewhere in the neighbourhood, an electric lawnmower is turned off. Only now, once the noise is gone, do I notice it. The silence immediately starts to swell and fill the room.

'But I can tell you this,' he continues. 'That you must hand over the shrine. You must. To me, to your father or to Professor Llyleworth. Nothing will happen to you, no reprimand, no note in your file, no official report. I promise.'

'But I *have* been reported.'

'Already?'

'Oh, yeah. The police were at my place, snooping around.'

'The shrine is very valuable.'

'But I'm no villain.'

'Nor are they.'

'They broke into my place.'

'You stole the shrine.'

Touché.

'Why did you give them permission? For the excavation?' I ask.

'Strictly speaking, it was the Royal Norwegian Office of Cultural Heritage that gave its permission. It was only submitted to us for comment.'

'But why were they allowed to do it?'

'Bjørn . . .' He sighs. 'We're talking about the SIS, Michael MacMullin, Graham Llyleworth. What, were we going to say "no" to the world's foremost archaeologists?'

'Do you know Llyleworth well?'

'I've known him for a few years.' His voice hints at something more. 'It seems like you're doing quite a bit of research into this.'

'It hasn't really taken that much effort. Everyone seems to know a little. If I talk to enough people, maybe I'll understand what this is all about.'

He chuckles. 'I suppose it's not a coincidence that the words "research" and "search" are almost identical. Who have you talked to so far?'

'Several people, including Grethe.'

'Ah, Grethe. She knows what she's talking about!'

'What do you mean by that?'

'She was very active at Oxford. In so many ways.' He glances at me quickly. 'She was a visiting lecturer and adviser when your father, your actual father, was writing that treatise of his along with Llyleworth and Charles DeWitt.' He shrugs. His eyes follow a fly on the ceiling.

'It's a Norwegian find,' I say. 'No matter what's in the shrine, no matter where it's from. It is and will remain a Norwegian find, which belongs in Norway.'

Viestad takes a deep breath. 'You're like an ill-tempered little terrier, Bjørn, who's barking at a bulldozer. You have no idea what you're up against.'

'Woof.'

He smiles. 'Such youthful, self-righteous indignation. But you don't know the whole story.'

'Well, I know the Cultural Heritage Act! Which prohibits the export of Norwegian archaeological artefacts.'

'You don't need to tell me that. Did you know that I helped draft the legislation? I am intimately familiar with every single paragraph.'

'Then you should know that what Llyleworth was trying to do is against the law in Norway.'

'It's not quite that simple. The fact that the shrine was found here in Norway is just incidental. The shrine isn't Norwegian.'

'And how do you explain that?'

'Can't you just trust me? And give the shrine back to your father?'

'Professor Arntzen is not my father!'

'To Llyleworth, then?'

'Professor Llyleworth is a prick.'

'And what about me? What am I?'

'I don't know. I don't know what to believe any more. What are you?'

'A piece.' Viestad knocks his knuckles against his desk. 'I'm just a piece in the puzzle. We're all just pieces. Insignificant pieces.'

'In what puzzle?'

He refills his glass. I see now, for the first time in all the years we've worked together, why so many of his young female students fall for him. When the stern, world-weary demeanour recedes, he looks like some indeterminate American movie star from the thirties. He has a strong chin, high cheekbones. His eyebrows arch across his forehead like two colourless rainbows. He gives me a penetrating look, his eyes dark.

'Not a puzzle for you and me, Bjørn,' he says.

This sudden intimacy embarrasses me. I pretend to cough.

'I have some questions,' I say.

He watches me in silence, waiting. 'Yes?'

'How did Professor Llyleworth know where to dig to find the octagon?'

'They found a map or some new information.'

'Why did he claim we were looking for a ring fortress?'

'Well, you *were*. It was built around 970.'

'But the octagon is what we were looking for?'

'Yes.'

'And Llyleworth knew that a shrine was hidden in it?'

'Presumably.'

'Did you know the shrine is made of gold?'

His reaction tells me that he did not know that.

'What do you know about Rennes-le-Château?' I ask.

He seems genuinely surprised. 'Not that much. It's a French village in the mountains where some manuscripts were supposedly found that aroused pseudo-scientific interest.'

'So you don't know anything about a historical treasure?'

His facial expression grows increasingly bewildered. 'Treasure? You mean at Rennes-le-Château? Or at Værne Monastery?'

'Does Llyleworth know what's in the shrine?'

'You ask question after question, but you need to understand that I'm an even smaller piece of the puzzle than the rest. I'm the blue piece in the top right corner of the puzzle, a piece that's only there to fill in the sky.' Snorting softly to himself, he leans forward over the desk. 'Bjørn,' he says quietly, and then the phone rings. He answers it in Norwegian with a terse '*ja?*' He conducts the rest of the conversation in English. No, he doesn't know. Then he says *yes* a bunch of times, and from his eyes I get the sense that one of these *yes*es is the response to a question about whether I happen to be there in the room with him. He hangs up. I stand up.

'Are you leaving so soon?' he asks.

'I gather that you're expecting company,' I say.

He walks around his desk and rests his hand on my shoulder. 'Trust me. Hand over the shrine. They aren't crooks. They're not bad. They have their reasons. Believe me, they have their reasons. But this isn't something for people like us to get messed up in.'

'People like us?'

'People like us, Bjørn.'

He follows me to the door, with his hand on my shoulder the whole time. Maybe he's considering keeping me here by force. But when I brush aside his hand, he doesn't object. He stands in the doorway watching me as I rush out.

From behind a curtain in a window on the second floor – I'm convinced it must be the bedroom – his wife waves. On my way down to Bolla I imagine that she's beckoning me closer and not waving goodbye to me. I don't always have such a firm grip on reality.

6

A white room, four by three metres, a bed, a table, a closet, a window, a door: that was my world for six months.

When I first got to the clinic I wouldn't venture out of my room. I would sit on my bed or on the floor and rock for long periods of time, with my face between my knees and my arms over my head. I just couldn't look into the eyes of the nurses who brought my medication in small, transparent plastic cups. When they stroked my hair, I would collapse like a sea anemone.

Every day at the same time they brought me to Dr Wang. He sat in a chair and spoke sensibly. I never looked at him. Four weeks went by before I glanced up and looked him in the eye. Still he sat there talking. I listened.

After five weeks I interrupted him. *What's wrong with me?* I asked.

You must look back to your childhood, he used to say.

Very original.

Things that happen to you when you're a child help make you who you are, he said. *Your emotional life is kneaded into shape in your mind.*

I had a happy childhood, I responded.

Always? Dr Wang asked.

I told him that I grew up as a pampered prince in a palace of purple silk.

And you never had any bad experiences? he asked.

Never, I lied.
Did they beat you? he asked.
Did they abuse you? he asked.
Were you molested? he asked.
Did they lock you in a dark room?
Did they say hurtful things to you?
Did they bother you?
Nag, nag, nag . . .

Outside his office, on the wall in the hallway, there was clock. Oh, the tyranny of time. All the clocks in the world are interconnected, ticking together as one, but this clock was different. This was one of those ones that's controlled remotely by radio waves from an atomic clock in Hamburg, Germany. I could follow the second hand's sweeping flight across that clock face for hours.

I looked Dr Wang up again early this summer. I wanted help processing some memories that had sneaked up on me under the cover of darkness, the circumstances surrounding my father's deadly fall, all the small peculiarities that I hadn't really understood as a child. Each little episode is a thread in a tangled web. The doctor was happy that I was finally talking about what happened the summer my father died. Something must have opened up inside me.

He said he understood more now. *Bully for you*, I told him.

Dr Wang was the one who recommended that I write down my memories. *It helps make everything more real*, he said. *It helps you see more clearly. It's as if you've been transported back in time and are re-experiencing the whole thing.*

Well, alrighty, then, I said. And wrote.

When I was a kid and someone would call me paleface or throw a brick at my head, I sought refuge from my mother.

I park Bolla on the driveway's rust-red pavers. Warm light and Prokofiev's *Romeo and Juliet* pour out of the open living-room window. I catch a glimpse of my mother as she peers out, a fairy in the resplendent light.

It would be unfair of me to say that my mother tried to forget or drive me away. But her love was replaced by a distant sort of courteous care. She makes me feel like a beloved relative on holiday in the old country.

She is standing in the doorway as I walk up the steps. 'You're late,' she says. Her voice has the round clang that it always takes on in the evening, one that says that she's been sipping at a drink all day and topped it off with cocktails when the professor came home.

'I had a few things to take care of.'

'You know we always eat dinner at seven thirty.'

'Mum, has Professor Arntzen ever mentioned something called the Q manuscript to you?'

'*Trygve*,' she corrects me cheerfully. Her patience knows no boundaries in her attempts to bring us closer together.

'The Q manuscript?' I repeat.

'Oh, help me out here! What's a cue document?' She giggles.

We go in. The professor tugs the corners of his mouth into the taut, born-again grin that for twenty years he has believed will make me accept him as my new father and my mother's faithful friend and devoted lover.

'Bjørn,' he says. Coldly, distantly. All the while still smiling to please my mother.

I say nothing.

'Where is it?' he says through clenched teeth.

'Boys,' my mother scolds, 'are you guys hungry?'

We proceed into the living room – an oasis of thick carpets and soft sofas and velvety wallpaper and china cabinets and chandeliers that tinkle merrily in the summer breeze. In the middle of the floor there's a Persian carpet no one is allowed to walk on. The French doors between the living room and the dining room are open. On the table candles flicker in many-armed candleholders, reflecting in three hand-painted porcelain plates. From the kitchen I hear the dog's claws clicking as it gets up – it's half deaf and has only just realised that a stranger has entered the house. I hear how its tail eagerly thumps against the kitchen cabinet.

'Where's Steffen?' I ask.

'At the movies,' my mother says, 'with a girl, a really pretty girl.' She giggles again. 'Don't ask me who she is. He has a new girl every month.' She says it coyly, proud, as if to emphasise that that's a pleasure I've never afforded her. On the other hand I've also never contracted AIDS or oozing genital warts.

I've never been that close to my half-brother. He's a stranger. Like his father, he took over my mother. And left me out on the doorstep, in the cold.

The professor and I take our places. We have assigned seats around here, he and my mother each at their end of the table, me in the middle of the long side. It's a ritual.

When my mother opens the kitchen door and disappears to her pots and pans, the professor's pointer pads out. It's four-teen years old and named Breuer. Or Brøyer. I've never bothered to ask how they spell it. People give dogs the stupidest names. Breuer looks at me and wags his tail then stops. He never learns to recognise me. Or he just doesn't give a damn. The apathy is mutual. The dog collapses in the middle of the floor, as if someone had pulled a steel wire out of its spine. He's drooling. He watches me with those long-suffering eyes. Goop is oozing out of his eyes. I don't understand how it's possible to love a dog.

'You have to return the shrine,' the professor says. He whispers, barely audibly: 'You don't know what you're doing!'

'I was asked to keep an eye on things.'

'Exactly.'

'Professor,' I say in my iciest voice, which is very icy, 'that is exactly what I'm doing.'

My mother brings out the steak before darting back into the kitchen to get the potatoes and gravy and finally a small casserole pan of potatoes au gratin and broccoli for me.

'Don't blame me if the food is cold,' she says, both cheerfully and reproachfully. She looks from me to the professor. 'What was that you were wondering about Trygve and some cue thing?'

The professor gives me a startled look.

'A misunderstanding,' I say.

My mother turned fifty last year, but you would think she's only a few years older than me. Steffen was lucky to get his looks from her and not the professor.

The professor cuts the steak while my mother pours wine for them and light beer for me. I help myself to broccoli casserole. My mother has never understood why I decided to be a vegetarian. But she's good at making vegetable dishes.

The dog is staring at me. It has a two-foot-long, wet tongue that it has unrolled on the carpet.

The professor tells a joke I've heard before. He laughs dutifully at his own joke. I don't understand why my mother chose to commingle her life and her limbs with his. These are the kinds of thoughts that poison my temperament.

'Did you visit the grave today?' I ask my mother.

Her eyes flit to the professor. She finds no refuge there. He cleaves a potato in two and cuts a piece of meat, then he puts it in his mouth and chews. His ability to act as if he's oblivious has always impressed me.

'Didn't you go?' she asks, her voice a little too high.

Dad was buried on a Thursday, one week after the accident. The floor around his casket was covered with flowers and wreaths. I sat in the first row, between my mother and my grandmother. Every time I glanced up at the crucifix on the side of the altar, it reminded me how high up my father was when he lost his grip. Wreaths with black ribbons and expressions of condolence lay in front of the casket. The casket was white with gilded handles. Dad lay there with his hands folded, his eyes closed peacefully, in eternal sleep. His body was surrounded by silk. And otherwise battered beyond recognition. With a crushed cranium. And arms and legs that were broken in so many places that he was limp and weirdly double jointed.

'Delicious broccoli dish,' I say.

I don't need to say anything else about the grave. By asking the question I've managed to remind them that it was a senseless death which brought them together, and that actually a different man should have been sitting at my mother's table.

'Had it been tended? The grave?' my mother asks.

I look at her in surprise. There's an angry undercurrent to her question. She usually never engages me when I'm being disagreeable.

'I planted some lilies.'

'You hold it against me that I never go.'

The professor clears his throat and pushes his vegetables around.

I'm very good at pretending I don't understand. 'Well, can you blame me?'

My mother hates visiting my father's grave. I don't think she's been there since the burial.

'It was twenty years ago, Little Bjørn. Twenty years!' She

stares at me across the table. Her eyes gleam with rage and wounded self-pity. Her fingers clenched around her knife and fork. 'Twenty years!' she repeats, and again: 'Twenty years, Little Bjørn.'

The professor raises his glass of red wine and drinks.

'That's a long time,' I concede.

'Twenty years,' she says yet again.

For my mother, overstatement and self-pity are art forms that are much cultivated and practised.

The dog coughs and vomits up some mess that it then immediately licks up again with relish.

'Do you ever think about him?' I ask.

It's not a question. It's a spiteful accusation. I know it. She knows it.

The professor clears his throat and says: 'Great gravy, dear. Really great gravy.'

She doesn't hear him. She's looking at me. 'Yes,' she says tersely; something alien and intense has come over her. 'I think about him.'

My mother sets her knife and fork on the table. She folds up her napkin.

'I know what day it is today,' she says, subdued. Her northern Norwegian dialect slips through: 'Every year, every summer. Don't think that I've forgotten what day it is.'

She gets up and leaves the room.

The professor isn't sure whether he should go after her or let me have it. He should have done both. He just sits there and keeps chewing. He looks at my mother's empty chair. He looks at me. He looks down at his plate. Chewing the whole time.

'You have to give it back,' he says.

I look at the dog. Something in my eyes makes it shake its head and perk up its ears. It whimpers. Drool pours out of its half-open mouth, forming a nasty stain on the light-coloured carpet. It stands halfway up, then farts and walks off.

8

The first thing I notice when I park outside my building is the red Range Rover. It's empty.

They must think I'm stupid. Or blind.

The second thing is Roger. He's sitting just outside the entrance to the building, on the wooden box that holds the sand they spread on the ice in winter, smoking.

The light from a first-floor flat hits him from the side, leaving his face in the shadows. If I didn't know Roger, I doubt I would have noticed him. Boys like Roger are hanging out in suburbs all over Oslo, bored out of their minds. With his long hair and his wrinkly Metallica T-shirt, he looks like any old juvenile delinquent, just waiting to snatch a purse away from some old lady with a cane or seduce your thirteen-year-old daughter. But because Roger never usually hangs out by the front door, and because it's late at night, and because there's an empty Range Rover in the car park, the sight makes me nervous.

When he sees me he hops off the wooden box. 'Do you have guests?' he asks, holding the front door open for me.

I look at him as if to say 'huh?'

He presses the lift button. 'There's people in your place, man. They're waiting for you.'

We get out at the ninth floor and head into Roger's flat. I borrow his phone and call my flat. The answering machine has been turned off. Someone picks up the phone but doesn't say anything.

'Bjørn?' I ask.

'Yes?' the voice responds.

I hang up.

Roger is sitting on the sofa, rolling himself another cigarette. 'They came a few hours ago.'

I flop down into a chair. 'Thanks for waiting out front for me.'

With yellow fingertips, he twists the cigarette around and around. He moistens the glue on the rolling paper, gives the cigarette one last twirl between his thumb and fingertips and lights it.

'I don't know what I should do,' I say.

'Maybe call the cops?' Roger suggests with a smirk.

We wait by the window until the police car pulls in off the ring road and stops in front of our building.

Roger stays in his flat while I meet the policemen in the tenth-floor hallway as they get out of the lift. They're young, serious and authoritative, and I can tell from their dialects that they're not from Oslo but from somewhere around Ålesund. I hand them the key and remain out in the hallway. It's clear that the dispatcher didn't link this call to the investigation going on against me. That won't happen until one of the detectives browses through the log later in the morning.

They come out a few minutes later.

There are three of them. One is muscular, with a hard look in his eyes: my buddy King Kong.

The second is a refined-looking gentleman in a suit, with manicured nails.

The third is Professor Graham Llyleworth.

All three stop short when they see me.

'They were sitting there waiting,' the policeman says. 'In the living room. Do you know them?' His tone is surprised, vaguely accusatory, as if it's my fault they were there in my flat.

I look at each of the men for a long time. Then I shake my head.

'They're English,' the policeman says. And waits for an explanation that he's never going to get from me.

Professor Llyleworth's eyes are narrow and deep. 'You'll regret this,' he snarls.

The policemen shove them into the lift. Heavy-handedly. Even though all three go voluntarily.

Then the lift door slams shut.

9

An insect that realises escape is impossible will fold up its legs and play dead. Every once in a while I feel like doing that too.

Fear and adversity have a paralysing effect on me. Just at this moment, however, I am experiencing a new and unexpected reaction: I'm angry. I can't take any more! Like the insect, I intend to play dead only for a little while. Then I'll crawl behind a blade of grass and gather my strength, pluck up my courage.

I look at Roger for so long that it starts to bug him. 'Um, could I spend the night here?' I ask. I'm neither brave nor foolhardy. They're going to come back. It won't be long before they're impatient and cross.

'Sure.'

'I'm leaving on a trip early tomorrow anyway. I'll just leave right from here.'

Roger's not one to fish for more information or ask questions.

We go down to his place. He asks me whether I'm tired. I'm not tired, I'm wide awake. He puts on a CD. It's Metallica. And he brings in a few bottles of Mack beer from the fridge and lights a black candle, which reeks of paraffin. We sit there together drinking pilsner and listening to Metallica and waiting for the dawn.

III

The Lover

1

I'M A MAN who appeals more to a woman's instincts than to her urges. Women look at me and see a prodigal son.

When I was twenty-one, my mother asked me to come over one Sunday to talk about something. We were alone in that big house. The professor and my brother had been sent out hiking or something. My mother had baked biscuits and made tea. The scents of steak and sauerkraut and a casserole of vegetables au gratin for me wafted from the kitchen. My mother seated me on the sofa and sat down in a chair across from me. She put her hands in her lap and looked at me. From her bloodshot eyes I could tell she'd been bracing herself for this all morning. She was unusually pretty. I thought she was going to tell me that the doctors had discovered a tumour and that she had six months left to live.

Then she asked me whether I was gay.

She must have been thinking about it for a long time. To my mother, my albinism was invisible. I don't think she ever realised what a social handicap it is for a red-eyed albino to compete with pleasantly tanned Norwegian boys with their blue eyes and corn-blond hair for the girls' attention.

I remember the smile of relief that washed over her face when I assured her that I was attracted to girls. I neglected to mention that the girls were somewhat less attracted to me.

I often wonder whether it was my mother or I who inadvertently pulled the sliding door between our lives shut. After my father died, it was as if she didn't want anything more to do with me. I felt like a painful memory, an anchor dragging on her life, and dutifully took on the role of the outcast, the pathetic schmuck who doesn't want to intrude where he isn't wanted. I'm sure some people think I haven't been fair to her. Did I ever – just once – try to put myself in her shoes? Did I ever think about how her life had fallen apart and how she'd tried to piece it back together with her drunken delusions and the love of a man who was just taking what he could get?

In London, I checked into a hotel in Bayswater. If it weren't for the view of Hyde Park, the hotel might just as easily have been on Ludwigstraße in Munich or Sunset Boulevard in Los Angeles. I feel a certain sympathy for concert pianists and rock stars who, after four months on tour, have no idea what country they're in.

The room is narrow, with creamy yellow walls and generic-looking reproductions: a bed, a chair, a table with a phone and a binder of information and blank stationery, a minibar, a TV, a wardrobe with a few forlorn hangers, and a bathroom with white tiles and small, individually wrapped bars of soap which smells hysterically clean. I've never been here before, but it feels as if I have. I've spent my share of time in hotels. After a while they all look the same. Some men feel that way about women.

There have been a handful of women who have fallen for me – out of curiosity, affection and compassion – but what they all had in common was that they didn't know any better. No one has stayed with me for all that long. I'm easy to like, but I'm not that easy to love.

There's a particular type of woman who's drawn to me. They're older than me. They have names like Mariann and Nina and Karina and Vibeke and Charlotte. They're well educated and intelligent. And a tad neurotic. Schoolteachers, cultural consultants, librarians, economists, nursing supervisors – you know the type. They wear shoulder bags and glasses and are brimming with concern and kindness for society's losers. Spellbound, they stroke my chalky-white skin with their fingertips, and then they tell me what women enjoy. Breathlessly they show me how we should proceed. As if I've never done it before. I don't correct them.

I lie on the hotel bed for an hour and relax after my trip. I've showered. With my hands folded on my stomach, I rest the back of my head on the crisp, cool linens. The noise from Bayswater Road and horn music from Hyde Park fuse into an exotic cacophony that follows me into dreamland, but I sleep only for a few minutes.

2

'Charles who?'
'Charles DeWitt!'
The woman in the lobby is wearing half-moon-shaped glasses that have slid down to the tip of her nose, and she scowls at me over the top of the lenses with a look she has dug out of the darkest, frostiest, nethermost depths of some chest freezer. The name has ricocheted back and forth between us six times. We are both losing our patience. She's my age, but looks ten – twenty! – years older. Her ponytail is pulled so tight that it makes her face look tired, as if she's had several unsuccessful bouts of plastic surgery with an inebriated surgeon in Chelsea. She's wearing a snug-fitting, red dress.

She's the type of woman that I imagine might indulge in sadomasochistic games in the dead of night.

'Is Mr DeWitt not in?' I ask politely. The only thing that can help with a shrew of her calibre is being overly polite to the point of sarcasm.

'Let me enunciate more clearly, so – that – you – understand.' She moves her lips as if I'm deaf. 'There – is – no – one – here – by – the – name – of – Charles – DeWitt.'

I pull the business card that I found at Grethe's out of my pocket. The cardboard is yellowed, the type faint, but it is certainly legible.

Charles DeWitt, it says, London Geographical Association. I hold the business card out to her. She does not take it, but stares at my hand with indifference.

'Perhaps he retired,' I suggest, 'before you started here?'

From her expression I realise right away that this question was a tactical catastrophe. Behind her sleek reception desk, in her expensively panelled lobby with wall-to-wall carpeting that could use a trim from a lawnmower, with a secretary's phone on her right and an old-fashioned IBM Selectric typewriter on her left, with her colour photo of her distinguished husband and her charming children and their miniature schnauzer on her desk in front of her, she's the Uncontested Mistress of the Universe. This is her empire. From this perch, she rules the entire world, from the errand boy to the managing director. It would be an outrage to call her a receptionist or a switchboard operator. To suggest that she does not know everything there is to know about the London Geographical Association is blasphemy.

'I rather doubt that,' she responds.

I wonder what her voice sounds like when she cuddles up against her husband at night, all snuggly and aroused.

'I've come all the way from Norway to see him.'

She looks at me through her membrane of ice. This is how

they must have felt, those poor human sacrifices who stared into the eyes of the high priestess seconds before she plunged her dagger into their hearts.

I see that my battle is lost. I borrow a pen from her desk. She flinches in her chair. She's probably calculating how much ink I'm using.

'Well, ma'am, if anything should happen to occur to you, could you please be so kind as to contact me . . .' I hand her my own business card, on which I've written the name of my hotel. '. . . here?'

She smiles. I can't believe my own eyes. She smirks, and it must be because she can tell I'm about to leave.

'Certainly,' she coos, placing my card at the very edge of the desk.

Above the wastepaper basket.

3

For a seemingly basic architectural component like a column there's a body of aesthetic scholarship dedicated to categorisation and a level of vocabulary that can take your breath away.

The two marble columns I'm currently standing in front of and admiring are from the 2,500-year-old Ionic order. When describing an Ionic column, an art historian might say that 'the echinus is partially covered with scrolling volutes' or that 'the shaft of the column features channels or flutes'. Interesting how every branch of scholarship, every academic field, wraps itself in its own terminology and in-group vocabulary. The rest of us are left on the outside, staring in.

These columns are supporting a triangular gable and in the tympanum, or pediment, cherubs and seraphim are frolicking around the date '1900'.

Brass signs have been screwed on to the tile wall on either side of the entrance, polished so bright that they reflect the cars and the red double-decker busses passing behind me. The engraved letters are filled with silver. No one could accuse the Society of International Sciences of scrimping on the details.

The double door is made of blood-red beech. The door knocker functions mostly as a reminder not to make yourself too much at home. To my right – two metres below the surveillance camera up by the ceiling – there's a black plastic intercom set into the wall. As if to excuse this abominable breach of style, the doorbell is shaped like a flower (or is it a sun?) and made out of gold.

I press it. And am buzzed in. No questions asked.

The big, open reception area makes this place feel like the kind of bank where you would need to make an appointment to deposit your money. There's a hum of low voices and rapid footsteps. The walls feature deep brown wainscoting and above that oil paintings that must surely be on loan from the National Gallery. The ceramic mosaic tiles on the floor are buffed to a shine. A palm tree is growing in the middle of the reception area, emerging out of a square opening in the floor and proceeding up towards the sloped atelier windows in the roof up under the clouds; it looks as if it misses the Sahara.

The only thing that doesn't seem to fit is Grandma.

A grey-haired old woman is sitting behind a desk so large that you could play ping-pong on it, knitting. She looks at me. She's as happy as can be, just knitting away. Presumably my confusion is due to the fact that the setting doesn't seem to mesh with the sight of a grandmother knitting.

'Can I help you?' she asks cheerfully, her knitting needles clicking against each other.

'What are you knitting?' I blurt out.

'Socks! For my grandchild, a little boy, *such a little darling*! Was there anything else?'

Her question is meant as a joke. I love her. I could entrust my beating heart to the hands of a person with a good sense of humour.

I introduce myself and explain that I've come from Norway.

'Ah, *the land of the midnight sun*.' She smiles knowingly. 'Then perhaps you know Thor Heyerdahl?' Her laughter burbles and bubbles. 'Oh, what a charming man. He's in here all the time. What can I do for you?'

'I was hoping to see Michael MacMullin.'

Her eyes widen. She sets down her knitting. I feel like an extremely unexpected asylum seeker. From the planet Jupiter. Who's just asked whether she could give me change for the parking meter I parked my flying saucer in front of.

'Good gracious . . .'

'Is something wrong?'

'He . . . I'm afraid Mr MacMullin is out of the country. I'm so sorry. Did you really have an appointment with him?'

'Not strictly speaking. When do you expect him back?'

'I don't know. Mr MacMullin isn't one to . . . But perhaps someone else could help?'

'I'm an archaeologist,' I explain. My tongue can't quite keep up – the English word for 'archaeologist' has a few too many consonants all strung together. *Arrrrr . . . key . . . olo . . . jist*. 'Mr MacMullin is involved in an excavation project. In Norway.'

'Really?'

'And I need to speak with him. Is it possible to get hold of him? Maybe on his mobile?'

She emits a doleful chuckle. 'Unfortunately not. I'm afraid

that's quite out of the question. Quite. You must understand that, as chairman, Mr MacMullin has an office here, but he comes and goes without reporting to the rest of us, who,' she leans in closer, lowering her voice, 'are here to keep these ragamuffins in line. But perhaps our administrative director could assist you?'

'That would be great.'

'Mr Winthrop! One second.' She dials an internal number on her phone and explains that Mr Baltø is here from Norway expressly to speak to Mr MacMullin – *'yes, really. No, without an appointment. Yes, isn't it?'* – and would it be possible for me to see him instead? Then she says *aha* several times, says thank you and hangs up.

'Unfortunately Mr Winthrop is not available, but his secretary says he could meet you tomorrow at nine a.m. Would that work?'

'That would be great.'

'And to think you've come all this way from Norway.'

Even though they're technically closed for the day, Grandma lets me take a peek at their library.

I've been fascinated by libraries ever since I was a child, when the local branch of the Oslo Public Library would serve as my after-school sanctuary whenever my mother would shoo me outside to play with all those tanned boys with the good vision who wanted to play soccer or capture the flag. There's something about library shelves with their book spines that fills me with a sort of devotional awe: the quiet, the alphabetical, thematic organization, the scent of paper, the adventure, the drama, the thrills. I would wander through the Oslo Public Library for hours, pulling out books, browsing through them, and sitting down with some book that captured my attention. When I was a kid, I would run my fingers over the cards in the card catalogues, in all those long, narrow drawers. And then once it was all computerised, I would search the database.

There's an inexplicable peacefulness about the SIS library, too. It's like a church. I stand there in the middle of the room with my arms crossed, staring, taking it all in.

'I'm afraid we're closed.'

The voice is high, vaguely sarcastic. I turn towards it.

She must have been sitting there watching me, as quiet as a mouse. She was probably hoping I would disappear. If only she were quiet enough. She's sitting over by the filing cabinets. There's a stack of card catalogue cards in the lap of her tweed skirt.

'The woman out in reception said I could take a look around,' I explain.

'Ah, that's fine, then.'

Her smile transforms her little-girl's face into something more mature. I guess that she's about twenty-five. She has shoulder-length strawberry-blonde hair and a hint of freckles. Cute. What I'm most drawn to are her eyes. Her irises gleam in an assortment of colours, like a kaleidoscope. It has struck me before that there may be colours only I know about. You can't describe a colour. A scientist can say something about the spectral composition of the light, that red has a wavelength between 723 and 647 nanometres, but when you get right down to it, every colour is a subjective experience. Which means it's quite possible that we all see colours only we know about. It's a captivating thought.

That's what her eyes are like.

She sets the stack of cards on a book truck. She's thin, not that tall. Her fingernails are very long and sharp and done in a deep crimson nail polish. I've never thought of fingernails as something sensual, but I can't look at her nails without imagining how it would feel to have them clawing at my back.

'Is there anything I can help you with?' she asks.

The tone of her voice, her eyes, her petite figure – something about her tenses up the coiled spring that makes me tick. She has a nervous presence, a restless persistence.

'I'm not really sure what I'm looking for,' I say.

'Well, then it won't be easy to find, will it?'

'There are so many things I'm wondering about. You don't happen to have any good answers just waiting for me?'

'Um, what's the question?'

'I don't know. But if you manage to find an answer, I can always come up with a question.'

She shakes her head and smiles, and at that moment I fall for her. It doesn't take much.

'Where are you from?' she asks.

'*Norway*,' I say, trying to say it very clearly.

She raises her eyebrows. '*What do you mean – nowhere?*'

I roll my 'r': '*NoRRRway! I'm an ...*' I take a second, concentrating on pronouncing it correctly, '*archae-olo-gist.*'

'Are you working for SIS?'

'Not exactly, no. Kind of the opposite, you might say.' I laugh tensely.

'You're here to do some research?'

'I came to see Michael MacMullin.'

She looks at me quickly, surprised. She's about to say something, but then stops herself. Eventually she just says, 'Oh.' The sound rounds her lips into a cute little pout.

'I have a few questions for him.'

'Don't we all.'

I smile. She smiles. I blush.

'What kind of library is this?' I ask.

'Mostly non-fiction: history, theology, philosophy, archaeology, cultural history, mathematics, physics, chemistry, astronomy, sociology, geography, anthropology, architecture, biographies, and so forth ...'

'Ah,' I say, 'the trivial details of life.'

She laughs again and looks at me with curiosity, perhaps wondering what sort of creature I am and who picked up the rock and set me free.

'And you're the librarian?' I ask.

'One of them. Hi, I'm Diane.' She holds out a hand with red fingernails. I take it.

'I'm Bjørn.'

'Oh? Like the tennis player, Bjørn Borg?'

'Don't you see the resemblance?'

She sizes me up, chewing on a pencil. 'Well,' she says, teasingly, 'he may have a bit more colour than you.'

4

I eat dinner at one of the main hangouts for serious vegetarians in London. Excited, I choose one of the most expensive dishes on the menu, composed of Brussels sprouts, morel mushrooms and asparagus, in a garlic cream sauce.

I should be thinking about the shrine and Llyleworth's brazen manoeuvre. I should be contemplating the cloud of mystery surrounding Charles DeWitt. I should call Grethe. No doubt she could explain. Maybe DeWitt quit. His business card doesn't exactly look new.

Instead I'm thinking about Diane.

That could be because I see a potential girlfriend and future wife in every woman I oh-so-easily fall in love with. A smile, a voice, a touch . . . I'm not repulsive. I'm pale, but I'm not ugly. They say I have kind eyes. Red eyes, sure, but kind red eyes.

As I'm contemplating my inner mysteries, I eat the Brussels sprouts and morels and asparagus and empty the carafe of wine.

Then I burp and go.

5

One of my Norwegian teachers once asked me a question.

'If you were a flower, Bjørn, instead of a human being, what kind of flower would you be?'

She always came up with the strangest questions. I think she liked messing around with me. I was an appreciative victim. I was seventeen. She was twice that.

'A flower, Bjørn?' she repeated. Her voice was compassionate, pleasant. She leaned over my desk. I still remember her scent: warm, spicy, full of moist secrets.

The classroom was quiet. Everyone was wondering what kind of flower Bjørn would be. Or they were all hoping I would stammer and blush, as I was wont to do whenever she leaned over me with all her scents and heady temptations.

But for once I had an answer to one of her incessant questions.

I told her about the Haleakala Silversword.

It grows only in and around Haleakala volcano on Maui. It spends twenty years as a modest ball covered with shimmering silver hairs, storing up its energy, and then suddenly one summer it explodes extravagantly into bloom in yellows and purples. Then it dies.

My answer flummoxed her. For a long while she just stood there by my desk, staring at me.

What the heck had she been expecting me to say? A cactus?

6

The message is handwritten in a girlish hand full of swoops and flourishes on a slip from the hotel that has A MESSAGE FOR OUR GUEST pre-printed on it in a sans serif font:

To Mr Bulto, room 432:
   Please call Ms Grett Lidwoyen imidiatly.
      Linda/Reception/Thursday 2.12 p.m.

'Are you Linda?' I ask the girl at the front desk.

'No, sorry. Linda's shift ended at three o'clock.'

So Linda must've been the long-legged puma who was working behind the desk when I checked in. *Linda the foxy ferret*. She may have many fine qualities. I'm sure she's pleasant and all. She's pretty. Under the skilled hands of a torturer I probably wouldn't deny that my eyes had been drawn to her backside. But spelling is not Linda's strong suit.

With the note and my keycard in my hand, I take the stairs up and let myself into my room.

I dial the number and let the phone ring.

Outside the window the noises sound different to how they did earlier in the day. A bus, maybe a lorry, makes the windowpane vibrate. I sit down on the bed. Sunlight is filtering down over the wallpaper. I kick off my shoes, pull off my socks and massage my feet. I have lint between my toes.

Someone on the other end picks up. It's quiet for a long time.

'Grethe?' I ask.

'Hello?' Grethe's voice. Distant, shut in.

'It's Bjørn.'

'Oh.'

'I just got your message.'

'Yeah.' She sighs. 'I didn't mean to . . .' She sighs again.

'Grethe? Is something wrong?'

'Huh? No, nothing.'

'You sound so far away.'

'It's . . . the pills. Can you call back later?'

'Sure. You mentioned that there was some hurry?'

'Yes. But I . . . Now's not the best time.'

'Grethe? Who's Charles DeWitt?'

She starts coughing. It's quite a rattling fit. With a bang she slams the phone down on the table, and I imagine that I hear someone thumping her on the back. After a long while she picks up the receiver again and whispers: 'Can you call back later?'

'Grethe, are you ill?'

'It . . . will . . . pass.'

'Is anyone there with you?'

She doesn't answer.

'You need to call your doctor,' I say.

'I'll . . . manage.'

'Who's there with you?'

'Little Bjørn, I . . . just can't . . . talk right now.'

Then she hangs up.

My childhood made me leery. When you're an introverted albino, you develop a sense for the rhythm of language. Even over a telephone line that stretches from Bayswater, London W2, to Thomas Heftyes Gate, 0264 Oslo, through cables under the North Sea and a telecommunications satellite in geostationary orbit, I could sense Grethe's distress. I could tell she was lying.

I lie back on the bed and flip on the TV. I surf through the channels.

I call Grethe back an hour later. She doesn't answer.

I take a quick shower and watch the end of an ancient episode of *Starsky & Hutch* before I dial the number again. I let it ring twenty times.

I spend an hour reading the book my father wrote with Llyleworth and DeWitt. It doesn't work well as a sleeping pill. Their claims are so far fetched that I don't know whether they're being serious about everything. Their most extreme assertion is that finding the Shrine of Sacred Secrets would change the current social order, but then they hedge that claim so many times – the way academics usually do – that the statement becomes meaningless.

As I'm flipping to page 232, a sheet of stationery falls out of the book. It's handwritten and the date is 15 August 1974. The letter is not signed, and it doesn't say who it's to. At first I think it's from my father. The handwriting is identical to his, but that can't be right, can it? Even though I recognise the loops under his 'g's and 'j's and the line over his 'u's. In the letter he is describing the plans for an expedition to Sudan. What I don't understand is why there's a letter from my father in a book that has been sitting on Grethe Lid Wøien's bookshelf for the last twenty-five years.

There's something about nights.

For me, nights are something I'd just as soon sleep through and be done with. The darkness interferes with everything. I feel sicker. The trivialities of everyday life churn around and lose all sense of proportion.

I should be tired. I should be exhausted, but I'm lying here with my eyes wide open, staring out into the dark hotel room. A steady stream of cars passes by outside my window. Some tourists in a partying mood holler. I think about Grethe. I think about the shrine I hid at Roger's place. I think about Professor Llyleworth and Professor Arntzen and Charles DeWitt and Michael MacMullin. I think about my father. And my mother.

But mostly I think about Diane.

At 2.30 in the morning I startle awake and turn on the bedside lamp. Bleary eyed, I dial Grethe's number.

Somewhere in a small country, in a small city, in a flat in a building near Frogner Park, a phone sits ringing, unanswered.

7

There are pleasant ways to wake up – a kiss on the cheek, birds singing, Schubert's string quintet in C major, the chug of an outboard motor on a small wooden boat going by on the fjord.

And then there are unpleasant ways, which is most of them. Like a phone ringing.

I fumble around for the phone. 'Grethe?' I mumble.

It's 8.15. I overslept.

'Mr Belto?' a woman asks.

I recognise the voice, but can't place it.

'Yes?'

She hesitates. 'I'm calling from the London Geographical Association.' Her voice is tense, cold, distant, and just at that moment the image of that fury behind the desk pops into my head. The S&M dominatrix has once again left her leather skirt and whip at home and donned her stylish secretarial outfit and bitchy tone.

'Yes?'

She hesitates again. She does not want to be making this call. 'There seems to have been a misunderstanding.'

'Oh?'

'You were here asking for a . . . Mr Charles DeWitt?'

'Yes?' My lips curl into a malicious grin.

'*I'm terribly sorry* . . .' The tone of her voice is so dry that I could've plucked the words apart and crushed each letter into dust. '. . . but it appears that we actually do have a Charles DeWitt affiliated with us.'

'Really?' I exaggerate my surprise to prolong her humiliation.

The way she inhales tells me that she's pursing her lips. I enjoy that.

'Perhaps you forgot about him?' I fish.

She clears her throat. I realise someone is standing next to her, listening.

'Mr DeWitt is very interested in seeing you. Unfortunately he's not in London at the moment, but we are expecting him in on a flight this morning. He asked me to set up a meeting with you.'

'How nice. Perhaps you'd like to join us? So you can meet him?' It's a problem I have. Sometimes I'm a bit sarcastic.

She manages to restrain herself and not respond. 'If you could suggest a time that would . . .'

'One second,' I interrupt. I want to play hard to get. I've never hidden the fact that I can be a real pain in the ass. 'Have Mr DeWitt get in touch with me once he's back. I have a very tight schedule.'

'*Mr Belto!* He explicitly asked me to . . .'

'Just be a dear and give him my number at the hotel. I can probably fit him in some time in the afternoon or evening.'

'*Mr Belto.*'

'The front desk can take a message.'

'But . . .'

'And please give Mr DeWitt my regards! I look forward to hearing from him.'

'*Mr Belto.*'

Laughing, I hang up and swing my legs on to the floor. I take a pair of underpants, socks and a shirt out of my suitcase. I get dressed before I call Grethe. I'm no longer surprised when she doesn't answer.

I go to the bathroom. My urine smells after last night's asparagus. I was surprised to learn that only a small percentage of people can actually detect the smell from asparagus in urine. I cling to everything that makes me unique.

8

'Ah, the mysterious Mr Balto.'

Anthony Lucas Winthrop, Jr, is a short, heavyset man with a round, hairless head and a bubbly laugh that makes him seem like a clown who's been hired to entertain spoiled children at a fashionable birthday party. He holds out his hand to me. His short fingers look like hairy sausages with gold rings on them. His eyes twinkle merrily at me, his face overflowing with sincerity and paternal solicitude.

I don't trust him. There's something about his voice.

The grandmother with the knitting escorted me up the wide marble staircase to the third floor and down the long, open colonnade with its echoing footsteps and low murmur of voices and around a corner to Winthrop's outer office.

He escorts me into the office.

It's not an office. It's a universe.

Far away, over by the arched windows, I can just make out his desk. At the other end, by the door, there's a decent-size sitting room. Between these two areas there's an enormous hanging display of stellar nebulae, comets and black holes.

'Am I meant to understand,' I ask, with a teasing grin, 'that you like to play God?'

He smiles uncertainly. 'I'm an astronomer. By profession.'

He holds out his hands, palms up, in a self-conscious gesture, as if to let his career history explain the strange fact that he has converted his office into a miniature cosmos.

A while ago I read a piece in the paper about an international group of astronomers who had discovered a celestial body that emitted matter which apparently moved faster than the speed of light. News of the discovery caused quite a stir at COSPAR's scientific assembly in Hamburg, but the newspapers did not consider something as abstract as the speed of light to be any big deal, so they didn't write anything else about it. A group of astronomers using a radio telescope discovered the mystical celestial body thirty thousand light years from Earth. A ways away, in other words. If their observation is correct, it would obliterate the most absolute limit of all the laws of nature – the speed of light. The corollaries are staggering. I suppose that's another reason why it didn't get much media attention.

We stroll through the solar system and deep into the cosmos, past Proxima Centauri and the Andromeda Galaxy, to his desk. My walking through them has caused the galaxies to quiver and sway on their nylon threads.

'I understand you're going to meet with Charles DeWitt later today?' he asks hesitantly.

'You people are very well informed.'

Chuckling nervously, Winthrop takes a seat in a strikingly high desk chair. I sink into an equally strikingly low chair. It's like sitting on the floor. I think – in one of my constantly recurring attacks of pure maliciousness – that behind a shiny desk even a clown can elevate himself to the level of a god.

'*Mr Balto!*' he exclaims in delight as he rocks in his chair and claps his hands together, as if he's been waiting for this day for years. 'So . . . What can we do for you?'

'I'm looking for some information.'

'That's what I understood. And what brings you to SIS? And to Michael MacMullin? Yes, as you understand, he isn't here.'

'We found something.'

'Oh?'

'And I think MacMullin knows something about it.'

'Really? What did you find?'

'Mr Winthrop,' I say with exaggerated politeness, 'let's not beat around the bush.'

'Excuse me?'

'We're both intelligent men, but we're bad actors. Let's just skip the whole song-and-dance routine.'

His mood undergoes an almost undetectable yet nonetheless perceptible transformation. 'That's fine, Mr Balto.' His voice has cooled, becoming businesslike, suspicious.

'I'm sure you know who I am?' I say.

'You're an assistant professor at the University of Oslo, the Norwegian inspector on Professor Llyleworth's dig.'

'And I'm sure you must also know what we found?'

He shrugs. Winthrop is a man who does not perform well under pressure.

I help him. 'We found the shrine.'

'So I understood. Truly fascinating.'

'What can you tell me about the myth of the Shrine of Sacred Secrets?'

'Not much, I'm afraid. I'm an astronomer, not a historian. Or an archaeologist.'

'But you're familiar with the myth?'

'Superficially. It's like the Arc of the Covenant. The Shrine of Sacred Secrets? A message? A manuscript? That much I know.'

'And I'm sure you know that this shrine was what Llyleworth was looking for?'

'Mr Balto, SIS doesn't waste its time with superstitions. I hardly think Llyleworth was hoping to find some shrine.'

'Well, what if this didn't actually have anything to do with superstition? But, let's say, with a reliquary made of gold?'

'Mr Balto.' He emits a sort of gasp of mock hopefulness and raises his two bundles of sausages. 'Have you brought it with you – the artefact? Here? To London?'

I make a pfff sound as if to say *you wish*.

'I hope it's in a safe place?' he says.

'Of course.'

'Is it,' he asks vaguely, 'a question of money?'

'Money?'

Sometimes I'm a little slow on the uptake. He looks me in the eye, and I stare back. He has blue-grey eyes with very long eyelashes. I try to read his mind.

'How much were you thinking?' he asks.

At that moment I realise where I know his voice from. I talked to him on the phone, two days ago, when he introduced himself as Dr Rutherford from the Royal British Institute of fucking Archaeology.

I start laughing. He looks at me in confusion. Then he chimes in with his own clown laughter. We sit there cackling like that in mutual distrust.

Behind us, at the opposite end of the universe, a door opens. An angel swoops over to us with a silver tray bearing two cups and a porcelain teapot. She pours the tea for us without a word and disappears.

'Help yourself,' Winthrop says.

I tip a cube of sugar into my tea, but don't touch the milk. Winthrop does exactly the opposite.

'Why won't you hand over the artefact?' he asks.

'Because the find is Norwegian property.'

'Now you listen to me,' he starts in irritation, but then stops himself. 'Mr Balto, isn't Professor Arntzen your boss?'

'Yes.'

'Why aren't you obeying a direct order from your boss?'

Orders, regulations, decrees, commands, directives, laws, rules, instructions, mandates … to most British people there's something safe about all of life's rules, but I resist them all.

'I don't trust him,' I say.

'You don't trust your own stepfather?'

A shiver runs down my spine. They know even that!

Winthrop blinks and makes a clicking noise with his tongue. He pays attention.

'Tell me, Mr Balto, you're not suffering from a touch of paranoia, are you?'

It wouldn't surprise me if he'd read my medical file. And my journal. Sometimes even paranoid people are right.

'What's in the shrine?' I ask.

'As I said, Mr Balto, let me remind you that it's your duty to hand over something you simply don't own.'

'I'll hand it over.'

'Wonderful.'

'As soon as I know what's in the shrine and why so many people are so damned eager to smuggle it out of Norway.'

'Mr Balto, honestly.'

'I was the inspector on the dig.'

Winthrop smacks his lips. 'True, true. But no one actually told you what they were looking for?'

I hesitate. I understand that he is going to share something with me now that I wasn't meant to know, but I also know that he will probably offer me a carefully prepared lie, an alluring dead end.

'A treasure map?' I suggest.

His eyebrows form two perfect Vs turned upside down.

'A treasure map, Mr Balto?'

'Have you been to Rennes-le-Château lately?'

'Where?' He genuinely seems to have no idea what I'm talking about.

I concentrate on the pronunciation: 'Rennes-le-Château. You know, the medieval church? The treasure maps?'

'I'm sorry, I really have no idea what you're talking about.'

'Well, then maybe you can tell me what they were actually looking for?'

He shrugs uncomfortably and lowers his voice. 'They had a theory.'

'A theory?'

'Nothing more, just a theory.'

'Which was?'

Winthrop makes a strange grimace, maybe meant to show that he is having a profound thought but which ultimately just looks like a strange grimace. He says: 'Isn't it amazing how ancient civilisations just weren't as primitive as you might have thought?'

'I suppose you could say that.'

'They possessed knowledge, both technological and intellectual, that people at their stage of development just shouldn't have had. They knew the universe better than many of today's hobbyist astronomers. They had mastered abstract maths. They were amazing engineers. They practised medicine and surgery. They had an inconceivably good understanding of distances and proportions, geometry and perspective.'

I scrutinise him, trying to read between the lines by studying his face and eyes.

'For example: have you ever wondered why the pyramids were built?' he asks.

'Actually, no.'

'So, do you know why?'

'Weren't they burial chambers? Monuments to the pharaohs' grand reputations?'

'Picture the Pyramid of Cheops, Mr Balto. Why, almost five thousand years ago, would a primitive civilisation decide to build such an unbelievably massive project?'

'Well, maybe there wasn't anything else to do in the desert back then,' I joke.

He rewards me with a soft chuckle. 'There have been a lot of theories. Take the best known of these magnificent burial chambers, the Pyramid of Cheops. One hundred and forty-four metres high when it was erected by the fourth-dynasty Egyptian king Cheops. Archaeologists and grave robbers have uncovered a King's Chamber, a Queen's Chamber, shafts, galleries and narrow corridors. Altogether the known open spaces occupy about one per cent of the pyramid's volume. Are you following?'

I'm following.

He leans in over the desk. 'Using modern technology, scholars started X-raying the pyramid. They soon found that there were far more cavities than had been discovered. And the hollow spaces actually account for nearly fifteen per cent of the volume.'

'Not so surprising.'

'No, not at all. But fifteen per cent, Mr Balto! That's quite a lot. And not just that: the sensitive equipment received reflections back that suggested a large object made of metal was located seven metres below ground level under the pyramid.'

'Buried treasure?'

'I understand that you're preoccupied with treasures, and you could certainly say that everything found in a pyramid can be considered treasure by definition. The presence of metal in an Egyptian pyramid shouldn't surprise anyone per se, but this was no coffin made of gold or store of copper or iron. The size and sheer mass of the metal object were such that the scholars had to take the measurements over and over again before they felt confident they had the numbers right. And by positioning their X-ray equipment at different angles and locations, they were able to put together an outline of the metal object, its contours.'

'And what was it?'

Winthrop stands up and strides over to a cupboard that contains a safe. He punches in a code. The door opens with a gasp. Winthrop pulls out a black portfolio that he brings back to the desk while opening the zipper.

'This is a copy showing the outline of what they found,' he says.

The piece of paper that he hands to me is enclosed in a

transparent plastic cover. At first glance the computer drawing looks like a space shuttle.

Then I realize that it actually *is* a space shuttle: oblong hull, small wings, rudder. I glance up at Winthrop.

'Last year we dug down to the gallery where the ship is located,' he says.

'What is this?'

'Don't you see it?'

'It looks like a space shuttle.'

'A spaceship.'

'A spaceship?'

'Exactly.'

'Now wait a minute. A spaceship that botched a desert landing so badly that it ended up stuck underneath the Pyramid of Cheops?' I ask sarcastically.

'No, no, you misunderstand. The Pyramid of Cheops was constructed over the spaceship,' Winthrop says.

I give him my best hangdog look. The one that says, 'You don't really think I'm going to buy this bullshit, do you?' And then I sigh deeply.

He says: 'Maybe you're familiar with the controversial theories of Swiss author Erich von Däniken?'

'Sure. About extraterrestrial beings visiting the Earth at some point in the past?'

'Quite right.'

I look down at the piece of paper with the drawing of the spaceship-like vessel. I look at Winthrop.

'You can't be serious?' I blurt out.

He pulls some sheets out of the portfolio, on which every inch of space is covered with mathematical equations. 'Calculations,' he says, pushing the paper over to me. 'NASA has evaluated the ship's aerodynamic properties. They are going to incorporate aspects of this design into their future space shuttles.'

I fold my arms across my chest. I don't feel well – not because I believe him but because the lies seem to be hiding a secret that might be even more frightening.

'A spaceship underneath the Pyramid of Cheops,' I say. My sarcastic tone has no effect on him.

'I suppose it's not an easy thing to believe,' he adds, as if he's already managed to convince me.

I tilt my head to the left and then to the right, as if I have a kink in my neck. I take a sip of my tea. It's lukewarm and tastes like something a rich Bedouin might serve you in his tent in the desert.

'So you are asking me to believe that the Pyramid of Cheops was built over a prehistoric space shuttle?' I say slowly.

'Let me reiterate – a spaceship. We presume it was one of the landing vessels for a larger mother ship orbiting the Earth.'

'Of course.'

'You look sceptical?'

'Sceptical? Me? No, not at all. But tell me, how do you explain why the Egyptians built an enormous pyramid over the ship? Surely a "garage" wasn't really a concept five thousand years ago?'

'They believed the spaceship was sacred, the heavenly ship of the gods.'

'I bet it really pissed the aliens off when they eventually returned and found an enormous, heavy pyramid on top of their ship.'

He doesn't even smile. He thinks I believe him.

'Something may have gone wrong,' he says. 'Maybe they had a crash landing, maybe the ship couldn't take off, maybe sand in the machinery? Or maybe their astronauts couldn't survive the Earth's atmosphere or our bacteria. We're not sure. It's still all conjecture at this point.'

'So you guys haven't tried turning the key in the ignition?'

'We haven't really tried yet.' He hesitates. 'There's another theory.'

'I'm sure there is.'

'Maybe the spaceship never planned to go back. Maybe its mission was to bring a group of beings here, obviously ones who resembled humans, who would stay here on Earth,' he suggests.

'And what were they going to do here?'

'Maybe they wanted to colonise our beautiful planet? Maybe they wanted to procreate, for all we know. Some people believe the stories in the Bible about beautiful, stately angels were based on these beings. They were bigger, taller than us and unbelievably beautiful. We know from religious history that the angels occasionally had the misfortune of getting our earthly women pregnant. So genetically, we must have had a common origin.'

I laugh.

He says nothing.

I say: 'And you believe this?'

'It's all about accepting the facts, Mr Balto.'

'Or the lies.'

I look at him. For a long time. Eventually the redness appears, two roses on his round cheeks.

'And the shrine?' I ask. 'What's the connection?'

'Perhaps we'll find out when you hand it over to us.'

I emit something between a snort and a laugh.

He says: 'We hope that the contents of the shrine can lead us to these extraterrestrials. Not necessarily the original ones who landed, of course. They were hardly immortal. Although, who knows,' he looks up towards the heavens, 'their descendants, their line. Perhaps we'll find a message. From them to us.'

I leave us in silence.

Recently in the paper I read about Finnish doctor Rauni-

Leena Luukanen-Kilde, who's not only an expert on down-to-earth conditions like sinusitis and haemorrhoids, but also on the pacifistic philosophy of beings from other solar systems. She's in regular telepathic contact with the humanoids who criss-cross the heavens over our heads. Of all the things they've confided in her, I'm particularly fascinated by her claims that they function in six dimensions, travelling through time and space, and that a delegation of them was waiting to greet Neil Armstrong when he took his first step on the moon. The most fascinating of all Luukanen-Kilde's claims, however, is that they are vegetarians just like me. And that the humanoids' favourite food is strawberry ice cream.

I laugh loudly. It's possible that he senses a hint of scepticism emanating from me.

'You can believe what you like,' he says vehemently.

'And I do.'

'I've presented you with the facts, everything we know, and which we believe. I can't do any more than that. You can believe what you want. Or not believe it.'

'I promise you I do.'

He clears his throat and moves his chair.

'What is SIS?' I ask.

'Ah!' He claps his hands together. The question pleases him, an innocuous question, the kind of question that he could hold forth on for an hour or two at the cocktail parties he frequents with his beautiful, young wife who's surely having an affair with her tennis instructor.

'S-I-S,' he says, enunciating each letter clearly. 'SIS is a scientific institution founded in 1900 by the leading researchers and academics of the day. Its purpose was to consolidate knowledge from many different branches of science into a common repository.'

It's as if he's turned on a recording that they play to visiting schoolchildren on field trips.

'Think back in time.' He gestures with his arms. 'To the beginning of the last century when there was a new optimism. Growth, progress, idealism. Big, new industries were springing up in the business world, a new era was flourishing, but the problem – do you know what the problem was?'

'No.'

'No one was thinking beyond his own specialised little field. And that was the great idea behind the founding of the Society of International Sciences: to keep tabs on scientific advances, to consolidate, to introduce scholars who might benefit from each other – in short: to bring a comprehensive vision to this maze of specifics.'

'That sounds wonderful. And what about SIS today?'

'We receive financial and intellectual support from all branches of the sciences. We receive funding from the state as well as our owners in addition to grants from universities and research institutions from around the world. We have over three hundred and twenty full-time employees. We are home to a vast number of scholars working on research contracts. We have contacts at all the best universities. We have representatives everywhere where important research is being done.'

'I'd never heard of you.'

'Well, that's odd.'

'Not until I discovered that SIS was behind the archaeological excavation I was asked – ha! – to inspect.'

Winthrop seems lost in thought, looking at some papers on his desk.

'What can you tell me about Michael MacMullin?' I ask.

Winthrop looks up from his papers. 'A great man,' he says reverently, 'the chairman of SIS, a very affluent, older chap, a gentleman, very cosmopolitan, appointed professor at Oxford right after the war, left academia in 1950 to dedicate his life to SIS.'

'Where is he now?'

'We're expecting him back any moment. You will have the opportunity to meet him soon. He's very eager to meet you.'

'What was he a professor of?'

Winthrop raises his eyebrows. With his bald pate it looks as if there are elastic bands on the back of his head pulling the eyebrows way up on to his forehead. 'Don't you know? He's an archaeologist. Like yourself. And your father.'

9

Diane sits behind the counter squinting at the green text on the computer screen. She's cute when she squints. She's cute when she's not squinting, too.

The sun streams through the enormous windows, filling the library with soft light. I stand just inside the doorway. I'm clutching a rolled-up brochure about SIS that I got from Winthrop in my hands. When we parted he laughed his ridiculous clown laugh and said he was glad I was so willing to cooperate. Willing to cooperate? I suppose he imagined he had done his job and that I was planning to run home and find that darned shrine for him. He must think I'm easy to convince and more than a little dumb.

With a discreet *ahem*, which echoes in the cathedral-like silence, I take a step into the library. Diane glances over towards me absent-mindedly. Her look of concentration relaxes into a smile. The light is playing a trick on me; I think I see her blush.

'Oh, it's you again,' she says.

'I was just up with Winthrop.'

She stands up and comes over to me. She was very careful this morning when she decided what to wear (I can picture her): she's wearing a cream-coloured silk blouse, a tight black skirt that suits her figure, black nylons, and high heels.

'Ah, we call him the *Man in the Moon*,' she scoffs, and places her hand on my arm. I humour her with a forced *har, har*. Her touch releases a cascade of hormones in my head.

'Diane, can you help me?'

She hesitates for a second and then says, 'Of course.'

'It may not be that easy, what I need help with.'

'I'll give it my best shot. But the impossible is going to take a bit longer.'

'This is about information you have in the computer system.'

'What about?'

'Is there somewhere we can talk? Where we,' I lower my voice another notch, 'won't have to whisper?'

She grasps my hand (softly, tenderly) and leads me through the library into an office with a frosted-glass door. It's an impersonal office. Bookshelves filled with fat three-ring binders, an ancient desk with a nice, brand-new computer monitor on top of a fancy base, a keyboard with a curly cable to the computer down on the floor, an empty ashtray, a plastic mug with dregs of old coffee and cigarette butts in it, a wobbly desk chair. Diane sits down on the chair. She looks up at me. I gulp. I'm overwhelmed by the thought that I'm alone with her, and that I (purely hypothetically) could lean over and kiss her. And, if she kisses me back, and perhaps sighs affectionately, I could (still theoretically) lift her up on to the desk and make love to her hard and shamelessly. And write a letter to a men's magazine about it afterwards.

'So – what's you're problem?' she asks.

My problem is that I have a few too many problems.

The straight-backed chair creaks under my weight. 'Are you good at doing searches?' I ask, nodding towards the computer.

'Um, yeah? It's, like, my job.'

'I need to know more about MacMullin.'

She looks at me quickly. I can't quite interpret the look. 'Why?' she asks coldly.

'I don't know what I'm looking for,' I say honestly.

She doesn't look away. Only once she notices how uncomfortable I'm feeling does she pull the keyboard over, press F3 for Search and type *Michael & MacMullin* incredibly fast. The computer mulls over the question and hums before it responds: *16 documents found, 11 locked.*

'Do you want a print-out of the files that are available?'

'Available?'

'Eleven of the files are protected. Which means you need a password to access the information.'

'Don't you have a password?'

'Obviously. But watch this . . .'

She enters her password.

Unauthorized. Level 55 required, the machine responds.

'What does that mean?' I ask.

'We have different security levels. All users have access to Level Eleven, even outsiders. Level Twenty-two means the data is protected and you need to document that you have authorisation to access it, things like current research projects, etc. Level Thirty-three protection means the data can't be made public. Library employees have Level Thirty-three clearance. Level Forty-four is for personnel files and human resources information. And then there's a Level Fifty-five. Who knows what that protects? In other words, SIS bigwigs only.'

'Are you connected to a database?'

Diane looks at me as if that's a stupid question. I suppose it *is* a stupid question.

'We *are* a database,' she says. 'Haven't you heard of us? SIS Bulletin Board or www.soinsc.org.uk? We're the world leader in our field. We have subscribers at universities and research institutions all over the world.'

'What kind of data?'

'You name it! Everything related to any kind of science or research that SIS has ever been involved in – in other words, pretty much everything. The database consists of all our own material, historical and updated versions, and includes cross-references. All of the reports and field notes are in there. We also store relevant articles from Reuters, the Associated Press, the London *Times*, the *New York Times* and a number of other important media outlets.'

'Can you do a search for anything?'

'Just about.'

'Try the Shrine of Sacred Secrets.'

'The what?'

'It's a shrine, a reliquary.'

'What's it called again? *The shrine of what?*'

I repeat it and she types it in. We get nine hits. The first is the book my father, Llyleworth and DeWitt wrote in 1973. The second is a summary of the myth:

The Shrine of Sacred Secrets: a myth concerning a sacred relic or a message in a golden shrine. According to the philosopher Didactdemus (approx. AD 140) the message was meant only for the 'innermost circle of the initiated'. The contents of the message are unclear. The reliquary shrine was kept at the Monastery of the Holy Cross between about AD 300 and 954, when it was stolen. The Crusaders are thought to have handed the shrine over to the Knights Hospitaller in AD 1186, but there are few definite traces of the shrine after the fall of Acre in AD 1291. Oral tradition suggests that monks hid the shrine in an octagon. According to various versions of the story, the octagon might be in Jerusalem (Israel), Acre (Israel),

Khartoum (Sudan), Ayia Napa (Cyprus), Malta, Lindos (Rhodes), Varna (Norway), Sebbersund (Denmark).

Cross references:

Arntzen/DeWitt/Llyleworth	ref 923/8608hg
Bérenger Saunière	ref 321/2311ab
Dead Sea Scrolls	ref 231/4968cc
Varna	ref 675/6422ie
Knights Hospitaller	ref 911/1835dl
Monastery of the Holy Cross	ref 154/52830c
Cambyses, King of Persia	ref 184/0023fv
Rennes-le-Château	ref 167/9800ea
Shroud of Turin	ref 900/2932vy
Clement III	ref 821/46520m
Schimmer Institute	ref 113/2343cu
Prophet Ezekiel	ref 424/9833ma
Q	ref 223/9903ry
Nag Hammadi	ref 223/9904an

You needed a password to access the other documents – a strange list of references including old European myths, royal dynasties, noble families, occultism, hermetic traditions and many that were incomprehensible. Diane enters her password. The computer responds *Unauthorized. Level 55 required.*

'Strange,' Diane says. 'General data isn't usually password protected, just personnel records. Maybe one of these kings or prophets worked for us?' She titters.

'Maybe as a visiting scholar?' I suggest.

She glances up at me. 'What is this reliquary, anyway?'

'Who knows? Do a search for Ezekiel.'

'Who?'

'The Prophet Ezekiel. He was one of the cross-references listed.'

She gets four hits. Three are locked. The open one refers to the Schimmer Institute.

'Do you know what the Schimmer Institute is?' I ask.

'A centre that does basic archaeological and theological research. Among other things.'

'Try Varna. V-A-R-N-A.'

We find eight documents. One refers to Dad's book. One leads to information about the Knights Hospitaller. One refers to a monastery in Malta. One has to do with Professor Llyleworth's current excavation. One is about the Schimmer Institute. The other three are locked.

'Do a search for Rennes-le-Château!'

She looks at me.

'Rennes-le-Château,' I repeat.

She clears her throat and makes a couple of attempts before managing to spell it correctly, including the 'â'.

We get eight hits, but we're not authorised to look at most of them.

Diane prints out the information that is accessible, which describes a poor, young priest who found some parchments, the contents of which remain unknown, but which somehow left him with a fortune. It hints at connections to the Crusades, the orders of knighthood and conspiracy theories about the Freemasons and clerical orders.

'Can you do a search for all of the excavations SIS has been involved in?' I ask.

'Are you crazy? We'd be here all day!'

'What about excavations that MacMullin and Llyleworth have led for SIS?'

'Sure, but it might take a while.'

It takes a while. The list is long. As I skim through the list of places and years, my eyes happen to stop at Ayia Napa on Cyprus, Xifenggou in China, Tyumen in Siberia, Karbala in Iraq, Aconcagua in Chile, Thule in Greenland, Sebbersund in Denmark, Lahore in Pakistan, Coatzacoalcos in Mexico, and Khartoum in Sudan.

In the margin next to several of the items it says ASSSA and a date. Diane explains that ASSSA means there is an Archaeological Satellite Survey Spectro-Analysis Available. That's a satellite photo based on magnetic and electronic measurements of the ground. This type of geophysical image can detect ruins many metres under the current ground level. The reference also appears in the margin next to *Varna (Vaerne Monastery) Norway*. The satellite photography was done last year. I've read about this technique in international journals.

'The satellite was launched in January of last year,' Diane says.

'Can you find the image for me? The one from Varna?'

With a patient sigh and a smile that she probably doesn't give every demanding academic, Diane goes down into the closed stacks in the basement to find the satellite photograph. But it isn't there.

Graham Llyleworth signed the file out personally.

'Let's move on to the next one,' I say. 'What do you have on the Knights Hospitaller?'

She has a lot. We find cross-references to the Schimmer Institute and to the Shrine of Sacred Secrets, which refers us on to the Monastery of the Holy Cross south-west of the Old City in Jerusalem. The monastery was erected around 300 on the site where legend and biblical history claim that Lot planted the walking sticks of three wise men sent by God. The sticks took root and grew into a tree. Legend says that the cross used in Christ's crucifixion came from the wood of this very tree.

According to the myth of the Shrine of Sacred Secrets, the shrine was kept at the Monastery of the Holy Cross until the year 954. It was then stolen and hidden again in a secret location. There are no other historical references to the shrine until the Crusaders surrendered it into the custody of the Knights Hospitaller in 1186.

'Search for Graham Llyleworth,' I say.

The computer finds forty documents. They're almost all newspaper articles and write-ups from academic journals. But the last four documents are locked.

'Search for Trygve Arntzen.'

The computer finds five documents. All are locked.

'Try my name.'

Diane looks at me, questioningly. In a flash she types in *bjorn & 1 belto*.

The machine responds: *0 documents found.*

'Try spelling it with an "oe",' I suggest.

She types *bjoern & 1 beltoe*.

Wow, she transliterated the Norwegian ø just right. I should be honoured.

The Society of International Sciences actually has a record of the famous Norwegian albino, Bjoern Beltoe, in its computer. *1 document found.*

And not just that. The record is locked. Whatever they know about me is a secret.

'Enter your password,' I say.

We look at the screen.

Unauthorized. Level 55 required.

Four words, no big deal, just four words in a luminous green typeface.

10

They say that criminals who've been in jail for many years long to return after they're released – back to the community behind those walls, the daily routines, the camaraderie, the absurd safety of being surrounded by bandits and rapists doing time for murder.

I can understand them. That's how I feel about the clinic.

Diane knows of a homey little lunch place, a café just off Gower Street. I don't find it that homey. All the decorations, tables and counters are made of glass or mirrors. No matter which way I turn, I see my own confused face.

As I tell her about finding the golden shrine, about all the confusing things that happened in Oslo, about Grethe's veiled innuendos and what brought me to London, I enjoy the attention she's paying me and how interested she seems. I feel like an adventurer on an exciting expedition. This is how I think Diane must see me as well.

On our way back to SIS to pick up the print-outs that we'd forgotten there, Diane asks whether I have any plans for tonight. Her question detonates a fragmentation bomb of anticipation. I leap to the side to avoid stepping on a nonchalant London pigeon and tell her that I don't think I have any particular plans. I don't need to sound completely desperate. Four steps later she asks whether I want her to show me London. I'm filled with equal portions of bliss and panic. 'That sounds nice,' I say.

I wait outside SIS while Diane runs in to get the print-outs about Michael MacMullin. It takes her a while. When she eventually comes back out and passes me the stack of print-outs she rolls her eyes and emits a strained laugh. 'Sorry that took so long,' she says with a fake-sounding groan. It looks as if she's planning to give me a quick kiss. Hesitantly, faltering, she says: 'You know ... um ... maybe that thing about tonight wasn't such a good idea ...?' Her question trails off into nothing. She looks into my eyes. 'Oh, piffle!' she suddenly exclaims. 'King's Arms pub. Seven thirty.' I still haven't opened my mouth. She takes a breath to say something else, but stops. A motorcycle speeds by. 'You know . . .' she says. 'I have a friend who works in the library at the British Museum. You want me to call her? Maybe she could help you?' 'That would be great,' I say. And wait for the kiss that never comes. She looks at me. I can't tell what she's thinking. There's something she's not saying. 'See you tonight,' she says. Then she smiles and is gone.

In a store where vast walls of CDs disappear into the horizon, I buy a compilation CD for Roger. It's called *Satan's Children: Death Metal Galore*. There's a picture on the cover of the devil playing an electric guitar. Sulphurous flames lick at his legs. It's a charming little trinket that Roger will appreciate.

11

Even I have my bad habits. When you've won the race from the balls to the egg, and have tumbled your way through childhood without being mown down by a drunk driver, when you've lazed your way through your teen years without succumbing to a heroin overdose in some blue-lit stairwell, when you've endured life in a dorm for more than four years and found yourself a nice, secure public sector job to boot, when you haven't been afflicted with kidney failure or a brain tumour, well then, why not squeeze the fucking tube of toothpaste from the middle or leave the toilet seat up when you're done pissing. Bad habits are a human right. I'm glad I don't have a wife.

I like to leave my toothbrush on the very edge of the sink. That way I know where it is. OK, it's a bad habit. It isn't rational. I don't give a fuck.

But now my toothbrush is lying on the tile floor.

It's not a big deal. It might have been housekeeping. I did

leave the window open a crack. It might have been a gust of wind. It might have been Henry VIII, resurrected in a cloud of vapour and brimstone.

I pick it up and put it back on the edge of the sink so that the maid can have the pleasure of putting it back in the plastic cup on the shelf below the mirror.

When I was little, it wasn't the fairy tales about cannibalistic witches or bloodthirsty trolls which scared me the most. It was the story of Goldilocks and the three bears.

When the bears roared, 'Someone's been sleeping in my bed,' it plunged me into a bottomless pit of terror. I think it has something to do with my excessive respect for the inviolable nature of home.

The zipper on my shaving bag is closed. I always leave it open. So that I'll have instant access to the pack of condoms (MicroThin, no lubricant) when I stumble into my hotel room at night with my harem of nymphs and fashion models.

It's 3.30 in the afternoon. I dial Grethe's number on the old-fashioned hotel phone. It has a rotary dial.

I let it ring ten times, then hang up.

A pinch of fear makes me call Roger. It sounds as if I woke him up, which I probably did. I ask whether everything's all right. He grunts something that probably means 'yup'. I ask whether the shrine is still safe. He grunts, 'Yup.' Someone giggles in the background.

Then I call Caspar to ask him to check and make sure nothing happened to Grethe.

'Where are you calling from?' he asks.

'London.'

He whistles softly into the phone. He sounds like the whistle on a boiling tea kettle.

'Be careful,' he says.

'What do you mean?'

'You're in London because of the shrine?'

'Yeah. So?'

'Someone broke into your place, you know.'

'I know.'

'You do? Oh. But can you guess *who* broke into your place?'

'Wait. How do you know that someone broke in?'

'Because the Royal Norwegian Office of Cultural Heritage had to send someone, and when I say someone I mean Sigurd himself, in person, down to the police station and the Ministry of Foreign Affairs to vouch for *his almightiness* Graham Llyleworth.' Caspar's dry laugh sounds like paper crinkling.

'I already know it was him. I saw them.'

'But do you know who he had with him?'

'Let's hear it.'

'One of the thieves had diplomatic immunity. How do you like that? Diplomatic immunity! Rumour has it that he's in intelligence. The British embassy made a tremendous stink. You would've thought it was a matter of national security, or something. It went all the way to the top, Bjørn, all the way to the top. The Foreign Ministry has been trying to smooth things over as best it can. What the hell did you guys find?'

I kick off my shoes, fling myself on to the sofa and unfold the metre-long print-out of information on Michael MacMullin.

First I read the biographical highlights: birth date and location not given, special scholarship to Oxford where he became a professor of archaeology in 1946, guest lecturer at the Hebrew University of Jerusalem, a key figure involved in the translation and interpretation of the Dead Sea Scrolls after their discovery in 1948, chairman of the SIS starting that same year, honorary professorship at the Weizmann Institute, named chairman of the London Geographical Association in

1953 and of the Israeli Historical Society in 1959, one of the co-founders of the British Museum Society in 1968, and chairman of the London City Finance and Banking Club in 1969.

I read on in articles drawn from academic journals and newspapers. MacMullin has participated in archaeological, theological and historical seminars, conventions and symposia all over the world. He has been SIS's representative on the most important archaeological digs. He's financed a whole string of projects through the SIS. When the Dead Sea Scrolls were found at Qumran, MacMullin was one of the first Western scholars summoned. Over the years, he's worked as a mediator in the conflict between Jewish and Palestinian scholars over who owns the manuscript fragments that are divided between the Hebrew University of Jerusalem and the Schimmer Institute. A few more details come to light in the exhaustive list of references: since 1953 he's been head of the International Friends of the Shroud of Turin, and since 1956 he's been on the Schimmer Institute's board of trustees.

I call Caspar back and ask him to do me yet another favour. I ask him to recommend me for a position as a visiting scholar at the Schimmer Institute, totally spontaneously, but I have a funny feeling that it may come in handy. Caspar doesn't even ask why. He promises to send the recommendation the next day. By fax. Bearing the official stamp and seal of the Royal Norwegian Office of Cultural Heritage. I'm sure that'll get them to fling open all their doors, and drawers, and cupboards to a nosy busybody from Norway.

12

It's not that easy for me to get all spiffed up.

Women can do wonders with make-up. The unattractive

ones become pretty. The pretty ones become irresistible. Men can do their hair, add a little colour to their skin with facial bronzer, grow out their beards. With my complexion, none of that makes any difference.

For formal occasions, I compensate with clothes.

For this evening I put on grey CK boxers, my Armani suit, a white shirt, a silk tie featuring hand-painted lotus blossoms, black socks and leather shoes. I finish it all off with gold cufflinks.

From the collar down I look pretty good.

I splash a bit of Jovan aftershave lotion on my cheeks. I put some gel in my crew cut. When I was younger, I used to try to add a bit of colour to my colourless lashes and eyebrows with mascara I stole from my mother. I don't do that any more.

I walk over to the big mirror by the door and inspect my appearance.

Certainly not a Greek demigod, but decent.

I break the seal, open the box of Cho-San condoms I brought with me, and rip one off. I'm an eternal optimist. And down in my pants there's a swelling of hope.

Linda at the front desk looks me over as I pass her my keycard. 'Very nice, Mr Balto,' she says, smiling approvingly. Is she perverted? Do albinos turn her on? *Linda the libidinous.*

'I didn't know you were in,' she says. 'I have a message for you.'

She hands me the slip: 'Charles DeWitt called while you were out. Please call him back as soon as possible.'

'When did he call?' I ask.

'Did I forget to write the time? *Whoops, I'm so sorry.* A couple of hours ago. No, more than that. Right after I started. Maybe around four.' She smiles coyly, apologetically; I'm supposed to understand that she was meant for bigger things in this world than remembering when she took a message for some overdressed albino at the front desk of a two-and-a-half-star hotel in Bayswater.

I look at my watch: 7.30.

I go up to my room and call the London Geographical Association. The nightwatchman answers. He's grumpy. He probably just woke up. He's never heard of Charles DeWitt; I'll have to call back during business hours. I ask him to check the phone list just to be sure. There's a bang as he slams the receiver down on to the desk. I hear him flipping through some pages. In the background I hear a hysterical sports commentator. Then he's back. It's as he said; he didn't find any DeWitt on the phone list. I'll have to call back during business hours.

In the phone book I find only one DeWitt: Jocelyn, Protheroe Road. I dial the number.

'*DeWitt residence*,' says a woman with a West African accent.

I introduce myself and ask whether I'm speaking to Jocelyn DeWitt. I'm not. Mrs Jocelyn isn't home. I'm speaking with the housekeeper.

'Perhaps you can help me. Is this by any chance the family of Charles DeWitt?'

Silence. Eventually she says, 'Yes, this is the family of Charles DeWitt. But you'll have to speak to Mrs Jocelyn about that.'

'When do you expect her back?'

'Mrs Jocelyn is spending a few days with her sister in Yorkshire. She'll be back tomorrow.'

'And Mr DeWitt?'

Silence. 'As I said, you'll have to speak to Mrs Jocelyn about that.'

'Just one question: is Charles DeWitt her husband?'

Hesitantly: 'If you'd like, I can leave Mrs Jocelyn a message that you called.'

I leave my name and the phone number at the hotel.

13

Diane is waiting for me at a barrel table at the back of the pub. Through the cigarette smoke I don't recognise her until she waves to me nonchalantly with her fingers.

The alluring idea of a soulmate, the notion that we're on a lifelong quest for our lost other half – it's the most romantic idea I can think of, metaphysically speaking. It's total rubbish, of course. Still, it's a tempting thought. I can't ignore the speculation that Diane could be my soulmate. Although, of course, I think the same thing about everyone I go out with.

The men sitting near Diane look up to see whom she's waving at. When they see me, they look at Diane again, maybe to check whether she's nearsighted or developmentally disabled, or a social life skills coach taking her client out for a night on the town, or maybe a call girl that I hired for the evening.

I pardon my way through the raucous crowd and squeeze in between Diane and a German guy who's singing a drinking song. There are over seven thousand pubs in London and in lots of them you'll find only tourists. The British have their own secret hangouts. I can see why. I order two pilsners at the bar and we drink them quickly.

Traffic flows past us like a metallic river. Neon signs create fountains of light that are distorted at the edges of my thick glasses. I feel lost, as if I'm on another planet. For Diane, London is home. She's tucked her arm in mine and is chatting away, filled with the self-confidence that came from seeing her reflection after hours over her make-up box and delving in her wardrobe. She's wearing sheer red stockings, a black skirt and a red blouse under a short velvet jacket. I can only fantasise about what's underneath. She has a small purse on a strap that rests snugly at a diagonal across her chest. She's gathered her hair into a ponytail with a bit of ribbon.

'I remembered to talk to Lucy. Aren't I a good girl?'

'Lucy?'

'At the library at the British Museum. She'd be more than happy to help you.'

'More than happy?'

She giggles. 'Lucy is so curious about all the various men in my life.'

While Diane discusses the convivial Lucy, I wonder whether I'm a man in her life.

I like quiet women, slightly shy, introverted women, not the ones who whistle at men in bars. I like women who are full of thoughts and feelings, but who don't share them with the whole world. I have no idea what kind of woman Diane is. Or why I'm so attracted to her. I have even less idea what she sees in me.

There's a French vegetarian restaurant on Garrick Street that's known for its amazing *menu potager* and its steep prices. I mean, if you're going to go to the trouble of inviting a beautiful woman out for a vegetarian dinner, you might as well do it right.

I convince Diane to try a Tuscan white bean stew with a Stracchino-stuffed focaccia. I order myself an eggplant parmesan and whole asparagus with a vinaigrette. As an appetiser we settle on spinach and mushroom crêpes, which our lisping waiter, who blinked a little too often, reluctantly recommended. One good thing about vegetarian restaurants is that the waiters aren't prejudiced. They're every bit as

151

condescending to an albino as they are to all their other guests.

After the waiter has taken our order, lit the candle and disappeared, Diane puts her elbows on the table, folds her hands together and looks at me. Because the restaurant is dark, and because my face is bathed in shadows that will hide my blushing, and because simple details like this provide me with a bit of shelter, I pluck up my courage and joke about the unspeakable: 'I know why you went out with me.'

My words catch her off guard. She sits up. 'Oh?'

'You're curious to see what happens to albinos at midnight,' I tease.

She stares at me uncomprehendingly, then she relaxes into a grin.

'Well, tell me why, then,' I say.

She clear her throat, takes a breath and cocks her head to the side: 'Because I like you.'

'You like me?'

'I've never met anyone quite like you.'

'Well, now *that* I can believe.'

'Don't get me wrong. I mean it in a good way.'

'Oh. Uh, thanks.'

'You don't give up easily.'

'I think *stubborn* is another word for that.'

She chuckles and looks at me. 'You don't have a girlfriend? At home, I mean?'

'Not at the moment.' That's a slight exaggeration. I don't want to seem pathetic. 'How about you?'

'Not right now, no. But I'm sure I've had hundreds.' For a second she vacillates between laughter and despair. Luckily laughter wins. 'That arsehole!' she says, kind of to herself.

I don't say anything. Dealing with other people's broken hearts is not my forte. I have enough trouble with my own.

She looks into my eyes. I try to return the look, which isn't that easy. I've developed a sort of twitch in my eye muscles because of my poor vision. The condition is called nystagmus. The doctors think it's caused by the eye trying to simultaneously focus *and* distribute the light flooding in through the iris. But to most people it just makes me seem shifty, as if I'm constantly scanning for danger or something.

'You're not like the others,' she says.

Our appetiser arrives. We eat in silence.

It isn't until our waiter has served our entrées, refilled our wine glasses, hissed *bon appetit* at us, bowed and disappeared back into his damp, dark hiding place in the kitchen that Diane perks up. For a long time she sits and looks at me while alternately smiling and biting her lower lip. She stabs a bean and puts it in her mouth.

'So – why did you become an archaeologist?' she asks.

I tell her I became an archaeologist because I like history, classification systems, deductive reasoning, interpretation and understanding. Theoretically I could've been a psychologist. Psychology is the art of mental archaeology. But I'm way too shy to be a good psychologist. Besides, I'm not really that interested in other people's problems, not because I'm self-centred, but because my own are plenty big enough for me.

'What's the deal with this shrine, Bjorn?' she asks.

I push an asparagus spear back and forth across my plate as I respond: 'They're hiding something, something really big.'

'What could it be?'

I look out of the window. A delivery van with tinted windows is double parked just outside. I stick my fork into the asparagus and shudder. I'm picturing cameras and microphones inside those black windows. Sometimes my paranoia acts up.

'Something that's big enough that they'll go to great lengths to keep it secret,' I say quietly.

'Who are *they*?'

'Everyone, no one, I don't know. MacMullin, Llyleworth, Professor Arntzen, SIS, the Royal Norwegian Office of Cultural Heritage, all of them. Maybe you, too?'

She doesn't say anything.

'That last one was a joke,' I say.

She winks and sticks her tongue out at me.

'They must have found something in 1973,' I say. 'At Oxford.'

'Oxford?'

'All of the threads lead there.'

'To 1973?'

'Yeah.'

A pained wince slips over her face.

'Is something wrong?'

Behind us someone in the kitchen knocks over a bottle. Our waiter rushes over there with a reproachful snap of his fingers.

Diane shakes her head. 'No,' she says distantly.

'There are just so many things that don't add up,' I continue. 'Things that don't make sense.'

'Maybe it's you. Maybe there's some kind of big picture you're not seeing,' she suggests.

'What do you think?' I ask. 'How could SIS know exactly where the shrine was buried?'

My question startles her. 'We knew?'

'Clearly. Professor Llyleworth, DeWitt and my father had speculated as early as 1973 in their book that there was a relic at that site, but they didn't get around to looking until this year. What's that all about?'

'That's not so strange. We didn't get the satellite images that revealed exactly where the octagon was until last year.'

I should have realised that.

'The real story is never quite what we perceive it to be,' I say. 'Someone is pulling on strings we can't see.'

'What do you mean by that?'

'They knew exactly what they were looking for and where to look for it. And they found what they were looking for. And then I came along and got mixed up in it.'

'That's what I like about you! You got mixed up in it.'

'Well, they sure don't seem that excited about my part in all this.'

'They have only themselves to blame.'

'I'm like a pebble in their shoe right now.'

'Serves them right.'

I laugh. 'You've really got it in for them, haven't you?'

'They're just so . . .' She shakes her head and clenches her jaw.

'Did you like your stew?'

'It was delicious.'

'So, do you think you might become a vegetarian?'

'No chance! I'm far too fond of meat,' she says, and winks at me.

It's not every day that I stroll through London with my arm around a beautiful girl. Well, actually, it's not every day that I stroll anywhere with my arm around a beautiful girl.

The air is warm, stuffy, charged. Or maybe it's me. I wave at the cars driving by. I wink at the girls. A beggar is slumped over, snoozing in a phone booth. Diane slides her hand down into my back pocket.

I never told Diane which hotel I'm staying at. And yet she leads me up Oxford Street and then to Bayswater Road. Or maybe I do it subconsciously. I take a chance and put my arm around her shoulders.

'I'm glad I met you,' I say.

We run across a side street against the red light. A Mercedes honks.

'Really glad,' I say, pulling her to me.

Suddenly she stops short and waves her hand. I have no idea what she's doing. I look around for mosquitoes. Are there mosquitoes in downtown London? A cab swerves over to the kerb. When she turns to me, her eyes flood with tears. 'I'm sorry,' she says. 'Thanks for a nice night. You're sweet. Sorry!'

Then she slams the door shut behind her. I open my mouth to say something, but there are no words in there to come out. Diane says something to the cab driver. I can't make out what. The driver nods and the cab speeds away. Diane doesn't turn around. The cab turns a corner. Perplexed, I stand there on the pavement looking at all the cars.

For a long time.

Linda is still on duty behind the front desk, that minx. *Linda the long-legged leopard.*

'Have a nice evening?' she asks professionally.

I give a sullen nod.

'I have a message for you and a letter.' She passes me her handwritten memo and an envelope.

I read that DeWitt called and would like me to contact him.

On my way up to my room I open the envelope. It contains a white piece of paper with a brief message:

You will receive £250,000 for the shrine.
Please await further instructions.

I wonder how much it would cost to buy me: my pride, my self-image, my self-respect. I'm really not sure, but £250,000 doesn't even come close to tempting me.

I should really be seeing a psychologist.

14

'Diane has sort of a strange relationship with men.'

I'm sitting on a hard chair in the reading room in the British Museum library. The ceiling curves above me at a dizzying height of thirty-two metres. The desks radiate out from the circular centre of the room. Here is the written memory of Anglo-Saxon civilisation. A pile of thick tomes is stacked on the desk in front of me. Two cardboard boxes of documents from the manuscripts archive sit on the floor. Everything – the air, my clothes, my fingertips – smells of paper dust. But Lucy smells of Salvador Dali.

I've been browsing and taking notes for four hours. I've filled twelve A4-size pages with notes, comments and observations. Now Lucy comes back. She's planted her cute rump on the unused desk next to mine and is sitting there swinging her legs back and forth. She's a redhead with her eyelids done up with blue eyeshadow and wearing a baggy sweater. And a miniskirt. It's obvious that she thinks I'm proof of Diane's peculiar taste in men.

I'm not used to being discussed as 'men'. I'm not used to women talking about me at all. Unless they're feeling sorry for me.

'Well, there's men and then there's men,' I mumble, trying to camouflage how uncomfortable I feel.

'I can think of a couple things they're good for,' she purrs.

'Did you find anything else? About Værne Monastery?'

'Sorry, you've got it all right here.' She's hoarse, as if she goes out on the town a bit too often, and stays out a bit too late. 'Mostly letters and references in manuscripts. But we do have plenty more about the Knights Hospitaller if you want to look through that. Why are you interested in all this?'

'It has to do with an archaeological find.'

'Ah, Diane said you were an archaeologist. Are you finding what you're looking for?'

'I don't even know what I'm looking for.'

She clucks. 'Hm, she said you were an odd one.'

The Knights Hospitaller were a monastic order dedicated to St John the Baptist founded for charitable purposes at a Crusader hospital in Jerusalem in AD 1050. The monks cared for the elderly and sick, but – inspired by the Knights Templar, who were founded in 1119 – they later evolved to provide military protection for Christian holy sites as well.

When Saladin recaptured Jerusalem from the Crusaders in 1187, the Knights Hospitaller moved their headquarters to the Crusader fortress in Acre. From there, the monks continued to fight the Muslims alongside the Knights Templar. During this same period, the monks started to travel widely – oddly enough, even to places as remote as Norway. When Acre fell in 1291, the Knights Hospitaller moved their home again to Cyprus, and then to Rhodes.

The Knights Hospitaller careered through the centuries from battle to battle, from flight to flight, from valour to defeat, and then to valour anew. The order became powerful and rich. They received gifts from kings and princes. The Crusaders brought magnificent treasures home from their raids. The fact that the order still exists to this day says something.

While the military branch of the Hospitallers was fighting powerful enemies throughout Europe, their pastoral brothers who settled in at Værne Monastery initially enjoyed a great deal of protection in Norway. The Pope issued them with letters of protection from Rome, and the local population and the Norwegian king watched over them. Before long, however, Værne Monastery also started encountering opposition, and their holdings and property were seized. In a letter to the Bishop of Oslo, Pope Nicholas II asks that this seized property be returned to the monks, but it never was. It is not clear what was really going on behind the scenes.

The order's Grand Master did not acknowledge the authority of any king or prince over the order but only that of the Pope, which freed the three classes within the Knights Hospitaller – Knights, Chaplains and Brothers, who cared for the infirm – to spread the order throughout Europe. In the monasteries they still tended to the elderly and the sick, but beneath all this piety lurked each new Grand Master's desire to acquire even more land, gold and jewels, and power.

The Hospitallers and the Knights Templar eventually came to be seen as dangerous competitors to kings, princes and the clergy. By 1312, Philip IV of France had made quick work of dissolving the most powerful order, the Knights Templar, and the less dangerous Hospitallers then took over much of the Templar's vast riches. This prosperity was short lived, however, as much of their wealth was ultimately seized as well.

In 1480 the Hospitallers initially repelled an Ottoman attack on Rhodes but ultimately capitulated to the Ottoman sultan, Suleiman the Magnificent, in 1522. The Ottomans allowed the Grand Master to travel to Messina on Sicily. After negotiations there, the Hospitallers convinced Holy Roman Emperor Charles V to give them Malta, Gozo and Tripoli in 1530.

Two years later the Knights' days at Værne Monastery came to an end.

Lucy is wearing red nylons. They're distracting me. The nylon makes a scratching sound between her thighs every time she moves her legs, a sound that easily gets my imagination going.

I ask: 'Who was he? The last guy?'

'George, an arsehole. He was just using her. She's so trusting.' Her facial expression tells the whole story. 'She caught him with a . . . slut.'

'Did she dump him?'

'Diane? Ha! She was all in a tizzy over him. I told her: he's just a body. Nice muscles, nice arse, no brain, but she didn't care.'

'She seems smarter than that.'

'Diane is razor sharp. But being smart doesn't make you an expert on men. Diane, she's a genuine free spirit. She's searching. I don't know what her deal is. She's a little peculiar.'

'She seems normal to me.'

'I guess, but she had a sad childhood. That'll do something to a person.'

'Sad how?'

'Diane grew up in boarding schools. Her father would come to visit her once a month. She idolises him. And hates him, I think.'

'Did he leave her?'

'Her father?'

'The last guy, George.'

'You bet he did. He moved right on in with that slut of his. I guess she was curvier than Diane, but ten times dumber. A better fit for him, if you ask me.'

'And you? Are you married?'

'Me?' She lets out a little yelp. In the silence around us everyone looks up. She slams her hand over her mouth to silence herself. 'Married? Me?' She whispers, 'I'm only twenty-three!'

As if that were some kind of explanation.

If it hadn't been for Lucy, it would've taken me a whole day just to get into the library and see the manuscripts. Lucy got me a Reader's Pass and a Manuscript Pass without the usual wait. They took my picture and I had to leave my

Norwegian passport with them and filled out a two-page form.

I've written down some data in my big, lined notebook, but I have no idea if it's significant. Large parts of the archive from Værne Monastery – *Domus hospitalis sancti Johannis in Varno* in the Latin sources – were intact in 1622. The oldest of the papal letters of privilege, signed by Pope Innocent III, was issued to the *giffuett munckenne ij Werne closter* in 1188. In it, the Pope excommunicated King Sverre. Hence the monastery must be older than that. The latest one is from 1194. More likely from 1188 – right after the Knights had to leave Jerusalem and move to Acre. Then Pope Clement III (who was never recognised as pope) wrote a letter to the Knights' leader. Scholars have had trouble interpreting its significance. Basically the letter commanded the Order to comply with the sacred assignment to hide and guard the shrine. As far as religious historical documents go, this letter is hardly important. It's not even complete. But on the copy of the fragment of the document that's left, in the middle of a torn edge, I see three letters: V-A-R. I'm sure no one has bothered to contemplate these letters. As I said, it's just one of many thousands of documents. But it certainly can't be ruled out that at one time the letters were part of the word Varna.

Late in the day Lucy brings me to an office where the phone receiver is off the hook, waiting for me.

I hear Diane's voice.

In a near-whisper she apologises for last night. Her voice sounds cool and distant. As if she doesn't quite know what she wants or how she feels. She hadn't meant to run off so suddenly, but she hadn't been feeling good. She hopes I didn't take it the wrong way.

I say that maybe she just isn't cut out to be a vegetarian.

She asks whether I was hurt.

Hurt? I scoff bravely, pretending to have no idea what she's talking about. *We were wrapping things up anyway, weren't we? Ha, ha.*

She asks whether she can make it up to me. If I'd like to see her again tonight? Maybe come over to her place?

Why not? I say. *I don't think I have any plans.*

15

I noticed him an hour ago. An older man wearing a cashmere overcoat that's far too warm for the weather. His features are a bit exotic, as if one of his distant ancestors had been an oriental prince who happened to stop in London for a bit of fun. His hair is silvery white and longer than normal for a man of his age. He must be about seventy. He's tall and thin, distinguished. His eyes are almond shaped and vigilant. He potters around, pulling out books and filing cards at random, but the whole time he keeps a watchful eye on me. Now, slowly, he approaches the desk I'm sitting at.

I'm tired. I've spent the whole day poring over books and documents that don't solve any mysteries. I've read page upon page about knights and religious myths and the Crusades. I've just found a bundle of documents that have to do with the events at Rennes-le-Château. I've read treatises on the worldview of medieval monks and about the historical development of the Church's stance on material possessions and property. Every now and then I ask myself why I'm doing all this. Does it even matter? Couldn't I just give them the damned shrine? It isn't mine. It's not my problem. But something in my nature resists. And wants to know.

'Mr Beltø? Mr Bjørn Beltø?'

He's the first Englishman who's managed to say my name

right. His 'ø's sound crisp, not muffled. At some point in time he must have learned to pronounce the sound correctly. For example, perhaps because he was my father's colleague and friend.

Perhaps at Oxford.

Perhaps in 1973.

Charles DeWitt . . .

I've finally found him. Although actually, of course, he found me.

I shut the odd booklet on Rosicrucian codes (which was with the documents on Rennes-le-Château for some reason) and look up at him.

'That's me,' I confirm, setting the booklet down on the desk.

He's leaning over me a little with one hand resting on the little cubicle wall separating the carrels. With a quick glance, he peeks at the booklet and then his eyes come to rest on me. His exudes charisma. He reminds me of an old-fashioned aristocrat – an eighteenth-century lord who's stepped out of his era. Normally I would cower under the intensity of the look he's giving me. But I look right back at him with a reckless grin.

'Given my appearance, I have a pretty hard time hiding. Even in London,' I say boldly.

I can't properly describe the next few seconds. In fact the only thing that happens is that he smiles at my self-deprecating joke. But there's something about the smile and the eye contact that raises us both up out of the British Museum and into a vacuum where time has stood still. Somewhere deep in the back of my head I hear the clicking and whirring of the inner workings of the grandfather clock in my grandmother's house by the fjord, I hear my mother whisper, 'Little prince, Bjørn.' I hear my dad scream, I hear Grethe say, 'I was hoping you would never find out' – words, voices, sounds woven together in a flood of memories glimpsed for a second, as if by a bolt of lightning.

And then reality clicks back into place. I shiver in my chair. He doesn't seem to have noticed anything.

'You've been asking for me?' he says.

I think: Good God, if this happens again, I'm going to have to call Dr Wang when I get home.

'I have,' I mumble. I feel dazed and confused. What the heck just happened?

'What do you want from me?' he asks.

'I think you know, don't you?'

He shakes his head, but doesn't respond.

I sigh. 'Everyone knows more than they're willing to admit,' I say. 'But they're all pretending they don't know anything.'

'That's usually how it is.'

'We have quite a few things in common,' I say.

'We do? How interesting. Such as what?'

'I have some questions. And I think you have some answers.'

'That will depend on the questions, of course,' he says.

'And on who's asking them.'

He stands up and surveys the room. 'Truly a fascinating place. Did you know that this library started out with just the fifty thousand volumes Sir Hans Sloane bequeathed to it in 1753? And that when the museum's collections were catalogued in 1966, that the catalogue alone was two hundred and sixty-three volumes?'

'Someone forgot to mention that to me.' I smile.

'I'm sorry I've made you wait, Mr Beltø – I've been out of the country. I have a car waiting outside. Perhaps you would do me the honour of accepting an invitation to my home for a cup of tea? Then we can discuss what we have in common in a somewhat more private setting.'

'How did you know I was here?'

A reserved smile crosses his lips. 'I'm very well informed.'

I don't doubt that.

He lives in a fashionable neighbourhood with wide front steps leading up to the front door and a narrow staircase (behind a wrought-iron fence) leading down to the kitchen entrance. A limousine with tinted windows pulled up to collect us as we stepped out of the British Museum. For twenty minutes the chauffeur, whom I could just make out through the privacy window, wound his way through a labyrinth of side streets. I wonder whether he did that to confuse me, so I note the street sign where we stop. Sheffield Terrace.

Jocelyn DeWitt's address was on Protheroe Road.

DeWitt unlocks the door. Two screw holes and a darker shade indicate where the name plate should have been.

It's a distinguished home, and like many distinguished homes it seems uninhabited and freshly redecorated. The furniture, the pictures, the carpets . . . none of them give it a homey feel. I don't see any clutter, nothing that seems personal, no small meaningless object that seems out of place but stays front and centre because the resident associates fond memories with it. Everything is sterile, as you might expect of a recently divorced man who's just moved out of his home to establish a new residence.

'So your wife got to keep the housekeeper?' I say as we hang up our coats.

DeWitt gives me an aggrieved look. 'My wife?'

I should have bitten my tongue. That was an indelicate and rash comment. Typical me. The kind of tactless comment you might permit yourself with a close friend. But for a blue blood like Charles DeWitt, the divorce – obviously he and Jocelyn must be getting a divorce – must be a social catastrophe. Not suitable fodder for jokes from a complete stranger.

'Sorry,' I say meekly. 'I looked you up in the phone book and called her, your wife, but she wasn't home.'

'I beg your pardon?' he says. He seems confused.

'Jocelyn?' I say, tentatively.

'What?'

'I couldn't get hold of her.'

'Oh!' he exclaims suddenly. He looks at me cheerfully. 'Jocelyn! I understand. Ah . . . I understand.'

We go into the living room and sit down by a window where the sun is slicing columns of silver through the suspended dust particles.

'You wanted to talk to me?' he asks.

'You may know what this is about already.'

'Maybe. Maybe not. What brings you to me? To us?'

'I found your name in the book. At Grethe's house.'

'Grethe.' His voice sounds fragile, tender; like a father discussing his daughter in a distant land.

'You remember her?'

He closes his eyes. 'Oh, yes,' he says simply. Sadness clouds his face, leaving him with an agonised look.

'Do you know her well?'

'We were sweethearts for a while.' The word *sweetheart* casts a saccharine light over the romance. If I know Grethe the relationship was anything but saccharine. But at least that explains some of her behaviour. Then something surprising happens. His eyes grow shiny. He scratches at the corner of one eye.

'Please,' he chuckles, embarrassed, 'don't look so surprised. Grethe has always been a – what should we say? – passionate woman, warm blooded, and a kind soul. Far too nice and compliant. It's not surprising that she had many male, um, friends over the years. This was many years ago, all this.'

'I went to see her for some advice. About an archaeological find. And I came across this,' I say, passing him his business card from the London Geographical Association.

He stares at the yellowed business card with a distant expression. He's struggling to hold something back.

'They've never heard of you there,' I say.

'It's all due to a misunderstanding.'

'What misunderstanding?'

'Don't worry about it. But of course they should have recognised the name Charles DeWitt.'

'I came because of an archaeological find.'

'Yes?'

'We found a shrine.'

'Interesting.'

'Made of gold.'

'Perhaps you brought it with you?'

'Why?'

'So we can take a look?'

'You don't understand. The thing is, I have to protect the shrine.'

He raises his left eyebrow. 'Really?'

'They were trying to steal it. They wanted to take the shrine out of the country.'

'Who are we talking about?'

'Llyleworth, Arntzen, Loland, Viestad. My superiors, all of them. Everyone is involved. In one way or another.'

His laughter does not sound genuine.

'You think I'm exaggerating?' I ask. 'Or that I'm making all this up?'

'I think you've misunderstood a great many things. Not surprising, when you get right down to it.' He looks at me. 'You sound like a distrustful person, Bjørn. Very distrustful.'

'It's possible I'm being paranoid. But maybe that's because I have reason to be.'

He's clearly delighted at something, although I have no idea what.

'So, what did you do with the shrine?' he asks.

'I hid it.'

He raises his eyebrows again. 'Here? In London?'

'No.'

'Where?'

'In a safe place.'

'Well, I should hope so.' He takes a deep breath, trying to collect his thoughts. 'Can you tell me why you're so committed to this?'

'Because everyone wants to take it from me. Because I was the inspector. Because they tried to trick me.'

His face takes on a self-satisfied look. 'The protector,' he whispers.

'Excuse me?'

'You see yourself in the role of the protector. That's nice.'

'I would prefer it if I didn't have to protect anything.'

'I can understand that. Tell me about the dig.'

'We were working in a field by an old medieval monastery in Norway. Graham Llyleworth from SIS was leading the dig. Under Norwegian supervision from Professor Trygve Arntzen and Director-General Loland. I was the inspector on site. Ha ha. We were looking for a ring fortress. Or so they claimed. Then we found the ruins of an octagon. Perhaps you're familiar with the myth? And in the ruins we found the shrine. *Et voilà!*'

'And from this you have inferred some kind of conspiracy?'

'Professor Llyleworth ran off with the shrine. Then they ferreted it off to Professor Arntzen, my boss.'

'Still, I get the impression that at least up until this point everything was going according to plan? Why did you intervene?'

'Because they were planning to smuggle the gold shrine out of Norway.'

'How?'

'Probably on a private jet. They called someone in France.'

'Really? And how do you know that?'

'I was listening at the door.'

He gives me a look and laughs out loud. 'Now I see. That explains a lot. You were listening at the door.' He laughs with gusto, can't quite seem to stop.

'I took the liberty of stopping this little conspiracy in its tracks.'

'You could say that.'

'I stole the shrine back.'

'So dutiful.'

I can't tell whether he's making fun of me or not.

'And why is it that you've sought me out?' he asks.

'I was hoping you could explain what the deal with the shrine is.'

'And why do you think I would know anything about it?'

'Everything leads back to Oxford, 1973. And that book.'

'Is that so?' he says undecidedly.

I wring my hands. 'I'm going out on thin ice here, but since you weren't involved in the dig, I imagine – I hope – that you can help me.'

'How?'

'By telling me what it was that you guys found twenty-five years ago.'

He thoughtfully strokes his chin as he contemplates me. 'Let me be honest,' he says. 'Let's both be honest with each other. I know more than I'm letting on.'

We size each other up.

'Do you know what's inside the shrine?' I ask.

'First I want to know where it is.'

'In a safe place.'

'And you haven't opened it?'

'Of course not.'

'Good! Bjørn, do you trust me?'

'No.'

My straightforward response causes him to dissolve into laughter yet again.

'My friend,' he says, 'I understand you. I understand your scepticism, but think about it . . . You don't know the scope of what you're doing. There's so much you don't know. You have to give the shrine back.' His eyes are pleading, insistent.

'Why?'

'Can't you just trust me?'

'No. I want to know what's in it.'

He closes his eyes and breathes through his nose for a while. 'Believe me when I say I understand you. You're curious, suspicious, unsure. And afraid? And you think that ultimately it has to do with money.'

'That thought had occurred to me.'

'But it's not like that.'

'So what does it have to do with?'

'It's a long story.'

'I have time.'

'It's a complicated, involved story.'

'I'm a good listener.'

'I don't doubt that.'

'I'm just waiting for an explanation.'

'I understand that. But I must ask you to accept that the solution to the mystery is so delicate, so sensitive, that it can't be shared with you.'

'What a bunch of arrogant bullshit!'

My outburst amuses him. 'Well put, Mr Beltø. I must say.

Well put. You seem like a man who can be trusted with a secret.'

It isn't a question. It's a statement. Or a command. But I don't say anything.

'One might say that I don't have a choice,' he continues. He's not talking to me. He's talking to himself and letting me listen to the conversation. 'I'm simply going to need to let you in on our little . . . secret. Going to need to,' he repeats. 'I have no choice.'

I still don't say anything. I think: *I don't think he could possibly be any more melodramatic than this.*

But I'm wrong.

He moves to stand up, but then changes his mind and stays seated. 'Mr Beltø, will you swear an oath?'

'An oath?'

I think about the oath that Director Viestad took so seriously.

'I must ask you, as a gentleman and a scholar, to promise never to reveal what I am about to tell you.'

It's hard to tell whether he's joking.

'Do you promise?' he asks.

I half expect the wall to open up and reveal a twenty-man team from *Candid Camera* who will rush into the room with flowers and microphones and laughter. But nothing happens.

'OK, I promise,' I say, but I'm not sure that I mean it.

'Good,' he says to no one in particular, still not really addressing me, but more some spirit hovering somewhere over my head.

'Where should I begin?' he asks himself. 'Well . . . You could call it a gentleman's club, a club for the initiated, for the well informed, a gentleman's club for archaeologists.'

'An archaeology club?'

'Not for just any old archaeologists. We're the leaders. We

just call it the Club. It was founded by Austen Henry Layard a hundred years ago. Layard gathered fifty of his day's leading archaeologists, explorers and adventurers. The number of members can never exceed fifty. When a member dies, the others gather to vote on who they'd like to invite into the club, not unlike a papal conclave. Well, not as important, of course,' he adds in a way that leaves a little doubt as to whether he means it or not.

'And you're lucky enough to be a member of this Club?' I ask.

He doesn't seem to notice my sarcasm.

'In all modesty,' he says, taking himself far too seriously, 'I'm the president.'

He watches me as he waits for this revelation to impress me. To no avail. But of course I could always pretend.

'It's imperative that you understand the importance of our little club. Informally and in a convivial atmosphere, the world's fifty leading archaeologists gather. Completely confidentially. It happens twice a year. Most of us hold professorships at major universities. We talk, we swap stories, we contemplate theories. And, of course, we enjoy ourselves.'

'Oh, what fun!' I exclaim.

He scrutinises me. 'Quite,' he says. My attitude confuses him. He must be used to being treated with more respect and grovelling admiration.

'You wouldn't happen to have an opening for an albino assistant professor from Norway, would you?'

'Mr Beltø, I don't think you're taking this seriously.'

I just stare at him, because of course he's dead right.

His eyes narrow and he stares off into space. 'Our club discussions have resulted in some of the most sensational archaeological discoveries in recent decades. Completely unofficially, of course. The Club never takes credit for something one of our members accomplishes. Although the

Club as a group might well be the reason a specific excavation was undertaken or why it was done in that specific location. The Club is a way for us to pool our expertise, to create a sort of intellectual database to which we can all contribute knowledge, and from which we can in return reap rewards in the form of the collective expertise of our fifty members.'

I lean back in my chair and cross my arms. It's so easy for knowledgeable people to lapse into pompous platitudes when they talk about their fields of expertise. They simply aren't aware that they're doing it.

'Perhaps you think we're a bunch of dried-up, humourless old academics?' He laughs. 'Ah, my friend, we enjoy the pleasures of the table, the best wines and the finest sherries.'

'And perhaps a couple of cute young coeds later in the evening?'

He gives me a hurt look. 'No, but we play.'

'Play?'

'We have contests, challenges. They're really something quite unique, a combination of historical rebuses, cartography and of course archaeology. Call it an advanced treasure hunt. Every five years we present a new challenge. The first one to find the solution and bring us the artefact we've hidden is named co-president. There are currently five of us.'

I'm starting to have an inkling of where he's going with all this.

'Last time we hid a rune stick in a Mesopotamian tomb. Quite an amusing anachronism.' He chuckles. 'We designed a rebus based on Layard's five-legged winged bulls in the British Museum, which led the clever ones to Nimrud.'

'And this year,' I interrupt, 'you buried a golden shrine at Værne Monastery.'

'You're clever. But it's not quite that simple. This year we're celebrating the Club's anniversary. So we wanted a special challenge. We broke up the challenge.' He clears his throat, then pauses. 'We put Michael MacMullin in charge of coming up with the rebus. He based it on the myth of the Shrine of Sacred Secrets. When your father was a student in the 1970s he wrote a book – along with Graham Llyleworth – in which he hinted that the shrine was buried in an octagon in Værna, Norway.'

I don't point out to him that he has humbly neglected to mention that he himself was the third author of the book.

'It was a very ingenious rebus,' he says. 'Solvable, but difficult. A brilliant challenge.'

I know what he's going to say. 'And then something went wrong,' I suggest.

'So it did. Unfortunately. So it did. It's quite an awkward situation. For our anonymous little club. For SIS. For the British Museum. Actually for the whole of British archaeology.' He grimaces. 'It could have been quite scandalous. Such a delicate situation.' He stares at me. 'And the scandal has not been averted yet.' He takes a breath. 'Let me tell you about Michael MacMullin. He's one of the Club's most distinguished members and the co-president. He's a prominent professor. Perhaps you're familiar with his work? MacMullin is a man of great vision, but also few inhibitions. He stole the shrine from the British Museum.'

'Stole it? The shrine?'

'The golden shrine you found is an artefact that was originally excavated in Khartoum in 1959. It's been in the British Museum since then.'

This information fills me with an uncomfortable bewilderment. Khartoum, Sudan, is the place my father wrote about in the letter that was tucked inside Grethe's copy of the book. Why didn't anyone know, or mention, that the reliquary had been found forty years earlier? Is Grethe hiding something from me?

I don't want him to figure out what I know and what I don't know, so I let him continue.

'MacMullin left the museum with the shrine in his briefcase,' he says. 'Evidently he buried it at Værne Monastery in Norway.'

I could have pointed out that I was there when the shrine was unearthed. If he hadn't been an archaeologist himself I would have explained to him about soil formations, about how dirt and sand are compacted over the centuries in parallel layers that are destroyed when someone digs a hole and fills it back in again. I could have explained how the earth around the shrine was packed tight, and how the layering in the area was undisturbed. But I don't.

'This was a bit of a scandal. He really overstepped the bounds. I should mention that the Club has never experienced a scandal of this proportion. But there was really only one thing we could do – clean up the mess. Of course, we figured out where MacMullin had buried the shrine. The problem was knowing exactly where. Until we found the satellite photo he'd specifically ordered. It was taken with infrared film so we could see the underground structures. And there it was. Actually there *they* were – an octagon and a ring fortress – both there in the grounds at Værne. The rest was relatively simple. We even gave the operation a code name. *Operation Shrine.* We organised the excavation. It would have been impossible to locate the octagon without a certain tolerance based on the satellite photos. We would've been caught if we'd tried to secretly dig up the shrine. So we proceeded the way we would if we were looking for a ring fortress. We played by the rules. We applied for a permit. We paid all the fees. We even agreed to a Norwegian inspector, a clever young chap who would ultimately create some unanticipated problems for us.'

He smiles and looks at me.

'The British government has alerted the Norwegian authorities to the magnitude of this affair. The British embassy in
Oslo is providing us with assistance. Mr Beltø, I hardly think
you have a choice. You're going to have to give the shrine
back.'

This all feels like being a kid at Christmas. After the
presents have been exchanged and you sink back into the
corner of the sofa, warm and empty and weak because all
the excitement over. Your parents and grandparents and
aunts and uncles are all sitting there around you, smiling
and sipping from their glasses, and you realise it's all over and
that it will be a whole year until it happens again. No matter
how fantastic his explanation is, it's like a cold shower. It's
anticlimactic.

'I understand,' I say. This time I'm the one staring off into
space.

'You . . . understand?'

'You'll get your shrine.'

'I'm so glad. Truly. Do you have it with you?'

'Unfortunately not. I left it in Norway.'

He gets up. 'Come,' he says, 'I have a plane waiting at
Stansted.'

'I have an appointment tonight. An appointment I have
absolutely no intention of missing. But we can go
tomorrow.'

'With a woman?'

'With a goddess.'

He winks at me. If the years have cooled his passions, they
still smoulder on in his memory.

I stop to use the bathroom on the way out. The roll of toilet
paper is still glued shut. The soap hasn't been used. The hand
towel is freshly ironed. But the mirror is still covered with
fingerprints and smears and no one has bothered to remove
the price sticker: £9.90. A steal if you ask me.

DeWitt clasps my hand as I leave. We agree to meet outside my hotel at ten the following morning. He thanks me for being so cooperative.

The limousine pulls up to the pavement as I descend the front steps. I open the door and get in. DeWitt waves. He looks like someone's rich, eccentric uncle. The limousine starts moving. I haven't said where I'm going, but five minutes later it stops in front of my hotel.

16

'I'm going home tomorrow,' I say.

Diane has sealed herself off in a bubble of indifference. She looks up at me. 'So soon?' she asks. There's something tired about her expression. Honestly, I wonder whether she isn't stoned or something.

She lives in a flat on the nineteenth floor of a high-rise with a view that makes me ask her whether that isn't the Eiffel Tower I see in the distance. The hall is a chessboard of black and white, made to seem longer by the mirror mosaic on the far wall, and with an archway leading to a narrow bowel-like kitchen. The living room opens out on to the sky; the whole far wall is windows. At this height, Diane must have to go out on to the balcony every morning to wipe away the clouds.

The leather sofa gleams black and red. The glass table is so thick that you could seek shelter underneath it if anyone ever decided to shoot you with a bazooka.

I stand by the window. Below me London unfolds as a fan of buildings and streets and parks.

'This is an amazing view,' I say.

She says thanks.

Something vibrates between us. But I can't quite put my finger on what it is.

'This is quite a flat,' I exclaim. I'm about to add that it looks as if it was decorated by an interior designer. But I don't know whether she'll take that as a compliment or think I'm being sarcastic.

'It's mostly Brian's doing.'

'Who?'

'This guy. Who I was with. Brian. He was an interior designer.'

An emergency vehicle is moving through the streets below, a glow of blue light.

'Lucy helped me out today,' I say. 'She was wonderful.'

'Did you get anywhere?'

'Not at the museum, but something happened while I was there.'

'She called me. She thought you were cute.'

'Cute?'

'And very odd.'

'Odd?'

She laughs at me. 'So what happened at the museum?'

'A man I've been trying to get in touch with found me.'

'Who?'

'His name's DeWitt, Charles DeWitt.'

She doesn't say anything, but I can tell that she recognises the name and is amazed. I still can't quite bring myself to ask her about him.

She's made a vegetarian meal from a recipe in a magazine that's still sitting open on the kitchen worktop.

'I hope I did it right,' she says, clapping her hands together with a nervousness that's both touching and typical of so many people, who think that vegetarian food requires some special insight that only the chosen few are privy to.

I take a seat at a round dining table in the corner of the living room that's closest to the kitchen. Diane scurries back and forth, constantly remembering things she's forgotten. I help myself to summer squash au gratin and salad. She pours the white wine and passes me a baguette, from which I tear a piece, and a bowl of garlic butter. She stands there with her hands on the back of her chair, watching me expectantly.

'Delicious,' I say with my mouth full of food.

She smiles and smooths her skirt over her thighs before sitting down. There's something primal and feminine about the way she does it. She raises her wine glass and nods at me. The wine is dry.

'Fascinating guy, this Mr DeWitt,' I say.

'Was he able to help you?'

'He tried.'

'So, what did he tell you?'

'A long story, full of holes.'

'Really?'

'Yeah, bizarre things.'

'You don't trust him?'

'I'm wondering about all the stuff he didn't tell me.'

'The world is full of liars,' she says to herself. Her eyes seem to glaze over.

'I think they followed me here,' I say after a bit.

'What?'

'A car followed me from the hotel. I hope that doesn't matter.'

'They followed you?' she asks indignantly, surprised. 'Here? Those bastards.'

She's about to say something but stops herself. Her eyes lock on to mine. It's as if she wants to give me some bad news. Maybe that I shouldn't take this dinner invitation too seriously. That I shouldn't think we were meant for each other. But that I'm a nice guy and she's considering adding my name to her list. Along with Brian and George and the ninety-eight other guys.

We eat almost without exchanging a word. She's made a delicious mousse for dessert. At the bottom of the bowl, buried under the mousse, I discover a strawberry and a piece of chocolate. She calls the dish Archaeologist's Delight.

Diane puts on an old Chicago album, an actual record on an actual record player. She dims the lights. She lights the two red candles on the glass coffee table. Her nylons shimmer in the flickering glow of the small flames.

The leather creaks as she sinks down on to the sofa next to me. Much as the music creaks. She must have played this record many, many times. For several minutes we sit there in silence, uncertain, afraid to get too close. Or afraid not to.

She asks whether I'd like a drink. I say *yes, please*. She goes to the kitchen and returns with Beefeater gin, Schweppes tonic, two glasses and ice cubes. We say cheers and giggle as we clink our glasses together. Then we sit and drink in silence. Neither of us knows who should start. I try to think of something romantic to say, something that could defuse the awkwardness.

She beats me to it: 'Do you think you're getting anywhere? With your enquiries?'

OK, maybe that wasn't so romantic, but it sure beats the oppressive silence.

I say: 'I know just as little as when I came. And yet I'm even more confused.'

She laughs softly. 'It's so strange to think that you have a . . . life back in Norway.'

'Well, there are lives and then there are lives. I suppose as lives go, mine isn't all that earth-shattering.'

'I don't know the first thing about you.'

'Well then, that makes two of us.'

'Tell me about yourself.'

I tell her about myself. It doesn't take long.

Outside the window London flickers below us, a billion points of light.

'Those arseholes!' she whispers to herself.

'Who?'

'They think they own me.'

'Who does?'

'My dad and all those eager little minions of his. *Do this, do that. Be a good girl, Diane. Do as we say, Diane.* They make me sick.'

Diane has drained her glass. My glass is still half full. From her eyes I can tell that she's starting to get drunk. She pours herself another drink and puts on a new record. *Hotel California*. She has a CD player but tonight she's playing only records from the 1970s. *On a dark desert highway . . . Cool wind in my hair . . .* A little flicker of nostalgia wells up in me. *Warm smell of colitas . . . rising up through the air . . .* I close my eyes and lose myself in my memories.

'You remind me of this boy I used to know,' she says.

I open my eyes and look at her in silence.

She takes a couple of sips of her drink and the ice cubes clink in her glass. 'His name was Robbie, Robert. We called him Robbie.'

I still don't say anything.

'Actually, I didn't realise it until just now, who you reminded me so much of. But now I see it. You remind me of Robbie.' She looks at me and past me at the same time. 'Robbie Boyd. We dated for a summer.'

'A long time ago?'

'We were fifteen. We were each going to a different boarding school.'

'Was he an albino?'

She looks surprised.

'You said I remind you of him,' I explain.

'Not like that. You're similar people.'

'And where is he now?'

'He died.'

'Oh.'

'Car accident.'

'Oh.'

'I just happened to hear about it. No one knew we were dating. I couldn't tell anyone. In some ways I've never got over him. Every time I'm with a man, it feels like I'm cheating on Robbie. Maybe that's why I've never been able to commit to anyone.' Diane chuckles, lost in thought, takes a deep breath and then slowly exhales. 'Do you ever feel lonely?' she asks, running her hand over my hair.

'Occasionally.'

'I don't mean, like, single or on your own. I mean – lonely.'

'Sometimes.'

'When I was young, I felt like the loneliest person on the planet. I never had a mother. She died when I was born. And my father, he . . .' She takes a sip.

'What about him?'

'He . . .' She shrugs. 'He was always so distant. He might as well have been a nice uncle. I suppose that's why I fell so in love with Robbie. It was like I'd finally found someone, if you know what I mean.'

'I lost my dad when I was a kid.'

'That must have been worse,' she says. 'You knew him. You lost someone you loved. I never had a mother to lose.'

'Then she didn't leave a void behind?'

'Or maybe the void is so big that I haven't even noticed I'm in the middle of it.' She looks at me. 'Sometimes I feel so fucking lonely. Even when I'm with a guy.'

'You can feel alone in the middle of a crowd.'

'Have you been with many girls?'

'Not that many.'

'I have! Well, not girls, I mean. Guys. Men! And you know what?'

'No?'

'You still feel fucking lonely. Even when you've been with a hundred men, you still feel just as fucking alone.'

I raise my shoulders. To me a hundred women is purely theoretical. As with Fermat's last theorem, I don't even understand the question.

I ask: 'Have you been with a hundred men?'

She snickers. 'It feels like it. Ninety-nine! I don't know. In a way I've only ever had one boyfriend: Robbie. The others were just . . . you know . . .' She leans in towards me. I put my left arm around her shoulders.

'Sometimes I hate him,' she exclaims.

'Robbie?'

'No, my father. Don't get me wrong. I love him. But sometimes I hate him so much.' She sighs, turns towards me and carefully studies my face. 'Has anyone ever told you that you're really cute?'

'Um, yeah. After two or three drinks.'

'I'm not kidding. It's so easy to like you.'

'Diane, I know what I look like.'

'You're cute.'

'So are you.'

She laughs loudly and pokes me in the side with her index finger. 'Such flattery!'

She stares deep into my eyes. 'I'm so glad I met you,' she says.

'Why?'

'Because I like you. Because I've never met anyone like you, someone who's so totally and completely themselves, who doesn't give a damn about being like everyone else. You're your own person.'

'It's not like I have a choice.'

'You *believe* in something. You never give up. No matter who you're up against. I've always admired people like you. All the while, those arseholes . . .'

'Who?'

'They think they can just . . .' She stops herself. 'If you only knew . . . Oh, screw them!' she says intensely.

Now something's going to happen, I think.

Then she leans over and kisses me.

The first time I kissed a girl I was sixteen. She was fourteen. Her name was Suzanne. She was blind.

Kissing Diane makes me think of Suzy. I don't know why. I haven't thought about Suzy for years. But something about the way Diane kisses (a clumsy sort of insistence, as if she wants to and doesn't want to at the same time) opens a drawer of forgotten memories. I remember Suzy's slender body, not fully formed, how we breathed heavily into each other's mouths.

Diane's breath smells of gin. Her tongue wiggles playfully. I don't know where to put my hands.

She pulls back a little, holding my face and looking at me. Her eyes have that confused, bloodshot look that people get when they're not used to drinking. And there's something else in there, too. Anger? Sorrow? Confusion?

Without a word she starts unbuttoning her blouse. Numb with anticipation, I follow each motion. Once it's unbuttoned, she takes my hand and leads my fingertips to her bra.

She steals a quick look at me. *Bjørn the kind albino*. One in a hundred.

She leads me into the bedroom. The walls are crimson. A black bedspread with a bold, golden lightning pattern covers the queen-size bed. A stack of glossy fashion magazines sits on the bedside table.

She flings back the bedspread, crawls into the bed and wriggles out of her skirt. She's dressed for the occasion. Her transparent red bra matches her panties. She rolls around in the bed while she waits for me. I unbutton my shirt and struggle with my belt. I always have trouble with this belt when an impatient woman is watching me take it off, although that's not a problem I have to contend with very often.

I sit down on the edge of the bed and she leans over and kisses me hungrily. I feel stupid, helpless. I know what I should do, but I don't do it. I sit there perplexed and let her take charge.

For a while, anyway. She opens the drawer of the bedside table and pulls out four short silk ropes.

She snickers nervously. 'Do you want to tie me up?'

She's drunk. Definitely drunk.

'Uh, pardon me?' I mumble. I heard what she said, but it's not really sinking in.

'Do you want to tie me up?'

I stare at the ropes.

'Are you shocked?' she asks.

'Uh, no.'

As if all I ever do is tie women up and love them to distraction.

'You *are* shocked. I can tell from the look on your face.'

'No, no, not at all. I've read about this.'

'You don't want to try? Just tell me if you don't want to.'

But it is clear that I want to. I'm just not quite sure how to proceed. She shows me how to do it. I tie her wrists and ankles to each of the four bedposts. She's breathing hard. We all have our desires.

I've never done it like this. I'm not a prude, but I've always just got right down to business.

Uncertain how to proceed, I snuggle in against her. My fingertips turn her on so much, she seems hardly able to stand it.

And then there's a problem, one I've never encountered

before. She's still wearing her panties, but her legs are splayed. And tied. If I untie the ropes, the magic will disappear. I contemplate how I can get rid of the panties. Finally I give up and just pull the stretchy material aside. Enough said.

Afterwards, lying entangled together under the bedspread, she asks: 'Hey, do you think I could come with you? To Norway?'

She misinterprets my silence.

'I don't mean to be pushy. Sorry,' she says.

'No, no, no. That sounds . . . nice.'

'I have a couple weeks of holiday coming up,' she says. 'I thought it would be fun. To see Norway. With you.'

'I'm going home tomorrow.'

'That doesn't matter. If you want me to come, I mean.'

'I would definitely like you to come.'

At 3 a.m. she wakes me up. 'You hid it well, right?' she asks.

I have no idea what she's talking about.

'The shrine,' she says. 'I happened to think of something, something you said. I hope it's in a safe place?'

I'm so tired I see two of her, the enchanting Diane twins.

'It's in a safe place,' I mumble.

'You wouldn't believe how good they are at finding stuff, when they want to. These guys are good.'

'What makes you say that?'

'I want you to know that I'm on your side. Even though I work for SIS and all that. I know you can't trust me completely. But no matter what happens, I'll always be on your side.'

'Obviously I trust you.'

'I hope so, but don't, OK? Maybe they put a microphone in my purse or something like that. So you can never tell me where you hid the shrine or anything else important, OK?'

'He's a friend. You don't know him. And I trust you,' I say, and turn over. She snuggles up against me. Her breasts press into the sensitive skin on my back, and I slip back into sleep like this.

17

I haven't seen this receptionist before, a man. He's tall with light blond hair and he looks like an Aryan war god. But when he opens his mouth his voice is so nasal and his tone so coy that I think he's making fun of me. With a wink and a smile he tells me I must be quite popular. Then he hands me two messages. One is a fax and the other is a handwritten note from the queen of the night, Linda. Her message is short and almost free of spelling errors. Jocelyn DeWitt called.

The fax is handwritten on Royal Norwegian Office of Cultural Heritage headed paper:

> Bjørn
> *I've been trying to call you. Where the f . . . are you?*
> *Can't get hold of Grethe. Sorry. Does she have relatives*
> *she might be staying with?*
> *Give me a call, OK?*
> C—

Everything in my room is the way I left it, almost. Before I went out, I stuck a toothpick under the lid of my suitcase under the bed, just to be sure, to convince myself that I'm being a paranoid idiot. But now the toothpick is on the floor.

In the shower I wash off all of Diane's scents and dried juices.

Then I change and, before I start packing, I call Jocelyn DeWitt. Not because I need to talk to her, but because I'm a polite person. And – I must admit – because I'm curious.

The housekeeper answers. Even though she puts her hand over the receiver, I hear her saying that it's the gentleman who called about Mr Charles.

Jocelyn DeWitt picks up another extension.

I introduce myself. Bjørn Beltø, archaeologist from Norway.

'Archaeologist?' she exclaims. 'Ah, I understand. That explains a lot.'

Her voice is soft and gentle and sounds as if it's coming to me from a bygone century.

'What does it explain?'

'Well, my Charles was an archaeologist when he was alive, although that was so many . . . well. It was so long ago now. Twenty years.'

Something stops me. 'There aren't many DeWitts in London,' I say.

'My husband's family was French. They moved to England during the Revolution. What was it you were wondering about Charles?'

I admit that I just randomly called the only DeWitt in the London phone book.

'Of course, you've really piqued my curiosity,' she says. 'I'm so curious about what you might want and who you could be. You must excuse me, but it's been so many years since Charles died. What can I help you with?'

It's 8.30. They're coming to get me in an hour and a half.

18

Jocelyn DeWitt is a graceful woman with a swan-like neck, fluid movements and a drowsy sort of voice that somehow evokes crystal and foxhunts and late afternoons in the cool shade of the summer house. Her eyes possess a casual, jovial self-confidence. Everything about her says she's never had to force herself out of bed at the crack of dawn to stoke a hearth fire. Which makes it all the more shocking each time a hearty swear word sneaks its way into her refined speech and explodes like a grenade on her lips.

She directs her plump, black housekeeper with quick finger gestures. They must have developed a code. The way masters and servants do when they've been together so long they've become one organism. The housekeeper understands when the waving and snapping means *leave the room immediately and close the door behind you* or *bring the banana liqueur* or *why don't you offer this Norwegian gentleman a cigar.*

I've never been here before. It isn't even the same neighbourhood as when I visited Charles DeWitt's house. Or his ghost's house.

We're in a living room weighted down by chandeliers and arched windows, Gobelin tapestries and thick carpets, baroque furniture, a massive fireplace and – why, I'll be – a tile stove in the corner.

She takes my hand and leads me over to the elephantiasis-afflicted fireplace.

'Here he is,' she says. 'My beloved Charles and the others. This was taken in 1973.'

She has the grainy, enlarged photo hanging behind glass in a frame in the place of honour above the mantel. The colours have faded. The men have long hair and are wearing T-shirts with psychedelic patterns. You are filled by the awareness that these people are staring at you with a look that is frozen in time.

They're crowded around an excavation shaft. Some are resting on their shovels. Some are wearing handkerchiefs on their heads to protect them from the sun.

On the far right, behind Grethe, is my father.

Grethe looks different, young and attractive, playful. Her eyes sparkle. She's holding her hands over her stomach.

Charles DeWitt towers with his arms crossed on top of a pile of dirt, so that he dominates all the others. He looks like the slave driver who owns the whole damned lot of them. So it was him. That old man didn't trick me. He has only tricked his wife.

I don't know what secret he's hiding. Or why he pretended he was dead. Or how he managed to live in hiding for all these years. Without being revealed. In the middle of London.

I think: I'm too much of a coward to tell her the truth.

Maybe he got tired of her? And moved in with another woman? Or did he meet an irresistible little altar boy? Maybe he discovered something in Oxford in 1973, along with my dad and Llyleworth, something that made him cease to exist?

Mrs DeWitt shows me into a parlour decorated in Louis XVI style. We sit down with our legs crossed at the ankles. Like a genie from a lamp, the housekeeper appears with a crystal carafe. 'A little banana liqueur?' Mrs DeWitt urges. I nod politely. Mrs DeWitt has trained her housekeeper not to look anyone in the eyes, so she pours two small glasses without our eyes meeting. The liqueur coats my mouth in sugar. 'Damn good,' Mrs DeWitt says, smacking her lips. It's surely not her first glass of the day.

'So, what was it that you wanted to know?' she asks, leaning towards me in an intimate way.

'As I said, I'm an archaeologist . . .'

'But why were you asking for Charles?'

'I found something that has required some investigating. And in the course of these investigations, your . . . deceased husband's name came up.'

The banana liqueur is like syrup in my mouth. I sit here sliding my tongue over the roof of my mouth.

'How so?' she asks.

I realise that I have no idea how I'm going to explain anything to her. Particularly that her husband is alive and in the best of health. I try to evade her curiosity: 'You mentioned something about the DeWitt family fleeing from France during the Revolution?'

'Charles was immensely proud of his heritage. Friggin' French frogs! They were this close to being guillotined, a family of social climbers, if you ask me. But they cultivated the company of the king and the aristocracy, especially the women – upper-class whores! Then they nipped across the Channel. Charles's great-grandfather founded a law firm, Burrows, Pratt & DeWitt, Ltd. His grandfather and father took charge of it in turn. Charles was expected to take it over after his father. Charles was . . . educated, you know. He started studying law. Then, completely unexpectedly, he flung himself into archaeology. It was Professor Michael MacMullin who I suppose you could say converted him. To Charles's family this was mutiny. Fucking mutiny! His father refused to speak to him for years. It wasn't until Charles became a professor that his father got back in touch. To congratulate him. But he never forgave him.'

'And your husband died in . . .?'

'1978,' she says.

That answer sends a shiver through me. I picture a rocky cliff face, a rope, a heap at the base of the cliff.

She doesn't notice the wave of emotion tearing at me.

'So, out with it, young man. What is it that you'd like to know?' she asks.

'What do you know about the circumstances surrounding your husband's death?' I stammer.

'They were searching for some kind of treasure, those lunatics. He was very secretive. Usually he told me more than I wanted to know about his work. Oh, how he could bore the daylights out of me with his yammering. Academic mumbojumbo! But this time the only thing he told me is that they were looking for a shrine. Some goddamned prehistoric relic.'

No way . . .

'Did they find it?' I ask.

'Who the hell cares? When Charles died, I went to live with my sister in Yorkshire. I stayed with her for a year. To . . . get over the shock. Have you ever lost anyone close to you?'

'My father.'

'Then you know what I'm talking about. You need time. Quiet. Time and quiet to remember, reflect, work through the grief. Maybe find a psychic to help you contact your loved one, you know. Tell me, did Charles leave behind papers or something that made you come?'

'Just a business card. How did he die?'

'An infection. He got a cut on his left arm. A tiny little cut, actually.'

'And it killed him?'

'The wound got infected. If it had happened anywhere else it would have been quite harmless.'

'Why? Where was he when it happened?'

'In the middle of nowhere. He developed gangrene before they could get him to a hospital.'

'Where?'

'In his arm, I'm telling you. They amputated it! The whole arm. But those brainless baboons – pardon my French –

weren't used to dealing with complicated cases. He died two days after the amputation.'

'But where?'

'In that infernal jungle.'

I sit there in silence for a few seconds before I ask: 'A jungle?'

'Isn't that what I just said?'

'You mean . . . in Africa?'

She rolls her eyes. 'Well, I certainly don't mean at bloody Oxford Circus.'

'It didn't happen in the Sudan, by any chance, did it?'

'Why do you even bother asking if you've known the answer the whole time?'

'What happened with the dig?'

She shakes her head. 'No idea. Honestly, I've never thought about it. Or to be even more honest: I couldn't care less. He wrote to me before he died. A goodbye letter, as it turned out.'

She snaps her fingers. The housekeeper, who's standing in the corner like a stiff, plump Buddha, springs to life, opens a secretary desk and brings her mistress a box. The box contains five handwritten pages tied together with a black silk ribbon. She unties the bow and passes me the brittle pages.

I hesitate.

'Have at it!' she commands.

> *By the Nile, in southern Sudan*
> *Monday, 14 August 1978*

My dearest Jocy,

Talk about rotten luck! I wasn't paying attention (no smart remarks, please!) on my way from the tents to the dig site and I stumbled over a root and tumbled down a steep gravel and clay slope. Don't worry, dear, it wasn't much of a fall, but I did tweak my knee a bit and scrape my arm on a sharp rock. It bled quite a bit for a while, but a boy bandaged me up and helped me back to camp. And then it turned out that we couldn't find the first aid kit. Isn't that typical? MacMullin ordered me to stay in the tent and take it easy today so the wound can knit. It's really not terribly deep, so I'm hoping it won't need stitches.

But let's look on the bright side. Now I'm sitting here in the tent, bored, so I finally have a chance to dash off a few lines to you. I know, I know – I should've written sooner, but MacMullin is not a man who considers free time or idle hands to be good for humanity . . .

It's hotter down here than I'd feared – truth be told it's rather unbearable, but it's the humidity that really gets you. The air sticks to you like warm paint. Oh, and the bugs! (Since you're not overly fond of creepy-crawlies, I won't tell you how big they are – enormous!!! huge!!! – or where we find them all – in our beds! in our shoes! in our clothes!)

We've come quite far (or deep!!! ha ha ha) with the dig. I won't bore you with all the archaeological details, I know how dull you find my work, but: we are searching for traces of a Persian military campaign. I can't tell you how many times I've told MacMullin that the Persians never had the shrine. The Knights Hospitaller must have hidden it in the octagon at their monastery in Norway. But no one listens to me. Aside from Birger. God rest his soul . . .

Ooops, the food's ready! More later, my love!

Night

It's 1.30 (in the morning!!!). I can't sleep. The darkness outside my tent is filled with strange noises and heavy scents.

Night-time in Africa is unlike anything I've ever experienced at home. It whispers to you, like something is coming to life. I don't mean the animals and bugs, but something much, much bigger. Forgive me if I'm rambling.

I think I have a fever. I'm freezing. Even though it must be 35° here in the tent and as humid as a goddam greenhouse.

The gash on my arm hurts like the dickens. Shit, shit, shit. I'm going to try to sleep again. I miss you, darling.
XOXO

Tuesday
It's as I feared. I have a fever. Can you believe it – I think the darned cut on my arm must be infected.

Don't worry, Jocy. MacMullin has decided to bring me back to the village, where there's a little hospital. It's a day's journey by foot and then another by jeep. I must confess, I'm dreading it.

Tuesday evening
I've been lying in a stretcher like a hunk of proud flesh all day. There were eight of them taking turns carrying me. Natives. They were chatting and laughing with each other and I couldn't understand a word of what they were saying. Luckily MacMullin sent a couple of Englishmen along, Jacobs and Kennedy. They're keeping me company, but in all this heat we're not able to talk much.

The heat and humidity are just unbearable. The jungle is thick and steaming. I'm miles from the nearest ocean, but I'm seasick anyway.

There's something I have to tell you, Jocy. My arm is beginning to smell. At first I thought it was the sweat. Then other people started noticing it, too. And when they took off the bandage, the stench poured out like a poison cloud. I don't know if a bacterial infection can smell like this. Maybe it's gangrene, I don't know. I fear the worst. To be honest I don't feel that good. I started vomiting this afternoon. But now luckily we've reached the cars. We were planning to set up camp here tonight, but the others think we'd better start driving right away, although it will be sheer hell negotiating these roads in the dead of night. I feel bad to be causing such a fuss.

Have to leave off, we're going now.

What a night. I'll tell you more about it later, once I'm home.

When we finally reached the hospital this morning there was quite a commotion. I don't think they've ever had a white patient before, which is promising – they'll treat me like a god, fallen from the heavens.

We're waiting for the doctor now. They have to go and fetch him from a village several miles away. Oh God, I hope it's not too bad, Jocy. The stench is disgusting. It must be gangrene. But luckily we're catching it early.

Not really feeling my best.

Oh, Jocy, Jocy, Jocy, sweetie. I have to tell you something dreadful. Promise to be a brave girl for me. Right?

They cut off my arm, Jocy!

Can you believe it? They amputated my arm!! Oh my God. When I look down to my left I see only a stump with a bloody bandage on it. It was gangrene, as I'd feared. Oh, Jocy!

Thankfully it's not as painful as I would have thought, but I can't seem to stop being sick all the time. They've got me stuffed full of morphine.

I'm so sorry to have to tell you such awful news and to have to do it by mail.

And to be coming home to you a cripple. I should have listened to you and stayed home.

Too tired to write more now.

Night

I miss you. I can't sleep.
Oh, how it hurts.
Freezing.

Saturday

My dearest, beloved Jocy,
Today – [illegible] – and I – [illegible] – to the priest.
But – [illegible] – my darling J, I love you. – Can you forgive – [illegible].

Night

It's [illegible] o'clock.
Jocy, my love, the fever is making me [illegible].
I'm exhausted!!!
I'll write more lat . . .

That's quite a captivating tale. Charles DeWitt must have had an evil glint in his eye as he described his own deathbed. The first page is written in vigorous, right-leaning cursive, the pen pressed firmly into the paper. He went to great pains to gradually make the handwriting weaker and harder to read. By the end the letters are a faint blur.

I set the pages down.

'He died in the early hours on Sunday morning,' Mrs DeWitt says simply. 'They found the letters in his bed with him.'

I don't know what to say.

'Quite a farewell, isn't it?' she says.

'It must have been awful reading this letter.'

'In a way. At the same time, it made me feel like I was there, like I knew what happened, what he was thinking and feeling. If you know what I mean. MacMullin brought the letter back from Africa himself. And gave it to me in person.'

She takes a sip of her liqueur. I stand up and walk back over to the photograph over the fireplace. Mrs DeWitt joins me.

'Do you know who this is?' I ask, pointing to Grethe.

Mrs DeWitt scoffs. 'That strumpet! An oversexed nymphomaniac from Norway.'

Then she remembers that I'm Norwegian too, and that theoretically that woman could be my mother, and that maybe that's why I'm here. 'Do you know her?' she asks meekly.

'I've met her,' I lie. 'She taught at the university.'

'She got pregnant,' she says.

My mouth falls open.

'Pregnant?' I stammer. *Was the baby my father's?* I ask myself. *Or DeWitt's?* I mean, he said himself that they were sweethearts. But I'm too chicken to ask the question.

'Everyone pretended they didn't know.' She sniffs.

I point to Charles DeWitt. 'And this,' I say quietly – I have to concentrate so as not to give away how agitated I am, 'this was your husband?'

'Oh good heavens, no.' She laughs. 'Not that I would have objected to that!'

Chuckling at her own racy remark, she points to a shy, swarthy guy squatting at the far left side of the picture. He looks like a disgruntled salesman at some open-air Spanish market. 'That's my Charles. God rest his soul.'

'But then . . .' I stammer, uncomprehending, tapping my finger on the man towering in the middle of the picture, 'who's he?'

'That,' she says, 'is the man in charge of the dig, a very renowned archaeologist and scholar, a good friend of my husband's. Didn't I mention him? Michael MacMullin.'

19

The moving van is as big as an oil tanker, and it fills the pavement along Sheffield Terrace so that the pedestrians are forced quite a way out into the street. I ask the cabby to wait. Filled with an inexplicable doomsday fear, I run over to one of the movers. He has vacant eyes and arms like logs. I ask who owns the house. He doesn't understand me. He yells to a guy who must be his foreman. I repeat my question. They look at me and laugh rudely at my Norwegian accent. I'm some kind of carnival attraction to them, in the flesh, a flustered jumping jack, white as a sheet, dangling right in front of their faces. 'The house's owner?' the foreman eventually repeats. 'Dunno nuthin' 'bout 'im.' 'Who lived here?' I shout over the rumble of a passing motorcycle. They shrug. 'It's important,' I plead. 'I'm a foreign surgeon. It has to do with a heart transplant. There's no time to lose. A child's life hangs in the balance!' They look at each other hesitantly, then the foreman climbs into the cab of the truck and makes a call. When he comes back, he looks confused. 'You must have the wrong address. This is a rental,' he says. 'We don't have a name. We can't reveal our clients' names, you know. *Company policy . . .'* The five-pound note I stuff in his shirt pocket distracts him and he leans closer. 'And besides, you'd have to talk to the government, wouldn't you, since they own the place. This isn't just any old house, you know.'

Of course it may be a coincidence. The funniest things can happen by coincidence. Every once in a while they stack up and begin to form a pattern.

Charles DeWitt, my dad's school chum and fellow scholar at Oxford in 1973, passed away in a Sudanese jungle one night in August 1978. Just a month after my father plunged to his death in an accident that the police gave up investigating owing to lack of evidence.

Lack of evidence.

Those words send a shiver through me. It doesn't mean nothing happened. It just means there's no proof.

The London Geographical Association isn't open on Saturdays. But I keep ringing the doorbell until a grumpy voice answers the intercom. I ask for Michael MacMullin. *We're closed*, the guard says. I raise my voice and ask for Michael MacMullin again, *it's important. You'll have to come back on Monday*, the guard says. I ask him to call MacMullin and tell him that *Mr Beltø from Norway is here to see him, it's extremely important that he get the message. You miss a bell thrum from nowhere?* the voice crackles. *Beltø!* I yell so loudly that people walking by look at me in alarm and scurry past. *Tell him the crazy albino wants to talk to him!* The crackling noise stops. I ring the bell several times, but he doesn't answer. I can picture him in there behind the lens of the security camera: fat, smug, safe and secure behind thick doors and metre after metre of camera cabling. With my lips I mouth the words *you call MacMullin right now you motherfucking son of a bitch!* It's possible he can't understand me. I give him the finger and run back down to my cab.

It's gone. The driver didn't even wait for his money.

20

'Oh, Lordy, you're here. Already?'

Even garbled over the SIS door intercom, I recognise her voice, my old friend the grey-haired grandmother with the knitting. I flash my toothiest smile up towards the camera and wave with two fingers.

Language is a funny thing. It sets us apart from animals. *Already*. Such an innocent word, but it tells me something. It tells me that she knew I was coming, because someone told her that I was on my way.

'Oh, Lordy! There's not really anyone here yet. No one said that . . .' While she's talking she buzzes me in and as I walk in she's still behind the desk with her finger on the button, chatting to me over the intercom. Her coat is over her arm. I don't know whether she just got here or whether she's on her way out. She eyes me with a frightened, sheepish look. I feel sorry for her. She doesn't really know what to do with me.

'Are you guys open today? On a Saturday?' I ask.

'No, of course not. I mean . . . no, not usually. But today . . . Uh, I don't know . . . Can I help you with something?'

'I need to talk to MacMullin.'

Some of the tension leaves her face. She shakes her head. 'Oh, how funny. He's on his way. He was hoping you'd be here. You two had an appointment . . .? To meet . . .? To go to the airport . . .? He said that if you . . .' She gives up and hangs her coat over the back of the chair. 'Well, he'll be here soon. Maybe we should head up to his office.'

She leads me up the marble stairs and down the colonnade. The acoustics emphasise the fact that we're the only people in the whole building. We walk across the mosaic tiles, past Mr Anthony Lucas Winthrop, Jr's universe and around another corner. Which brings us to the double church doors leading into Michael MacMullin's office. His name is screwed securely to the dark wood with small, brass letters. When you hold all the power in your hands, you can afford to be discreet.

The waiting room for Michael MacMullin's office is as big as a conference room back home in Norway. The parquet flooring gleams. The secretary's desk is next to an elegant French seating area where his guests can sit and wait until it pleases His Excellency to invite them into the inner sanctum. His bookshelves are weighted down by first editions of books you've only read about. Two windows face the street: long shafts out towards the light. The big copy machine and computer equipment are shoved as far back into the shadows as possible. The door leading into the actual office, where MacMullin resides, is equipped with one normal lock and two deadbolts. The door frame is reinforced with metal. A red light bulb on the wall is flashing in a box with a numeric keypad on it. Every day MacMullin must feel like a safe, happy little piggy bank in the world's most secure bank vault.

'Well, you go ahead and make yourself comfortable while you wait,' Grandma says. She's out of breath. Then she backs out of the waiting room and shuts the door.

I take a seat on the windowsill. As I gaze down at the street, I mull over what I'm going to say to MacMullin.

It doesn't take long before a beige BMW 745 rounds the corner. It took the corner so fast that a woman in the crosswalk had to jump back up on to the pavement. Which is why it caught my attention. Drivers who do stuff like that really piss me off.

The car comes to a sudden stop on the pavement below me. The tyres practically squeal. Four men get out. I've never seen the driver before. Then MacMullin (aka DeWitt) gets out. And my good old buddy Graham Llyleworth.

But the last one is the one that makes me nervous. We've met before. It's King Kong.

I wonder why they're bringing their muscle along if all they want to do is chat with me.

As I let myself out of the waiting room, I hear the group being buzzed in down below on the ground floor.

Grandma's voice: 'He's up there!'

I take off my shoes and run down the colonnade with one shoe in each hand. When I catch sight of the four men on the stairs, I jump to the side and press myself up against a column.

If they look in my direction as they pass by they will see me, but they don't.

I wait until they've gone around the corner before I run to the stairs and storm down them. At the bottom I put my shoes back on.

Grandma turns around. 'But . . . What are you . . .?' she asks, surprised, glancing up the steps. 'How did you . . . um . . . here?'

'Exactly,' I respond.

There's a yell from up by MacMullin's office.

'But . . .' she says, taking a step towards me as I go by. As if she has a black belt in jujitsu and is planning to fling me to the floor herself.

'Stop him!' a voice shouts.

She shuffles after me, following me to the door, whimpering anxiously.

I rush outside and try to blend into the crowd.

21

Diane's suitcase is already packed and sitting in the hall. Her facial expression seems to suggest that she's been sitting on it waiting for me for the last five hours.

'Finally,' she snaps. 'Where have you . . .'

I cut her off: 'I think they killed them.'

Diane can't quite close her mouth.

'We have to get out of here!' I urge.

'Who,' she stammers, 'killed who?'

'My father and DeWitt.'

'Who did they kill?'

'No, they *were* killed.'

'Now I'm completely lost. Someone killed them? Why?'

'They knew something.'

'Oh God. About the shrine?'

'I don't know. But they died practically at the same time. In accidents.'

'So?'

'There must be a connection.'

'I don't think . . .'

'Diane! You don't know the first thing about this. Come on! Are you ready to go? Come on, let's get out of here.'

'What's the big hurry?'

'They're after me!'

'Now just hang on a second.'

'We don't have time!'

'Who's after you?'

'MacMullin! Llyleworth! King Kong! The CIA! Darth Vader!'

'Uh . . .'

'Come on!'

'What do you mean, *after you*?'

'I just barely escaped before they got me.'

She gives me a worried look. '*Bjorn* . . . Don't you think you're exaggerating *a little*?'

'Diane!'

'OK, we're going, we're going. Is your luggage down there?'

'It must still be at the hotel.'

'But . . .'

'I have my passport and money.'

'*Bjorn*, I'm scared. What happened?'

'I'll tell you later. Come on! We have to hurry if we want to make the flight.'

'But shouldn't we . . .?'

'Shouldn't we what?'

'I have to call my dad.'

'Now?'

'Well, he . . .'

'Call him from the airport! Call him from Norway!'

'It'll only take a minute. A few seconds!'

'OK, call him. Hurry!'

Diane picks up the phone. I look at her. She looks at me. She sets it down again.

'Never mind,' she says. 'I can call him from Norway.'

Just then the phone rings. Confused, she picks it up. She answers 'yes' several times, impatiently, dismissively.

'What do you mean?' she says.

And listens.

'Why?' she grumbles, and rolls her eyes.

'Explain what?' she shouts into the receiver. Then she hangs up. 'Work,' she says. 'You'd think the world was ending just because I'm going on holiday.'

I carry her suitcase over to the lift. Diane locks up, but remembers that she forgot to pee. Women! She lets herself back in. She takes for ever. I've been holding the lift; I set the suitcase in front of the sensor. The door pings as it finally closes behind us. Diane presses a button with an outline of a car on it. The lift hums softly. I feel my stomach lurch.

In the garage she opens the boot of her Honda and I put her suitcase in.

Diane backs out of her parking space. Her tyres squeal as she accelerates, the echo sounds hollow. I sink back into the seat and take a breath. My legs ache.

We have to wait for an opening before Diane can pull out of the garage into traffic. One of the cars that passes us, and which slams on its brakes in front of the main entrance to the apartment building, is a beige BMW 745. I can't see in. But surely there's no way it could be them.

PART 2

The Son

IV

Secrets, Lies, Memories

1

IT WAS SUMMER when my father died.

The gash where the trees have been clear-cut around the power lines defiantly splits the old growth forest in two. It's been twenty years, but when I close my eyes, I can still see images and feelings from that summer holiday. Cosy crannies in my private memorial grove: the long car ride ... The sky was translucent above us. The radio was crackling, the station fading in and out. Drowsy and carsick, I sat there in the back seat glancing out of the half-open window. Along the verge swarms of gnats hovered over the tall, yellow grass. The heat was thick with scents. Chilly lakes glittered like shards of mirrors between the tree trunks. I remember a decrepit logging cabin that was being devoured by moss and rot, a flimsy plastic bag with an ad for Ali coffee hanging from a branch, a discarded car tyre, enormous boulders, and streams that burbled on the hillside then disappeared into grey concrete pipes. We passed small black mountain lakes surrounded by thickets. I swallowed each time I vomited a little. My mother stroked my forehead. My father was sitting behind the steering wheel, quiet and distant, Trygve Arntzen was sitting next to him, howling in high spirits, his legs up on the dashboard.

Muddy tyre tracks from construction vehicles crossing the forest service road, farms with boarded-up windows and overgrown yards, relics from the past. An old man was sitting on a chopping block in one of the yards, whittling, like a forgotten gnome or someone's elderly uncle, frozen in time. He didn't look up. Maybe he wasn't really there.

The path wound its way up a grassy bank from the car park. It was dark under the trees. In the dim light the dried-out roots looked like petrified snakes. The damp moss padded the tree stumps. My father was quiet. My mother was humming. Trygve walked a little way behind her. I was at the back. We must have looked like four lost sherpas. The mountain air washed over us, fresh and raw.

'Little Bjørn!'
Mother's voice crept into my dream, far away and warm, like a caress.
'Bjørnaboo?'
The sun was blinding even through the canvas tent. It was almost nine. I looked around for Trygve, with whom I was sharing a tent. His sleeping bag was empty; limp, half inside out, like an old snakeskin. Half asleep, I burrowed into the clammy darkness of my own sleeping bag.
'Little prince, Bjørn.'
With a whoosh my mother opened the zip and stuck her head into the tent, the face of an angel surrounded by unruly hair.
'Breeeakfaaast!' she sang.
She started tugging on my sleeping bag. I fought against it, with determination. I'd started waking up with an erection, but I could hardly tell my mother that.
Breakfast was laid out on paper plates on a blanket between the tents: slices of bread cut roughly with a hunting knife,

butter, salami, cured mutton sausage, raspberry jam, eggs and bacon a little charred from the Primus camping stove.

Trygve gave me a friendly slap on the shoulder. He hadn't shaved in several days.

My mother didn't like my father going climbing. My father and Trygve had demonstrated the safety equipment for her – ropes and cams and pitons and carabiners and abseil anchors – but it didn't help. She was afraid something would happen.

After breakfast, my mother and I strolled down to the lake to bathe. The water was dark and glossy. I asked my mother whether she thought there were leeches hiding in the reeds. She didn't think there were. The water felt warm when we waded out into it. There were water lilies floating around us. It seemed enchanted. We swam across the small lake and climbed out on to a big, flat, sun-warmed rock on the far shore. My mother closed her eyes and folded her hands behind her head. A bird took flight in the woods, but I couldn't see it. I lazily watched the water droplets dripping off my mother's body in fits and starts; like raindrops on a window, they trickled down her skin, dripping down on to the rock below, where they would gradually evaporate.

Here's another moment:

I caught two fish and was quite pleased with myself. I whistled all the way back to camp, the fishing pole resting on my shoulder. The fish were in a plastic bag and they stank.

No one was there when I got back.

I leaned the fishing pole against a tree and hung the plastic bag on a broken branch so that a weasel or a grizzly bear wouldn't take the fish.

Then:

My mother's voice through the wall of the tent: 'You're being silly!'

I was startled. The woods were quiet all around me. I was a spirit, hovering by the tent – unseen, unheard.

Her voice sounded funny, not like usual. There was something different about it, something disgusting, something that wasn't meant for my ears.

Tender, gentle, full of sticky dampness.

Deep, good-natured mumbling, from a sleeping bag.

I stood there silently in the heather, listening.

My mother (like a sigh, almost inaudible): 'You're so good.'

Silence.

My mother: 'Hey, not now.'

Teasing laughter.

My mother (playfully): 'No!'

Silence.

My mother: 'Ah! They could be back any minute.'

Moving around.

My mother (purring, whimpering): 'Youuu!'

A wild animal growled from the depths of the sleeping bag.

My mother (giggling): 'You're crazy!'

Silence.

Purring.

Silence filled with sounds: the wind in the trees, the distant burbling of the river, the birds.

My voice, pleading, feeble, frail: 'Mummy?'

It was quiet for a long time.

Then the tent zip slid open. Trygve crawled out and looked around. When he saw me, he stretched sleepily and yawned. 'Back so soon?'

'I caught two fish. Is my mother here?'

'Two? Wow! Big ones?'

I took the plastic bag down from the tree and showed him the fish.

'Is my mother here?'

'Not at the moment. Should we go and clean them?'

He took my hand. He'd never done that before. I hesitated.

'Don't you want to clean them?' he asked impatiently, pulling me away.

Then we went and cleaned them. It didn't take long. When we got back, my mother was sitting on the big rock, sunbathing. She smiled at Trygve, slightly apologetically, mischievously. She thought the fish looked great and promised to fry them up for lunch.

When you think back, it's the small episodes which are hard to let go of. Meanwhile all the stuff you would expect to remember in minute detail just disappears, leaving no trace.

One morning my father and I went hunting at the crack of dawn. He woke me up at 4.30 in the morning. Neither my mother nor Trygve wanted to come. But Trygve gave me a cheerful wink as I got dressed. He was wide awake, ready to get up and chop down a dozen trees with that little Boy Scout axe of his.

The wan early morning sun was shining. A cold steam rose from the ground. Down in the hollow, by the big lake, long tendrils of fog stretched into the woods. I was shivering, still cold from having slept in the tent; tiredness filled my head like wet cotton behind my eyes.

Each lost in our own thoughts, my father and I strode along the river and past the cliffs where they usually went to do their rock climbing. There was a cool breeze coming off the river. My father was carrying his Winchester over his shoulder. The shells weighed heavily in my jacket pocket, clicking against each other like small pebbles at the edge of a river.

The woods were thick with undergrowth and there was no path. Toppled tree trunks, ravines, steep inclines covered in heather, the sky a misty mirror above the tops of the spruce trees, marshy ground and creeks trickling beneath our soles. We were surrounded by the bracing scent of waterlogged moss and stagnant water. Splintered tree stumps, root balls, ferns in the sunny clearings. Farther up the ridge a bird was calling. The same tone over and over again. If I were that bird it would've driven me crazy. The light was a shimmery blue you could almost touch.

Just at the edge of an area where the trees must have been harvested a while ago, because there was quite a bit of new growth, next to a spruce that had been toppled by some storm a long time ago, my father stopped and looked around. He nodded and made a clicking sound with his tongue, signalling to me that we should sit down. I passed Father a handful of cartridges. He loaded the gun. He was hoping to get a red fox. He wanted to get it stuffed and put it in the entrance to greet visitors when they came to visit us. Something he could point to and casually say: 'I shot it last summer up near Juvdal in Telemark.'

We lay there in silence, watching the clearing. It smelled like leaves and grass and marshland. Birds chirped and clucked in the undergrowth. But it was still early and their songs sounded half hearted and obligatory. It was hard to lie still. Every time I yawned, my father hissed *shhhh*. I regretted going with him. My mother was the one who'd been so terribly eager for me to go.

I saw it first. It stepped majestically out of the woods on the far side of the clearing. We were downwind, so it didn't sense us. A magnificent red deer stag.

Slowly and graciously, it strode out into the open. Tugging leaves off a low birch and staring out over the landscape as if he were king of all he could survey. His coat was reddish brown and glossy, like bronze. The points on his rack of antlers formed a crown.

I looked at my father. He shook his head.

It came even closer. We hardly dared breathe. We were lying on the ground, completely hidden behind the tree.

Suddenly the animal shook his head.

Took a step back.

Whirled around.

Then the shot rang out.

I whipped my head to the side. My father's Winchester was still resting against the tree trunk between us.

He moved his index finger to his lips.

The stag sank to his knees and tried to stagger to safety. The next shot brought it down. It collapsed on to its side. For a few frightening seconds it lay there, kicking and trembling.

From somewhere in the clearing below us a triumphant cry rang out. And then another.

I was about to stand up. But my father stopped me.

There were two of them, poachers, my father explained later. They came wading through the ferns and seedlings. One of them was making a kind of yodelling war cry.

They stopped in front of the dead animal. They stood there unsteadily, admiring it. One of them pulled out a hip flask, took a few swigs and passed it to his mate. He was wearing a big knife in a sheath on his thigh. He loosened the knife and burped. While his mate held the plastic mug from the top of a thermos under the animal's neck, he slit the artery. They filled the cup with blood. And mixed it with some liquor from the flask.

And drank.

They grabbed the front legs and rolled the stag over on to its back. In one long, fluid motion one guy opened its belly. He pulled its entrails out on to the ground, metre after metre of steel-blue, steaming intestines, emerging with a disgusting gurgling sound. Then came the rest of the entrails. The smell wafted over to my father and me.

They were both squatting. They had found what they were looking for, the warm heart. The guy with the knife stuck the tip of his tongue out of the corner of his mouth and squinted as he sliced the heart in two. As if he were in the middle of some kind of complicated cardiac surgery in the middle of the woods. He gave his mate one of the halves.

Then they started eating.

I felt dizzy. I could hear the smacking noises as they chewed. Blood was running down their chins.

My father held me as I vomited, silently.

They cut up the animal and dragged the carcass away through the clearing, hollering and singing. When my father and I scrambled back to our feet, the stag's head was still lying there on the ground, staring at us.

The flies were already staking their claim to what was left. I heard a flock of crows in the woods.

Some people think vegetarianism is a choice, something you do to make yourself interesting. Maybe that's true for some people, but there are a lot of us who never had any choice. We were forced into it. By the barbarism of blood.

2

Grethe's not home.

I had hardly expected otherwise. Still, I stood there for five minutes, fondling her buzzer down on the street, hoping that the intercom would suddenly groan or that she would come around the corner with a bag of groceries and a surprised 'Hey there, Little Bjørn!'

The Frogner tram jangles by, sounding like a load of scrap

iron, which isn't that far from the truth. On the granite façade above me a lascivious satyr frolics with a nymph. The image reminds me of Diane and myself.

Yesterday feels like a movie that I only just barely remember, sort of dreamlike, not quite real. I try to recall the frantic scramble to get to Heathrow, the plane ride home, the long drive in Bolla from Gardermoen airport out to my grandmother's country place by the fjord. But I can't quite picture any of it.

We arrived in the early evening. The water was calm. We made love in my attic room, among my Hardy Boys books and magazines and worn issues of *Reader's Digest* from 1969, surrounded by the scent of sun-warmed dust – summery sweet and intense. Later that night she got out her silk ropes and wanted me to tie her up and do it again, a little harder. We did that for a while until I untied Diane and left the silk ropes hanging from the four bedposts.

In the middle of the night I woke up because she was crying. I asked her what was wrong. But she said it wasn't anything to worry about. I lay there listening to her breathing in the warm night-time darkness.

An elderly woman, coming teetering towards me on the pavement, is staring at me. She stops and sets down her bags.

'Yes?' she says to me, right up in my face, loudly, like a challenge. As if she owns the building. And the pavement. And large tracts of downtown Oslo. And has misplaced her hearing aid.

'I'm looking for Grethe Lid Wøien,' I say just as loudly. The way inconsiderate people talk to the elderly or mentally disabled.

'Mrs Wøien?' she asks, as if Grethe had ever at any point been someone's wife. Then her tone softens. 'She isn't home. They came and got her.'

'Who came and got her?'

My question comes a little too quickly, sounds a little too urgent. She looks at me in fear.

'Who are you, actually?' she asks.

'A friend.'

'An ambulance,' she says.

Grethe is sitting up in bed, the newspaper spread out over the covers in front of her.

'Little Bjørn.'

Her voice is frail. Her face looks like a cranium covered with a little too much skin. Her hands tremble, making the newspaper rustle. It sounds like dry leaves in the wind early on a November morning.

'I tried calling you again from London, several times,' I say.

'I wasn't home.'

'I didn't know you were in hospital.'

'Just for a couple of days. I didn't want to worry you. I'm a tough old coot.'

'You can say that again!'

'I know, I know, but I didn't want you to worry.'

'How are you feeling?'

'That doesn't matter. How did it go? In London?'

'Everything is so confusing.'

'What did you find out?'

'I know less now than before I went.'

She smiles. 'That's how it is with knowledge.'

I sit down on the edge of her bed and hold her hand. 'You have to tell me something,' I say.

'Fire away, my boy.'

'Who's Michael MacMullin?'

'Michael MacMullin . . .' she says softly.

'And who's Charles DeWitt?'

Her eyelids slide slowly shut, their insides transformed into a screen for her memories.

'Michael . . .' She pauses and something happens to her voice. '. . . is a good, close friend. He was my boss when I was a guest lecturer at Oxford. Well,' the corner of her mouth curls up ever so slightly, 'more than a boss, much more. A smart, good man. If only everything had been different, he and I might have . . .' She opens her eyes and smiles. 'We've stayed in touch over the years.'

'And DeWitt?'

'Charles DeWitt, your father's friend and colleague. He co-authored that book along with your father and Llyleworth. A sweet little English chap, an eccentric fellow, married to a shrew of a woman. He died. In the Sudan. From a wound that developed gangrene.'

'And you knew all this?' I ask.

'Of course. They were my friends.'

'But you didn't tell me anything.'

She looks at me in surprise. 'What do you mean? Did you ask? Why does any of this matter?'

I give her hand a gentle squeeze.

'I have another question.' I hesitate, because I know how crazy it's going to sound. 'Could they have killed him?'

Grethe's reaction is completely normal: surprise. 'Could who have killed whom?'

'Could someone have killed DeWitt?'

'What are you saying?' She looks at me quizzically. 'Who would have done something so awful?'

'MacMullin?'

'Michael?'

'Maybe because DeWitt knew too much? Or figured something out that he wasn't supposed to know?'

She laughs briefly, dismissively. 'No, you know what? It's out of the question.'

'Maybe someone else? Someone at SIS. Llyleworth? I don't know, someone . . .'

She chuckles. 'You've been reading too many books, Bjørn.'

'Something happened. In 1973. At Oxford.'

She stiffens. There's something she's not telling me.

'What was it, Grethe? What did they learn? Something that has to do with the shrine. What was it?'

She gives a deep sigh. 'If only I had some idea . . . they got messed up in something, Bjørn. But I don't know if they even realised it themselves.'

'Who?'

'Your father, DeWitt and Llyleworth.'

'Well, two of them are dead.'

'I should have been in on it, too.'

'But?'

She turns to look out of the window. She does not make eye contact when she says: 'I got pregnant.'

The silence is heavy.

'It was an accident,' she says. 'These things happen.'

'I . . .' I begin, but don't know what to say.

'It was a long time ago.'

'What happened?'

'I went away for the last several months and had the baby. In Birmingham. No one knows about it, Bjørn. No one.'

I don't say anything.

'I couldn't keep it,' she says.

'I understand.'

'Do you? I doubt that. But that's what happened.'

'Have you had any contact with . . .'

'Never!'

'But how . . .'

She holds up her hand. Her face is turned away from me. 'I don't want to talk about it.'

'It's not that important. I mean . . . not to me, not now.'

'Do you still have the shrine?' she asks.

'It's in a safe place.'

'Safe . . .' she murmurs, as if she were chewing the word, tasting it.

'Grethe, what's in the shrine?'

'I don't know.'

It sounds as if she's complaining.

'But what do you know about it?' I ask. 'Is it the Q manuscript? Or something else entirely?'

She sits halfway up in bed. It's as if she's trying to shake off the illness, the decline. The effort leaves her gasping for breath. She looks me in the eyes, filled with a stubborn enthusiasm.

'Did you know there are those who think that the oldest French and British aristocratic families are descendants of pre-Christian tribes who were driven out of the Middle East?' she asks.

'I suppose. Sort of.'

'And that some present-day royal families are descended from our biblical forefathers?'

'I guess I've heard speculations,' I respond vaguely. I wonder what kind of medication the doctors have her on.

'But what do I know . . .' she says to herself, as if my scepticism were contagious. 'People are allowed to guess, right? Deduce? Reason?'

Somewhere outside the door to Grethe's room I hear a young child euphorically shouting, 'Grandpa!'

'There's a . . . um, group,' she says.

Someone out in the hallway laughs. I see the grandfather lifting the child.

'I don't know that much about it,' Grethe explains. She alternates between talking to me and to herself. As if it's her, and not me, she's trying to convince. 'But I know it exists.'

'A group . . .?' I help her out.

'Its roots go back to old French nobility. An organisation.'

'What does it do?'

'Call it a Masonic order if you like, a hermetic sect. Secret. I know almost nothing about it. No one knows about it.'

'So, how do you know about it?' I start laughing. 'I mean, how can you tell me all this if it's so secret?'

She flashes me an angry scowl. As if I should know better than to ask. But then her expression softens. She says: 'Maybe I know someone who . . .' She stops herself. 'Even those who have been initiated into the order do not know who the other members are. No one member knows more than two or three others. Each individual knows the identity of only one superior. The structure is intricate and secret.'

'And what's your point with all this?'

'Maybe they're who's looking for the shrine, Bjørn.'

'A secret order?'

My question sounds pretty sceptical. Condescending would be a more accurate description. And it doesn't earn a response, either.

I ask: 'Then they must know what's in the shrine?'

Grethe looks straight head. 'They've always been searching. Always. I think the shrine is what they've been looking for. Everything is starting to fall into place, all of the pieces.' Grethe glances up at me. Her eyes roll. Suddenly I'm not sure whether she's fully lucid.

I get up and walk over to the window. The bright light makes me squint. Some workmen are erecting scaffolding around the building next door. It looks rickety, but I'm sure they know what they're doing.

'You're tired. I'm going to go now,' I say.

'So senseless,' she mumbles. Louder: 'I told Birger.'

I don't know what she's talking about.

'I warned him. I told him.'

She seems out of breath again, swallows, but then her eyes suddenly seem focused again. It's as if she's returning to reality, some kind of reality.

'Nothing is what you think it is, Bjørn.'

I give her hand a squeeze. 'It's time for me to go. You're tired.'

'There are so many things we don't actually want to know.' She looks at me, as if there's something she wants to tell me, or rather, as if there's something she wants me to understand.

'I know,' I say softly, 'but I should be going now.'

'So many things we don't want to know,' she repeats. 'Even if we think we do. So many things we shouldn't know, too. So many things it isn't good for us to know.'

'What are you trying to say?'

She closes her eyes, and even repeating the words to myself doesn't help make sense of them.

'Are you afraid, Grethe?' I ask.

She opens her eyes again. 'Afraid?' She shakes her head. 'You don't really die until there's no one left who knew you existed,' she says.

On my way out of the hospital I stop at a phone booth. I should probably get a mobile phone, but I like not having one. It gives me an absurd sense of freedom. No one knows where I am. No one can reach me, not unless I want them to.

I call Diane first, just to hear her voice. She doesn't answer. I'm sure she's sitting out on the patio.

Then I call Caspar.

He's agitated, shaken. Someone broke in, into both his house and his office. He can't understand why someone would break into both places. On the same day! He's too worked up to talk to me. Maybe that's just as well.

3

To be on the safe side I park Bolla in a side street down below my building and sneak up the path through the trees by the soccer field to let myself in.

Ten years ago the buildings were grey and functionalist – ugly as hell. Now they've had architects come and gussy them up: new façades, new colours, new balconies, new windows – ugly as hell.

I take the lift up to the tenth floor and let myself into my flat. The place smells stale, the way it smells when I've been on holiday. I detect another odour: old cigar smoke.

Things are still strewn all over the place after the break-in. They even pulled the sheets off the bed. My books are in heaps on the floor. The drawers are all open.

Something is wrong. I don't know what. It's my intuition again. I shouldn't have come.

I check my answering machine: four messages from my mother, eight from the university, one from SIS, six hang-ups, and three from Mr Squeaky Voice, each sounding progressively more irritated, insisting that I get in touch with the police ASAP.

With a sigh, I pick up the phone and do the unavoidable. I call my mother.

She answers immediately, reciting her phone number in a cool voice as if her last name is too personal to share with any old fool who dials her number.

'It's me,' I say.

She's quiet for a moment, as if she can't quite place my voice, as if I'm any old fool who's dialled her number.

'Where have you been?' she asks.

'Abroad.'

'I've been trying to get in touch with you.'

'I had to go abroad, to London.'

'Oh.'

'Work,' I add, in response to her unasked question.

'Are you back in Norway? Where are you calling from?'

'I just got home.'

'This is such a bad connection.'

'I can hear you fine.'

'I've been calling and calling. Trygve needs to talk to you, too. It's very important, Little Bjørn.'

'I had to leave at short notice.'

'I've been so worried about you.'

'Don't worry, Mum. I was just calling to apologise.'

'Apologise?'

She pretends she has no idea what I'm talking about, but she knows full well what I'm referring to. And she knows that I know.

'For . . . the other night. For what I said. I wasn't quite myself.'

'It doesn't matter. Let's just forget it ever happened.'

Fine for me. I'm not sure how sincere my apology is anyway.

The conversation fizzles out. On impulse I ask whether I can stop by to talk to her about something. I regret it the second it comes out, but she's so happy about it that I can't make myself take it back. My mother says goodbye and hangs up. I stand there with the phone in my hand.

Then I hear another click.

'Mum?' I ask.

But there's only silence.

'Ah, it's you, huh?' Roger says.

He's wide awake and dressed, even though it's only 12.30. He's got a cigarette butt in his mouth. He looks as if he's got something to tell me. He chuckles and lets me in.

His living room smells of sweet, heavy incense. You could

get high just from breathing in here. The smell spreads and swells and presses against the walls and windows to get more space. Roger snickers.

The stack of mail he's picked up for me is sitting on a dresser in the hallway. Along with all the newspapers, ads and bills, in an envelope from Caspar, I find a fax from the Schimmer Institute to the Royal Norwegian Office of Cultural Heritage. They would like to congratulate *Mr Bjoern Beltoe* for being named a visiting scholar, a position for which the Royal Norwegian Office of Cultural Heritage had recommended him. Not only that: they offer me a travel and research grant that will cover most of the costs. They would like to establish closer ties with Norwegian academia. They provide a phone number and a name: Peter Levi. He will be my contact person when and if I choose to come, which they hope I will, at my earliest convenience. All I have to do is call.

I put the letter in my inside pocket and tell Roger: 'I have something for you.'

He grunts in anticipation.

I give him the CD. He tears off the paper. When he's done reading all the names on the back, he clenches his fist as a sign of gratitude.

'So tell me, what are you smoking there?' I ask.

My question sets off an explosion of laughter. He tosses his head towards something behind me. I turn around.

A young girl comes trundling out of the bedroom. At first glance one might assume she's looking for her comfort blanket and little pink teddy bear. She can't be older than fourteen or fifteen. She's wearing make-up. She has a cute face and shoulder-length charcoal-black hair. She's wearing tight black panties and one of Roger's shirts. She has braided leather cords wrapped around her wrists and ankles. She has a tattoo on her upper arm that looks like a rune or an occult symbol.

'Nicole,' Roger says.

Nicole gives me a blank look.

'Bjørn,' Roger explains, 'the guy I told you about.'

She flops on to the sofa, puts one leg up on the table and the other up underneath herself on the sofa and starts rolling herself a cigarette. I don't know where to look. She's wearing black toenail polish. I discover yet another tattoo. On the inside of her thigh. A snake that is sort of slithering upwards.

'Nice, huh?' Roger says, giving me a jab, which knocks me off balance. I'm falling. My face is instantly red.

Nicole pouts at Roger. Her tongue is red and pointy. The tip of her tongue is pierced. She lights the cigarette. The way she blows the smoke out of her nostrils gives her a hardened look, as if she's really fifty years old and forty of them were spent in a whorehouse in Tangiers. Her eyes meet mine as I glance at her quickly. I can't seem to look away, although I try. Her eyes are icy blue and much older than her body. They are searching me, reaching in through my pupils and on into my brain, where they rummage around in the darkest corners and open the lids of trunks I thought were locked. They creep in – greased, smooth – around my pituitary gland and squeeze it, hard, and make me gasp. Then she releases her hold. She smiles at me, cute and girlish, a confidante who's privy to my secrets.

'You've had visitors again,' Roger says.

'Visitors?' I ask mechanically. I'm trying to clear and air out my brain after Nicole's entrance and don't understand what he's talking about.

'Twice. At least. I heard 'em.' He glances up at his ceiling.

The weight of it hits me mid-jaw. 'You mean they broke in? To my flat? Again?'

'Yup. Whatcha gonna do now?' he asks.

I have no idea what I'm going to do now.

'What are you guys talking about?' Nicole asks.

'Some stuff,' Roger says.

'What's going on?' she nags.

'Guy stuff!' he says, dismissing her.

'Bah,' Nicole says, jutting out her lower lip.

It's a coincidence that I go over to the window, and it's just as much of a coincidence that I spot the red Range Rover as it comes racing up the street.

'Uh-oh,' I say.

Roger looks out to see what I'm looking at. 'Oh, fuck. Are they watching your place or something?'

'Trouble with the cops?' Nicole asks. 'Sweet!'

'My bag!' I hiss quietly.

'*Uno momento!*' Roger replies. The bag with the shrine in it is in a locked drawer in his CD cabinet.

'Adios!' Nicole calls after us as Roger and I race out of the flat and down the stairs. The stairwell feels safer than the lift right now. I carry the bag under my arm.

On the ground floor I wait behind the door to the stairwell while Roger slips out to check. When he comes back, he rolls his eyes.

'Their car's outside,' he whispers. 'One of them is sitting in it. The lift's on the tenth floor.'

His eyes are ablaze. None of this is quite real to him. He's playing a three-dimensional, interactive video game.

Way up above us, a door into the stairwell opens. First one and then two faces peer down from the tenth floor. I hurry Roger off to the side – 'Walk out calmly and go for a long walk. And buzz Mrs Olsen on the first floor. The old caretaker's widow.'

The lift whirs, rapid footsteps come clomping down the stairs.

Mrs Olsen opens her door a crack. Rattling sounds come from her dentures, jewellery and the door chain. She squints at me with eyes overflowing with suspicion. Her entire existence revolves around the fear of being robbed in her own home.

'It's Mr Beltø,' I yell into her hearing aid.

'Sister Belter? What?'

'You recognise me, don't you?'

She nods distrustfully. We walk by each other on the way to the grocery store and always say hello. And chat by the mailboxes. And yet there's always the chance that my exterior is hiding an evil demon with red eyes and fangs.

'I have to inspect your new balcony,' I say.

'Eh? Something about a falconry?'

'BAL-cony! There's a risk that some of them may be coming loose.'

'I've never heard anything about that,' she protests. She eyes the bag I'm holding. As if it contains my portable torture paraphernalia kit.

'The association sent me!' I yell.

The lift stops.

Association turns out to be the magic word for an ageing social democrat of Mrs Olsen's ilk. Open sesame! She lets me in, following me through the flat, which is meticulously decorated and very clean. As if the lady from the Sophisticated Homes Society might be dropping by at any moment. She rambles on about incompetent craftsmen and how the community association should never have squandered its money on new balconies and that, of course, she had voted against it and that her Oscar, God rest his soul, would never have agreed to this sort of nonsense.

I open the balcony door and step out. For the sake of appearances, I pretend I'm inspecting the seam between the floor and the wall.

'Good news, everything looks fine on your balcony, Mrs Olsen,' I call. 'I'm sure your balcony will hang in there a while longer.'

'Hang in there? A while longer?' she repeats, flustered.

'Luckily you live on the ground floor. Ha ha! I mean, if things should take a turn for the worse. You have to look on the bright side.'

She's about to ask me something. I say: 'I've got a lot of balconies to inspect. I think I'd better take the most expedient route.' And with that I climb up on to the railing and jump down on to the grass below. I land badly. Mrs Olsen stands there watching me as I limp over to the path through the trees.

Once there I turn around. On the tenth floor, behind the reflections in my flat windows, I can make out the outline of a man.

On the floor below that Nicole is standing at the window.

I wave to her.

She waves back.

Mrs Olsen, still standing on her balcony, raises her hand and hesitantly waves it from side to side.

I vanish into the trees.

To confuse the enemy's heat-seeking missiles, I stroll through side streets in the neighbourhood for a long time. I nod cheerfully at cute young women with prams. I nod cheerfully at dogs and songbirds. I nod cheerfully at little children, who gawk rudely at the crazy, pale man.

Ultimately I risk approaching Bolla. They haven't found her, poor little car.

I set the bag containing the shrine on the back seat. I toss my jacket in on top of it.

4

The garden around the palace in Lower Holmenkollen is full of colours. The bushes are cheerfully blooming away.

Everything is so damn prosperous. Even the lawn is bursting with self-satisfaction.

I stand there hyperventilating on the steps for a few minutes before I work up the courage to ring the doorbell. When my mother opens the door, I can tell she's been drinking. Make-up fills her fine wrinkles like spackle. Her eyes are heavy from wine and Valium. Her lips look as if they've been kissed to pieces. It occurs to me that she looks like a madam who's just been converted by some obscure religious sect.

'Oh, honey, it's you. Already?' Mother says.

It wasn't meant as a question. She senses that she has been caught up in something inevitable.

'It's me. Where's the professor?'

'Trygve? He was called away. Quite suddenly.'

'Where to?'

'Why does it matter? Is something wrong? What are you up to these days? How are you feeling?'

The questions flood out of her. Every time I do something unusual, my mother thinks I'm suffering a relapse, that the staff from the clinic are running around town looking for me with their nets and straitjackets. It often seems as if she's ashamed of my nerves, would have preferred something more tangible like cancer, a stroke, Creutzfeldt-Jakob disease, AIDS. I've tried to tell her that, strictly speaking, the brain is just an organ, just like a heart or a kidney, a porridge of nerve cells and fibres and fat and fluid where our thoughts – everything we sense, everything we are – can pretty much be reduced to chemical and electronic signals. And that a mental disorder is nothing more than an imbalance. But my mother is the type who's shocked when people say they're struggling with their nerves. She pulls back. As if they were planning to cut off her head. And eat it.

We walk through the living room, in a wide arc around

the Persian carpet, and into the kitchen. Breuer lifts his head and burps. His tail thumps against the floor two or three times. That's all he can muster in the way of joy at seeing me again before he lets his head sink back down on to his paws.

I set the bag containing the shrine down on the floor. She probably has no idea what's in it.

Silence.

'So . . . you wanted to . . . talk to me?' she says.

My mother has never been good at sounding offhand and casual. She had meant for it to sound sincere, like *Oh, it's so nice of you to stop by*, but it comes out like a sob.

In my head I've been rehearsing this conversation since I was a teenager. So you could say I'm prepared. I've hammered out my responses, fine-tuned them, filed them down and polished them, and guessed at what my mother's responses would be. But all my preparation vanishes and I suddenly draw a blank.

I look at my mother. She looks at me.

Finally I just blurt out: 'I saw you guys.'

I don't know what she was expecting me to say, but that certainly wasn't it.

'Saw us?' she asks, not understanding.

'On the camping trip.'

'What camping trip?'

In the background I hear a hum of voices and laughter that confuses me until I realise that the radio is on in the next room.

I say: 'That summer. You and the professor.'

Each word is a depth charge. It takes a few seconds before it hits. She gives a start, four times. Each of the words has hit its target on the bottom of her soul.

At first she says nothing. Her eyes glaze over. I can see deep into her brain. It's rewinding. She's going back in time. In movie format, rewinding fast, I see how my mother recalls that summer and brings the professor's faded embraces back to life.

'Saw us?' she says again, as if to give me a chance to say *Ha ha, just kidding, I didn't see anything. I was just messing with you.*

But I just watch her.

'Oh my God, Little Bjørn. Oh my God, honey.'

I feel my jaw muscles clenching.

She takes a deep breath. 'It didn't mean anything,' she says. Her voice is cool, dismissive. You'd think she was defending herself to my father. 'Not then.'

'You married him, so it must have meant something.'

Her eyes are hurt, indignant. 'That was later. By then, of course, we had . . . But that summer . . .' She searches for the right words, but can't find them.

'You were unfaithful,' I say.

'Your father and I − we had an agreement. We never cheated on each other. Your father also . . .' She stops. 'If your father had lived . . .' The words stick in her throat.

'He was Dad's friend,' I say, accusatorily.

She takes my hand, nervously twining her fingers with mine. I pull my hand back a little too quickly. 'Even on the camping trip you guys were off doing your thing. Right in front of Dad and my eyes!'

'But Little Bjørn, honey. It never occurred to me that . . . I had no idea that you . . . I didn't think anyone . . .'

'Well, you thought wrong.'

She squeezes my hand. Hard. 'Oh God, Little Bjørn . . . I don't know what to say. I didn't know you'd noticed anything. Or understood. You were so young.'

'I was old enough . . .'

'I'm so sorry. Your dad and I were open with each other about this. We talked about it. It was a different time,

Little Bjørn, a different ... era. You have to try to understand.'

'I don't think Dad understood.'

My mother looks down at the floor. 'No,' she says, 'deep down I don't think he ever did.' Her voice keeps catching. 'You never knew your father the way I knew him,' she says once she's gained control of her voice again. 'He wasn't always ...' She avoids my eyes, suddenly sad. 'He always seemed like he was in full control, but inside he was ...'

We look at each other.

'But I don't believe he jumped,' she says. 'If that's what you're wondering.'

She must have been stewing over that question for twenty years. It amazes me that it just slips out of her lips like an offhand remark.

'There are so many ways he could have fallen,' I say.

She doesn't catch the innuendo and insinuation.

'Trygve took everything so seriously. About our relationship, I mean. Much more seriously than I did. For me it was just a ... I don't know. A jaunt? A flirtation? A diversion? A little variety? A break from everyday life?'

She looks at me expectantly, waiting for my response, but I really don't have one.

She sits there, thinking. 'It was just a fling, an affair, something that would have ended. But then the accident happened.'

We sit there quietly for a while.

'And you've been carrying this around with you for all these years?' she says, mostly to herself.

I give her a silent moment to let the magnitude of that rhetorical question sink in.

'Why didn't you say something?' she blurts out. Her voice has a sharp edge to it.

'My God, Little Bjørn. What must you think of me?'

I really don't want to answer that one.

'When your father died . . .' she starts, but can't seem to make it any farther. 'I hope you don't think it's been easy. I've tried to forget every single day.'

'Forget me, too?'

She shakes her head. 'You?'

I take a deep breath to get my voice under control.

She beats me to the punch: 'Have you ever asked yourself if you've been unfair to me?'

I just look at her and swallow.

'You're not the only one who lost someone when you lost your father,' she says. 'I lost my husband, whom I loved. In spite of . . . that business with . . . Trygve. But I don't think you've ever considered that, Little Bjørn. And now I suppose I understand why. God, you're being so unfair.'

'I . . .'

'Yes?'

'Nothing.'

She nods to herself. Her eyes are full of tears.

'No one ever wants their children to know about things like this. You must understand that,' she bursts out.

I feel like a jerk. Maybe because I am one.

'It was a shock for both of us,' I mumble. It's not much of an excuse. But it's meant as one.

'Trygve has never wanted to talk about what happened that day,' she says. 'Never. He blames himself, but he won't say why. He had swapped round the abseil anchors that morning when they left, because Birger had borrowed his. So actually Trygve was the one who should have fallen. But I haven't wanted to pressure him. People try to forget. To put things behind them.'

My mother is better at putting things behind her than I am. Maybe because I know more than she does.

The blue-eyed girl sitting at the receptionist's desk gives me a confused look and says: 'Well, well, Torstein, is that a new jacket?'

I've never seen her before. My name's not Torstein. This is not a new jacket. But I sweep past her with a wink and a nod and open the door into a climate-controlled jungle of thriving yucca palms and an abundance of plastic ferns. Here, in a rectangular office landscape that is pretentiously referred to as the central editorial office, three journalists sit, each in front of his own computer, looking as if they're trying to come up with the Ten Commandments. A poster hanging on the wall depicts a computer with arms coming out of the sides of its monitor. It's flexing its muscles and the caption reads: '*PC* – the Muscle Magazine for Norwegian Computer Users'.

I push open a frosted-glass door. An almost identical copy of myself is seated behind the desk.

Torstein Avner has pale skin and white hair and glowing red eyes. When people see us together, they think we're identical twins. When we were teenagers we used to fantasise about taking each other's girlfriends for a test drive. They would never have known the difference, but we never followed through on it. Neither of us ever had a girlfriend to share.

He squints at me through the lenses of his glasses, which are even thicker than my own, and when he eventually recognises me through the haze that clouds his vision, he gets up and starts hooting:

'My old buddy, Bjørn!' he yells, howling with laughter. 'Fucking A, it's you. I thought I was finally having some kind of out-of-body experience.'

We grab hold of each other's hands. 'Good old Bjørn!' he says, grinning. He doesn't want to let go of my hand.

I chuckle bashfully. 'Long time no see,' I say.

Eventually he lets go of my hand. He's got a very toothy smile.

'The receptionist thought I was you,' I say.

'Lena did?' Torstein sings in his northern Norwegian dialect. 'She does her best.'

Torstein and I got to know each other when we took a class on albinism together fifteen years ago. We've stayed in touch, off and on. He comes over to my place every once in a while. I've dropped in on him at work a couple of times in recent years. He started out at *PC* as a sort of handyman, with his salary being paid for by a government programme to support diversity in the workplace. Then he became a journalist and was given his own technology column: @vner's @dvice. He'd shown me some of the articles. I couldn't understand a thing. Now he's the lead technology editor. I understand even less now than I did before about what he does. If that's possible.

'Well, well. Did your hard drive crash?' he asks.

I feel like a greedy relative visiting a dying aunt. The only time I ever visit Torstein is when I'm having computer trouble.

'I need a little help,' I say.

'Since you're the one who's asking, I bet you need more than a little,' he says, chuckling softly.

'Can you help me find something on the Internet?'

'Sure. What are you looking for?'

I pass him a sheet of paper with a list of search terms I've written down in Norwegian:

Knights Hospitaller
SIS
The Schimmer Institute
Michael MacMullin

Værne Monastery
Varna
Rennes-le-Château
Bérenger Saunière
The Dead Sea Scrolls
Monastery of the Holy Cross
Shroud of Turin
The Q manuscript
Nag Hammadi

'Whoa!' he says. 'You're sure you don't want to add anything else to the list?'

'Why? Is that a lot? I suppose some of the search terms will
have to be translated into English. Like *Shroud of Turin* and
Dead Sea Scrolls.'

'Whoa.'

'I don't need it right this minute,' I say.

'You're going to have to give me at least an hour,' he says.

I don't know whether he really means that or whether
he's being sarcastic.

'If I could get the results tomorrow, that would be great,' I
say.

'What search engine do you want me to use?'

I try to act as if I'm contemplating the question. Truth be
told I don't understand it.

'Yahoo? AltaVista? Kvasir? Excite? HotBot? MetaCrawler?'
he asks.

'Huh?'

'I get it, I get it,' he says, smirking. 'Do you just want the
first five hits for each search term? As URLs?'

'Um . . . Could you make print-outs for me?'

'On paper?' he exclaims.

'Um . . . yeah?'

He rolls his eyes. 'Bjørn, Bjørn, Bjørn . . . Do you not get that we're living in a paperless society? I mean, we can be if we want to be. And we want to be. Think of the trees!'

'I know that, but I'm going kicking and screaming.'

'Why don't you just let me e-mail you all the websites instead?'

'Torstein, I'd really prefer print-outs. Besides, someone stole my hard drive.'

'Paper,' he says, full of disdain, as if he regarded paper as a medium as outmoded as cuneiform tablets and papyrus, which he's probably right about. 'Someone stole your hard drive?' he asks quickly, surprised, but he isn't really interested in the answer.

Before I leave I borrow Lena's phone to call Diane down at my grandmother's place. Lena stares at me in confusion as I stand there listening to the phone ring. Behind her even salon tan, her foundation and rouge, I can just make out a faint blush as she realises that I'm not Torstein.

Diane doesn't answer.

6

On my way back to my grandmother's place by the fjord, I hide the shrine in the last place in this world where anyone would think to search for it. I'm pleased with my own ingenuity. The feeling gives me at least the sense of having the upper hand.

The twilight breeze fills Bolla with a mild, salty, late summer scent. I rumble along in the wheel ruts on the side road to my grandmother's place. The trees around all the summer cabins are weighed down with cherries and plums so juicy they're ready to burst. The fjord shimmers between the trees, silver and seeming drowsy. Some children are hollering down by the pier. A small yacht has anchored a stone's throw past the Coastguard noticeboard. A seaplane pulls its shadow across the rocky shoreline.

I park Bolla next to the crooked pine at the end of the drive and call out cheerfully to Diane. The front door is open. The tablecloth on the picnic table out on the patio is fluttering in the breeze.

When I left her early this morning, she was sleeping with her mouth half open and her hair across her face. I didn't have the heart to wake her. The air was chilly, the windowpanes covered in condensation. I pulled the duvet up over her naked body, kissed her on the cheek and brushed the hair off her face. Before I drove in to Oslo, I wrote her a note to tell her where I was going and stuck it under the glass of water on the bedside table. To *My Angel*, signed *Your Prince*. Aren't we cute?

I honk – Bolla's horn sounds like a plastic party-favour horn, with spit in it – before slamming the car door shut and waiting for her to come running out. *'Bjorn! Finally!'* she'll yell, impatient but happy. Quivering with anticipation, I realise that the first thing we'll do after she's hugged me and asked why I was gone so long is have sex, hard and sweaty on the creaky sofa in the living room.

Slowly, whistling, to give her a chance to finish up whatever she's doing, I walk up the stone steps to the patio, through the door – *'Diane? It's meee!'* – and check for her in the kitchen. She's been to the little country store and bought a few odds and ends for dinner: eggs, onions, tomatoes, potatoes, beer. That must be why she didn't answer when I called. The receipt and a stack of five- and ten-kroner coins are sitting on the kitchen worktop. I wonder for a second where she got the Norwegian money from. She's prepared a plate of food for me; it's covered with cellophane. Scrambled eggs and diced vegetables. She wrote my name in big letters on a slip of paper and set it on top of the plate. As if to ensure that Goldilocks wouldn't help herself to it first.

I look for her: in the bathroom, where her toothbrush in the pink plastic cup on the glass shelf over the sink makes my heart go pitter-patter, in the living room, in my grandmother's bedroom, in the guest bedroom, in the attic room, where her suitcase sits open on the floor, in the storeroom, in the back garden.

She must have gone for a walk.

I take the food and a beer and go and sit on the patio. There's a man standing down by the shore, fishing. He must have come from the camping site, because anyone staying in the cabins would know that you can't catch fish so close to shore. A sailing boat slices through the waves in the middle of the fjord. A telescope on a yacht beyond the breakwater catches the sunlight.

Where could she be?

I eat the food and finish the bottle of beer and go back inside. I'm starting to get worried. She would hardly have gone off on a long walk when she knew I might be home any minute. I sit down in the green velour chair my grandmother was so fond of. Its springs squeak. The sound instantly takes me back to my childhood, when the springs' lament used to make my grandmother's fearsome Rottweiler, Grim, scramble under the sofa, where he would curl up, shaking and making a little moaning cry. It struck me even back then that there must be sounds that only a select few can hear. And when you look at it that way, there's also no reason why a few people shouldn't see ghosts, too.

I walk out into the back garden and lie down in the hammock, which sways gently. The air is full of birds. A speedboat races over the surface of the water. The line on the neighbour's metal flagpole chimes in the wind, making a hollow, cheerful sound. I look at my watch.

Only then does it hit me.

They've taken her.

They knew about the summer home. They've been watching us.

My having the upper hand was an illusion. I was deceiving myself.

I go in and search for anything she might have left behind: a note, a secret sign. I check all the rooms again. My head is buzzing, almost as if I have had too much to drink. In desperation I run down to the shoreline, all the way down to the edge of the water. As if I'm afraid I'll find her floating down there. With her face a few centimetres underwater.

As I approach the house again, I hear the phone ringing. I race up the stone steps, but just miss the call.

I grab a beer from the fridge and take a swig. My breathing is laboured.

I try to understand. Why would they take her? If that's what happened. Why her? Where is she? What do they want with her? Are they going to use her to get to me? I drink the beer in big gulps, burp and set the empty bottle on the windowsill among the dead flies.

The phone rings again. I answer and shout: 'Diane?'

'*She's OK*. Diane is with us now.'

The voice is deep, speaking in English, articulate. There's something pleasant about it that makes it sound somehow insincere.

I can't muster a response. The detailing on the living-room furniture stands out with a strange clarity. As if I've never seen it before.

'We'd really like to talk to you,' the man says.

'What have you done with her?'

'Nothing. You don't need to worry. Have you eaten?'

'Where is she?'

'Don't give it another thought. She's doing fine. Was the food good?'

'Screw the food! Why did you take her?'

'Calm down. Let's get together and talk.'

'I've heard more than enough of your talk. I'm calling the police!'

'Be my guest, but it won't do you much good.'

'Diane doesn't have anything to do with all this!' I yell.

'When can we have the shrine?'

I hang up and rush out on to the patio. I need air. My head is spinning. I stand there with hands on the railing, gasping for breath.

Way out on the fjord a cluster of small boats has converged over the fishing grounds. The gulls from Revlingen swoop and dive above the boats in a cloud of cries. An invisible international ferry drums its thumping rhythm over the sea's surface. I close my eyes and rub the bridge of my nose with my fingertips. Staggering, I lurch backwards and collapse into a wicker chair. I'm freezing. The cold spreads through me, radiating from my diaphragm out to my fingertips and toes. I grasp the edge of the table for something to hold on to.

What's wrong with me?

My right cerebral hemisphere starts swelling and tingling. My skull is too tight for my engorged brain.

My mouth is dry; my tongue sticks to the roof of my mouth. I make a few frightened noises, grab my head and try to yell. Only a gasp claws its way through my lips. I try to stand up, but my limbs are no longer attached to my body and are lying in a heap on the patio below me.

A car comes rolling down the drive. Its wheels crunch in the gravel. Its engine rumbles. It stops behind Bolla. I manage to just lift my head. It's the red Range Rover.

I put my hands over my mouth and make a rattling noise.

The car doors open.

There are two of them, two of my old acquaintances from the break-in: King Kong and the refined man in the suit.

They stroll up the steps on to the patio as if they had all the time in the world.

'Hello there, Mr Beltø,' the refined one says, British down to the manicured tips of his manicured nails.

I try to respond, but the words swell up on my tongue and come out as meaningless babbling.

'I'm terribly sorry,' the Englishman says. 'We had hoped you would cooperate. Then we could have avoided all . . . of this.'

They grasp me below the arms and drag me across the patio. My legs bounce down the steps behind me. They lift me into the back seat of the car.

And then I don't remember anything else . . .

7

When I was little, I was somehow always able to sense what day it was before I was really awake. Sunday's quiet doziness, Wednesday's whisper of boredom, Friday's shiver of antici-pation. I lost this ability as the years went by. Like so many other things. It often happens now that some time around dinner time I will catch myself wondering what day it is. And what year.

Shattering sunlight blazes through the six panes of the locked window.

I pull the quilt over my head and spend a few minutes com-posing myself, which isn't always such an easy task for me. But I peek out a few minutes later.

The room is bare. And so am I.

Someone has neatly folded my clothes and draped them over

the back of a chair. This disgusts me: someone undressed me! A stranger took my clothes off and put me to bed stark naked.

There's a door and a wardrobe, an etching of Jesus and the lambs, a lithograph of a stone castle, and a picture of Buckingham Palace.

My head throbs and aches.

There's a glass of water on the nightstand, next to my glasses. I swing my legs on to the floor. The motion makes my brain swell up to twice its normal size. I put on my glasses. I drain the glass of water in one go but am still just as thirsty.

The leather straps on my watch are spread out to the sides and it looks like something that has died. But it's ticking and says it is 11.30.

I stand up and stagger over to the window. I feel faint and cling to the windowsill. It's white and smells as if it's been freshly painted.

The garden isn't big. A few cars are parked on a strip of asphalt alongside the house. The chestnut trees block any view of the street below, where I hear a tram rumble past. So I'm in Oslo. On the second floor of a house with a garden.

I put on my clothes. I have some trouble getting my shirt buttoned. My fingers are shaking so much.

They haven't taken anything from my pockets. My wallet is still in my back pocket. And my money.

The door is locked. I tug at it. I hear voices and footsteps on the outside. As in a prison, a heavy bunch of keys jangles, then a key turns in the lock.

'Hello, my friend.'

It's Michael MacMullin or Charles DeWitt or whoever he's decided to be today.

The seconds drag out.

Eventually I say: 'For someone who's been dead for twenty years, you're in surprisingly good shape.'

Normally I'm not that good at improvising cheeky retorts. I'd thought of this one on the plane from London. I'd suspected the whole time that we would meet again.

'Let me explain.'

'Where's Diane?'

'She's in safe hands.'

'What have you done with her?'

'Later, my friend, later. I'm ever so sorry.'

Strangely, it seems as if he means that.

'Would you please come with me?' he asks.

Please?

The hallway is lined with red velvet carpeting and small sconces between old portraits of kings and queens, noblemen, knights, Crusaders and popes. They all follow me with their eyes.

The soft carpeting leads us down the long hallway and up a wide staircase to a heavy door. I don't know whether you would call this a conference room or a smoking room or perhaps, most likely, an assembly room – a showy and over-furnished drawing room full of beech and rosewood, heavy drapes and chandeliers. It smells of furniture polish and cigars.

The first thing I notice is an enormous oil painting of two druids at Stonehenge. The second is the long, dark, highly polished table with a green felt blotter in front of each of the twelve high-backed chairs. The third thing is that there are two men sitting in the corner of the seating area. I don't notice them until I see the cloud of smoke rising from their cigars. Both have turned to watch us with tense interest.

It's Graham Llyleworth and Director-General Loland.

They stand up. Loland doesn't know quite where to look. Llyleworth holds his hand out to me first and then Loland does the same. 'Nice to see you again,' he says awkwardly, as if he's remembering the last time we saw each other.

246

No one says anything.

There's a porcelain coffee pot on the table and four cups.

'Cream? Sugar?' Llyleworth asks, his cigar glowing between his index and middle fingers.

I don't like coffee.

In Norwegian I tell Loland: 'I'm not a criminal law expert, but I would imagine that kidnapping a foreign woman and then drugging and kidnapping a Norwegian would earn you somewhere between five and seven years in prison. Unless you're planning on sending me to the bottom of the sea with my feet in a barrel of cement. Then it's probably more like twenty-one years, with parole.'

Loland clears his throat nervously and looks over at MacMullin.

MacMullin gives a paternal chuckle, as if he understood everything I just said. 'I'm sorry, perhaps you would prefer tea?'

'Where's Diane?'

'You needn't worry. She's fine.'

'What have you done with her?'

'Not a thing. Please, don't give it another thought. Everything can be explained.'

'You kidnapped her!'

'Actually, no.'

'Who are you? Really?'

'I'm Michael MacMullin.'

'Funny. Last time we met, you introduced yourself as Charles DeWitt.'

Llyleworth looks at him in surprise: 'You did? Really?' He doesn't quite manage to suppress a brief laugh.

MacMullin pauses briefly for effect. 'Ah, but did I?' He gives me a playful look, furrowing his brow. 'True enough. When we received a message from our friends at the London Geographical Association that Bjørn Beltø from Norway had asked after Charles, we came up with a stupid little plan. You're quite right that I let you believe that I was good old Charlie. But in all fairness, I never did introduce myself.'

I ask: 'So why should I believe that you're Michael MacMullin?'

He holds his hand out to me. I grasp it reflexively.

'*I. Am. Michael. MacMullin*,' he says, emphasising each word.

His aura of safety and conviviality confuses me. Llyleworth, Loland and I are like jittery dogs growling around a bone that we all want. MacMullin is different. It's as if he's hovering above the rest of us, above petty bickering and mistrust. Everything about him – his warm eyes, his deep voice, his calm – radiates a gentle, gracious dignity.

Loland pulls out a chair for me. I sit down on the very edge of the seat. We all look at each other.

'You're a tough nut to crack, Beltø,' MacMullin says.

The other two laugh nervously. Loland winks at me. They seem to think we've all crossed some invisible line and are suddenly on the same side, and that we're sitting here swapping stories about something that's already been resolved. They don't know me very well. I'm a tough nut to crack.

'I'm actually pleased that you're so loyal,' Director-General Loland says. He has a smirk on his face. 'If only we had more like you.'

MacMullin senses my misgivings. He shrugs. 'Gentlemen, please. We owe our friend here an explanation.'

Sometimes it's best not to say anything, so I don't say anything.

They exchange glances as if they all hope someone else will start speaking first. Once again MacMullin is the one to speak.

'Where should we start?' he says.

'Let's start with DeWitt,' I suggest.

'DeWitt . . . That was dumb of me. I underestimated you. By quite a bit.'

'What were you hoping to achieve?'

'We figured everything would be easier if we let you think I was Charles. We thought you would trust him or, well, me. We hoped you would trust Charles with the shrine if he gave you the answers you were looking for. We were naive. I really must apologise.'

'So that I wouldn't discover that you offed him?'

'Huh?' they ask each other.

'The same summer my father died?' I look at each of them in turn. 'Do you mean to tell me that it was purely coincidental that the two of them died right about the same time?'

Their astonished expressions are so genuine that for an instant I consider believing them, but just for an instant.

'Why? Do you believe otherwise?' MacMullin asks.

Loland says: 'Really.'

'Purely coincidental?' I ask.

'Of course,' MacMullin says.

'We're not barbarians,' Llyleworth says.

Loland shakes his head. 'You've been reading too many detective novels. Your father died in an accident. Charles died from an infection. It was coincidental that both deaths occurred that same summer.'

Llyleworth says: 'Life is full of coincidences like this.'

'To say nothing of death,' I reply.

I look at each of them in turn. 'Let's drop it,' I say eventually. 'For now. I still don't understand why you haven't been able to tell me the truth. I have the shrine. All I'm asking for is an answer to what's inside it. Once I know the truth, I'll give it back. Why all the lies and wild-goose chases?'

'The truth. Ah . . . But what is truth, really?' MacMullin asks. He contemplates me – half smiling, half goading me – while he lets his question sink in.

I shrug my shoulders indifferently.

'And what entitles you to the so-called truth?' he asks.

'I represent the Norwegian government.'

'Rubbish!' Loland says. 'I represent the Norwegian government.'

'You?' I scoff. 'You're part of this whole conspiracy.'

'Bjørn, Bjørn,' MacMullin chuckles, 'don't be so angry. Try to see this from our perspective. We didn't know where you stood, if you were with us.'

'With you?' I shout.

'Yes, or against us. If you were on the up and up.'

'Up and up?'

'If you were in it for the money. We didn't know why you stole the shrine from us.'

'I didn't steal it. I took it back. Because you were planning to steal it.'

'You can't steal something you legally own,' MacMullin says.

'You don't own it. The shrine is Norwegian. It was found on Norwegian soil.'

'We can come back to that.'

'It never occurred to you that my intentions might be honest?' I ask. 'That I simply want to get to the bottom of all this?'

'We thought you were going to hand over the shrine,' MacMullin says. 'As you promised.'

'Well, then you started playing the part of a dead man and rented a house and furnished it for one day?'

He gives me a startled look. 'Um, no. We actually just borrowed it. It's a house that the authorities use for . . . ah, these kinds of things.' He stirs his coffee with a silver teaspoon. 'After our little chat I thought everything was squared away,' he says, 'until Diane told us how wary you were.'

A chill runs through me. Diane?

MacMullin notices. He says: 'Someday you'll understand. She doesn't have anything to do with this, not really. It wasn't until we became aware of your ... friendship with Diane that she was drawn into all this, rather against her wishes.' Something in his eyes darkens. 'We went and extracted her because it was in her own best interest.'

They wait for me to say something. I don't.

My silence has an impact on them.

'When we heard that you'd talked to Charles's widow, we realised we'd misjudged you,' MacMullin says.

'Totally,' Loland chimes in.

MacMullin continues: 'Things happened too quickly in London. You were smarter than us, one step ahead of us the whole time.'

I'm trying to understand how Diane fits in. None of this makes any sense.

MacMullin raises his cup and sips his coffee. 'In the end I realised that the only way to resolve this mess was to have a proper talk with you,' he says. 'Which is what we intend to do now. Explain things to you. Help you understand.'

'Oh really?' I mumble, distrustful.

'When you went to SIS we thought we finally had you and again we underestimated you. You're a tough nut to crack, Beltø. A tough nut.'

MacMullin glances over at Loland, who seems to be study-ing the plush carpeting.

'And all of this gives you the right to kidnap Diane and drug and kidnap me?'

'A harmless medication in your food, Bjørn, practically a sleeping pill. I'm truly sorry. But surely you would hardly have come voluntarily?'

'You're bloody right I wouldn't.'

'We need to make you understand.' He looks down. 'This occasionally requires us to resort to unusual methods. It's not that we're consciously looking for the most dramatic ways to solve our problems.'

'I have one question,' I say.

'Yes?'

'What's in the shrine?'

'It's not a Norwegian artefact,' Loland says quickly.

'The shrine is made of gold,' I point out. 'The value of the gold alone will amount to several million kroner.'

'On the commercial market, the shrine itself would be worth at least fifty million pounds,' MacMullin clarifies. 'But it doesn't matter to us what it's made of or how much it's worth.'

'Because there's something even more valuable inside,' I say.

MacMullin leans forward. 'And neither the shrine nor its contents are Norwegian.'

'It was found in Norway.'

'True enough, it happened to be in Norway, but it is not Norwegian. Which is why the Norwegian archaeological authorities have no objections to handing over the shrine.'

Director-General Loland nods his head a little too eagerly.

'Quite the contrary,' MacMullin continues, 'it's quite important that the proper authorities be able to analyse the artefact. Norway is a parenthetical interlude in the shrine's history. Although perhaps not in terms of time.'

'I don't understand what you mean. What history?' I say.

MacMullin takes a deep breath. 'A long history, isn't that so, gentlemen? A long history.'

Loland and Llyleworth chime in – *Yeah, it's a long history.*

'I've got plenty of time. Go ahead and fill me in,' I say, crossing my arms and leaning back.

'Let me start with the SIS,' MacMullin says, 'the Society of International Sciences, my support network. The society, in its current form, was founded in 1900, but its roots go back centuries. SIS unites scholars and researchers from many different fields. But behind the scenes, SIS is what you might characterise as a . . . uh, academic intelligence service. We gather data from all of the relevant disciplines and look for . . . clues. SIS has supervised, generally quite openly, all the important archaeological digs of the last one hundred years. Either by sending one of our representatives, such as Professor Llyleworth, under the pretence of some research project, or, as is more usually the case, by having the excavation leaders send us reports.'

'I joined in 1963,' Loland says. 'I've been in charge of supervising excavations in Norway. And I send SIS a copy of every single relevant report and dissertation that is written here.'

'How nice of you,' I say.

'And let me add,' Loland says, 'that everything that has been done has been on the up and up. We're not bad guys.'

'We work with good people – like Sigurd Loland and your stepfather, Professor Arntzen – all over the world,' MacMullin says. 'And engage men of Professor Llyleworth's calibre as our agents in the field.'

'Just like 007,' Llyleworth says flatly. It's the first time I've heard him make a joke. Even MacMullin and Loland look at him with surprise. He blows a smoke ring.

'Now we're getting to the heart of the matter,' MacMullin says. 'It turns out that the SIS has a secret, which is indirectly associated with the shrine.'

'Finally.'

He clears his throat. There is something ceremonious about him, something surreal.

A few seconds pass.

'This is how I picture it,' he says. 'I picture a river before me, and I want you to do the same. Do me a favour, Bjørn. Close your eyes. Picture a river before you.'

I picture a river. It is broad and flowing quietly, like melted steel under a tropical sun. It's late in the day. The insects are hovering in lazy clusters over the reeds along the shore. Small twigs and clumps of algae move back and forth in the ripples. The river is flowing through a desert landscape with cypress trees. There's a marble temple up on a cliff, but I don't see any people.

MacMullin lets the image sink in before he proceeds: 'And picture a group of travellers, not many, two or three individuals, maybe, on an expedition on a vessel moving down the river into a strange, mysterious landscape.'

The scene unfolds within me as if on a movie screen: the vessel is a raft, logs bound together with thick rope. There's a little covered area behind the mast made of woven branches and vines. The men are sitting on the front of the raft. One of them has stuck his bare foot in the water. Another is sucking on a pipe. The men are sweating in the heat.

'They've been chosen,' MacMullin says. 'Because of their qualifications and their courage. The journey is dangerous. Their travels take them through foreign lands through a landscape they've never seen or visited, only read about.'

I close my eyes to picture the images more clearly.

'The river is endless. It flows on and on and on.'

'Until it ends in the sea.'

'Oh, no. It doesn't end anywhere.'

'Really?'

'You must imagine that it has no outlet or estuary.'

'That would be some river.'

'It just keeps going and going, and the travellers' vessel can only drift – not with the current, but against the current. The expedition is bound to defy the will of the river. They can never turn around. They can never return to the source. They can only sail against the current.'

'Can they go ashore?'

'They can go ashore, but then they would be stranded. They won't get any farther. They can set up camp, but they cannot go back or move farther down the river.'

'Which never ends.'

'Quite right, which never ends.'

'A journey without end.'

'Precisely.'

'And without a goal?'

'The journey itself is a goal.'

'It must get boring eventually.'

He laughs. Then he puts his hands together, palm to palm, and spreads his fingers so that they form five steeples and says: 'They have no contact with those they've left behind and only with a select few along the way. But they leave a . . . well, let's call it a message in a bottle. Meant for those they left at home. Travel reports, you might say. In which they describe everything they have observed and experienced. Learned accounts. All viewed in the light of the knowledge they bring with them.'

'So the messages in the bottles can move backwards?'

'If they enlist time to help them.' He nods to himself. 'Because, well, can you tell me what time is?'

I cannot.

'Time,' he says, 'is an endless series of moments.'

I'm trying to understand his parable, but I can't. I hazard a guess: 'So, does this river,' I ask, 'represent space? And the expedition came from another planet? Out there in infinity?'

It's a weird question. I don't notice how weird until it is rolling off my tongue. Still, MacMullin looks at me in a way that makes me think I guessed right, that somehow that crackpot Winthrop was telling me the truth, that the parable is about a group of alien beings with technology so advanced they were able to journey across the light years separating an alien solar system from the Earth. That would explain a lot.

They could have arrived here hundreds of years ago and left their technological traces as a calling card, which would astonish the archaeologists who encountered them among the potsherds and arrowheads. Humanoids, highly advanced beings with a message for us earthlings.

'Is that what it is?' I ask, excited and incredulous.

MacMullin hands me a clipping from the paper, an announcement in *Aftenposten*:

Particles playing hide-and-seek with CERN scientists

MEYRIN, SWITZERLAND (AP). International researchers at the CERN Particle Accelerator announced this week that they have verified the disappearance of mass without emission of energy in several near-light-speed experiments conducted over the past six months.

Project head Jean-Pierre Latroc told the Associated Press that his team does not have any explanation for what he characterised as a 'physical impossibility'.

'According to the laws of physics, mass should not be able to simply disappear,' Latroc says. 'Now, we're focusing our efforts on finding what happened to the particles.'

'CERN,' MacMullin says. '*L'Organisation européenne pour la recherche nucléaire.*' His pronunciation is flawless, as if French were his first language.

'What's that?'

'The European particle physics lab. It was started in the mid-fifties. It's located in Meyrin, Switzerland. The place is huge! The lab is in a tunnel a hundred and seventy metres underground. It has a circumference of twenty-seven kilometres, the biggest in the world.'

'The world's biggest lab?'

'Particle accelerator!'

'What's that?'

'A peephole into Creation.'

'Huh?'

'A particle accelerator. It transforms a stream of particles moving close to the speed of light into mass.'

Sometimes I have trouble coming up with the right thing to say. 'Golly,' is all I come up with.

'Which allows us to study what happened during the first millionths of a second after the birth of the universe. In experiments we can recreate conditions like the ones that prevailed right after the Big Bang, the birth of the universe.'

'Golly.'

'To understand Creation,' he says, 'we must investigate the universe's smallest building blocks: atoms, electrons, protons, neutrons, quarks, antimatter.'

He pauses for a moment and I try to catch up.

'Golly,' I say for the third time. Not much of a contribution to the conversation, but physics has never been my strong suit, especially not experimental particle physics.

'Am I going too fast for you?' MacMullin asks.

'Fast or slow – it's not going to make any sense to me either way.'

He says: 'What the particle accelerator does is to smash the smallest particles up into, believe it or not, even smaller pieces.'

'I believe it.'

'The particles are sent around and around in the enormous accelerators using magnetic fields, until they're going at almost the speed of light.'

'That's fast.'

'And then they get the particles to collide head-on, to study the physical consequences.'

'OK, look. I don't understand the first thing about what

you're saying. What are you getting at? What does this have to do with the shrine?'

MacMullin hands me another clipping, this one from the *New York Times*:

Concept of time under the magnifying glass
By ABE ROSEN

Particle accelerator researchers at the European Organization for Nuclear Research (CERN) are focusing the enormous magnifying glass of the prestigious particle physics laboratory on time itself. If the researchers' ideas about time can be proved, their results will radically alter the foundations of modern physics.

During an experiment earlier this year, CERN physicists were astonished to find evidence of particles of matter disappearing without emitting energy.

The experiment – dubbed 'The Wells Experiment' after H. G. Wells and his 1895 novel *The Time Machine* – has been reproduced multiple times with the same result.

The project's leader, French particle physicist Jean-Pierre Latroc, says that scientists have not been able to find a satisfactory explanation for this physical paradox.

'At this early stage, our hypothesis is that the particles were accelerated through time,' Latroc says.

He cautioned that the idea should be viewed merely as a working hypothesis for the time being.

'If we manage to demonstrate that the particles have moved through time and stayed there,' Latroc says, 'then we're talking about a fundamentally new understanding of the laws of nature. We would no longer be able to talk about 'before' or 'after,' 'cause' or 'effect.' Instead we will have evidence of some kind of realm where there is no space-time. Some would define this as a dimension, a parallel universe, or hyperspace.'

Latroc is circumspect about drawing conclusions but points out that even well-known scientists such as theoretical physicists Stephen Hawking and Kip Thorne in recent years have been seriously discussing the possibility of time travel through so-called wormholes. Theorists suggest that black holes are the entrances and exits to these wormholes, which serve as a kind of shortcut between infinite distances in space-time. If this understanding is correct, then CERN scientists have already broken this 'magical' and absolute barrier of space-time.

The CERN team is also taking a fresh look at the quantum physics phenomenon of 'non-locality' in recent photodetector experiments run by Austrian quantum physicist Anton Zeilinger. Non-locality means that particles once connected to each other will remain connected regardless of where in the universe – and where in space-time – the individual particles are.

The Latroc team's hypothesis has caused a stir in academic circles among physicists at leading universities in Europe and North America.

One of Latroc's most outspoken critics, however, atomic physicist and Nobel Prize winner Adam Thrust, says that understanding time is one of the final bastions of science. 'Even in nature, there are absolutes,' Thrust says. 'And the speed of light is one of them.'

But criticism like this does not surprise Latroc and his team. 'We're the first to admit that our hypothesis sounds crazy,' Latroc says. 'Several members of my own team think there is an entirely different explanation. But given the data we have right now, I personally don't see any other explanation for what has become of those particles.'

I look up from the newspaper clipping.

'Now do you understand?' MacMullin asks.

'Not at all.'

'Don't you see the connection?'

'What connection? What am I supposed to be getting from this? What does all this have to do with the shrine?'

MacMullin takes a very deep, very slow breath. I feel like a not-so-bright student who didn't read the homework assignment well enough.

'Imagine,' MacMullin says, 'two hundred and fifty years from now that scientists finally manage to break the time barrier, the way NASA succeeded in sending people to the moon in 1969. Imagine the scientists of tomorrow making it possible for people to travel back through time.'

I try to imagine this, but I am not able to. 'You're talking about travelling back to the past?' I ask.

MacMullin exhales through his nose with a whistling sound.

'Imagine,' he says slowly, 'that these time travellers stumble out of their vessel in a distant past, just as awkwardly as Armstrong did on the moon. And then imagine them leaving a message, not exactly an American flag, but still a message to those they left behind in the future, a message that they made it there in one piece.'

'Wait,' I say, trying to wrap my head around this mind-boggling parable. 'Then they could read their own message – before they started out on their journey back through time . . . Because if they succeed in the past, then they would have to be able to read their own message in the future . . .'

'Ultimately, yes. But we're still facing the age-old paradox – what if you travel back in time and kill your own parents before you're born? We think it has to do with different timelines. Parallel universes or spheres.'

I'm quiet for a moment. Finally I say: 'Do you mean to tell me that that's what's in the shrine? A message from a group of time travellers?' I fold my arms across my chest.

All three watch me jubilantly. Time passes. If there's one thing I have plenty of, it's time. I let the seconds tick by.

'We found the time capsule,' MacMullin says. 'Their vessel. The time machine, if you will.'

'At Værne Monastery?'

'The golden shrine at Værne Monastery contains the message they left behind.'

'Uh-huh, right. Sure. And how did the shrine end up there?'

'It's a long story. The Egyptians considered the time travellers divine. When the golden shrine with their writings was brought from Egypt to the Middle East, it was considered sacred, a religious reliquary. Eventually the Knights Hospitaller took charge of the shrine. They also thought it contained divine writings. They thought Værne Monastery would be a safe hiding place, off at the ends of the earth.'

I nod to myself as if I finally understand. 'And where did you find this time capsule?'

'In Egypt.'

'Egypt?'

'It wasn't a spaceship they found under the Pyramid of Cheops. It was the capsule.'

At this point, I just can't hold it in any longer. I start giggling. It's a problem I struggle with.

Llyleworth looks as if he wants to trample me, all two hundred and thirty pounds of him.

'Honestly,' I exclaim.

Llyleworth sits down heavily and picks his cigar up from the ashtray. It's gone out. He pouts as he lights a match and sucks life back into the cigar.

'Yes?' MacMullin asks, sounding as refined as ever.

'Honestly,' I repeat. 'What do you people take me for?'

MacMullin studies me, his thumbs under his chin and his fingers forming steeples in front of his nose. If the situation had been different, I would have thought he was enjoying himself.

'You guys are pulling my leg, right?' I say. 'You must think I'm some kind of gullible idiot.'

'What makes you think we're pulling your leg?' Loland asks, sounding put out.

'Time travel? Honestly. Even a dim-witted associate professor of archaeology knows that's impossible. Pure science fiction.'

'They said the same thing about the moon landings. Many of the everyday amenities we take for granted now were science fiction fifty years ago.'

'Still! Somehow I'm supposed to believe that there's a message hidden in an ancient golden relic found at Værne Monastery in Østfold, Norway, that was left there by someone from the future after they travelled through time and ended up in the past?'

'Exactly.'

'Oh, please.'

I laugh and sigh theatrically, flinging out my arms and generally making a big production. 'Boys, you're forgetting one thing, one important detail.'

They look at me expectantly. They're power players, used to getting their way. They're confused by my reactions.

'You're forgetting that I know where the shrine is.'

'True, true.' MacMullin sighs.

I just can't stop myself from driving in the last nail: 'And I know about Rennes-le-Château,' I say.

MacMullin stiffens. He regains his composure a second later. But it's too late – I've already seen.

'You do?' he asks without skipping a beat.

I clear my throat meaningfully. 'So, was there anything else?'

MacMullin places his hand on my shoulder. 'In a bit,' he says, glancing over at Llyleworth. 'We'll talk about Rennes-le-Château a little later.'

With his hand still resting on my shoulder, he guides me out into the hallway and back to my room.

8

Restlessly I pace back and forth on the green carpet. The air is stuffy and warm. When I open the window a crack, I smell freshly mown grass and exhaust.

A bumblebee slips in through the crack in the window. It starts impatiently thumping against the glass. It doesn't like being in here, and I can understand how it feels. It's big and fuzzy. They say that strictly speaking, according to aerodynamic computations, bumblebees shouldn't be able to fly. There's something about bumblebees that I like. I'm not quite sure what. Maybe I can relate to their sense of defiance. I have a habit of identifying with all sorts of things.

I don't understand what they did with Diane or where they're hiding her. I ask myself how the police are going to respond if I file a report. Especially if I give them an explanation that's anywhere near the truth. I really doubt Mr Squeaky Voice is going to drop everything and rush to my aid. Oh my God, I don't even know Diane's last name. When I booked our plane tickets, she insisted – with a lot of giggling – on being called Mrs Beltø.

I'm no hero. Busting down the door to search for Diane in this maze of rooms is out of the question. Not that I would even be able to bust down the door – I'd probably dislocate my shoulder – and even if I did manage to escape from this room, some muscleman would scare me right back into obedience with a stern look.

I'm so jittery that I jump when I notice the envelope on the bedside table, an ordinary, white envelope with my name written on it in capital letters.

I open the envelope with the nail of my index finger and pull out the handwritten letter:

Dear Bjørn,

What can I say, my dear, other than to apologise? If only you can forgive me. Please? I'm so sorry . . .

They don't know I'm writing this. So don't show it to them or to anyone. These words are between you and me and no one else.

You must have so many questions. If only I could give you some answers, answers that would make sense, that would explain even a tiny portion of what's happened. But I can't. Not now anyway.

But I want you to know this: I love you. I never sold you out. I've never pretended to have any feelings for you that weren't true. Please believe me. I'm not a whore. But then maybe I am . . .

Whoever said that things were supposed to be easy? Life isn't an equation that just balances out if all the factors are right. Life is an equation that never balances out. And my life? One continuous catastrophe. A catastrophe that started the day I was born.

Bjørn, I'm sorry our paths ever crossed. Forgive me for falling for you and for getting you mixed up in all this. You deserve better. Someday maybe I'll learn. But here I am going on and on. And you don't understand the first thing. Because you're not meant to.

If you're worried about me, you have no reason to be. They haven't done anything to me. Maybe I'll get a chance to explain after this is all over. I don't know. Maybe not. But there's an explanation for everything.

If only we could have run away together. You and me. To a desert island. Where no one could bother us.

I should have known, of course. I should have known what would happen. But I'm so stubborn, so pig headed, so hell-bent on making my own way. If Daddy says, 'Wear the red dress. It looks great on you,' I wear the

264

grey slacks and the lavender blouse. If Daddy says, 'That boy's not for you,' I fuck his brains out. But you – I loved you, Bjørn.

Do you understand any of what I'm trying to say? I don't even know what I'm trying to say. Aside from this: I don't want you to hate me.

Just forget me! Forget that you ever met a dumb girl named Diane. Forget that maybe you thought she was a little bit cute. Forget that she fell for you. Here you go – here's an eraser. Erase her from your memory and your life.

Your angel,
Diane
XOXO

I rip the sheet in two and tie the ends together along with the duvet cover. I open both windows wide. The bundle of fabric tumbles out.

The bumblebee rejoices.

I tie the material around the narrow bit of wall separating the two windows a couple of times. Then I clamber up on to the ledge and lower myself down. I let myself drop the last metre and a half.

9

The scream lasted only a second or two, but the reverberation has been shrieking inside my head for twenty years.

The night before the accident, my dad was quiet and distant, as if he suspected that something terrible was in the offing.

When it got dark, Trygve lit the campfire. The logs were arranged in a tepee and surrounded by river rocks. A blackened coffee pot was suspended over the flames from a stick, a nifty little wilderness set-up, like a drawing you might find in *The Boys' Guide to Camping* or something.

Trygve was playing 'Blowing in the Wind' on his guitar.

The woods smelled of coffee and pine needles and my mother's perfume. My father had found a mosquito coil, which was reeking and stinking something awful, but apart from that didn't seem to be bothering the mosquitoes in the least. My father was lounging by the fire, leaning against a tree stump. My mother was sitting between his legs, using his body as her backrest. My father was talking about having found a trove of pearls, gold, silver, arts and crafts at Gaalaashaugen up by Nes in Hedmark earlier in the summer. My mother wasn't really listening, but I was spellbound, trying to picture the priceless treasure.

Trygve had a deep, pure voice. He closed his eyes as he sang. The flames made his long blond hair and stubble glow. He held the guitar tenderly between his powerful forearms. My mother kept sending him looks filled with invisible little kisses.

The sounds of the guitar floated up between the trees. The sky was white with stars. The lake twinkled through the canopy of leaves. Up in the meadow a willow warbler was calling it a day. The forest was closing in around us, vast and magical.

As the evening wore on, my father went to check the climbing gear. He was always so anxious. I can still picture him. He brought the backpacks back over to the tent, and he was standing there stooped over, fiddling with the equipment, when I caught him by surprise. He turned and looked up with a sheepish expression as if I'd caught him doing something. I forgot all about it a second later and that image of my father, stooped over the equipment bags, was frozen in time, something I wouldn't glimpse again until I recalled it again twenty years later.

Trygve opened a beer for him, but he wasn't thirsty. Later he emptied the bottle in one long swig.

My father went to bed early. My mother and Trygve stayed up – giddy and secretive, each with their bottle of beer and their low voices – roasting marshmallows over the fire.

It was dark and the stars were out when I crawled into the tent. I was a little queasy and worried. Before I fell asleep I lay there listening to the night and my mother's soft laughter.

I was sitting on a tree stump whittling a willow flute when my father fell. I wasn't that far away.

As I raced through the bushes, I was hoping with all my heart that the scream had come from Trygve, but deep down inside I knew it was my father.

Moments like that rend the consciousness into fragments. Fleeting images and snippets of sound become frozen, etched into memory.

The blue sky.

A bird.

Screaming.

The dull grey cliff face rising up from the accumulation of loose rocks at its base.

Trygve, a splotch of colour on a ledge way up above.

A shout: Bjørn, Go, go!! Go away!

The vertical line of the cliff.

The rope coiled in the sharp rocks.

My mother's wail.

Blood.

The heap of clothes at the base of the cliff. No, not clothes. My father.

A tree trunk behind me. Bark scraping the back of my neck as I collapse.

*

The rescue personnel weren't able to help Trygve down from the rock ledge until the next morning. My father had pulled the rope down with him when he fell.

There was an investigation. A report was written.

As the more experienced climber, Trygve had been responsible for safety, which is why he was still there up on the ledge to make sure that everything was the way it was supposed to be, which it wasn't. An abseil anchor had failed during the descent. Metal fatigue, the report said. Although no one could explain how the failure had occurred. It was the kind of failure that just wasn't supposed to be possible. My father didn't have a chance.

But no one wanted to blame Trygve, not my mother, not the investigation committee. He was really cut up about the accident.

Six months later he married my mother.

V

The Desert

1

THE SUN IS red hot. The sky is colourless.

I just opened my eyes. I shouldn't have done that. The sun's rays splinter in the back of my head. The light impales my pupils and bores through my skull. When I fell asleep, with my forehead against the cool window, it was still dark and a little chilly. The plane landed four hours ago. The sun has made very efficient use of that time. This place feels like a pressure cooker at peak pressure.

I angle my head away from the desert light and fumble around, pulling out the pair of sunglasses I bought at the airport in Oslo for 745 kroner, on sale. Sure, they're RayBans, but 745 kroner? On sale? If the saleslady hadn't been so cute, I would have scoffed scornfully and walked off, leaving the sunglasses on the counter, but now I slip them into place on my nose.

The road stretches straight ahead through a gold, undulating landscape. The line of asphalt disappears in heat waves that blur the shimmering horizon.

I'm in an air-conditioned bus in a rocky, desert wasteland, or maybe on another planet. Say, Jupiter. The rocks on the horizon are rust red. The odd stubborn plant grows amidst the rocks along the side of the road, looking like the kind of thing you might find in a terrarium or a herbarium or between the flagstones in a forgotten, tumbledown garden. Along the edge of the hill, there's a row of cypress trees, looking like the kind of biblical scene you might find embroidered on a cushion in the home of an overly religious old lady in conservative south-western Norway.

For the five thousandth time on this trip, I take out the letter from Diane and read it: word for word, line by line. I know it by heart, but it still doesn't make any sense to me.

It's just me and the bus driver. We're driving through a desert that never ends, without exchanging a word. There's something about the driver that makes me wonder whether he came pre-installed behind the wheel when the bus rolled off the factory assembly line. As if he was developed and designed by a team of talented bioengineers and geneticists and then constructed, meticulously and with great effort, in a separate wing of the production plant. He's wearing a short-sleeve shirt and has hairy arms, sweat rings under his arms, thinning hair, unshaved, strong eyebrows. Every now and then he glances at me in the enormous rear-view mirror, but he doesn't acknowledge my presence with so much as a nod.

It's never been easy for me to form connections with people. Over the years I've concealed my shyness behind a camouflage netting of faux cheerfulness and sarcasm. There are those who would seize this opportunity to engage the swarthy driver in cheerful banter about Jews and Arabs or sports cars and football, about Christianity and Islam, about fly fishing along the Namsen river or the prostitutes of Barcelona, but not me. And I can tell from his face that that's just as well in his book.

We round a rocky promontory; a lush oasis unfolds in the valley before us, a Garden of Eden with olive trees, frankincense bushes, sandalwood, camphor and cedar trees. A fig grove cloaks the hillside in silvery green. Spring water is flowing into carefully constructed irrigation channels, being pumped out of a well by a noisy diesel generator.

They decided to put the Schimmer Institute in this oasis. Don't ask me why. You could hardly get any farther away from people.

At least you can work in peace.

The institute is a striking example of how people are always trying to combine the ancient with the hyper-modern. With varying success. Monks established a monastery in the middle of the oasis seven hundred years ago, a building made of desert rock, hewn with geometric precision, finely polished and made to fit, and assembled into a complex of cells and hallways and larger rooms, a sanctuary for religious contemplation and prayer. Early in the 1970s, surrounding this centuries-old desert monastery, architects and engineers erected a mastodon of glass and mirrors and aluminium. A shock of modernity in an otherwise timeless setting. The institute does not tower upwards but spreads out flat like something swelling and growing, gleaming and sparkling in the sunshine.

2

'Bjorn, my friend, welcome!

The bus has manoeuvred around the lavishly planted roundabout, stopped, and released its air with a hiss after the long trip.

He's standing there waiting on the paved walkway outside the Institute's reception area. He's short and stocky, his eyes cheerful and warm. He has a bald spot and chubby cheeks, and if he were wearing a cowl, he would look like a parody of a monk.

His name is Peter Levi.

The Schimmer Institute is a research institute that attracts students and scholars from around the world. They rent rooms in the Institute hotel for weeks or months and otherwise ensconce themselves in the extensive library. In a separate wing they restore manuscript fragments and interpret words inscribed thousands of years ago on vellum or parchment or papyrus. The place is a blessed mix of theologians, historians, linguists, palaeographers, philosophers, archaeologists, ethnologists. They all want to shine the light of understanding on the past.

Peter Levi receives me with a level of enthusiasm that makes me sure he must think I'm someone else. But he exclaims 'Bjorn!' again and clasps my hand as he looks me in the eye and grins broadly.

'Welcome! Welcome to the Schimmer Institute. I hope we can be of service.' He speaks English with a thick, guttural accent.

We talked once before, two days ago. I called him from Torstein Avner's flat after I escaped from MacMullin. He was a name on the letter of invitation from the Institute, just a name, a random contact person. He will be my guide. Every visitor to the Institute is assigned a resident sponsor. But Peter Levi is acting as if we're old war buddies, who saved each other's lives in the trenches as enemy fire whistled over our heads and mustard gas hovered thick as porridge in the air around us, and, like brothers, shared a gas mask. Which leaked.

I don't know that I trust him, but I like him.

He insists on carrying my suitcase, which the driver has removed from the belly of the bus. With his left hand on my shoulder, Peter steers me into the reception office, where we pick up a keycard and register me:

NAME: *Bjørn Beltø*
TITLE: *Research Assistant/Archaeologist*
ORIGIN (CITY/COUNTRY): *Oslo, Norway*

ACADEMIC INSTITUTION: *University of Oslo*
ACADEMIC SPECIALITY: *Archaeology*
PURPOSE OF VISIT: *Research*

Peter shows me up to my room, number 207, which is in a different wing and which looks like a Holiday Inn room. He leaves me on my own here to 'wait until my soul has caught up with my body after the trip'. I unpack my suitcase and hang my clothes up in the closet. With a sigh that's due more to exhaustion than boredom, I sit down on the small green sofa. In my lap I'm holding all the print-outs Torstein Avner sent along with me.

He was efficient. Based on the search terms and names I gave him, he hunted around on the Internet and printed out all the web pages where he found information about what I was looking for. The information doesn't really seem very coherent. For example, the search term 'Knights Hospitaller' gave him thirty-two hits on AltaVista and seventeen on MetaCrawler: historical and quasi-academic websites about the Knights Hospitaller, Freemasons and hermetic sects. I flip through the print-outs with impatient irritation. I don't know what I'm looking for and am being bombarded with information I don't need.

Blaming Torstein for my irritation would be unfair. He did what I asked him to. I'm pissed off at my own powerlessness.

Where's Diane? What's her role in all this? What is she trying to get at in her letter?

Why are they lying about everything? Why did they drug me and then feed me a bunch of outrageously transparent lies? Are they trying to confuse me?

What's in the shrine? What secret are they actually hiding?

Are they trying to conceal one secret by making up an even more outrageous one? Questions like these keep running through my mind, but I'm not even close to finding any answers.

Torstein was bugging me to go to the police with everything I know and bring the shrine. I was tempted, but it's normal for anyone fighting something vast and not entirely perceptible to be a bit paranoid. I don't trust the police. They would just go by the book and logic and give the shrine back to the Antiquities Collection. And report me for simple burglary. And then we'd be in the same boat we're in now.

And how are the police supposed to find Diane? I don't know the first thing about her. Except that her name's Diane, and she lives in a skyscraper in London, and works for SIS, and that I was awfully naive to put any faith in her. Although at least I know that she never faked it when we made love.

I sit there for an hour browsing through the thick bundle of print-outs from Torstein. I read about the Knights Hospitaller and French nobility, about the Schimmer Institute's global reputation, about Værne Monastery, I read about Rennes-le-Château and Bérenger Saunière, about the Dead Sea Scrolls and the Monastery of the Holy Cross, about the Shroud of Turin and the Q manuscript and Nag Hammadi. I even find an article by Peter Levi about the Mandaeans' influence on non-Christian sects. I find thirty-four pages drawn from SIS's own home page, including brief biographies of both MacMullin and Llyleworth.

But nothing that results in any progress.

3

I lie down. My soul catches up with my body some time that afternoon.

After a slightly too-long nap, I pad aimlessly around the

Institute with the uneasy sense that I'm intruding. I often feel as if I don't belong. A hectic restlessness permeates the Schimmer Institute. This place is an academic anthill. I'm a visiting black ant, temporarily living among the industrious red ants. Their eyes focused on their own objectives, they scurry off following invisibly delineated paths. They stop, chat, hurry on. Enthusiastic students dart (*buzzing! gesticulating!*) along a hallway that seems to go on for ever. Maybe all the way to the queen's chamber? All the while they're eyeing me, sizing me up, analysing me, whispering about me. I'm sure Dr Wang would have said, 'You're just imagining that, Bjørn.'

What is it with this place? I ask myself. And shudder.

There's an island of ferns on the slate floor in the middle of the reception area surrounding a pillar with arrows and signs that point the way to various departments, labs, training facilities, lecture halls, conference wings, places to eat, shops, bookstores, a movie theatre, the library, studios, reading rooms.

Small surveillance cameras with red lights are mounted in the corners, up under the ceiling. I'm not unobservant.

4

Evening.

Peter Levi is sitting in a wing chair, drinking coffee and cognac in a dark, overcrowded hangout that everyone calls the Study, a fashionably appointed library bar thick with cigarette smoke, like some sort of British gentleman's club. The windows are covered, creating the illusion of eternal night. Tea lights on tables, soft piano music. All the voices are quiet, intense. Someone laughs loudly and is shushed. Heated conversations in foreign languages. When Peter sees me, he waves me over. His enthusiasm, and pleasure at seeing me, takes me by surprise.

Peter flags down a waiter, who hurries over with a tray bearing a cup of tea and a tulip-shaped glass of cognac. The tea is astonishingly spicy. I'm not sure whether the cognac is meant as a chaser. I think, *Tea?*

'I'm glad you were up to coming,' Peter says.

'Up to it?'

'You must be exhausted after your trip.'

'It's hard for me to say no to cognac,' I say.

We laugh a little to gloss over everything being left unsaid.

'We have a lot to talk about,' Peter says.

'We do?'

'Your research,' he explains, half as a question. 'Your interest in the Knights Hospitaller, the myth of the sacred shrine, and about how we can help you.'

I ask whether Peter knows Uri, who'd been sent from the Schimmer Institute to the dig at Værne Monastery. He does. Uri is still out on assignment.

Peter lights a cigarillo. He inhales with relish. He eyes me with curiosity through the cloud of smoke.

'Why?' he asks, rolling the cigarillo back and forth between his fingers. 'Are you really here?'

I explain. At least part of it. I don't say anything about all the lies and the mysterious high jinks associated with the shrine. Instead I pretend that I'm checking on the specific archaeological find. I explain that I'm searching for information about the Knights Hospitaller. And about anything that might have ties to Værne Monastery and the Shrine of Sacred Secrets.

'I know all that. But I asked about why you're *really* here.'

We scrutinise each other.

'If you are suggesting that I've got a secret, then you already know why,' I say ambiguously.

Peter doesn't say anything. He just looks at me and takes a

deep breath. The glowing ember at the tip of his cigarillo slowly eats its way down.

To fill the silence I tell him about the dig at Værne Monastery, which only moderately interests him. As I talk, he starts swirling the cognac in his glass. He stares into the golden-brown vortex, as if his thoughts are spinning around and around in the cognac. His eyes are tired. At this moment he looks like the kind of guy you'd expect to find sitting on a stool at a Formica counter in some side-street bar in New York City. Next to someone wearing black fishnet stockings and a world-weary expression.

When I finally stop talking, Peter gives me a look that seems indulgent but is probably purely and simply curiosity. 'Do you believe in Jesus?' he asks.

His question takes me by surprise. I do what he's doing: sniff the aroma of the cognac. 'As a historical figure?' I ask. Mildly inebriated, my blood is already starting to tingle. 'Or the Son of God?'

He just nods, as if I've answered his question, but that's not how I meant it. I ask him how he ended up here at the Institute. In a low voice, as if he really doesn't want anyone else to hear, he tells me about growing up in a poor neighbourhood in Tel Aviv, about a religious fanatic of a father and a devoted mother, about his search for faith, and about his studies. Peter is a religious historian. A specialist in sects that arose and died out around the time of Christ, and how they affected Christianity.

'Are you interested in the early Christians?' he asks in a way that strongly implies I should say yes.

'Definitely.'

'Good. I could sense that you and I have a lot in common. Lots to talk about. Did you know,' he continues, leaning across the table with a wry smile, 'that the Knights Hospitaller have a lot of similarities to the Mandaean Gnostics?'

'I don't think . . .' I respond slowly, pausing to take a sip of the strong tea. '. . . that I had fully grasped that.'

'But it's true. The Mandaeans rejected Jesus and considered John the Baptist their prophet. And they believed that salvation came through knowledge, gnosis, *manda*.'

I think to myself, *Boy, my mother must have been a Mandaean when I was a kid because she was all about the pursuit of knowledge.*

Peter continues, 'The Mandaeans' scriptures, the Great Treasure and the Book of John the Baptist, were five hundred years old when the Knights Hospitaller were founded. The Mandaeans have their King of Light. The point, my confused friend, is this.' He hesitates before he drops the bomb: 'Jesus and his contemporaries had *detailed* knowledge of the Essenes' writings.'

He gives me a triumphant, provocative look.

'So what?' I ask.

Crestfallen at my failure to appreciate what he has said and at my lack of enthusiasm, he drains his cognac glass in one long gulp. He gasps for air. Then he says: 'You're right. It's old news. You already know all this.'

I hem and haw. 'Well, not exactly all the details.'

He looks at me with his head cocked and then gives my shoulder a nudge and laughs quietly. I try my tea again and have to restrain myself from grimacing. Somewhere in the bar the pianist starts playing again. I hadn't noticed that he'd stopped. A waiter appears out of nowhere with a new glass of cognac for Peter.

'I'm sure you're dying to tell me about the Essenes,' I say.

'They're really interesting.'

He raises his glass of cognac. We toast.

He sets down his glass and clears his throat: 'The beliefs of the Essenes, or the Nazareans as they were also called, were heavily influenced by Babylonian religion. They believed that the soul was made of particles of light from a being of light that had been shattered by evil forces. These light particles were held captive in the human body until the host died. Then the light particles could be reunited with the being of light.'

'Peter,' I say, searching for the right words, 'why are you telling me this?'

'I thought you were interested.'

'I will be. As soon as I understand what you're trying to explain.'

He leans over and rests his tanned hands on mine. He's about to speak, but something makes him bite his tongue.

'I will have forgotten all this by tomorrow,' I say.

He hiccups. We chuckle.

Then he says: 'Maybe that's just as well. I'm talking too much.'

'If you could just explain the connection, I would actually find this very exciting.'

'Of course it's exciting.' My cautious praise triggers his enthusiasm: 'The point is that the Essenic influence on original Christianity seems to be far greater than was thought.'

'I didn't think it had had any effect at all.'

He lowers his voice, as if he is about to divulge a secret. 'Many people think that parts of the New Testament give a distorted and idealised picture of the religious underpinnings of Christianity.'

'Well . . .' I say, drawing it out, deciding to play along. 'It's all getting to be kind of a while ago now. Maybe that doesn't matter so much.'

'But we're still living in keeping with the spirit of the Bible.'

'Because a lot of people believe it's the Word of God,' I say.

'And because the Bible is the most inspiring book that's ever been written.'

'And the most beautiful.'

'A guide to how to live and die. With morality and charity. A primer on respect and the value of human life.'

'Those are big words . . .'

'It's a big book,' Peter says reverently.

We both stare off into space. The recessed lights in the ceiling slice like rays of silver through the fog of cigarette smoke. The voices, the laughter, the music – everything is a wall of sound that doesn't quite reach us. Peter puts out his cigarillo in the ashtray and turns to look at me. 'But is the Bible really the Word of God?' he says with surprising vehemence.

'Don't ask me.'

'God didn't write a single line of it. The twenty-seven books of the New Testament were selected through a painful and lengthy process.'

'With divine intervention?'

'I mean with out-and-out squabbling.'

I laugh, but stop the instant I realise that he isn't kidding.

He brings his cognac glass to his lips, inhales and drinks. He closes his eyes for a second. He gently sets his glass down on the table.

'It wasn't,' he continues, 'that a group of sacred authors sat down and *wrote* the Bible once and for all. The Church had a lot of manuscripts to evaluate over the centuries. Some were rejected, others included. It's important to understand that the New Testament became canonical during and as part of a power struggle, both within the Church and without, in a weakened and dying Roman Empire.'

'Power struggle? That sounds cold.'

'Well, remember that the Church was a dogged participant in the struggle over cultural, political and financial power in the vacuum left behind after Rome.' Peter looks around with a half-smile. 'If the fall of Rome hadn't coincided with the split between the Jews and the evolution of a whole new religion, the world would look completely different today.'

'I've never thought about that,' I admit. 'Our civilisation is a salad of Roman, Greek and Christian values and customs.'

'If we return to the Bible and its role in this process, almost four hundred years elapsed from when Jesus was born until the Bible settled into its current form. But many of the texts that were ultimately included in the New Testament and which are the crux of it today were quite contentious, anyway.'

'Who decided this stuff?'

'The clergy, of course. The early Church.'

'The priests . . .'

'More precisely the bishops, who received their authority directly from the Apostles.'

'The way the Pope does?'

'Same principle. They really bickered about what should be included in the Bible. The collection of texts that make up the Bible as we know it today was accepted by the synods that met in Rome in 382, in Hippo in 393 and in Carthage in 397. It certainly wasn't God who edited the Bible – it was the bishops and later religious communities. The Protestants, for example, don't recognise all the texts in the Old Testament the way the Catholics do. The Protestant Church uses the Old Testament canon that Hebrew scholars established in Jamnia in the year AD 90. They accepted only the thirty-nine books that were written in Hebrew and Aramaic. The Roman Catholic Church's canon was translated into Greek in Alexandria, Egypt, two hundred years before Christ and contains forty-six books. The New Testament cross-references this version more than three hundred times. And we haven't even touched on the sacred texts of the Jews yet.'

I can't stop myself from grinning. 'I'm picturing a bunch of corpulent clergymen, sort of casually giving biblical manuscripts the thumbs-up or the thumbs-down.'

Peter sucks air in through his front teeth, making a disgusting sound.

'Well, that's certainly a vulgarised and simplified take, but still, there's a hint of truth to it.'

'Powerful men.'

'Powerful, calculating, determined. What were their motives? Were they believers? Were they Christian? Were they con men who used the new faith as a springboard for their own ambitions?'

'Why are you even asking? It's all water under the bridge.'

'Because the question is whether the texts in the Bible give a representative picture of Jesus' teachings.'

'Well, they must, right? I mean, they're in the Bible, aren't they?'

'Hmm. But what if selecting and editing the texts in the New Testament was a political process? Part of a power struggle. It wasn't long after Jesus' death that the Church was split into denominations and sects with widely differing theological views. And what if the texts that were ultimately chosen were the ones that best suited the ambitions of the bishops and the Church. I mean, I'm just asking.'

I try to digest what he's saying. A growing suspicion is taking root in my gut. I can't quite put my finger on it. But I suspect that Peter is Jewish, that the Schimmer Institute is Jewish, and that something in the shrine from Værne Monastery will confirm the Jewish view of biblical history.

'Are you saying that the Bible distorts what really happened?' I ask.

He makes a protracted 'hmm' sound. 'I'm asking . . . I'm asking if the biblical texts that were chosen give a complete and correct picture of Jesus' teaching. I'm asking if someone needed to adapt the new religion to suit certain personal objectives of the bishops and the Church.'

I shrug. 'Lots of people would say that the Bible is a book about how the Jews viewed their world and their time.'

Peter reaches for his cognac glass, but changes his mind. 'Not to mention a set of rules to live by,' he says.

I empty my own glass of cognac and stand up. I'm tired. I've had enough of biblical history. Now I'm ready for bed.

'Personally,' I say, 'I'm inclined to consider Christianity a two-thousand-year-old superstition from the Middle East.'

5

An odd smell, like paper and burned caramel, fills the library at the Schimmer Institute.

It's early in the morning. The desert light is pouring in through the glass domes in the roof and falling like sloping columns on the rows of bookshelves. Dust hovers over row upon row of books and boxes filled with manuscripts on papyrus, vellum, parchment and paper. A menagerie of researchers and students sits bent over the reading desks: long-haired Americans, Orthodox Jews, women in shawls with ponytails, Asians, short men with glasses frenetically chewing their pencils. It occurs to me that I fit in as a natural part of this slightly eccentric scene.

The vast collection of books and manuscripts is particularly focused on the Middle East, Asia Minor and Egypt. There are separate sections devoted to books in languages that I can't even decipher the alphabets to. The English-language collection is surprisingly small.

And everywhere: women and men off in their own worlds in all the various specialities and fields, people who are world-leading experts in the most obscure topics – Sumerian cuneiform tablets, who actually wrote the Pentateuch, inter-preting the impact of old Babylonian myths and Egyptian death rites on pre-Christian dogmas. I wander around in this academic environment like a confused little schoolboy who's not quite sure what to do with himself. I'm not an expert in anything at all and I start despondently questioning our limit-less craving for knowledge about the past, which makes me an archaeologist who's asking why we need to know so much about the past when there's so much we don't know about the present.

I don't notice Peter until I bump into him. He's on his tiptoes looking for a book on a section of the bookshelves marked ANCIENT MYTHOLOGY – EGYPT/GREECE. I say oops. We say hello. He smiles inscrutably, as if the sight of me always fills him with delight. 'Thanks for a nice time last night,' he says with a wink.

'You too.'

'How are you feeling today?'

I think that is meant as a joke. Maybe he thinks I'm looking a bit pale today.

We mosey away so we won't disturb all the people who are absorbed in their books. 'My head is throbbing,' he says with a theatrical sigh.

We stop next to a counter of microfilm machines and look at each other expectantly, like two lovers each wondering how seriously the other took the previous day.

'You told me something,' I say expectantly.

'I did? Oh my, oh my. I'm sure I told you way too much. I get so chatty when I drink. I'm going to have to ask you to treat everything I said with discretion.'

'You know you can trust me.'

'I do? I hardly know the first thing about you. But you're right, I trust you.'

'What you said, it made me curious.'

'That figures, although I don't remember what it was that I said. Or shouldn't have said.' With a quiet laugh, he looks around the library. 'Come on.' He grabs my arm and leads me through a labyrinth of hallways, up stairs, down stairs, through doors, to a small office with his name on the door. The office is rectangular and narrow, full of books and stacks of paper. There are Venetian blinds hanging in front of the window. A ceiling fan is spinning.

He sighs with satisfaction. 'Here. This is a better place to talk,' he says, sitting down in his desk chair. For my part, I vanish into the depths of a beanbag on the other side of the desk. I have to struggle to hoist myself up into a position that feels even passably comfortable, let alone one that preserves a shred of dignity.

'So what's in all the manuscripts that you're analysing here?' I ask.

'Details, details, details. I'll tell you one thing: we're spending most of our time going through old manuscripts again.'

'Again? Why?'

'Because we've learned. We know more than the people who went through and translated the manuscripts the last time. We are reading and translating them in light of everything we know today. How precise are the translations of the biblical scriptures? Can contemporary scholarship shed a new light on our understanding and interpretation of the old scriptures? Do newly discovered manuscripts, like the Dead Sea Scrolls, affect our understanding of previously discovered manuscripts of the Bible?'

'You just keep asking questions,' I say.

'And I'm looking for new answers. Translating texts that are several thousand years old has just as much to do with new understanding and scholarship as with linguistics and understanding the language.'

'And maybe faith?'

'It has a lot to do with faith.'

'And what if you encounter facts that could shake that faith?'

He looks me in the eye. In the light that makes it through the blinds, I notice how murky the whites of his eyeballs look.

'Why do you think we're so secretive?' he asks through clenched teeth.

I wriggle in a rather futile attempt to position myself higher up on the beanbag.

'Let me give you an example,' Peter says. 'Did Moses part the Red Sea with God's help so that the fleeing Israelites could reach safety and so that Pharaoh's army drowned when the water streamed back?' He leans with his elbows on the desk, folds his hands and rests his chin on his thumbs. 'The institute has devoted many years to investigating the myth of Moses and the parting of the Red Sea. Our linguists have discovered a possible mistranslation or misinterpretation of the Hebrew expression *Yam suph*, which we now think means a place where it is so shallow that rushes or reeds grow. *Yam suph*,' he repeats, drawing it out.

I try to pronounce it, but it makes me sound as if I have some kind of speech impediment.

Peter pulls a historical atlas down from one of the bookshelves and looks up S – SINAI. 'In ancient times the Gulf of Suez reached much farther north,' he holds up the book and points to the map, 'and the whole area was green and covered with reeds and rushes. Our scholars – a multidisciplinary team of linguists, historians, geographers and meteorologists – seized on this linguistic detail. They figured out that the Israelites could have crossed the sea at what's known today as the Bardawil Lagoon.'

He presses his index finger firmly against the paper. I squint as I try to get my geographical bearings.

'We tested a number of models in our data simulator,' he says. 'The hydrographic mechanics here are such that if the wind were strong enough and lasted long enough, it could force out the three- or four-metre-deep water.' With his fingertips, he gestures as if sweeping the water away. 'And with that Moses could cross the almost dry sea. But . . .' He holds his index finger up. '. . . when the wind either subsided or changed direction, the water would come rushing back.' With a bang he slaps his palm against the atlas.

'Wow,' I exclaim. Which doesn't really sound that scholarly, but it's all I can think of.

He leans back in his chair, pleased with himself. 'Or what about the Flood? What really happened? Our archaeologists, palaeontologists and geologists have found evidence that a flood drove an agrarian society away from the Black Sea well over seven thousand years ago.'

'I thought the Flood affected the people living between the Tigris and the Euphrates?'

'Well, that's one guess among many. Everything is based on guesswork and hypotheses, but we've reconstructed what might have happened by studying old sources.'

'What sources?'

'Oh, lots of them: the Bible, four-thousand-year-old cuneiform tablets, the Gilgamesh Epic, the text of the Rig-Veda from India, and other, less well-known extant texts.'

'And what have you learned?'

'Let's start with the geologists. They found sediments containing seven-thousand-year-old saltwater animals in the Black Sea. These sediments were deposited quickly, like by a tidal wave. Remember that the Black Sea was originally a freshwater, inland sea separated from the Mediterranean by a spit of land at the Bosporus Strait. And picture how the Mediterranean gradually, and with increasing intensity, forced its way through that fragile land barrier. Until it burst.

What a sight that must have been! One sea inundating another
... The sound of the rushing water must have been audible
for hundreds of miles. It took three hundred days for the
water level to even out between the two seas. The Black Sea
rose by a hundred and fifty metres. But because the amount of
area to be covered is so enormous, it must have taken a long
time for the fertile agricultural areas in the north to flood.
Day by day the people would have been driven ever farther
inland by the rising sea.'

'That must have been a sight.' I shudder.

'And now we come to the next piece of circumstantial
evidence. Archaeological findings show that a very advanced
agrarian society showed up in eastern and central Europe
right around this same time.'

'Refugees from the Black Sea?'

'We don't know, but probably. Linguistic studies support
such a supposition. Almost all of the Indo-European languages developed from a proto-language. All these cultures
share a myth of a terrible flood. These surviving tales were
passed on orally until they were written down two thousand
five hundred years later, when the descendants of the Indo-
Europeans developed a written language. We think this may
have been the basis for the myth of the biblical Flood.'

'The myth? I thought you guys were dedicated more to
proving that the Bible was true?'

He makes an inexplicable grimace. 'I'm not saying that
God didn't have a hand in it.' Then he suddenly stands up, his
lecture over, and we head back to the library. Neither of us
says anything on the way. 'We'll talk later,' he mumbles, then
pats me on the shoulder and leaves me.

I stand there puzzled, alone and confused by all the un-
spoken insinuations.

From the top of the Potala a solitary kite was flying.

I've always been drawn to monasteries – the silence, the con-templation, the timelessness, the unassuming mysticism, the proximity to something bigger, something intangible – but nothing at the Schimmer Institute makes me feel as if I'm in a monastery. I think about the Potala Palace, the fabled monas-tery in Lhasa with its gilded roofs and domes framed by the peaks of Tibet. 'From the top of the Potala a solitary kite was flying.' That's the poignant last line of the book that gave me my first encounter with monastic life. The hippie bible, *The Third Eye*, from 1956, is an autobiography written by the Tibetan lama Lobsang Rampa, a captivating tale of life in and around the Tibetan monasteries, a life that included studies, tying themselves to kites and flying, prayers, philosophy and astral travels. I was quite surprised when I discovered that far from being a short monk wrapped in Eastern garb, Lobsang Rampa was actually a rather tall Englishman with a Devonshire accent and a fascination for New Age mysticism before the concept had been invented. Not only did he consider himself a Tibetan lama in an Englishman's body, but he also claimed that cats were sent to Earth from another planet to observe us. Is it any wonder that I can't stand cats?

I'm sensitive to illusions, things that aren't quite what we think they are. I feel as if I'm not quite getting the hang of the Schimmer Institute, which doesn't necessarily mean much. Sometimes I don't really get the hang my office at the Antiquities Collection either. Or my flat early on a Sunday morning.

After an afternoon nap, I sit and write in my journal for a long time. I like the scraping sound the pen makes against the paper. It's like listening to thoughts. One of my thoughts, which is currently scratching against the paper, is that the Schimmer Institute is a tool for MacMullin. It is possible that I'm being paranoid, but at least I'm consistent.

I allow my thoughts to wander into a dark, foggy forest of questions and fear. If the Institute has more of a Jewish perspective, maybe it's in their interest to expose the contents of the shrine in order to reveal once and for all that the Christians were wrong. But if the Institute has more of a Christian perspective, maybe they want to destroy the contents of the shrine to protect their faith, their Church, their power. The forest is a little too big for me, the fog a little too dense. All I have to do is choose: two conspiracies for the price of one.

7

Later that evening, burdened by my own obsessive thoughts and absurd preoccupations, I drag myself down to reception and then into the bar. I don't see anyone I know, but Peter comes hurrying in a few minutes later. We greet each other and find a table behind the piano. The waiter is attentive. He brings us coffee, tea and cognac before we request them. Peter raises his glass and says cheers.

'Can I ask you about something?' I ask tentatively, taking a sip of my cognac.

'Of course.'

'What do you think is in the shrine?'

'The Shrine of Sacred Secrets,' he says slowly, reverently. He furrows his brow in thought. 'Like any myth, it will be a distortion of the truth. The Church has embellished the story over the centuries, as the Church is wont to do.'

'What do you mean by that?'

'One of the manuscripts we've studied here at the Institute

– and we're talking about something that was written in the third century – suggests that Jesus Christ left behind a collection of texts that he dictated or wrote himself.'

'You're serious?'

'Mmm.'

'What kind of texts?'

'How should I know? No one has read them. Besides, it's just a hypothesis.'

'But what did it say in the manuscript where you read about this?'

'It suggested that they might be a set of rules to live by, commands, new commandments, if you will. The manuscript was in a sealed jar in an Egyptian burial chamber. We've been sitting on the information until we understand it better. In the beginning we didn't appreciate the scope of what we'd found, but then we realised the similarities to the myth of the Shrine of Sacred Secrets.'

'That's unbelievable.'

'The Vatican completely lost it when they found this out. We had a papal delegation on our doorstep here, but we never involved them. The Vatican has so many things to con- sider. The truth is just one of those things, and in all honesty it's pretty far down their list. Now the Vatican is in a bind; they know we know something, but they don't know what. They're not too keen on that.'

'Wait – are you saying that the golden shrine we found at Værne Monastery might contain a manuscript dictated by Jesus Christ?'

Peter flings out his arms. 'Anything is possible.' He shrugs.

'Could it be the Vatican that's been sending its agents after me? In their quest for the shrine?'

'Agents?' He laughs. 'The Vatican certainly has its methods, but they're so used to obedience that they hardly know how to handle someone who refuses to do as they say. No, I doubt the Vatican is after you.'

'If this manuscript exists, even if just in theory, then more people should have heard of it, shouldn't they?'

'Or someone needed to keep this knowledge secret.'

'Why?'

'I'm sure you can imagine.'

I take a swig of cognac. 'That would be something, deviant religious facts . . . Facts that would change our understanding of Christianity.'

'A scary thought for many.'

'Scary?'

'The most sensational news story in the history of the world, bigger than the moon landing: Jesus Christ's own gospel.'

The thought makes my head spin. Either that or it's the cognac.

8

The Study bar closes at eleven. Good little scholars go to bed early, at least in the desert, where there aren't many sins to enjoy. We trickle out into the glistening marble of the reception area, which is almost devoid of people. Peter is a bit drunk.

'Shall we go and get some fresh air?' he asks.

I say I think that's a good idea.

Outside it's pitch black and the stars are out. The air is nippy but smells sweet. Peter leads the way around the facility and up the hillside, into the grove of fig and olive trees. We make our way hesitantly in the faint gleam of the heavens and the lit-up windows of the Institute.

A short way up the hillside we stop under a tree whose

branches stretch above us like a ceiling. The bark has been furrowed by the claws of the centuries. The moon is glimmering through the leaves like a Japanese paper lantern. The surprisingly chilly desert air has a slightly intoxicating effect, as if there were a canister – maybe disguised as a cactus – around the next bend, leaking some kind of narcotic gas into the air.

'There was a natural oasis here at one time,' Peter says. He inhales deeply through his nose, as if sampling the scents. 'The monks planted these trees and tended them. It's a wonder that anything at all grows out here.'

'Who were they, the monks?'

'A group of Jews and Christians. Rebels, nonconformists. They wanted to found a new community.' He laughs, his laughter tinged with venom.

I look out into the darkness. From up here the Institute looks like a spaceship that crash-landed and is now glowing as it melts into the ground. Like some kind of prearranged special effect, a shooting star darts across the sky.

'What a sight,' I say.

'Strictly speaking a shooting star is nothing more than a grain of sand burning up as it meets the Earth's atmosphere,' Peter says.

Everything is dark, black and quiet. The atmosphere inspires a sense of intimacy in me.

'Who are you, Peter?' I ask.

Grinning, he pulls a flat, leather-bound flask out of his inside pocket. He unscrews the top and passes it to me.

'You mean as a part of the bigger picture?'

'Let's start with that.'

'Absolutely nothing,' he says.

I take a drink. The cognac burns all the way down. 'And what about a smaller picture?' I pass the flask back, urging him to take it with a nod.

Peter takes a swig, shudders, then another swig. 'In a

smaller picture, I'm just a really dedicated worker bee,' he exclaims.

We look at each other. He gives me a wink, as if he realises that his answer isn't an answer at all.

'You seem to know a lot about the shrine.'

'Theories,' he says softly. 'I'm an academic. Knowing things like that is my livelihood.'

'But what you know is so precise.'

'Who said I know anything? I'm guessing.'

'So let's keep guessing,' I say.

'What are you wondering?'

'If the Shrine of Sacred Secrets really exists, and if it's the reliquary that we found at Værne Monastery . . .' I begin and then wait, glancing over at him, 'why would it be important for someone to secure the shrine for themselves?'

'I would imagine they're after whatever's inside.'

'Who?'

'It could be so many people: scholars, collectors, the Vatican, clandestine groups.'

'And why?'

'Imagine that the message in the manuscript is of a delicate nature.'

'Like what? I mean, for example?'

'For example, something that could affect accepted dogma.'

'In what way?'

'In a way that would necessitate rewriting biblical history.'

'What difference would that make?'

'Now you're playing devil's advocate. The Bible does not contain any errors by definition. It can't be corrected.'

'But in practical terms what difference will it make if this manuscript overturns some ideas?'

Peter furrows his brow. 'You don't mean that, my friend.

Think about it. The whole Christian way of life could crumble. People will start to lose faith in it. It could threaten the position of the Church, little things like that.'

I whistle; the note sounds delicate, tremulous.

'That would be at its most extreme,' he adds. He raises the pocket flask and drinks as he watches me. He swallows slowly. 'But this is all just guesswork.'

'Exciting theories.'

'History *is* exciting. Particularly because history is all interpretation.'

'Interpreted with the benefit of hindsight.'

'Exactly. To his contemporaries, Jesus of Nazareth was predominantly a political figure.'

'And the Son of God.'

'Well, actually, it's mostly after the fact that people started focusing on his divinity.'

'After the fact?'

'From quite a bit later. To place Jesus historically, you need to consider both the Jews' thousand years of waiting for the Messiah and the political situation in Judaea and Roman Palestine.' He licks his lips and dries them with the back of his hand.

'I'm not really an expert on those things,' I admit.

'The Roman Empire had become so powerful,' he says. 'The province of Judaea was really a kind of local kingdom with Herod as its ruler, but in reality it was governed for Rome by Pontius Pilate. To its residents, Rome was a distant, yet irritating, pustular boil. Judaean society was a real menagerie of sects and groups, turncoats and traitors, clergy and prophets, bandits, murderers and con artists.'

'Like any big city today,' I say, taking the flask. The cognac tastes warm, numbing.

The expression on Peter's face is distant, the sort of engrossed face some people get when they're incredibly captivated by a topic and assume it must be just as fascinating to everyone else. 'They were rebellious times,' he says. 'The Zealots gathered the Pharisees, the Essenes and others into a political and military movement around the time of Jesus' birth. Jesus was born right at the beginning of a hundred-and-forty-year rebellion. And everyone, every last one of them, was waiting for the Messiah, a Saviour, a political and religious leader.'

'And they got one.'

'Well . . .' He wrinkles his nose. 'Did they? Let's look at the language, the semantics. To our modern ears, *messiah* and *saviour* mean something different to what they did back then. *Messiah* is *christos* in Greek – "Christ". In both Hebrew and Greek it means "the anointed one" or "the chosen one", a traditional way of referring to a kind of king or leader.'

'A born leader?'

'Exactly. Actually, all the Jewish kings who were descended from David bore the title of *messiah*. Even the priests that the Romans proclaimed as petty kings referred to themselves with the title *messiah*. But to the Zealots, none of these was the one true Messiah. Their saviour was supposed to be descended from David. Their dream of the Messiah bordered on hysteria. But remember, they were not waiting for a deity – they were waiting for a king, a commander, a leader. *Messiah* was a political title. The notion of the Son of God, as we think of Jesus today, would have seemed quite far fetched to them. On the other hand, they thought that the kingdom of God would be arriving any day.'

'But nowadays we believe in and worship the Son of God,' I say. 'Still. Hundreds of millions of people. All over the world.'

Peter picks up a rock and throws it out into the darkness. We hear how it hits the hill and bounces a couple of times before it stops. 'That's the way it is,' he says.

I take a swig of the cognac. 'But now you're telling me that this golden shrine might contain something that could shake that faith?' I ask.

'I don't know. I really don't know. Could be . . .' He takes a deep breath. 'Are you asking me what I think? I think your shrine contains something . . .' He stops, as if he has suddenly become aware of someone standing out in the dark, eavesdropping on us. I try peering into the night, listening for sounds, the rustle of fabric, a foot stepping on a branch. But I don't hear anything. I turn to Peter. He's looking away. I pass him the flask. He takes several small, quick swigs. Afterwards he cools his throat with deep gulps of fresh air.

We listen to the stillness.

'You were saying,' I say, 'that you think the shrine contains something . . .'

'. . . that could change our understanding of history,' he continues. 'And of Christianity.'

I don't say anything. But I realise that that would actually explain the insane level of interest in the shrine.

He finds a new stone and throws it out into the night. It may have lain there undisturbed for five hundred years. Hurtling through the air in the dark must come as a bit of a shock to it, but now it's still again. Maybe for another five hundred years.

'Could you be more precise?' I ask.

He shakes his head weakly.

'But why does the manuscript necessarily have to be so important?' I ask. 'Maybe the shrine contains . . . psalms? . . . poems? . . . a pope's secret love letter? Or something like that.'

He laughs, kicking his shoe against a root that's just barely sticking up out of the ground. 'My friend, a manuscript in a reliquary made of gold that someone brings to a monastery at the end of the world does not contain instructions for buying and tending donkeys. That much I can tell you.'

'So what do you think it might be about?'

He considers. While he's contemplating my question, he studies me unabashedly. 'Something about Christianity?' he asks. Or maybe it's a statement. I'm not really sure.

'The Q manuscript?' I suggest.

He grunts in agreement. 'Maybe, maybe not. It wouldn't actually surprise me. But I have a feeling . . . no, I don't think it's the Q manuscript.'

'Why not? That would fit with your hypothesis.'

'Bjørn,' he parries, 'what do you know about the Schimmer Institute?'

I glance down at the glowing sprawling structure. 'One of the world's leading research institutions for Jewish and Christian historical studies?'

'Right. That's our academic alibi and reputation.' He leans closer, and his breath smells strongly of cognac. 'I'm going to let you in on a secret.'

He doesn't say anything, and I wait. He passes me the flask. I take just a small sip.

'Most of the research we do is published in the leading international journals. Or is released in the form of reports, dissertations, monographs. But we're also involved in research that we never share with colleagues. Research that is meant for a very select few.'

'What about?' I ask.

'Old texts.'

Luckily he doesn't look over at me, because I'm sure I don't look very impressed. I suppose I was hoping for something more exciting. Maybe hidden treasures, forgotten royal burial chambers, the riddles of antiquity that have never been solved, the secret of the pyramids, mystical maps to remote and inaccessible mountain valleys where the fountain of youth flows, sparkling and blue, out of the prehistoric glaciers. I have a rather limited imagination.

'Old texts,' he repeats, smacking his lips, 'the DNA codes of civilisation and knowledge, if you will, the sources for our understanding of the past and hence our understanding of who we are today.'

'Kind of a pretentious way to put it, but I know what you mean.'

'Original manuscripts, notes and traditions, letters, laws and ordinances, hymns, gospels, biblical passages, the Dead Sea Scrolls, Nag Hammadi, manuscripts that could easily have been part of the Bible, but never made it in because someone wanted it that way.'

'Not God?'

He snorts. 'Certainly not God.'

I say: 'If no one knows what's in the golden shrine, or what might be in whatever manuscript is inside it, then why are they so desperate to get hold of it?'

Peter looks up. The air is clear. The stars look like milk through the leaves. I'm overcome by the thought that the lights twinkling in the sky are the past. The farthest stars stopped shining long before the Earth was here.

We stroll a few steps. Peter sits down on a rock. 'If I could hazard a guess,' he says, 'I think it might have something to do with biblical passages.'

I sit down next to him. The rock feels cool through the fabric of my trousers. 'Do you mean original biblical manuscripts?'

'For example. Either completely unknown ones, but still important texts, or original manuscripts of familiar passages, which prove how the contents have been altered after the fact.'

'In the Bible?'

He nods his head. 'Does that surprise you?'

'Actually, yes. Do you mean someone dared to tamper with the Bible?'

'Of course.' Peter pulls out a cigarillo and lights it. The flame from his lighter forms a sea of light in the darkness. I sense swarms of insects that we can't see. The smell of the smoke drives away from the oasis the scents of the flowers and trees.

'The Bible was never written as a single, definitive entity,' he says. 'The Bible was a collective understanding and interpretation. Someone started it, others finished. In between, the stories were doctored.' He inhales and blows the smoke out through his nostrils. 'To understand the New Testament, we also have to understand the history,' he says. 'You can't read the Bible outside the context of the historical reality of the lives of the prophets and evangelists.'

I grunt and take another swig. Someone turns the light on in the library. The glass domes in the ceiling flicker, neon blue and recalcitrant, as if the fluorescent tubes had fallen deeply asleep and were resisting being woken.

'I have trouble seeing the connections between the history of the Bible and the Knights Hospitaller,' I say.

'They came much later, as managers and protectors of the knowledge that the shrine hid. And still hides. When Jerusalem fell in 1187, the Knights Hospitaller moved their headquarters to the Crusader fortress in Acre. They were there for over a hundred years.' He hesitates. 'There aren't many people who know this, but the Knights Hospitaller divided into two groups during the Acre period.'

'Divided into two groups?'

I sense that this information is important, but don't know why. In the darkness, his eyes seem to glow. 'It may seem insignificant. Only a very few historians and religious scholars know that the order had split up, and far fewer know why. The branch that is historically well attested moved to Cyprus and Rhodes and then on to Messina and Malta in 1530.'

'And the other group?'

'Disappeared – or, to be more precise, they went underground.'

'Why?'

'I don't know.'

'But?'

'Let's speculate. What if the hidden branch is protecting a secret? What if its only purpose is to carry on some knowledge? And to protect this knowledge?'

'And who's supposed to be in charge of all this?' I ask.

'Maybe there's still a Grand Master?'

'You mean that the Knights Hospitaller still have a Grand Master?'

'A Grand Master that not even the members of the Order of Knights Hospitaller know about, a secret Grand Master.'

'What's the point of him if he's so secret?'

'Maybe he's the one who's carrying on the knowledge about the past. Maybe he's the one who needs the manuscript.'

'Is that a question?' I say.

'I'm guessing.'

'You *know* something.'

Peter rolls his eyes. 'Me? What do I know? What in the world were the Knights Hospitaller doing in Scandinavia? Remote, frozen Norway? Why would it even occur to them to hide anything at all in an octagon near the ends of the Earth?'

I don't respond. I also don't comment on the fact that he's aware of the octagon even though I never mentioned it to him. He must be exceptionally well informed.

'Maybe,' I suggest, 'it contains some kind of directions?'

'To what?'

'To a treasure?'

'Treasure?' Peter doesn't seem to understand. 'What treasure?'

'Well, I don't know . . . The hidden and long-forgotten fortune of the Merovingian dynasty?'

He bursts out laughing. 'So, you're one the people who believes those fairy stories? Who believes that at some point in history there were ever people who actually hid their fortunes so well that they still haven't turned up?'

'I don't believe anything, actually. I'm just speculating. Like you.'

'Let me just say this: like the historical conspiracy theories about Freemasons and Jews, these tales of buried treasures are some of the most persistent and pervasive there are.'

'What's wrong with that? Maybe there's something to them?'

'The problem is that they assume that an incredibly rich person would decide to do something so incredibly stupid as to bury or hide his fortune instead of putting it in safe keeping with someone he trusted.' He sneers. 'Remember that rich people usually get rich because they love money and all the trappings that come with it. No one would stash away all their wealth without letting those who are nearest and dearest to them know where.'

'Well, if anyone could figure that out, I suppose it would be all of you,' I say.

He says something under his breath that's presumably an affirmation.

I clear my throat nervously. 'Peter, would you say you're a Christian or a Jew?'

He takes a deep breath, making a strained, whistling sound. 'What I believe,' he says softly, 'doesn't matter. I'm mostly interested in what I know.'

Later, after we empty the flask and stumble back to the Institute, Peter trips on a tree root. Only my quick reaction keeps him from tumbling down a cliff. He mutters a thank-you meant either for me or for a god whose flame is burning in Peter's heart at just that moment.

We say goodnight in the reception area.

I'm drunk and dizzy and more than a little nauseated. Before sinking into bed and swirling off to sleep, I kneel (not unlike a monk) in front of the shiny white porcelain toilet and vomit.

9

After a breakfast that I consume so late that it wouldn't be unreasonable to call it lunch – and which consists of toast, undercooked scrambled eggs, prune yogurt and freshly squeezed orange juice – I hurry down to the library. In the old-fashioned alphabetical card file I flip my way to VARNA, which refers me one centimetre back to VAERNE, where I find references to four books and a manuscript collection that I spend forty-five minutes tracking down on a shelf located two metres high in stacks in the library's basement. A librarian, who seems like a Chilean military academy graduate who wants, more than anything, to brush up on what he learned in Refined Torture T101, lifts the manuscripts out of the box and places them on a felt-covered table. But I can tell right away that they're not going to be of any help to me: they're all in Hebrew.

I spend the next hour browsing through a British work about orders of knights in which over two hundred pages are dedicated to the Knights Hospitaller and three times that to the Knights Templar. I find an American doctoral dissertation from 1921 that analyses St Luke's literary techniques. According to the scholar, Luke (who was a physician and likely a travelling companion of St Paul's) is the closest we have to a modern novelist in the Bible. Luke writes with an epic flair that appealed to his educated, sophisticated, Graeco-Roman readers. In his gospel and in the Acts of the Apostles, he paints a picture of Jesus as a majestic, Old Testament prophet. Inspired by the Greek poets, Luke portrays him as a half-divine hero figure. I keep reading.

I find a sixty-year-old dissertation that discusses Luke's and John's portrayals of the break between Judaism and nascent Christianity. Apparently Luke coined the term 'Christian' to describe the spread of the new faith within the Roman Empire. Surprised, I read that Luke himself had been a pagan and his readers were predominantly those wondering whether it was possible to be a contented citizen of the Empire and a Christian at the same time. By contrast, John isn't quite so pragmatic. More than the other evangelists, he is preoccupied with spirituality, the godhead, divine mysticism. The dissertation was written by a J. C. Schulz, who was born in 1916 according to the title page, and who emphasises how John lets Jesus speak in long monologues where he openly proclaims himself divine. John describes how Jewish Christians were expelled first from the synagogue and then from Judaism. But this is more than a theological struggle, the author claims. The fight between the Jews and the Christians is a struggle for political and financial power. In short, for control.

I sit for hours, absorbed in other people's thoughts and interpretations. I'm looking for something that can help me proceed, bring me understanding. But I don't know what I'm looking for, and I don't find it.

When I notice that one of the computer terminals is free, I scurry across the room and beat a scholar wearing a suede kippa to it. The terminal is linked to the library and Institute databases.

I log in using a guest username that's written in felt pen above the screen. Searching the database is simple: I can search by subject, key word or author. And combinations of these.

To start, I type in *shrine of sacred secrets*. I get nine hits. The first is the book written by my father, Llyleworth and DeWitt. A flash of pride washes over me. Then I find a summary of the myth. Then a string of cross-references to Bérenger Saunière, the Dead Sea Scrolls, Varna, the Knights Hospitaller, the Monastery of the Holy Cross, Cambyses, Rennes-le-Château, the Shroud of Turin, Clement III, Ezekiel, the Q manuscript, Nag Hammadi and the Schimmer Institute Library. The other documents about the myth are password protected.

Something about the references stirs up a vague, uncomfortable tingling in the back of my mind. As when you recognise the face of your childhood tormentor waiting in line for the bus.

I flag down one of the librarians and ask whether he knows the password that will give me access to the blocked documents. He asks me to look away while he types in the secret characters. Then he clears his throat understatedly. I look at the screen.

Unauthorized. Level 55 required, say the glowing letters.

A cold chill races through me.

10

Absorbed in my thoughts, I shuffle down the long hallway to my room. The carpet in the corridor is dark green. My footsteps make no noise. I fish the key out of my trouser pocket and let myself in.

I notice it right away.

My stack of Internet print-outs is sitting exactly where I left it, but the piece of grey thread that I stuck in between two of the pages is gone. The little piece of cellophane tape that I stuck to the top of the wardrobe door has come loose. The match I had stuck into the crack on my suitcase is lying on the floor.

This does not scare me. It pisses me off. I'm mad at them, at myself for not realising they're everywhere, even here. Maybe here more than anywhere else. Peter Levi may be getting his pay cheques directly from the SIS for all I know. Maybe he's Michael MacMullin's personal assistant. Maybe Llyleworth is sitting in a room full of monitors and speakers and keeping an eye on me using his surveillance cameras and microphones and laughing at all the lies Peter is feeding me to cover up whatever's in the shrine.

I turn and look at the ceiling and shake my fist at the powers that be just in case they are watching me through some invisible lens.

11

You've got to respect your habits, even the habits that are hard to keep up. I like to take a nap after lunch, even if I haven't eaten lunch. It's a way to turn off my brain.

I switch off the light, pull the beige curtains shut and climb into bed, pull the cool, stiff sheet over me, and curl up into a ball of legs and skin and hair.

I sleep for two hours. My dreams bring me no peace. They're fast paced, frightening, harried. I feel surrounded by disdainful enemies sneering at me. I notice Professor Arntzen and my mother among them, MacMullin and Llyleworth, Sigurd Loland and my father. They whisper, insinuate, sneer, but then pull away and disappear in the dream fog when I try to approach them.

When I wake up, I feel as if I'm full of holes and that

everything inside me is pouring out on to the floor. It takes me forty-five minutes to fully wake up.

Peter Levi is sitting there waiting for me, half hidden in the shadowy bar, when I arrive later in the evening. His eyes reflect the flame from the candle. He raises his cognac glass in greeting. I wave back.

'We can't keep meeting like this,' I joke, taking a seat.

'Did you find anything exciting today?'

'Did you guys?' I counter.

He pretends he doesn't understand.

'I just woke up from a nap,' I say.

'So late in the day?'

'I sleep when I'm tired, not when my watch tells me I should.'

'But then you won't be able to sleep at night,' he points out thoughtfully.

'Not a problem. There'll be plenty of time to sleep when I'm dead.'

He chuckles.

'You said something that interested me,' I say.

'Well, I should hope so.'

'Something about how the Bible was a process. And how the stories were doctored.'

He grabs my forearm. 'I don't like to talk about these things in here. So many ears . . .'

'Why don't we go up to the grove? It was nice there.'

He drains his cognac glass. Without a word we get up and leave the bar. It feels as if a hundred eyes are watching me leave, but when I turn around, no one is looking at us.

12

We stroll along the paved walkway, over the asphalted square and into the grove. Everything is quiet. I'm starting to feel at home under these trees.

'To understand my train of thought,' Peter says as we stroll up the hillside, 'you first have to understand the time period we're talking about. I suppose most people have some idea in their heads of what things were like when Jesus was alive, but it's been tainted by the version in the Bible. And everything in the New Testament revolves around Jesus Christ.'

'And that's not how it was?'

'Jesus lived in turbulent times, and things didn't get any better after his death. The gospels were written a long time after Jesus lived and died. The chroniclers reiterated what they themselves had been told. They paraphrased written sources. But they were children of their times. Coloured by their surroundings and the *zeitgeist*.'

We help each other over the trunk of a fallen tree. The branches are full of healthy-looking leaves, which still seem to think the tree is in great shape. Peter brushes the bark off his trousers before we continue.

'We have to start with the Jewish revolt,' he says, 'Jerusalem's fall and the destruction of the Temple. And the way the Jews saw themselves after that humiliating loss. The most ardent rebels fled to the cliff fortress of Masada. When the Roman soldiers ultimately captured the fortress, they found no one there. Absolutely no one. They had all committed suicide, rather than submit to the Romans. Which is how Masada came to symbolise Jewish honour.'

'Even though they lost?'

'They suffered a defeat, sure, but still a defeat filled with pride and fearlessness. There were too few of them, the opposing force too great. But the failed revolt sowed the seeds of doubt among both the Jews and new Christians. They needed answers. Jerusalem had been destroyed. The Temple lay in ruins. Where was their God? What did He want? What was His intention? Without the Temple as a gathering place, the old clergy lost its power base.'

'But someone was ready.'

'Absolutely. Namely the Pharisees – in other words, the rabbis. They filled the void that the clergy left behind. The rabbis were the ones who led the Jews along their current path.'

'And the Christians?'

'The new Christians were still a part of Judaism. They were even more confused, if that's possible. What had become of the promised Kingdom of God? Where was the Messiah? These were all the questions Mark was seeking to answer. He wrote his gospel in AD 70. Forty years after the crucifixion. He wrote his gospel first, even though it comes second in the New Testament. But he wrote it forty years after the death of Jesus. That's a long time.'

We stop. Peter lights a cigarillo, turns it around and watches the glowing end as he traces circles in the darkness.

'During these years, the story of Jesus was passed down as oral histories and hymns,' he continues. 'In small Christian communities, people gathered around campfires and hearths and passed on what they had been told by others. Some of them modified the stories a little, took out a few things, added a few other things. They told of Jesus' parables and miracles, of his words and deeds. They were sharing memories, but coloured by hopes, dreams and historical aspirations from the past. Facts blended with legends and myths and hymns.'

Somewhere not far away the diesel generator for the irrigation system starts humming.

'Many scholars think that Mark wrote from Rome, others think it was Alexandria or Syria. But everyone agrees that

Mark and his readers were in exile, outside their homeland, that they spoke Greek, and that they weren't all that familiar with Jewish customs.'

'Almost like outsiders?'

He nods pensively. 'In a way. These people were searching for their roots. The Gospel of Mark was written right after the unsuccessful Jewish revolt. Imagine the mood! They were desperate, indignant. They needed new faith, they needed hope. Like Jesus on the cross, Mark's readers felt their God had abandoned them. They were scorned and pushed around.'

'So they turned to Mark for comfort?'

He draws the tobacco smoke down deep and releases it as he speaks: 'Mark viewed himself as a source of inspiration. As someone who could rally the Jews around a new hope. Many of them had suffered physical abuse by the Romans.'

A pleasant breeze flutters through the grove. It brings mild scents that for a brief instant supplant the smell of perfumed tobacco.

'In keeping with the spirit of the times, he presented an image of Jesus as mysterious, mystical and divine. For Mark, Jesus is not a rebel the way many had viewed him up until the revolt. Jesus had a deeper dimension, a trait that led to what religious historians call the messianic secret.'

'Which means . . .?'

'People are supposed to suspect, but not understand, who he is. He shrouds his identity in fog. Only Jesus knows what Jesus must do. His mission on earth is not to perform miracles. At that time, pretty much every other wise man could perform miracles. But only Jesus knew that he was the Son of Man. He came to the Earth to suffer and die, to redeem humanity.'

'No small matter,' I say.

Peter holds his cigarillo between his fingertips and inhales the smoke, his eyes half closed. Down at the Institute I see a light wink off in one room and come on in another. I sense a shadow behind a curtain. Peter pulls out his flask and hands it to me. It's full. I take a swig of the cognac and pass it back. He stares straight ahead, sips it, and hands it back to me again.

He says: 'Matthew had a totally different readership to Mark's. Matthew was a Jewish Christian who wrote his gospel fifteen years after Mark. He had read Mark and incorporated most of it into his own gospel. Matthew's readers were Christians and Jews at the same time. They had fled to the villages north in Galilee or south in Syria. Here, too, the rabbis had assumed a lot of the power. The Christians were in the minority. It was important for Matthew to underscore that Jesus was a Jew, as good as anyone. It was no coincidence that Matthew opened with Jesus' family tree, which goes back to Abraham. Even though it's a paradox that he's following Joseph's lineage, while the whole time Joseph isn't exactly regarded as Jesus' father.'

We chuckle softly.

'Matthew was trying to create a Moses-like depiction of Jesus,' Peter explains. 'In Matthew, Jesus speaks to his people from a mountain, like Moses, and five sermons are ascribed to him, corresponding to the five books of the Pentateuch. I suppose I think Matthew wanted his readers to think of Jesus as an even greater Moses. The Pharisees are so prominent in Matthew because the Pharisees would get Matthew's readers all riled up. Their power increased after the revolt. The Pharisees and the Christians were struggling to control the future of Judaism.'

Peter pauses for a moment and sighs softly. He looks at his cigarillo, crushes the ember between the tips of his fingers and tosses the butt aside.

'Then there was another Jewish rebellion that divided the

Jews from the Christians once and for all,' he says. 'Sixty years after Masada, a popular Jewish revolutionary, Bar-Kokhba, led a new revolt against the Romans. He called himself a descendant of King David and described himself as the new Messiah. The Jews started stirring again. Was he the one they'd been waiting for? Had their Saviour finally come? Many people rallied around the new hero, but not the Christians. They already had their Messiah. Bar-Kokhba led his followers to some caves not far from Masada. The Romans found their hiding place and laid siege to it. Some of the Jews surrendered, others starved to death. Archaeologists recently found forty skeletons of women, children and men in the Cave of Horror. In the Cave of Letters they found letters from Bar-Kokhba saying that he had hoped to stand his ground. It didn't work out that way. The Jews' hope of a new Messiah died with Bar-Kokhba.'

'And the Christians?'

'. . . were still waiting for Jesus to return as he had promised.'

'But nothing happened?'

'Not a darn thing. The hopes about the Kingdom of God became more abstract, more spiritual and less concrete, for both the Christians and the Jews. You could say that Christianity has two founders: Jesus with his warmth and fundamentally simple teachings, then the apostle Paul, who transformed Jesus into a mythological, divine figure and who brought abstract religious and spiritual dimensions to his teachings.'

'But if Jesus was just a political figure, then there goes the foundation of Christianity,' I say.

'And one of the pillars of Western civilisation's cultural heritage,' Peter adds.

We stand there staring out into the darkness as we contemplate these thoughts.

Something starts beeping. At first I don't understand what the sound is, but it's coming from Peter.

'My pager.' He smiles apologetically. He fishes the little device out of an obstinate pocket and squints at the message in the narrow window.

'It's chilly out here,' he says. 'Should we head back? There's just enough time to get something warm to drink before they close.'

With our eyes on the dark path, we cautiously make our way back down towards the Institute.

'Do you think the manuscript in the shrine could reveal something like that? Something that casts our understanding of Jesus in a new light?' I ask.

'It's not an unreasonable assumption.'

'I wonder what it could be.'

'Well,' he says with a little laugh, 'you're certainly not the only one wondering that.'

13

The reception area is warm and inviting, full of sounds – dinner music and the hum of voices from the Study. A telephone rings impatiently. Behind the desk an electronic alarm beeps quietly, urgently.

Peter pushes me into the bar and asks me to order while he ducks out for a second. 'My bladder, you know . . .' he whispers, rolling his eyes. When he returns he has a strange look on his face.

'Is anything wrong?' I ask.

'Not a thing.'

I lower my horns: 'Peter . . . Are you familiar with SIS in London?'

'Of course.'

His admission surprises me. I had expected him to keep playing dumb.

'What do you know about them?'

He raises his eyebrows. 'What do you want to know? They fund a lot of our research. We're working together on a number of projects.'

'Do any of them involve me?'

'I wasn't aware that you were a topic of study.'

'I'm a topic of interest at any rate.'

'For SIS?'

'Definitely.'

'Strange. They're arranging a conference here this weekend. "New Insights into Etruscan Etymology".'

'Strange,' I repeat.

'Why are they interested in you?'

'Surely you already know that. They're after the shrine.'

'Ah.' He doesn't say anything else.

'And I'm starting to see why.'

'Have you ever considered that they might have a legal claim to it?'

I was waiting for that, the sign that Peter, too, is more than a random satellite orbiting my life.

'Perhaps . . .' I say.

'They probably just want to study whatever's in it.'

'Sure.'

'Why so mistrustful?'

'They're trying to trick me, all of them. You too, I'm guessing.'

His lips curl into a grin. 'So this is somehow personal, all of this?'

'Extremely personal.'

The waiter who brought us the coffee and tea comes over with a slip of paper that he discreetly hands to Peter, who glances at the note and sticks it in his pocket.

'Is something going on?' I ask.

He stares down into his glass. 'You're a tough nut, Bjørn Beltø,' he says. It sounds like admiration. And for the first time he almost manages to pronounce my name.

'You're not the first person to say that,' I point out.

'I like you.'

When he finishes his drink, his eyes are tired and distant. Then he surprises me by getting up and wishing me good-night. I had been expecting him to grill me for answers or offer me money, maybe a veiled threat. Instead he shakes my hand, squeezing it firmly.

After he leaves, I sit there drinking my lukewarm tea and watching the people around me — low, boisterous voices, shrouded in smoke and laughter.

Sometimes it feels as if everyone else is just an extra in your life, hired to hang out wherever you are at any given time but not notice you, and all the buildings and landscapes are set designs hurriedly constructed to perfect an illusion.

Tea has an extremely diuretic effect on me. After two cups I have to snake my way through the crowded room, past the emergency exit and out to the men's lavatory, which is spotlessly clean and smells antiseptic. I try to avoid looking at myself in the mirror while I pee.

It's all sheer luck: when I come back out, I just happen to glimpse, through the throng of arms and heads, the waiter talking to three men. I freeze. If anyone had glanced over at me, they would have thought I'd turned into a pillar of salt, completely white and completely motionless.

Through the crowd I see Peter. I see King Kong. And I see my good old pal, Michael MacMullin.

Outside the main entrance I find a rack with bicycles, modern mountain bikes, which are used for getting back and forth between the buildings in the complex. They're not locked.

They're there for people to use. I mean, who would steal a bicycle in a desert?

14

The moon gleams. Everything around me is dark and endless. I sense the mountains in the distance, not with my eyes but from my sense that the darkness is curving. Everything is big and flat and black. It feels like bicycling through thin air. My attention alternates between the sky arching above me and the vibrating puddle of light from the bicycle's headlight, which drags the bike along the asphalt behind it.

I'm freezing. I'm scared. I'm sure this is exactly how an astronaut would feel as he floated farther and farther away from his spaceship.

There are no sounds, no howling coyotes or distant train whistles or chirping crickets. All I can hear inside this cone of silence is the creaking of the bike.

The night has no end. The moonlight is flat and cold. In the pitch-black darkness, the light from my headlight eats the centre line metre by metre.

Towards morning a yellow strip steals over the horizon. I've been trying to bike up a sweat, but my teeth are chattering from the cold.

I stop by a rust-coloured boulder, out of breath and shivering. I sit here on the hard bike seat and enjoy the dawn.

15

When I was eight, my father and Trygve took me into a sauna for the first time. We'd just come back from a long day of cross-country skiing in the freezing cold, and when they invited me into the sauna it was like being initiated into a secret grown-up ritual. I sat there stoically for the first few minutes, gasping for air. Then my dad dumped a ladleful of water on to the glowing stones in the stove.

In the desert, there's no wooden door to dart out through.

The heat surrounds me like a scalding towel. The air is heavy and saturated. The heat tightens around my body. It hurts to breathe. The sun's rays drill right through me, squeezing me.

I bike with mechanical motions. Every rotation of the pedal is a victory. Suddenly I discover that I've climbed off the bike and am walking next to it, pushing it.

The air quivers. The heat is a wall of sticky rubber.

I hear the car long before it comes into view. Which gives me time to push the bike off the road and hide in a ditch. A few minutes later it sweeps past.

A Mercedes with tinted windows.

To be on the safe side, and to gather my strength, I stay there, lying in the ditch. At one time there was a creek here, a long time ago, some time around the Palaeozoic.

I'm thirsty. I didn't bring anything to drink with me. It wasn't this hot when I left. I figured it would take me four or five hours to bike from the Institute to civilisation. I mean, I go without water for four or five hours all the time, right? That's what I was thinking, if you could call that thinking.

Shale and rust-coloured sandstone lie in uneven layers in the dry creek bed. The little channel runs towards a distant, violet escarpment. An insect with long legs jumps right in front of my eyes. It looks like a radioactive mutation, a cross between a beetle and a spider. Well, at least there's something alive out here.

The sun claws at my face and hands and presses impatiently on my shoulders. The sun's rays weigh several kilos. If my mouth weren't so dry, I would spit on a rock to see if the water would sizzle and evaporate.

I push the bike back out on to the road. After only a couple of minutes flames start crawling up my back. I try dismounting and pushing the bike for a bit. The asphalt is boiling. I'm trudging through glue. Heat waves quiver over the road. My heart is pounding. Sweat from my forehead pours down into my eyes. The oxygen is slowly being sucked out of the air. I gasp, have to concentrate so as not to hyperventilate. Through a film of tears I'm on the lookout for a stream, a well, anything that casts a shadow. The horizon closes in, as when you look through a telescope the wrong way, but the thirst hasn't driven me crazy yet. If only I could experience a mirage, a Fata Morgana, a super-colourful Disneyland oasis, but all I see is a golden sea of rocks and heat and mountains in the distance.

16

Kneeling on a slab of rock by the edge of a depression that at one time might have been a water source, I snap out of it. The bike is gone.

I stagger to my feet and stand there wobbling, searching for the road, for the bike, for anything at all that catches my eye. My tongue sticks to the roof of my mouth and makes dry, clicking noises. My head is exploding. I'm nauseous. I vomit, but nothing comes up. I sink to my knees and groan. I glance up. The sun burns white.

That's the last thing I remember.

VI

The Patient

1

THEY DRILLED A red-hot bolt through my skull and painted my face with caustic soda and stuck my hands in pots of boiling lava.

I hear the pulse beats of an electronic device. The sound reminds me of the echo of the ticking from the wall clock at home in that crazy old house I grew up in. Hollow and steady, time breathing. Every hour it would erupt in chimes.

My mother stopped winding it the day my father was buried. Immobile, it bears witness to my father's passing, along with its own internal, quiet death.

2

'Bjørn Beltø, you're a tough nut.'

The light has been dimmed. I cautiously take a breath, release it and inhale again. The pain is smouldering.

Little Bjørn ... time to wake up ... Bjørnaboo ... Little prince ...

I'm lying in a room with an extremely high ceiling. The room smells old. The brick walls are clean and whitewashed. A hairline crack cuts across the ceiling, which has water stains on it.

'Wake up,' the voice says.

The bed is surrounded by a rack supporting a light green, almost transparent curtain.

When I moisten my cracked lips with the tip of my tongue, my skin cracks open from the corner of my mouth to my temples. My face is a porcelain mask that was left in the oven too long, and crackles if anyone bumps it with the tip of a finger.

Little Bjørn, wake up . . .

They've stuck a needle in my forearm. There's a tube hanging down from an IV bag over the bed. Fluid is slowly seeping through the coiled line and into my blood. Truth serum? I wonder. Sodium Pentothal, which lubricates the brake pads of the mind with oil and fat.

The voice: 'Are you awake?'

I don't know whether I'm awake or dreaming. Maybe I'm in a hospital. It looks as if they've crammed a random room full of medical equipment. To take care of me. Or maybe to trick me.

I hold up my bandaged hands. It's like lifting two burning lead weights. I whimper.

'Sunburn,' the voice says.

There's something familiar about it.

I let my head flop to the side.

I see his knees.

His hands folded in his lap.

Like a concerned grandfather, Michael MacMullin is sitting in a chair at my bedside. His eyes scan up and down my body. 'Second- and third-degree burns on your hands, head and neck,' he says. 'Heat stroke, of course. Dehydration. That could have ended really badly.'

I moan. Carefully, I straighten my head. To be honest, it feels as if it *did* end really badly. With stiff motions I try to sit up. My head starts to swim. I hold on tight to the stainless-steel handrails on the bed.

'We only just found you in time,' he says.

He's not armed, but of course that doesn't mean anything. They must surely have more humane ways of doing away with troublesome albinos, such as a hypodermic needle, or maybe they tie us naked to poles out in the desert and give the ants a whistle.

I sense a figure, like a grey shadow, behind the curtain; leaning over slightly, listening.

It can't have been that many days. Time flies when you're having fun. Leaves rustle outside the window. Oak? Aspen? I'm lying too low down to be able to tell. But I have a feeling I'm not in the desert any more. The sun is nicer, the light softer. The air smells of fertiliser and vegetation.

'Where am I?' I croak. The desert coated my vocal cords with sand.

'It's safe here, Bjørn. Don't be afraid.' His voice is pleasant, gentle, warm.

I can't take my eyes off the shadow on the curtain.

'They're giving you morphine for the pain,' he says. 'And a first-rate ointment made from aloe vera. The morphine might make you a little drowsy and dizzy.'

An icy pain slices through me.

He rests his hands lightly on the covers. 'Bjørn, my brave young friend, this has gone way too far. Please, won't you tell me where you hid the shrine?'

As I look at him, without answering, my eyes decide to slide shut all on their own. A little later I hear him leave.

The shadow is gone.

That night I drink about a thousand litres of water. A nurse comes in at regular intervals to check whether I'm all right and whether the morphine is working. It's working great, thanks. My fantasies are delightful. Most of them involve Diane.

In a delirium, I await their next move.

*

It's Diane.

A soft knock on the door wakes me from my dozing early in the morning. I struggle to think of the right words until I realise that *kom inn* in Norwegian and *come in* in English sound exactly the same.

A high voice says: 'How are you doing today?' The tone is warm and cold at the same time – shy, formal, enquiring – as if I've been off at war for two years and have been brought home to my beloved without arms or legs.

Diane walks straight over to the window. She stands there, her back half turned to me. She clenches her fists and presses them against her sternum. From her back I can tell that she's breathing quick and hard. Or crying.

We both wait for the other to say something.

'Where am I?' I ask.

She turns slowly. Her eyes are red around the edges and full of tears. 'Oh, how you look!' she says.

'I went for a walk. In the desert.'

'You could have died.'

'That's what I was afraid of. That's why I ran away.'

She says: 'He's my father.'

She's so cute standing there, angelic.

'Did you hear me? My father!' she repeats.

'Who is?' I ask.

'Michael MacMullin!'

I look down at my hands, the bandages, the fingertips that caressed her.

'He's my father,' she repeats.

I put on my poker face. Not a single feeling shows on the surface. Not a word escapes. I look at her. She's waiting for me to say something apropos. I don't. I'm just trying to understand.

'You mustn't misunderstand,' she says softly. She comes closer. Hugging her fists to her chest. 'It's not what you think.'

I don't make a sound.

'We met each other by chance,' she says. 'You and me. And . . . liked each other. It was chance. I was infatuated with you. I'm sorry . . . They discovered the searches I'd done on the computer,' she explains, and clears her throat. 'Daddy asked for my help.'

Eventually I look her in the eye. 'And you helped them?' I ask.

'You mustn't think that . . .' She doesn't get any farther. The words get stuck in her throat.

Even I'm having trouble breathing. My heart is really pounding. 'Well, that explains why you just had to come back to Norway with me,' I say.

She takes a step towards me and stops. 'Bjorn, it's not like that. It's not how you think. Everything is so hard. I didn't mean to . . . I didn't want to . . . There's so much you don't know, so much you don't understand.'

'You're right about that.'

'It's not like anyone planned it. It's not like I was doing a job for them. You and I . . . that would have happened anyway. The stuff with my father – it just ruined it for us.'

'You could say that.'

'Couldn't you just give it to them? The shrine? You don't need it.'

The way she's standing, Diane reminds me quite a bit of my mother, both her figure and the way she's gesticulating. Weird that I hadn't noticed that before.

'Do you hate me?' She sits down on the edge of my bed and looks deep into my eyes.

'No.'

'Don't you hear what I'm telling you?' she says urgently. It sounds as if she can't stand what she did. 'I helped them so it would put an end to all this. For your sake.'

I digest her words, one by one. Like irresistible canapés

dipped in a slow-acting poison. I study her eyes to see whether she means what she's saying or whether she just has an arsenal of clichés and phrases to use in situations like this.

'But there's something else . . .' she starts.

'Yes?'

'We . . .'

'What?'

'You and me . . .' she starts again.

'What are you trying to say?'

'*Bjorn*, we . . .'

She squeezes her eyes shut so hard that it looks as if she's trying to wring tears out of them.

I encourage: 'Yes, Diane?'

'I . . . can't . . . take . . . it . . . any more!' Every word is a major effort for her.

I rest my bandaged hand on top of hers. We listen to our breathing together, the hum of the machines. Outside I hear a tractor in the distance. The wind rushes through the leaves. Someone is hammering. A moped with a defective silencer starts up and is slowly swallowed by silence.

'Can't you just accept that this is too big for you?' she asks quietly.

'What are you doing here, Diane?'

'They came and got me.'

'From London?'

'They flew me here.'

My pulse echoes in my breath. 'What's really going on?'

Then she does something strange. She starts to laugh, high pitched, loud sobs of laughter, bordering on hysteria. I don't understand what is bothering her, but her laughter is contagious. I smile, and the smile makes my face burst into flames of pain, knocking me out.

When I wake up again, she's gone.

*

Later the nurse comes in with a gigantic hypodermic needle. She chuckles when she sees the frightened look on my face and waves her hand dismissively. 'Medicines,' she exclaims in broken English, and points to my IV bag. 'Is good for you, *oui*?'

'Where am I?'

She inserts the needle into the three-way port on the line and nods comfortingly as she injects the fluid.

'Please . . . Where am I?'

'Yes, yes.'

My eyes follow the yellowish liquid as it slowly slides down towards the needle in my forearm and erases my pain and my questions.

3

MacMullin visits me again later that afternoon. The ointment and the morphine dull the pain, but my skin tingles and itches, and the morphine turns my brain into a watery soup that my thoughts slosh around in.

'Ah, you look so much better!' he exclaims.

He's lying.

He pulls the chair over next to the bed.

I try to sit up. My skin is two sizes too small. Despite the morphine's numbing membrane of indifference, I can't stop myself moaning.

'It will pass,' he says. 'The doctor assures me that the burns are superficial.'

'When can I go home?'

'As soon as you're up to it.'

'I'm not a prisoner?'

He laughs. 'Well, I suppose we're all prisoners. But you're not my prisoner.'

'I've got a number of things to think about.'

He runs his fingers through his silver hair. 'I don't suppose you've ever done anything rashly, have you, Bjørn?'

'I can be spontaneous, if I have enough time to work up to it. Where's Diane?'

'Diane?' His eyes darken. He doesn't say anything. He opens his mouth, but then stops. I try to read the expression on his face.

'I know you're her father,' I say.

He doesn't respond right away. It's as if he has to think about it, but then he says: 'Yes.' Quietly – it sounds like a sigh, as if he's not quite sure.

'That explains a lot.'

He looks sternly into my eyes. 'Listen to me! She never treated you badly. She never betrayed you. Never.'

'She . . .'

He raises his hand dismissively. 'No more,' he says. 'Not now.' A thought that obviously amuses him makes his face light up. He mouths something silently, half smiling. Mesmerised, I watch his internal scene change. It's like eavesdropping on a conversation that a hermit is having with himself. 'We're two pig-headed old mules, Bjørn,' he says.

'Speak for yourself.'

'You don't want to hand over the shrine until you've extracted everything I know.'

'I'm not after everything you know, MacMullin.'

'What do you want, then?'

'Just the truth. About the shrine and what's in it.'

He looks me in the eye, his breath sounding strained. 'That, my friend, is a secret that people have died to protect.'

'Sometimes,' I say, 'you can be a tad melodramatic.'

His startled expression dissolves into happy, rollicking laughter. Insults never bother him, which is terribly inconvenient for those of us who use irony and sarcasm as weapons.

'Strange how two old fogies like us will stand here, each pulling on our end of this rope,' he says. 'I want to have the shrine and protect its secret. And you don't want to hand it over until you find out what I'm hiding.'

'Well, you mustn't think I envy your position.'

'And I'm certainly not asking you to.'

'So tell me, why should I believe you?'

He shakes his head, wondering what I'm getting at.

'You told me about a time machine. Winthrop claimed it has to do with a spaceship. Peter was talking about those flimsy theological theories of his. What am I supposed to believe? You're all lying, the whole lot of you.'

He watches me for a long time. His smile is sly. 'We wanted to confuse you,' he says.

'You succeeded. Congratulations! Mission accomplished. I'm confused.'

'There's a reason for everything we're doing.'

'Well, I promise you, that that much I believe.'

'But try, if you can, to understand. The shrine was never intended to wind up in your hands. You're just a disruption, Bjørn. You shouldn't judge us because we're doing what-ever's necessary to get it back.'

'Whatever's necessary?'

'You know what I mean.'

'Right. You guys wanted to confuse me . . .'

'. . . and give you an answer that no one would believe if you took it to anyone else, but one that was still incredible enough that it would explain all the lengths we were going to to rescue the shrine.'

'Rescue it? Um, hello? I have it.'

'Exactly.'

He gets up and cautiously grasps my bandaged hand. He

looks at me for a long time. In the end I have to look away. He leans down and runs his hand over my hair. His eyes seem watery. It must be the way the light is reflecting.

'Who are you?' I ask.

He looks away. He doesn't answer.

'Really.' I push. 'Who are you *really*?'

'We'll be parting ways soon, for ever. You're going back to Oslo. They say you'll be over the worst of this in a couple of days.'

'They?'

'You'll be given some ointment to take with you, to help with the burning and itching.'

'How nice.'

'We'll arrange a flight for you.'

'We?'

'You're so mistrustful, Bjørn.'

'I'm not used to having everyone out to get me.'

'Maybe you're not what they're after.'

'Ha ha.'

'Maybe they're out to get something you've taken possession of?'

'Maybe I'm willing to give it up,' I say.

'For what price?'

I'm tempted to say ten million kroner, a Ferrari and a week in the Maldives with a Peruvian stripper who's always fantasised about being with an albino, but I make do with this: 'An explanation.'

'What more do you want to know?'

'The truth, not just a piece of it.'

'You haven't figured it out yet?' he asks.

'No,' I say. 'But then some people think albinos are a little slower than other folks.'

He laughs obligingly.

'Is it the Q manuscript?' I ask.

He raises his eyebrows. 'Q? In the shrine? That *would* be a disappointment, although I can't rule anything out.'

I watch him, but he doesn't seem to be planning to tell me anything else.

'There's something else I'd like to know,' I say. 'Something totally different.'

'What now?'

'The connection between the deaths of my father and DeWitt.'

'There was no connection.'

'Knock it off! It all fits together.'

'They died. Neither one was murdered – coincidences, accidents, circumstances. Everyone dies sooner or later.'

'How do you know for sure that they weren't killed?'

'I knew them both. I was even there when DeWitt died. We were on a dig in Sudan. I had a theory that the shrine might have been buried during a military campaign that followed the course of the Nile. Charles was just as convinced that I was wrong, that the shrine was buried in Norway. He tripped. It was a silly infection in a cut. We were in the tropics, far from help. Things went the way they went, but no one killed him. And no one killed your father.'

'You sound so sure.'

'Let bygones be bygones.'

'How did my father die?'

'Ask Grethe.'

'I asked Grethe. She wouldn't say anything. What does she know?'

'Grethe knows most things.'

'What does that mean?'

'You'll have to ask her. Grethe and I . . . we . . . we . . .' For a brief moment he's at a loss for words. Then he seems composed again. 'We were lovers, as perhaps you know. It calmed down as the years went on. Eventually I became her friend.

Everything I know about your father's death, I know because she told me.'

'She wasn't even there when it happened, but I was.'

'She knows. And therefore we know.'

'How can Grethe know anything about my father's death?'

'She was a close friend of your father's.'

'They were colleagues.'

'And friends, close friends.'

A thought sends a shiver through me. 'Lovers?'

'No, but as intimate as two people can be.'

'She never told me that.'

'Why should she?'

I bite my tongue.

'They wrote letters,' MacMullin says. 'We have them in the archive. Thousands of letters in which they put all the thoughts and feelings they had into words. You could say that they used each other, as friends, as therapists. Which is how we know.'

4

That night I don't sleep well. My face burns and stings. Every time I doze off, I'm startled awake by all the dreams knocking and wanting to come in.

I lie there in the darkness thinking about my grandmother. She lived on the ground floor of that rambling old house. At night she looked like a ghostly spectre who used to make a din in the darkest reaches of the house. She would leave her teeth in a water glass on the bedside table and wear a white nightgown that dragged on the ground. When my mother and father went out in the evenings, I never wanted to spend the night in that stuffy, dark bedroom of hers that smelled of camphor and balsa. I preferred the fears of my own room and just knowing that she would hear me if I screamed.

In the daytime, she was a sweet, merry, grey-haired lady. When she was younger, she'd been a beautiful, much-admired singer. It was hard to imagine how that stooped figure had ever ignited men's passions, but old men would come up to her on the street and ask her whether she had performed at the Tivoli theatre after the war. And by that they meant the First World War.

In her bedroom, in the drawer of her bedside table, my grandmother kept a programme from a revue performance from 1923. It contained an oval picture of her. She was unrecognisable. Like a silent movie star, she beamed up at me from the yellowish brown paper. Her maiden name appeared below the picture: Charlotte Wickborg. And if I covered everything except her eyes with my fingers, I could tell it was her. In a bygone era.

I don't know much about my grandfather. There was something crestfallen and nasty about him. He was scrawny and wore trousers that were much too big, which he hoisted way up over his chest with braces. His breath smelled of camphor drops and snuff. And under all those scents a stiff whiff of aquavit, which he drank from bottles he kept lying around in hiding places he thought we didn't know about. Vital deposits in my grandfather's existence.

I don't know when I finally fell asleep, but it's already pretty late in the day when I struggle my way out of the sticky membrane of sleep.

5

His eyes are warm with a faint blaze of understanding. His pupils are as dark as small mountain lakes. Looking into them is like sinking into lukewarm water and resigning yourself to a slow death by drowning, as if the only thing you want in this life is to lose yourself in those eyes and to venerate him for showing you mercy and allowing you to look him in the eye.

I slept, and woke up and looked into those eyes. A piece of myself is still lingering in the lunacy of my dreams.

Michael MacMullin says: 'Well, here we are again.'

He's standing by my bedside, his arms crossed, watching me with a look that I can't characterise as anything other than tenderness. I'm trying to wake up, to snap out of it, to become myself again after sleeping.

'I suppose you're here to bring me another fruit basket?' I say.

'You're a tough nut, Bjørn Beltø.'

Somewhere inside me, something contracts.

Solemnly he says: 'I'm here because I'd like to talk to you.'

It's evening out, or night. The window is dark, a surface so black that the darkness could have been painted on the glass. I still don't know where I am – whether I'm in the infirmary at the Institute or in a hospital in some city somewhere.

'What do you want to talk about?' I ask.

MacMullin turns and walks slowly over to the window. His face is reflected. In the glass his wrinkles disappear, his features are erased and softened, and he looks like a young man.

'Have you ever,' he asks, 'had a secret so serious that you wanted to take it to the grave with you?

I think of my father, my mother and the professor, Grethe.

He's still standing there, facing away from me, and addressing his own reflection. 'I inherited my destiny,' he says.

That must have been a bit of a burden for you, I think. *Maybe that's why you've grown so pompous as the years have passed.*

'My father, and all of my forefathers before him, guarded our secret with their lives.' He turns to face me with a disarming expression: 'Forgive me if I sound melodramatic, but this is very hard for me.'

'If it's any consolation, it hasn't been that easy for me either.'

'How much have you guessed?' he asks, and sits down.

'Not much.'

'I understand you were talking to Peter?'

I don't respond.

'That's fine,' he says quickly. 'He didn't do anything wrong.'

'What's in the shrine?'

His mouth forms a thin line. His eyes house something profound, indefinable.

'I still think it's the Q manuscript,' I say.

'I wonder if it is. Let me expand on one of the things Peter must undoubtedly have divulged to you. When the Knights Hospitaller split in 1192, it was because of a disagreement over a reliquary that later came to be called the Shrine of Sacred Secrets. They referred to it as the Shrine, a reliquary, a sacred item that many people have tried to trace – kings and lords, princes and high priests, Crusaders and popes, both back then and since.'

'Because it contains something valuable?'

'The strange thing is that no one, or at least only a very few, knows what's in the shrine. Aside from the fact that the contents were something fantastic, something sacred. Many have guessed. Some called the shrine the Ark of the Covenant, which is pure fiction, nothing more than medieval mythologising.'

'Is the thing we found at Værne Monastery the Shrine of Sacred Secrets?'

'After the split in 1192, the secret half of the order took control of the shrine. But where could they hide it? Who could they trust? Everyone was after it. They had to hide it as best they could. And then they had a stroke of genius. They joined the brothers who had been sent to Værne Monastery; three monks – called the "Guardians of the Shrine" – tagged along to the distant reaches of Scandinavia, in secret. No one knew their true mission. They were three highly regarded, well-respected monks. One was the Grand Master. The brothers they travelled with did not know they belonged to a branch that had broken off from the Knights Hospitaller. They were on a sacred mission and no one asked questions. Everyone tacitly accepted that those three simply came all the way to Norway and lived there at the monastery, isolated from the other monks. Their only claim to fame, as far as the other monks were concerned, was that they built an octagon, to which they ascribed a sacred power.'

MacMullin looks down. Something in me starts to quiver. We're starting to get to the heart of the matter.

'There was one little snag to this arrangement,' he says. 'Those three monks were the only ones who knew where the shrine was hidden.' He bites his lip. 'That would prove to be disastrous. One of the three died from an illness in the autumn of 1201. The second was attacked and killed by highwaymen on his way to Nidaros in 1203. And the following year, in 1204, the Grand Master set out to return, to make sure that knowledge of the shrine and its hiding place would be passed on to his heir, his son, the next Grand Master.'

MacMullin sighs. As if reflexively, he runs his fingers through his grey hair.

'And how did he fare?' I asked.

'The Grand Master fell ill on the journey. A priest in a church in a northern Italian mountain village tended to him, but he died after just a few weeks. And from that point on the stories differ substantially. Some claim that he left written information. Others think that the information he left his son was brought to the order and to his son by a messenger. The message conveyed was, to say the least, garbled. The message explained that the reliquary was hidden in "the octagon". But no one knew where he was returning from. Do you see? The knowledge that he had been in Norway was lost. No one knew. No one was able to put all this information together and see the big picture.' MacMullin shakes his head and takes a deep breath. 'At some point or other over time, awareness of the three monks' mission was lost. Everything took on an air of mystery, mysticism. The only thing the secret order has had to hold on to for all these centuries is the knowledge that the missing shrine was in an octagon.'

I don't respond. I sense that I'm finally being told the truth, at least parts of it, the parts that MacMullin wants me to hear.

He gets up and again stands over by the window. 'There has been a Grand Master to this day,' he says.

'How do you know?'

He doesn't answer right away. 'No one knows who he is or where he is.'

'So how does anyone know that he exists?'

'He exists because it's inconceivable for him not to.'

'That's the kind of argument a believer uses to prove that God exists.'

'The Grand Master is no god. He's just a person.'

'But hardly just any old person?'

'Like the Grand Masters before him, he is descended from the very first Grand Master.'

'And who is he?'

'The Grand Master's lineage can be traced back to the Bible, to the noble houses of ancient France, to the Merovingian dynasty, the clan of Frankish chieftains who first founded the great empire of the Franks and held on to its crown until the middle of the eighth century.'

'Well, that's quite an impressive . . .'

'But again, Bjørn, in practical terms, no one knows who he is. The Secret Sect has a Council consisting of twelve men. These twelve are the only ones who know his identity and they have pledged their loyalty to him. Even the seats on the Council are hereditary. The blood ties go back for centuries – well, even longer than that – for thousands of years.'

He turns back towards me. I don't say anything.

'The Council does not consist of fanatic believers,' he says. 'It's much more than that. These are powerful men. Like the Grand Master, many of them have royal pedigrees. Some have titles. They own magnificent castles, enormous estates. They're all rich, unbelievably rich. The families' riches can originally be traced back to medieval Church taxes. Some of them are famous: for their wealth, for their accomplishments. But no one outside the Council knows who sits on it. No one knows what the Council is, no one knows what secret the Council is hiding. Hardly anyone even knows the Council exists.'

'So how do you know all this?'

'In 1900, the Council founded and funded the SIS. They wanted to intensify the search for the reliquary. It was the dawn of a new century, a new era. They realised they needed a way to coordinate all the information that was out there in various academic circles, research institutes, universities, among scholars and amateurs. And so, *voila*: SIS.'

He clears his throat and wrings his hands. I realise, without being able to explain how, that he's both telling me the truth and concealing it.

'Which is how we eventually discovered the answer,' he says. 'After eight hundred years. We had known for a long time that there was a legend about an octagon at Værne Monastery. But despite decades of study and fieldwork from the 1930s until a few years ago, it was impossible to find so much as a tiny trace indicating where the octagon might be. Until modern technology came to our aid practically overnight, at least from a historical perspective. Archaeological Satellite Survey Spectro-Analysis. We gained access to satellite photographs last year that clearly and plainly showed us where the octagon at Værne Monastery was. Just like that.' He snaps his fingers. 'A metre and a half underground.' He chuckles softly. 'Can you imagine how excited we were? After eight hundred years we finally had a chance to recover the reliquary, to open it, to remove the wooden case and reveal the golden shrine, to open the golden shrine and find its contents.'

He's breathing heavily through his nose.

'The rest was easy,' he continues. 'We secured a permit to excavate. You must remember that the Council possesses unlimited resources, money, contacts ... The Royal Norwegian Office of Cultural Heritage is a friend of the SIS, as was your father, as is Professor Arntzen. But not even they know a fraction of what I've told you here this evening. You've been granted quite a privilege.'

'My profoundest thanks.'

Some thought makes him chuckle, but his laughter is directed inward. I don't move. It's as if I have no right to be here, as if the slightest sound, the slightest movement, from me will startle him into silence.

'We wanted to do things on the up and up,' he says. 'So obviously we did not oppose having a Norwegian inspector assigned to the dig, an associate professor. Honestly, we didn't really think about him at all. Our contacts assured us that he wouldn't cause any trouble, that he was an amenable and agreeable young man, someone we hardly needed to give a second thought to.'

'Well, I suppose you were wrong about that.'

MacMullin gives me a serious look and then does something unexpected: he winks at me and thumps me gently on the shoulder with his fist. 'You can say that again, my friend. We were wrong about that.'

A nurse comes in with a bedpan, but turns and goes back out again the instant she spots MacMullin.

'I still don't understand what's in the shrine that's so unbelievably valuable,' I say. 'Or is it just the value of the gold itself that everyone wants? Is that all it is?'

'The shrine is just the packaging, the wrapper.'

'So . . .'

'It's the contents we want, Bjørn, the contents.'

'Which are . . .?'

'Information.'

'Information?' I repeat.

'Information, knowledge, words.'

'A manuscript?'

'Which is only valuable in the right hands.'

'Which are yours?'

'Not even mine. I just hold the key to understanding it.'

'I still don't understand what you're getting at.'

'Think about it. A manuscript!' He sits down again.

'So it is the Q manuscript?' My question comes out like a sigh. I sound so disappointed. After all I've been through, I was hoping for something a little more tangible: Jesus' crown of thorns, a piece of the cross.

'A manuscript,' he repeats softly, reverently. 'Handwritten, passed down, but if it's not interpreted correctly, the manu-

338

script is nothing more than a two-thousand-year-old historical artefact. The manuscript must be read by the right eyes in order to be understood.'

'Two thousand years,' I repeat.

'For the thousand years before the Knights Hospitaller took charge of it, the manuscript was well looked after. The Grand Masters personally stored it in their castles and churches until the fourth century, when the shrine was hidden in the Monastery of the Holy Cross. We know that several attempts were made to steal the shrine. Fear that someone would eventually succeed was probably the reason that the Knights Hospitaller got involved. A disagreement among the Knights about the fate of the manuscript resulted in a schism within the order.'

'The manuscript, what does it say?'

As he sits there, MacMullin's face is almost translucent. I see a network of minute capillaries beneath his skin. I feel as though, if the light were different, I could see right through him. He opens his mouth so that he can breathe more easily. He has a secret that he's having a hard time letting go of.

I say: 'Two thousand years . . . Can I guess? This has something to do with Jesus, right? The historical Jesus.'

His lips tilt into a smile. 'You've definitely been talking to Peter.'

'And now you want me to believe that Peter wasn't doing your bidding?'

MacMullin stares at me.

'And that he didn't disclose to me precisely what you wanted him to disclose?' I persist. 'That he didn't pump me full of facts and half-truths at your bidding?'

With a coy expression, MacMullin shakes his head. He makes a tsk-tsk sound with the tip of his tongue. But he still doesn't address my allegations.

'I think you're enjoying this game,' I say. A hint of anger has sneaked into my voice.

'Game?'

'Wild-goose chases, lies, innuendos, elaborate shows of secretiveness ... It's all some kind of game to you, a competition.'

'In which case, you're a worthy adversary.'

'Thanks, but you never explained the rules of the game.'

'True. But you haven't fallen for any of our tricks. I like that.'

He presses his fingertips together. 'My young friend, have you ever asked yourself the question: who was Jesus Christ?'

'Nope,' I say, a little faster than he was expecting.

'Who was he really?' He watches me. 'God's only begotten son? The Saviour? The Messiah, King of the Jews? Or was he a philosopher? An ethicist? A rebel? A disciplinarian? A politician?'

Surely he doesn't expect me to respond to that. And I don't.

'Some would say he was all that and more,' he says.

'I don't understand where you're going with all this. Peter's already gone over all this with me, chapter and verse. You don't need to repeat it. Get to the point.'

My impatience doesn't seem to affect him.

'Why do you think,' he asks, 'the crucifixion is the single event in human history that made the biggest impression on us?'

'I have no idea,' I practically snarl. 'And, honestly, it's not something I really care to know, either.'

'But have you ever thought about it? Was it the brutality of the crucifixion? Was it because God sacrificed his son? Or because Jesus let himself be sacrificed? For the sake of man? For your sake and mine? For the salvation of our souls?'

'MacMullin, I'm not a believer. I've really never thought about it.'

'Still, you must have some thoughts on the matter. What is it about the crucifixion that created a religion?'

'Maybe it's because Jesus rose from the dead?'

'Bingo! Exactly. Everything begins with the crucifixion. Our Western cultural heritage begins with the crucifixion. And the resurrection.'

I'm trying to interpret his expression – what's his point, where's he going with all this?

'The crucifixion . . . Try to picture the whole thing, Bjørn . . .' His voice is frail, whispering, his eyes filled with images that only he can see: 'Jesus is force-marched to Golgotha by his Roman guards. He's exhausted. The skin on his back is shredded from whippings. The crown of thorns tears at his skin, causing blood to mix with his sweat, tracing light red streaks down his cheeks. His skin is wan, his lips chapped. The spectators cheer derisively. Shrill, contemptuous voices scream at him. A few people cry out of compassion, look away. The smells . . . the scents from the fields and groves of trees mingle with the rank stench of the sewers, of urine, sweat, reeking goats, donkey manure. Jesus carries the cross-beam that his hands are tied to on his shoulders. He falters under its weight. Occasionally he falls to his knees, but the soldiers yank him back on to his feet, brutally and impatiently. When they meet Simon of Cyrene, the soldiers force him to carry the cross for him. A little later they pass a group of crying women. Jesus stops to comfort them. Can you picture it? Can you imagine what it must have been like? The atmosphere is charged, electric . . . Once they reach Golgotha, Jesus is given wine mixed with soothing, numbing myrrh. But he takes only a small sip.'

MacMullin stops; his eyes are distant.

I lie still in my bed.

'Then they nail him to the cross,' he says.

'Yes,' I say eventually, to fill the silence.

MacMullin clears his throat before continuing: 'Someone carved his name into the cross, "Jesus, King of the Jews". While he's still hanging there, on the cross, his face contorted with pain. The soldiers divvy up his clothes by drawing lots. Imagine it: they divvied up his clothes, while he was hanging there, nailed up like a sacrifice, following everything with his eyes. They divvy up his clothes among themselves. Then they sit there guarding him. At one point, he cries out in despair to his father and asks him to forgive them. Exhausted, his voice barely audible, he addresses his mother Mary, who is being comforted by three women, including Mary Magdalene. Spectators, priests and scribes – yes, even the two thieves who are being crucified on either side of Jesus – start taunting him and daring him to save himself from his predicament. Then, Bjørn, then a darkness falls over the land. Maybe the clouds rolled in, maybe the sun darkens. Jesus yells: "My God! My God! Why have you forsaken me?" The wind picks up. Or maybe the heat trembles lifelessly over the ground. We don't know. Someone brings a sponge with vinegar, attaches it to a stick and lets him drink. Jesus says: "Father, into your hands I commit my spirit." And then he dies.'

MacMullin glances at the clock. Without looking at me, he gets up and goes over to the door. It's heavy. The wood is decorated with a carved floral pattern.

'Where are you going?' I call after him.

He opens the door and turns to face me.

Confused, I ask: 'Wasn't there something else?'

'Something else?'

'Why did you tell me all this?' I ask.

'Bjørn, think about this . . .'

He hesitates, staring off into space.

'. . . what if Jesus never died on the cross?'

Part of my brain understands what he's saying. Another part gums up seconds before he speaks those words and can't quite keep up with him at this unexpected turn.

'Huh?' I say, even though I heard what he said.

He shuts the door quietly behind himself and leaves me to my questions and the night.

6

At some given point in a person's life, is there a turning point – an instant when one event shines the light of understanding, illuminating everything that's happened to you so far in your life and lighting up the path ahead?

Life is a circle. The beginning and end of life are connected at one point, which religions use as leverage for all they're worth.

For the Maya, time was a circle of repetitions. The Stoics believed that the universe would perish, but that a new universe would arise from the old one.

I find something comforting in that.

But for the Christians, time is a straight and unalterable line that leads right towards Doomsday.

If you elevate all this to a cosmic perspective, maybe they're all correct.

It can be tricky in this kind of unending cycle for a poor sunburned guy with peeling cuticles and an expired monthly tram pass to find his rightful place.

There are so many riddles. I wasn't meant to figure them out, which doesn't really matter that much. I don't really care.

7

Dawn. The fields are pieced together in a supple patchwork, rectangles of subdued colours in a puzzle of ochre and green, yellow and grey. The hills are gentle, rolling. Patiently and modestly, the farmers have tamed the countryside and breathed life into the soil. But there's something defiant and stubborn about this lushness. The landscape has fought back, resisted. Rock juts through the farmland like tumours. Sharp cliffs shove the earth aside. Rocky wounds tear up the fields.

I survey the countryside through a window, a window in a fortress, a medieval fortress of reddish-grey stone. I suppose there are those who would call this a castle. The window ledge is so deep that I sit in it.

The castle is on an overgrown ridge. I have no idea where I am. I'm guessing Tuscany or maybe the Spanish highlands? Alternatively maybe it's an asylum where everything that happens to me, everything I'm seeing and experiencing, is happening in my head. At the moment, that latter alternative appears to be the most likely. And the most attractive.

8

'Where am I?'

MacMullin meets my question with a slightly raised eyebrow. He's standing in the doorway. I'm still on the deep window ledge. I've been sitting here for several hours now, but the countryside has not revealed any of its secrets to me.

'You've made it out of bed, I see. I'm glad to see you're on the path to recovery.'

'Thanks. Where am I?'

'In Rennes-le-Château.'

Something in me sinks.

Rennes-le-Château. Ladies and gentlemen, the show is about to begin. Yet another section of the stage curtain has been pulled back, the actors are waiting in the wings, but first our esteemed author has to finish writing the play.

MacMullin shuts the door and comes into the room. 'In the eastern Pyrenees, in southern France.'

'I know where it is,' I say quietly. 'The priest's village.'

'You have a good memory.'

'What am I doing here?'

'You were brought here.'

'How? Why?'

'On my private plane.'

'I don't remember that.'

'You were unconscious.'

'For how long?'

'A little while. They felt they had to give you some sort of anaesthetic, something to help you relax after we found you in the desert. You really were on death's doorstep.'

'So I was drugged. Again.'

'We didn't have any choice.'

'You guys have a really nasty little habit of doing that.'

'It was for your own good.'

'Why was I brought here?'

'The infirmary at the Institute isn't really anything to write home about.'

'But why here?'

'We could have brought you to a private hospital in the nearest city, or London, or Oslo for that matter. But we just went ahead and brought you here, because I really wanted to invite you here to Rennes-le-Château, to my home. You'll understand why soon.'

'What kind of building is this?'

'To be perfectly frank, it's a castle.'

'Your own private little castle, huh?'

'An old Crusader castle, actually. It's been in my family for some time.'

'I know what you mean,' I say. 'My family has a few medieval castles lying around, too.'

Later MacMullin follows me out of the room, down a dark corridor and up a broad granite staircase. We walk slowly. He's supporting me under one arm.

At the top of the stairs he opens a thick door, and then we find ourselves on a roof, in a narrow passageway surrounded by a parapet topped with towers and spires. The view is spectacular. The air is sultry and full of scents.

We gaze out at the scenery. 'Beautiful, isn't it?' he asks.

He points toward the south east. 'That mountain you see over there is called Le Bézu. There's a medieval fortress there where the Knights Templar used to hang out and train. There are hundreds of churches around here. Many of them were erected on sacred ground. There are reported to be forgotten graves containing apostles, prophets and saints, hundreds of them. To the east of us,' he turns a bit and points, 'lay the ruins of the Château de Blanchefort. The fourth Grand Master of the Knights Templar, Bertrand de Blanchefort, lived there in the twelfth century.'

'Well then, I guess if you ever decide to get rid of the castle your estate agent could safely call this a well-established neighbourhood,' I say.

MacMullin chuckles politely. 'In the Middle Ages, this area was practically overpopulated,' he says. 'Some estimates say that close to thirty thousand people lived here in the area around Rennes-le-Château. The region was close to the Mediterranean and the trade routes, close to Spain and Italy, and, well, in a part of France that was quite centrally located relative to most things.'

'Are you planning to offer me a deal on the castle? Or are you going somewhere with all this?'

MacMullin walks over to the wall and sits down in one of the arrow slits. 'In the 1960s, a French magazine published a story that piqued the interest of readers who were able to read between the lines,' he explains. 'The article helped contribute to the authors of a bunch of pseudo-historical documentaries trying to guess the answers to the riddles this place was hiding. These books have led to an increasing number of tourists to the region.'

'Riddles?'

'The magazine told the story of Bérenger Saunière.'

'The priest . . .'

'A thirty-three-year-old man who came here to Rennes-le-Château as the village's new priest in June 1885.'

'And what was the deal with him?'

'There was a mystery about why he wound up here, in a remote village with only a few hundred souls. As a student he had mapped out a magnificent future for himself. Something must have happened. Since he was relegated to this outpost it seems likely that he provoked one of his superiors.'

'Well, it's pretty nice here, actually.'

MacMullin leans against the wall. 'In the years between 1885 and 1891, Saunière had a modest income, just enough to get by respectably. After all, there wasn't much for him to spend his money on here.' He glances out over the desolate terrain. 'Saunière was a dedicated priest. He started studying the local history with the help of a priest from the neighbouring village, Abbé Henri Boudet in Rennes-les-Bains.'

MacMullin points to show me where Rennes-les-Bains is located. A cloud darkens the hillside.

'Saunière had been wanting to fix up the dilapidated church for a long time. The church dated from 1059, but had been built on the foundations of an earlier church from the sixth

347

century. Saunière began his renovations in 1891. He borrowed a small sum from the village coffers and set to work. One of the first things he did was to remove the altar stone, which revealed two balusters, one of which was hollow. Inside the cavity, he found four rolled parchments inside sealed, hollowed-out wooden tubes. Two of the parchments were said to contain genealogies. The other two were said to be documents written in 1780 by Saunière's predecessor, the Abbé Antoine Bigou. Bigou was also priest to the Blanchefort family, one of the largest landowners in the area prior to the French Revolution. Bigou's texts were from the New Testament, transcriptions, but the documents were bizarrely garbled. There were no spaces between the words and completely superfluous letters were italicised and strewn through the text, seemingly at random, as if the documents contained a hidden message. Some of these apparently coded texts have proved to be indecipherable, even using computers. Saunière couldn't understand the text or the codes either. But he did understand that he had found something that might be important. He brought the parchments to his superior, the Bishop of Carcassonne, who took one look at them and sent him on to Paris to see his superiors at his own expense. Saunière spent three weeks in Paris. What happened there remains unclear, but the poor village priest was granted access to the innermost circles. Rumour has it that he began a relationship with the celebrated opera singer Emma Calvé. She called on him here in the village several times in the following years. After his stay in Paris, he returned to Rennes-le-Château and continued renovating the church. What's inexplicable, however, is how well off the village priest suddenly was. He no longer had any trouble financing his church renovations. He entered into a lengthy correspondence with people both in France and abroad. He engaged in business transactions. He had a modern road built to Rennes-le-

Château. He bought exclusive porcelain, collected valuable stamps, and amassed an impressive library. He installed a zoo and an orange grove. He lavished the parishioners in his village flock with money and delights. He received distinguished visitors from France and abroad. Believe it or not, by the time of his death in 1917, he had managed to spend the equivalent of several million pounds. Where did all that money come from? He refused to say. A suspicious new bishop tried to transfer him, but Saunière did something unheard of. He refused. He became the victim of malicious accusations and was suspended from his post. But then the Vatican itself stepped in and reinstated him as village priest. He had a stroke on 17 January 1917. He died a few days later. But people in this village are still asking themselves: where did his sudden wealth come from?'

MacMullin stands up and moves towards me.

'I think you can see a connection,' he says. 'And you're asking yourself: what was in those parchments he found in the hollow baluster under the altarpiece? What was in the documents that he took to Paris – before money turned the once impoverished village priest into a prosperous and secretive man?'

'Search me,' I say. 'But you're right that I am asking myself some questions.'

'I guessed as much. You're curious by nature.'

'And you have no doubt that you know the right answer?'

He grabs my arm, as if he's about to faint, but lets go of it again a second later.

'But you're not planning on telling me what it is?' I ask.

'The parchments contained a coded genealogy, a pedigree, a family tree if you will, that traced the royal line all the way back to the start of our current calendar. And the parchments described how to interpret the revelations about the bloodline.'

'A royal family tree?'

'Name by name, king by king, queen by queen, country by country, for century after century.'

'Does that have anything to do with what you were hinting at last night? About Christ's crucifixion?'

'That,' he said, 'would not be an overly unreasonable assumption.'

With a firm grip on my arm he leads me back to the door. 'But the documents that were found in the church in 1891 contained only one set of information,' he says. 'We don't know its source. We don't know who was sitting on the information or how it was passed down, but it did give us our first insights into what had become of the Shrine of Sacred Secrets. It gave us the key to the quest, which is why SIS was founded nine years later as a direct result of the coded information. Finally we had some tangible leads to follow. We knew more about where we should be looking for the shrine and the octagon. But it still took us almost one hundred years to succeed.'

He locks the door with an impressive key that makes the lock mechanism emit a rusty creak.

'Strictly speaking,' I say as we descend the stairs, 'it seems a little premature to say that you've succeeded.'

9

My mother always dragged me to church with her on Christmas Eve. It was always when I was in the middle of watching a cartoon on the Swedish channel. She would walk in humming, with her shiny nylon legs, surrounded by a cloud of perfume and laughter, and start getting ready to go to church. 'We must cling to tradition,' she used to say. She was very partial to clichés. She never understood that cartoons were a far more important tradition to me than church. I'm not saying that, if it was snowing and the church bells were chiming and the lanterns were flickering along the path through the cemetery, the experience didn't put me in a bit of a Christmassy mood. But not as much of one as the cartoons did.

The same thing happened again before every summer holiday, but then the elementary school was responsible. Year after year they forced us to attend church services. I've never been a Christian, but under that mighty altar, with Jesus' arms spread wide, hypnotised by the rush of the organ and the minister's chanting voice and warnings, I would obediently put my childish hands together in prayer. At moments like that the believer in me woke up; a little freak of nature who would take comfort wherever he could find it.

The religious ecstasy would last for about fifteen minutes, then summer started.

Later on I found other ways of soothing that little freak of nature's longings. When I grew up I would find the same comfort between a woman's thighs, a desire to be surrounded by the warmth and tenderness of someone who cared about me and wished me well, as pathetically simple as that is.

I lie quietly in bed. It's dark. My face and hands burn and itch.

The room is big and empty and quiet.

A thought buzzes around in my head like a fly that never settles down. The thought is this: is there only one truth?

I don't want to believe in MacMullin's conspiracies. They're too much for me, too unrealistic: the crucifixion, Crusaders, Templars, medieval fortresses, dogmas, mystic Freemasons, unbelievable fortunes, hidden treasures, timeless secrets . . . These things have no place in reality, not in my reality, at any rate. Did they really manage to keep something secret for two thousand years? I don't think that's possible.

Somewhere in the castle, almost inaudibly, a heavy door closes.

Layer by layer MacMullin is peeling away the lies and wild-goose chases and revealing the core of the matter. But maybe even the core is an illusion?

I don't know whether MacMullin is lying. I don't even know whether *he* believes what he's saying. Or maybe he really is telling the truth.

I always used to feel the same way about the minister. I would sit there on that hard wooden pew staring up at the pulpit and I would wonder whether even he really believed all the stuff he was saying. Or did doubt creep up on him as well, leaving in tatters his hope that everything on heaven and earth really was the way he said it was in his preaching.

10

I doze off for a while and I wake up when the door opens and I hear Diane's light step behind the curtain.

I must be getting better. My first thought is that she's here for a quickie. I push myself up on to my elbows. I'm more than happy to play the part of the helpless patient at the mercy of the lusty nurse. In my imagination, I'm an enthusiastic adherent of even the most obscure fetishes.

But her face looks sad. She plops down on to the chair, not wanting to look me in the eye. Something is bothering her.

'Diane?'

'We have to talk.'

I wait a while until she continues.

'Daddy said that . . .' she starts. Then she stops.

Moving cautiously, I get up and get dressed. Without looking at me, she takes my hand, tenderly, as if she's afraid of hurting me, and together we walk out of the room, down the broad staircase and out into the grove of trees in the courtyard.

It's dark. A lantern has lured a swarm of insects and isn't letting them go. The breeze is cool and soothing on my skin, which tingles and smoulders the whole time. I think: she's going to tell me something I don't want to know.

She leads me down a gravel footpath to a bench by a decorative pond where the algae have long since gained the upper hand and the fountains have stopped working. The water smells putrid.

'*Bjorn*,' she whispers. 'There's something I have to tell you.'

There's something unfamiliar in her voice.

I take a seat on the bench. She stands in front of me with her arms crossed. She looks like the beautiful, white statue 'The Solitary Nun' in the cloister garden at Værne Monastery.

Suddenly I know what she's going to say. She's pregnant!

'I've thought about this,' she says. Her breathing sounds fragile. 'First I didn't want to, but it's only proper. That I just say it, that you understand.'

I still don't respond. I've never pictured myself as a father. It's a strange thought. We'll have to get married, I think. If she'll have me. And she will, won't she? I picture the happily married couple, Bjørn and Diane, surrounded by drooling, toddling kids.

She had let go of my hand, but now she sits down and grasps it again, a little too hard. *Will we live in Oslo or London?* I wonder. I wonder whether it will be a boy or a girl. I look at her flat stomach. My next thought: how can she know she's pregnant after such a short time?

'Sometimes,' she says, 'you find out things you never wanted to know.'

'Although you never know that until it's too late,' I say. 'Because it's only once you know them that you realise you didn't want to know.'

I don't really think she's listening to me, not to mention that that came out sounding rather cryptic.

'It's about my mother,' she says.

A frog starts croaking over in the stagnant water. I try to see where it is, but it's just a sound.

'What about her?' I ask.

Diane sobs. The frog issues a tentative response from over in the pond.

'It's weird that I had to meet you to find out who my mother is,' she says.

'What do I have to do with your mother?'

She closes her eyes.

'I thought your mother was dead,' I say.

'I thought so too.'

'But?'

'They never let me get to know her. She didn't want to know about me.'

'I don't understand. Who is she?'

'You may have some idea. You know her.'

I try to read it from her face.

At first I think: my mother?

Then: Grethe?

'MacMullin was with Grethe,' I exclaim. 'At Oxford.'

She doesn't say anything.

Now my breath is the one that catches and jerks. 'Is Grethe your mother?'

The frog has moved. Now the croaking is coming from a completely different direction. Or maybe another frog is finally responding to him?

'There's more,' she says. 'I'm my father's only daughter, his only child.'

'So?'

She shakes her head.

'Well, that doesn't matter, not when it comes to us, at least not in my mind.'

'It means everything. Everything.'

'You're going to have to explain.'

'You know, Daddy isn't . . .'

Pause.

'Isn't what?' I ask.

'When he dies, I'll . . .'

Pause.

'Yes? When he dies, you'll what?'

She stops. 'I can't help it, believe me. But that's how it is.'

'I don't understand.'

'It's just never going to work,' she says.

'What won't work?'

'You. Me. Us.'

'Rubbish, there's nothing we can't work our way through.'

She shakes her head.

'I thought you were serious,' I say.

'You know . . . When we met, you were so different, so refreshing, so totally different from all the men I've ever met. What I felt then was . . . something real, something I've never felt, never in that same way. But then Daddy came along and ruined everything.'

'But you kept going. You flung yourself at me.'

'Not to please *them*. The opposite, to spite them. Try to understand, Bjorn. If I used you, it was for my own sake, out of defiance, because you mean something, because I wanted to show *them* that I wasn't part of their game. But still . . .' She shakes her head.

'We can make it work, Diane. We can put it behind us.'

'It will never work. They ruined everything for us.'

'All the same, couldn't we . . .'

'No, Bjorn.' She leaps up suddenly. 'That's just how it is,' she says. She doesn't look at me. 'I'm sorry.' Our eyes meet and she gives me a brief, sad smile.

Then she turns on her heels and walks quickly down the path. The last I hear of her are her footsteps crunching in the gravel.

When my father died there was a lot of back and forth between my mother and the funeral home about whether the casket would be open for the memorial in the chapel. The undertaker had advised us to go with a closed casket so that we could preserve the memory of him the way he was. It wasn't until my mother refused to go along with that that the undertaker was forced to become unpleasant.

'Ma'am, he fell thirty metres, right on to a pile of rocks.'

My mother didn't seem to understand. She wasn't quite herself. 'Can't you put some make-up on him?' she suggested.

'Ma'am, you don't understand. When a body hits rocks after a thirty-metre fall . . .'

In the end, it was an open casket.

The chapel was decorated with flowers. An organist and a violinist played hymns. Four men from the funeral home stood by a back door. They wore professional expressions and looked as if they might burst into tears at any moment. Or laughter.

The casket sat on a platform in the middle of the room.

Adagio. Delicate tones in the silence, subdued sobbing. The sadness and the music intertwined.

They had folded his hands, which had not been injured, and stuck a bouquet of wild flowers between his fingers. What little was visible of his face shone though an oval hole that they'd cut in the silk sheet that surrounded his head. To

356

protect us. They must have worked on him for a long time, trying to recreate his appearance with cotton and make-up. Still, he was unrecognisable. That wasn't my father lying there. When I touched his fingers they were stiff and ice cold. I remember that I thought: it's like touching a corpse.

11

Morning. The light is dim. The colours on the hillsides haven't woken up yet.

Numb with fatigue, I sit with my elbows on the window-sill. I've been staring out into the vast, black emptiness all night, watching the darkness dissolve into a pale shimmer and the bats dancing in front of the stars. Ever since dawn the songbirds have been flitting and twittering in the tree outside the window. Like hyperactive dots, they've been chasing insects way up into the air. Down in the yard, a greyish-black cat stops and stretches luxuriously. A sleepy flatbed lorry chugs its way along the country road laden with fruit and vegetables.

Diane is gone. I watched her leave. Someone carried her suitcases out to a van in the middle of the night and drove her away. I followed the slow globe of light for several minutes until it was swallowed by the night.

12

'Has it ever struck you that nothing in this life is quite the way you think it is?'

He's sitting in the firelight by the fireplace in the library. It's evening. A Neanderthal with clenched jaws and shifty eyes came and fetched me from my room and led me, in silence, down the castle corridors to what MacMullin with exaggerated modesty refers to as the 'Reading Nook'.

The walls of this grand room are lined with books, thousands and thousands of old books, from floor to ceiling; a mosaic of golden-brown spines and bindings with ornate titles in Latin and Greek, French and English. The room smells of dust and leather and paper.

MacMullin has poured two glasses of sherry. We clink glasses without a word. The logs in the fireplace spark and crackle.

He clears his throat. 'I hear you spoke to Diane.'

I gaze into the flames. 'Grethe is her mother.'

'Indeed.'

'We have a lot in common, you and me.'

'I'm sorry it had to end this way,' he says. 'With you and Diane and . . . everything . . .'

'Why is your name MacMullin?' I ask.

He looks at me, surprised. 'What would you rather have it be?'

'You're descended from an old French family, so why do you have a Scottish name?'

'Because I like the sound of it.'

'So it's just a nickname?'

'I have so many names.'

'Really? Why? And why Scottish?' I ask again.

'That's the name I like best. One of my ancestors, Francis the Second, married Maria Stuart, who grew up in the French court and had strong ties to France. I'm sure you know your history. Before he suddenly up and died, he had an affair with a noble lady from the powerful Scottish MacMullin clan.'

He takes a sip of sherry. A membrane of mutual uncertainty vibrates between us. MacMullin is lost in his own world. My eyes and attention set off to explore this grand room.

In the end, the silence is too much and I'm forced to speak. 'You wanted to see me?' I ask.

He looks me in the eye with a playful twinkle. As if he's trying to see just how far he can stretch my patience.

'Yesterday,' he says, 'I told you about the parchments that the priest Bérenger Saunière found as he was fixing up the old church.'

'And what will you tell me tonight?' I ask, laughing, challenging him. I feel as if I've been transported into *A Thousand and One Nights*, although of course I'm sure Scheherazade was a bit more appealing to look at than MacMullin.

'Tonight,' he says, 'I want to tell you what the parchments revealed.'

'Something about a family tree?'

'A genealogy, and something more.' MacMullin takes a deep breath, holds it and then exhales through his lips. It sounds like a single long sigh. 'Hints about what actually happened,' he says.

'Actually?'

He rubs his hands forcefully, as if he's trying to take off a pair of invisible gloves. 'The other day I told you something that must have been hard for you to accept.'

'You mean about the crucifixion?'

MacMullin doesn't respond right away. It's as if he's reluctant to give away anything at all.

'The crucifixion of Christ,' he says, 'was symbolic for both history and religion. Christianity is based on the dogma that Jesus arose from the dead.'

Leaning forward in my chair, I ask, 'MacMullin, what faith are you?'

He pretends not to hear my question. 'If Jesus didn't die on the cross, and if the resurrection is false, well then, who was he?'

'A rebel, a preacher, and a great humanist philosopher,' I suggest. 'We've been over all this.'

'But not a divine being,' MacMullin adds. 'Certainly not the Son of God.'

'So you must be a Jew?'

'My faith,' he says, 'has no bearing on this. I do not belong to any church. I believe in a Force that cannot be described in words or captured in a book. And which is certainly not the property of priests or prophets.' He shakes his head. 'But we can delve into what I believe, and why, another night.'

'Explain to me,' I say, 'why you believe Jesus survived the crucifixion.'

MacMullin holds his sherry glass up to the light and rotates it, watching the light refract in the prisms in the crystal. 'I'm tempted to ask you the opposite.'

'You mean, why did he die?'

'Or rather, why did he die so quickly.'

'Quickly?'

He sets his glass down on the low, round table between us. 'There isn't much in the gospels to substantiate the fact that the injuries Christ suffered, really just flesh wounds, would result in a rapid death.'

'He was crucified!' I exclaim. 'Nailed to a cross! He suffered. Why wouldn't he die quickly?'

MacMullin presses the tips of his fingers together. 'Every believer, every doctor, every historian is entitled to his own opinion. But it's a fact that unless you're very ill, or suffer serious internal injuries, it takes a long time to die. The body is a robust organism. All its functions are geared towards survival.'

'As far as I recall, Jesus was hanging on the cross for hours, right?'

'That doesn't mean anything. People who were crucified had to wait days for death to claim them, often many days.

Unless the guards were merciful enough to break their bones or finish them off with a spear.'

I try to imagine their agony.

'In order to understand my chain of thought,' he continues, 'you have to understand how the Romans carried out their crucifixions. Everything followed specified routines.'

'I'm not really sure I want to hear about this.'

'In the summer of 1968, a group of archaeologists under the direction of a man named Tzaferis found four cave-tombs at Giv'at ha-Mivtar north of Jerusalem. There were thirty-five skeletons in the tombs. The timing of the deaths could be dated to some time between the second century BC and AD 70. Every single skeleton had a gruesome tale to tell. A three-year-old had had an arrow shot into his skull. A teenager and a woman who was a little older had been burned to death. A woman who was about sixty had been struck by something, which crushed her skull. Another woman, who was in her thirties, died in childbirth; the remains of the foetus were still in her pelvis. But the most interesting was a man who had been crucified.'

'Jesus?'

'No,' MacMullin says, 'that would have caused quite a stir. This man was several years younger than Jesus. But the young man, who according to the ossuary was named Jehohanan, was crucified in the same century as Jesus. And not only was he crucified more or less at the same time, but also at the same place, near Jerusalem, and by the Romans. Therefore we can assume there were many similarities between this man's crucifixion and Christ's.'

'I'd really prefer not to hear all the details.'

'As a method of execution, crucifixion is nothing short of gruesome; it's indescribably brutal. After sentencing, the victim was whipped and weakened. Then using straps or nails his arms were attached to a heavy wooden crossbar which was placed horizontally behind his neck and shoulders. He was forced to carry this beam to the execution site, where the beam would be raised on an upright stake.'

MacMullin rests his hands on his thighs and clenches his fists instinctively.

'What's interesting about Jehohanan is that the lowermost part of his forearms showed signs that a nail had rubbed against the bone,' he says. 'In other words, he wasn't nailed to the cross through his palms, but through his forearms. The palms cannot support the weight of a grown man. Furthermore, Jehohanan's legs were pressed together and twisted to the side so that his knees pointed straight out from the stake. A nail had been driven through both of his heels. Scholars speculate that the cross was equipped with a small plank that Jehohanan could rest his buttocks on. In other words, he was hanging in a very unnatural and contorted way.'

MacMullin takes a sip of sherry. We gaze into the flames in the fireplace.

'Hanging forward by the arms like this made it difficult to breathe,' he continues. 'Devious as they were, the executioners often prolonged the crucifixion victim's suffering by providing a support for him to rest his feet or buttocks on. This way, he was standing more than hanging, if you follow. With a support for his feet, a strong, healthy man could live for a day or two – sometimes close to a week – on the cross.' MacMullin looks at me and swallows. 'It's hard to think of a more inhumane form of execution. The victims did not die from pain or blood loss. They died from exhaustion, from thirst, from strangulation, or blood poisoning.' He massages his cheekbones with his fingertips as he seeks to maintain his composure. 'Sometimes the executioners took pity on the condemned, paradoxically enough by breaking their legs, which was a way of helping them die. Because with their legs broken they weren't able to hold up their bodies and they suffocated. This is what happened to Jehohanan. While he was hanging on the cross, his legs were crushed. For his own good.'

'And Jesus?'

'Jesus' feet were attached to the cross. He had good support for his body. All the same, he was hanging on the cross only for a matter of hours before he expired. There is no medical reason for him to have died so quickly. Nothing in the biblical descriptions suggest that by itself the torture he was subjected to – scourging, the crown of thorns, nails, spears – should have resulted in a rapid death.'

'Why not?' I object. 'Couldn't he simply have been so weakened from the torture that the crucifixion was too much for him?'

'The Romans had a fair amount of experience. Even Pontius Pilate was surprised at how quickly Jesus died. He was so perplexed that he called an officer over to confirm Jesus' death.'

I squirm in my chair. I don't know whether I should let myself get swept along by MacMullin's odd enthusiasm or whether all this is yet another wild-goose chase meant to confuse me and cloud the truth.

MacMullin gets up and walks over to the mantel. He turns and crosses his arms. 'What could Jesus have died from so quickly? Certainly not from being nailed to a cross. Not from the spear wounds in his side, which, according to the scriptures, he suffered after he was dead. The only probable cause of death is, as you suggest, exhaustion from the strain prior to the crucifixion itself. But Jesus was a healthy, robust young man. He had far too much stamina for it to be likely that he would die from exhaustion.'

I say: 'I've always thought of crucifixion as something indescribably gruesome, a quick and painful death.'

MacMullin sighs heavily. 'Gruesome, yes, but not quick, quite the contrary. Crucifixion was a slow and painful way to kill someone.'

He sits back down in his chair again and empties his sherry glass in one quick gulp. 'And another thing: Jesus was given a sponge with vinegar to drink right before he expired. Vinegar? Why would they give him vinegar? Vinegar is a stimulating drink that's meant to keep the victims conscious. Instead of speeding his death, drinking vinegar should have revived him.'

MacMullin rolls his empty glass back and forth between his fingers. 'But now we can begin our mind game, our intellectual experiment.' He's lost in some internal monologue for a few seconds. 'What if,' he says, 'the sponge doesn't contain refreshing vinegar but something completely different? An anaesthetic, narcotic drug, for example, a drug that causes Jesus to faint, to collapse. To everyone observing the crucifixion it would look as if he had suddenly died.'

I try to picture it, but I'm still not sure what to believe.

MacMullin leans back in his chair and regards me with a cautious smile, the corners of his mouth curving ever so slightly. As if he's extremely familiar with what's going through my head right now.

'When you start reading the gospels with a critical eye, the questions start piling up,' he says. 'According to the Bible, the crucifixion took place at Golgotha, which translates as Skull, near a garden . . . a garden with a private burial grotto carved out of a rocky hillside. The garden belonged to Joseph of Arimathea, one of Jesus' disciples. Not just anyone could have his private grave in this garden. He had to be from the upper class. At the same time, crucifixion was a method of execution the Romans reserved for the lower classes. The whole thing is rather nonsensical. The depictions in the Bible suggest that the crucifixion may have been held privately on private land and not at the public execution grounds at all. Even though it was a public event.'

'Why would someone have staged a scam like that?'

'What would you say,' he says quietly, 'to the claim that the crucifixion was an illusion supported by the people in power?'

'What do you mean? That the Romans were in on the scam?'

'Why not? Who was Pontius Pilate if not a corrupt scoundrel? How hard do you think it would have been to bribe him to look the other way over a fake crucifixion? A clever little arrangement that also took care of all his problems with Jesus, that Jewish insurgent.'

I roll my eyes, but he doesn't notice.

'We have to view the circumstances surrounding the crucifixion in the light of a contemporary understanding of Jesus,' MacMullin says. 'Who was he to them? A political insurgent, not a god. Remember, the region was crawling with self-proclaimed prophets back then: preachers, soothsayers, fakirs, fortune tellers, oracles . . . Every other charlatan could perform miracles.'

'So why are we still worshipping him today? Something must have set him apart from the crowd.'

'He had a way with words. Words.'

'And that's all?'

'His words were different. The way he saw humanity was different. He created a new worldview, one based on the value of human life. Jesus was smart, gentle. He didn't threaten his followers into obedience like the prophets of doom in the Old Testament. He introduced the gospel of love. He taught us about kindness, piety, love for thy neighbour. With all due respect, there really wasn't much of any of that back then.'

'But as you said, he wasn't the only prophet.'

'Only a very small group of people believed that Jesus was the Old Testament Messiah. The Jews didn't want him at all. He contradicted the scribes. He attacked ancient Jewish tenets. The image of Jesus as a divinity was created after the fact by the apostles and evangelists – by doctoring the history of Jesus' life and teachings, by tailoring the gospels to their readers and their contemporaries. They left some things out, added other things in. Others embellished and added even more. Why should we trust such old and unreliable copies of copies? There's no written documentation about Jesus from his own lifetime. All we have to hold on to was written down after the fact.'

'You keep going on and on. None of what you're saying confirms that the crucifixion was faked.'

'It wasn't faked!' MacMullin exclaims, leaning toward me. 'Listen to what I'm saying. The crucifixion happened. What I'm explaining to you is that what really happened afterward is completely different to what's described in the Bible.'

'And you're basing this absurd claim on circumstantial evidence?'

MacMullin chuckles. 'Boy, are you stubborn. I love it. I'm not trying to prove what I'm saying. I know the truth. I'm trying to demonstrate to you how some of the paradoxes in the Bible and history start to make sense when you view them with this new understanding.'

'New understanding? What understanding? I don't understand what you're saying at all.'

There's a cheerful twinkle in his eye. 'Let me give you yet another example.'

'Some kind of proof?'

'Circumstantial evidence. After the crucifixion, Pontius Pilate broke all the Roman rules by allowing Joseph of Arimathea to have Jesus' body. In the Greek translation of the Bible, Joseph asks for Christ's *soma* – a living body.

Pilate responds with *ptoma* – a corpse. How would a discrepancy like that occur?'

'You're asking me? Bible translations really aren't my forte.'

'Why would Pilate allow Jesus' dead body to be given to one of his followers at all? Why risk letting them create a martyr out of him? People who were crucified often weren't buried at all. They were usually left there to the forces of nature and the birds. To the Romans Jesus was primarily a troublesome rebel, a rabble-rouser and agitator. They would have preferred him to just go away and for people to forget about him. To them, the claim that he was the Son of God was pretty much just a wacky idea. They didn't really understand why the Jews' Jehovah would sire the Son of Man with a poor young girl who was engaged to a carpenter. The goodwill the Romans showed after Jesus' crucifixion was unheard of at the time – unless Pontius Pilate had been paid off by powerful men.'

'You seem so sure.'

'You've been to the Schimmer Institute yourself. There are other manuscripts, things that have been handed down, secret documents that suggest what might have happened. But in all the known texts, you will find only traces that support the theory.'

MacMullin goes over to the bookshelf and pulls out a red leather-bound Bible.

'Let's look at the Gospel of Mark,' he says, moistening his fingertip and flipping to the right page. 'The Gospel of Mark was the first one written. In the original, oldest manuscripts – the copies – the story ends with Jesus dying and being brought to his grave. When the women come to the grave, it's open and empty. His body is gone. A mysterious man dressed in white – an angel? – tells them that he rose from the dead. The women run away in fear. And, shocked as they are, they don't tell anyone about their experience. According to Mark.

It's a bit of a mystery how he found out about this little incident. But: this was not the kind of happy ending people back then wanted. No one was going to accept a meaningless ending like that. So what did they do? They changed it. They wrote a new ending.'

'Who did?'

'The writers, the other evangelists.'

With frenetic enthusiasm, he flips to Chapter 16 and reads aloud:

Now when the Sabbath was past, Mary Magdalene, Mary *the mother* of James, and Salome bought spices, that they might come and anoint Him.

Very early in the morning, on the first *day* of the week, they came to the tomb when the sun had risen.

And they said among themselves, 'Who will roll away the stone from the door of the tomb for us?'

But when they looked up, they saw that the stone had been rolled away – for it was very large.

And entering the tomb, they saw a young man clothed in a long white robe sitting on the right side; and they were alarmed.

But he said to them, 'Do not be alarmed. You seek Jesus of Nazareth, who was crucified. He is risen! He is not here. See the place where they laid Him.

But go, tell His disciples – and Peter – that He is going before you into Galilee; there you will see Him, as He said to you.'

So they went out quickly and fled from the tomb, for they trembled and were amazed. And they said nothing to anyone, for they were afraid.

MacMullin looks up: 'That's where Mark's gospel ends.'

'But there's more!' I say.

'Yes, there's more, but Mark didn't write it. Mark, the first of the evangelists, the one the other evangelists base their texts on, ends his own version with the mere promise of the risen Jesus. And do you see how naturally the story ends here? But people weren't satisfied with this ending. They wanted an ending that was more tangible and concrete, an ending with panache, an ending full of promise and hope, so someone added the rest. And note the change in style – notice how phoney and cursory the rest of the verses are:

Now when *He* rose early on the first *day* of the week, He appeared first to Mary Magdalene, out of whom He had cast seven demons.
   She went and told those who had been with Him, as they mourned and wept.
   And when they heard that He was alive and had been seen by her, they did not believe.

'And note this,' MacMullin says. 'They didn't believe her when she told them what she'd seen. And there's more:

After that, He appeared in another form to two of them as they walked and went into the country.
   And they went and told it to the rest, *but* they did not believe them either.

'And this is striking,' MacMullin says. 'Because Jesus predicted his own second coming. Those who were closest to him were waiting for him. According to the Bible they were expecting him to come back. So why don't any of his closest followers believe it when it happens? Jesus lives up to all his promises – and none of his followers accepts it? They should have been celebrating. They should have been praising the

Lord. But no, what happens? They don't believe it. They reject it. If you read these verses carefully, you soon see how the whole revelation seems like something that was added later. Why? Well, the manuscripts were tinkered with, amended, improved, just like a film manuscript. The writers and the other evangelists had Jesus rise from the dead, flesh and blood, with his instructions to preach the gospel to the whole world, a much more reader-friendly ending. You would think Hollywood wrote the script.'

MacMullin pulls his finger down to verse 14 and reads:

Later He appeared to the eleven as they sat at the table; and He rebuked their unbelief and hardness of heart, because they did not believe those who had seen Him after He had risen.

And He said to them, 'Go into all the world and preach the gospel to every creature.'

'Do you see how the author is suddenly gripped by enthusiasm?' MacMullin asks. 'How he's trying to bring the narrative to a head, to a rousing literary climax? And then he takes off completely – first with promises and then threats:

'He who believes and is baptized will be saved; but he who does not believe will be condemned.

And these signs will follow those who believe: In My name they will cast out demons; they will speak with new tongues; they will take up serpents; and if they drink anything deadly, it will by no means hurt them; they will lay hands on the sick, and they will recover.'

MacMullin furrows his brow. 'Are we supposed to take this literally? Exorcism? Speaking in tongues? Resistance to any deadly thing? The laying on of hands? Or is this a case of an

370

author filled with passionate faith and enthusiasm who wants to bring a story to a spirited climax? Here's the ending:

> So then, after the Lord had spoken to them, He was received up into heaven, and sat down at the right hand of God.
> And they went out and preached everywhere, the Lord working with *them* and confirming the word through the accompanying signs. Amen.

MacMullin shuts the book.

'Mark's ending was vague, unclear, unfinished. Even after Mark's original ending had been jazzed up by the people who copied and disseminated his writings, it was still anaemic. The other evangelists weren't satisfied with his version at all. *Action!* They have the resurrected Jesus, not some angel, meet the women at the sepulchre. They have Jesus meet his disciples face to face. Which version is right? Which evangelist is telling the truth and which one got it wrong? Then I ask myself: what do the other evangelists know that the first one, Mark, simply wasn't aware of? Why are they so much better informed than Mark was? None of them was there – they're all relying on the same sources. How can they go into so much detail and be so precise in their depictions of Jesus' resurrection and revelation – when the first one to write wasn't at all?'

Maybe MacMullin means that as a question, but I don't even try to respond.

'The gospels,' he says, 'came to be because of the primitive Church's need to confirm its faith in Jesus as the risen lord of the Church. The dogma about Jesus' resurrection was a premise, a necessity. They needed the resurrection as a foundation for their portrayals, because when you get right down to it, without the resurrection they didn't have a religion. The evangelists weren't that concerned with the historical Jesus.

They were portraying the spiritual Jesus. And they believed in him. They were convinced that Jesus' spirit was among them. They never sought to provide a historical or chronological view of Jesus' life. Preaching was their only goal, convincing their readers that Jesus was God's risen son. They compiled their gospels from the primitive Church's numerous traditions. But if you take the resurrection out of the Bible, you're left with a bunch of uncontextual stories about the heroic life of a great humanist.'

He refills both our sherry glasses. We sit there in silence. The minutes go by.

I ask: 'So if everything you're telling me is right, then what really happened?'

He takes several swigs of sherry and makes a smacking sound with his tongue to appreciate each little nuance. Slowly and with concentration – as if he's lifting a weight just with his mind – his eyes move from the flames in the fireplace over to me.

'It's not easy to give you an explanation that will immediately seem credible,' he says, setting down his glass.

I nod slowly.

'When one version has been hammered into us for two thousand years,' he says, 'it's quite difficult to accept a totally different version. People simply aren't open to believing a new version.'

'You've already told me the most important thing: Jesus survived the crucifixion.'

It's only now that I notice how tired MacMullin looks – old and tired. It's as if this conversation has sapped his strength. His skin is sallow and clammy, his eyes dull.

'I'm sure there are those who would call this a conspiracy,' he says. His words are slow, meditative. 'Others would call it a stroke of genius. No matter how you look at it, it must be one of the biggest frauds in the history of the world.'

'But what happened to Jesus?'

His face undergoes a transformation. It's as if he's telling me about something he witnessed himself, but he's having trouble remembering it because it happened so long ago.

He says: 'What happened?' He sits there in silence for a long time before continuing: 'Unconscious, Jesus was lifted down from the cross and wrapped in the shroud that would later become so famous and contentious. Yes, it was his imprint on the Shroud of Turin, a chemical process, nothing more nor less. His apparently lifeless body was brought to the sepulchre. Only his innermost circle was with him, the ones who knew he wasn't dead. To everyone else – the spectators, the soldiers – he had obviously left us.'

'And then?'

'No one knows the particulars of what happened next. We have only the veiled references in ancient, hermetic texts to go on. But at some point or other, when it was considered safe, and probably under the cover of darkness, Jesus was removed from the shroud, which was left in the sepulchre. He was brought to a secret hiding place. We assume that he must have spent several weeks in hiding, while the women tended his wounds and cared for him and generally made sure to spread the story about the angel and the empty sepulchre.'

'Which the evangelists kept on doing more than forty years later,' I fill in.

MacMullin watches me with an inscrutable expression on his face.

'Keep going,' I pester.

'We don't know that much about this specific time. But we can certainly assume that he slowly regained his strength. I picture him behind a curtain in a rich man's home. Surrounded and tended to by those who were most loyal to him. And when he was finally healthy and ready . . . then he escaped from the Holy Land.'

'Escaped?' I blurt out. A connection that had been hidden until now is starting to dawn on me.

'His time was up. He didn't have any choice, aside from death. He fled from a superior force along with those who were closest to him. He left Jerusalem in disguise along with Mary Magdalene, Joseph of Arimathea and a group of his most loyal and devoted followers. Not even all the apostles knew about his escape. They were fed a cover story: the resurrection, the official story. And as you know quite well, they bought the story. It became a historical fact. And a religion.'

'What happened to Jesus?'

'He went away.'

'Where to?'

'Somewhere where he could live safely.'

'I read something about how he supposedly went to Kashmir and founded a congregation there?'

'The Kashmir legend is a cleverly constructed lie.'

'So what did happen?'

'Jesus and his group travelled west, by land, to the coast, where there was a ship waiting. From there they travelled to a safe hiding place.'

'Where?'

He looks at me in surprise. 'You haven't figured it out yet?'

'Figured what out? Where did they go?'

'They came here,' MacMullin says. 'Rennes-le-Château was Jesus' final hiding place.'

13

Sometimes you have to look to the natural world to see yourself: to the bumblebees who break the rules of aerodynamics, to foxes that gnaw off their own paws to escape a trap, to the fish who merge with the coral to avoid being devoured. In the plant kingdom, I've always been partial to *Argyroxiphium sandwicense*. I'm sure you remember the plant I told my teacher I wanted to be like? The Haleakala Silversword. Year after year it grows, unpretentious and humble, not really doing much. It reminds me of me.

It slowly grows until it's a half-metre-high ball covered with glistening silver hairs. And then the ball shoots up a two-metre-high stalk.

After twenty years, it suddenly blooms with a bloom so extravagant that it is quickly followed by the plant's demise.

You just have to admire that kind of tenacious patience.

14

MacMullin comes and gets me at the crack of dawn. I open my eyes in the middle of a dream and in the viscous light it seems as if he's hovering over me like a ghost tethered to the earth.

I'm trying to wake up. I'm trying to understand what he wants and whether he's a part of the dream that is still holding me in its thrall.

'What is it?' I mutter. The words slosh around in my skull like some insistent, rasping echo.

He seems unsure of himself for the first time. He rubs his fist in the palm of his left hand. 'Bjørn,' he says, as if there's something he'd rather not tell me.

I sit up, trying to shake off the sleep. The room expands in all directions. I'm seeing two MacMullins. My head drops back on to the pillow.

'They called,' he says.

I squeeze my eyes shut and then open them wide, squeeze

them shut and open them wide. This probably makes me look a little odd, but I'm just trying to wake up.

'Who called?' I ask.

'It's Grethe.'

'Did she . . .'

'No, not yet. But she asked for you.'

'When can we go?'

'Now.'

15

The private jet is waiting at the airport in Toulouse. MacMullin's white limousine moves through the barriers and security checkpoints and glides to a stop by the Gulfstream. We're in the air twenty minutes later.

'Soon we'll be at the end of the road,' he says.

I'm sitting in a deep armchair by a large, oval window with a view opening right on to the sky. The incredible interplay between aerodynamics and engineering has lifted us to a height of seven thousand feet. Below us the ground is a patch-work of watercolour nuances and shadows.

There's a tabletop mounted in the fuselage between MacMullin and myself. There's a bowl of red and green apples in the middle of the table. MacMullin catches my attention. 'I suppose this isn't so easy for you to wrap your mind around,' he says.

'No,' I respond ambiguously, because I don't know whether he's referring to everything he told me or to Grethe, 'it's not so easy.'

The two Rolls-Royce jet engines on the Gulfstream create a steady drone of background noise. I spot a cloudbank in the distance that reminds me of white paint pouring into water.

MacMullin pares an apple for himself. He peels off the red

skin in one long spiral with a little fruit knife. He quarters the apple and slices out the bit of core. 'Would you like some?' he asks, but I shake my head.

'When you get right down to it,' he says, putting a piece of apple into his mouth, 'a lot of things in life are based on illusions. We just don't know it. Or we don't want to admit it.'

Once again he's making it hard for me to give him any kind of concrete response. I don't understand what he means. 'This is all a bit much for me . . .' I mumble.

He sits there chewing and nods. 'I'm not expecting you to believe me,' he says.

At first I don't respond. Then I say: 'Maybe that's why I do.'

He puts another piece of apple into his mouth. The bitter juices in the fruit make him scrunch up his face. 'Believing is a choice,' he says. 'Whether it's believing something someone tells you or believing the Word.'

'It's hard to know what to believe,' I say evasively.

'Doubt and scepticism are inherently valuable, because they show that you're *thinking*.'

'Maybe. I still don't know what to think about everything you told me yesterday.'

'Nor would I expect you to.'

'These things you're asking me to accept aren't exactly trivial.'

'You don't need to accept anything at all, Bjørn. As far as I'm concerned, you can dismiss everything I've said. As long as you give me the shrine,' he adds with a quiet laugh.

'You're discounting the entire Bible,' I say.

'Ah, but what is the Bible, actually? A collection of old texts about a *zeitgeist*: instructions, rules to live by, ethics, handwritten traditions, interpretations and dreams, embellished and edited, tales that have been passed on orally and eventually collected between two covers and stamped *approved* by the clergy.' He munches on the last of the apple wedges and moistens his lips with the tip of his tongue.

'And your version?' I ask. 'How does your version of the story end?'

'It's not mine. I'm just passing it on.'

'You know what I mean.'

'There isn't much that we can prove with certainty,' he says. 'Not after so much time has passed. Only a few things have been passed down, murky snippets, scraps of information.'

'Hm, like my life over the last couple of weeks.'

MacMullin chuckles quietly and rocks ever so slightly in his chair, as if he's not seated comfortably.

'Do you actually know what happened after the crucifixion?' I ask.

'We know quite a bit – far from enough, of course, but we know a bit.'

'Such as that Jesus went to Rennes-le-Château?'

'We know a lot about his escape. Basically because we are in possession of manuscripts from two people who travelled with him. They describe their escape from the Holy Land and the journey to Rennes-le-Château.'

'And?'

'After Jesus had regained enough of his strength following the crucifixion, he escaped in a ship that was waiting, along with a group of his close followers. They went to Alexandria first, in Egypt. From there they travelled north to Cyprus, west to Rhodes, Crete and Malta, and finally north again to "Vieux Port", the old harbour in Marseilles. From there they travelled south-west along the inland road and established themselves in Rennes-le-Château.'

'That's hard to believe.'

MacMullin purses his lips and glances out of the window of the plane. There's a drone from the engines. Then he flings out his arms with a self-confident expression. 'But when you

378

come right down to it – is the Bible version really that much more credible?'

I ponder that question for a moment.

'You're really convinced that this is true,' I say.

He eyes me. For a long time.

'How old was he when he died?' I ask.

'We don't know that. But he had several children with the woman he married, Mary Magdalene.'

'Jesus got married? And had kids?'

'Why wouldn't he?'

'It just sounds . . . I don't know.'

'They had seven children. Four sons and three daughters.'

A flight attendant, who had been standing in the little galley at the back preparing the food, serves us breakfast on warmed plates. She smiles at me. I smile back. MacMullin gazes down at the food and smacks his lips in satisfaction. We slice our rolls in half, pour orange juice into narrow glasses with ice cubes, and open the small glass jars of home-made marmalade.

MacMullin takes a bite of his roll and dabs the corner of his mouth with a napkin bearing his monogram.

'Jesus' children guarded the secret of their origin,' he says. 'His sons and grandsons, not Jesus himself, laid the foundations for what a thousand years later would become the orders of knighthood, the Freemasonry movements and hermetic societies, small conspiratorial organisations whose purpose was to protect a secret they kept so well they no longer even know what it is.' He shakes his head in wonder. 'There are hundreds of them: sects, clubs, movements, lodges, every single one of them hinting at the margins of the truth. Hundreds of books have been written. Poets have elaborated on the pseudo-scholarship and myths. There are dedicated chat rooms on the Internet and home pages devoted to speculations and guesswork. But none of them is seeing the big picture. None of them has understood things right. They're like flies who don't realise they're bumping into a pane of glass.'

'Or bumblebees,' I say quickly, but of course that doesn't mean anything to MacMullin.

I grip my cold glass. The orange juice is freshly squeezed and refreshing. 'What ended up happening to Jesus' descendants?' I ask. I'm sucking and chewing on an ice cube, which rattles and squeaks between my teeth.

'That's a question that can't really be answered.'

'Why not?'

'Because nothing really happened to them. They lived their lives. They had children and their descendants are still living among us, a proud and powerful family, right here in our midst.'

'Do they themselves know who they are?'

'Almost none of them. Very few of them know the actual truth. Fewer than a thousand. And now you as well.'

'His descendants are still alive,' I say, enthralled, lost in thought.

'Well, yes, sure. Of course. But two thousand years have elapsed. You mustn't forget that this bloodline, too, has been watered down. We are talking about a lot of generations, after all. Jesus' oldest son was the first Grand Master. He was the one who procured the gold shrine and sealed it. When the first Grand Master died, his eldest son assumed responsibility for the shrine. And thus the Shrine of Sacred Secrets was handed down from father to firstborn son through the centuries. Until the shrine disappeared.'

'But what about all the hints that Jesus was the progenitor of all the royal families in Europe?'

'As with so many things, that's an exaggeration. But there is a pinch of truth to it. After a few centuries, Jesus' descendants married into the Merovingian dynasty, and became part of the clan of tribal leaders who ruled the Frankish kingdom until the year 751. But with the exception of a few royals and the chain of Grand Masters and their very innermost circles, almost no one was aware of the big picture, of the secret. And by that I mean almost no one knew about Jesus' escape or his descendants. And eventually this too became a myth, something that even those who were in on the secret weren't really sure if they should believe.'

I finish my roll and drink the rest of my juice. This is getting to be a little much for me.

'And,' I ask, 'what is in the shrine?'

MacMullin looks as if he would like nothing more than for me to withdraw the question.

So I ask it again: 'What is in the shrine?'

'We think,' he hesitates, 'we think there are two things in it.'

He folds his hands on the table. He swallows. He does not want to reveal the secret. Silence is a reflex for his central nervous system. He's never revealed the truth to an outsider. He bristles against it, but he realises he has no choice. I'm a tough nut.

He gives me a beseeching look. 'For the last time, Bjørn . . . will you give me the shrine?'

'Sure.'

My response catches him off guard. 'Really?'

'When you tell me what's inside it.'

I sense the last, tenacious remains of his ability to resist crumbling within him.

He squeezes his eyes shut. 'Directions,' he says. 'Probably a map.'

'A map?'

'Directions showing the way to Jesus' grave, probably a sepulchre where he was laid to rest, his earthly grave. But even more important . . .'

He opens his eyes, but doesn't look at me.

I wait in silence.

He looks past me. 'The gospel of Jesus,' he says. 'The story Jesus himself wrote about his own life, his work, his faith and his doubts. And the years following the crucifixion.'

MacMullin turns to look out of the window at the sky, the ground beneath us, the soft light, the clouds.

With a series of short, quick breaths he releases all the little demons that are playing havoc within him at the moment.

I give him the time he needs.

After a while he turns to me, his eyes empty.

'That's it,' he says.

'A manuscript,' I say. 'A manuscript and a map.'

'That's what we think.'

We sit there in silence for a while.

'It sounds like some kind of Jewish conspiracy,' I say.

'You seem preoccupied with conspiracies.'

'What if you're the head of some Jewish network that aims to prove to the world once and for all that Jesus wasn't the Son of God.'

'Anything's possible.'

'If the manuscript proves that Jesus never died on the cross, and that he was also never resurrected, it will cause the world's religious order to collapse.'

'Quite right. But I'm not Jewish.'

'On the other hand, if you're Christian, it would be in your own interests to destroy the evidence that reveals that Christianity is based on a lie.'

'Another keen analysis. But I don't have any hidden reason to believe that the world wouldn't benefit from knowing the truth. I'm being quite open with you. It's best for everyone that we keep this secret. The alternatives are far too frightening. No one, absolutely no one, will benefit from learning the truth. We have no right to tear up history.

No good will come of that. We'll destroy millions of lives. Take away the beliefs of nations. It's not worth it. Nothing is worth that.'

'A manuscript written by Jesus . . .' I say quietly. 'Directions to his earthly grave . . .'

'That's what we think is in it.'

'You *think*?'

'We can never be one hundred per cent sure, not until we've opened the shrine and looked for ourselves. But regardless of what's in the shrine, we know that the first Grand Master – Jesus' eldest son – sealed it and guarded it until he left it to his firstborn, the next Grand Master, and on down the line. Every single one of them dedicated his life to guarding the shrine. Until it disappeared and was out of our hands, at Værne Monastery in 1204.' Then he adds: 'Yes, and then into your hands, of course. Eight hundred years later.'

'And the shrine has never been opened?'

'Of course not.'

'So what will happen to it now?'

'I will personally bring it to the Schimmer Institute.'

'That doesn't surprise me. Perhaps Peter is one of the people waiting for it?'

'Peter, of course! David, Uri, Moshe . . . And several dozen of the world's leading scholars, recruited by SIS. Historians, archaeologists, theologians, linguists, philologists, palaeographers, philosophers, chemists.'

'You've invited all your pals, I see.'

'We built a special wing that is ready to receive the shrine. We can't risk humidity or dry air, cold or heat causing the manuscript to disintegrate. Our scientists have developed a method that will ever so slowly acclimatise the two-thousand-year-old atmosphere inside the shrine to the air in our laboratory. It's estimated that it will take months just to open the shrine.'

'When you look at it that way, I guess it's a good thing that I didn't open it in my office.'

MacMullin shudders.

'Once we've finally opened the shrine,' he says, 'we need to carefully remove the contents, page by page. The papyrus may have disintegrated, requiring the pages to be glued together, bit by bit, like a puzzle. We will need to photograph the fragments and preserve them. We don't know what condition we'll find them in. But the same way you can interpret the writing on a flake of ash, we will be able to decipher the letters. The work will be painstaking, first from a technical perspective, then a linguistic one. We will have to interpret the handwriting, then translate it, understand it based on a context. If it's a long manuscript, the work will take years. Many years. If we find a map or directions to Jesus' grave, Professor Llyleworth is ready to rush off with his team of archaeologists. Everything is arranged. All we need is the shrine.'

My eyes can't seem to settle on anything to look at.

'So,' he sighs, 'now it's all up to you.'

'It has been the whole time.'

'I realise that.' He looks out of the window again. We're heading into a bank of clouds. 'Bjørn.' He turns to me. 'Please, will you give me the shrine?'

The look he's giving me feels as if it weighs several tons. I look at him. I get who he is. I don't know how long I've known, but I no longer have any doubt.

Something inside me relaxes. Even a maximally stubborn person has to give in eventually. I think back on the experiences of the last week, the lies, the wild-goose chases, the people who have tricked me, quite a long list of them. Everything is falling into place. I have to accept MacMullin's explanation, because I trust him and because I no longer have any choice.

'Of course,' I say.

He shakes his head, as if he can't quite grasp what he's hearing.

'You'll get the shrine,' I confirm.

'Thank you.'

He's quiet. Then again he says, 'Thank you, thank you very much.'

'I have a question.'

'That doesn't surprise me.'

'Why did you tell me all this?'

'Did I have any choice?'

'You could have made up some lie that I would have believed.'

'I tried that, several times, but it didn't work. You're a sceptical son of a bitch.' He says the last part with a grin.

'What if I tell somebody the whole thing?'

His expression is thoughtful. 'Of course, that is a possibility.'

'I could go to the press.'

'Yes.'

'I could write a book.'

He looks as if he's biting his tongue.

'Of course you could,' he says. Then, after a brief silence, he adds, impishly: 'But would anyone believe you?'

Circle's End

1

She looks as if she's dead. Her little sparrow's head is resting on a big pillow. The skin clings to her skull. Her mouth is half open, her lips dry and colourless. There's a green oxygen tube sticking out of one of her nostrils, attached to her cheek with white adhesive tape. Her skinny arms, flecked with blue, are crossed on top of the blanket. Fluid is moving into a vein in her forearm from an IV bag on a pole.

They gave her her own room. They meant well, but I remember she once told me that her biggest fear was dying alone.

The room is overflowing with warm light. I get a chair from over by the sink. The metal legs scrape against the floor.

Cautiously, I take her hand in mine. It's like lifting a luke-warm leather sack full of knuckles. I stroke her skin and fold her limp fingers in my own.

Sounds: her voice, the ticking of an electronic device, the revving of a car engine down on the street, a sigh from her lips.

On the wall over the door there's a clock that's five minutes behind. The second hand struggles in jerky motions to keep up with the ticking. Something in its inner workings is about to break.

There's a bouquet on the bedside table in a shiny hospital vase. The card is hanging half open. The note was written with a fountain pen, the penmanship rather formal:

Peaceful journey, Grethe.
Eternally yours,
MMM

MacMullin gave me a morsel of truth, nothing more. A morsel of truth. Maybe I don't know anything. I don't know which explanation to believe. I don't even know whether I should believe any of them. But I do know this: when I hand the shrine over to MacMullin, the shrine and its contents will be gone for ever. If they've kept their secret for two thousand years, they can certainly keep it under wraps for two thousand more. Værne Monastery is never going to be an international tourist attraction. The fields will never be turned into overcrowded car parks, American tourists will never stand impatiently in line to peer down at the exposed octagon through bullet-proof plexiglas windows, or study copies – translated into six languages – of the manuscript in the shrine. Because people will never know about this.

It will be as if this never happened.

Her eyelids flutter. She opens her eyes a little. Something about them seems heavy, misty, rooted in a dreamless darkness. She slowly recognises me.

'Little Bjørn,' she whispers.

'Grethe . . .'

Her eyes try to focus, to establish an image of a reality that she is no longer a part of.

'You look terrible!' she mumbles.

At first I don't respond. Then I realise what she means.

'Oh, it's just sunburn,' I explain.

The light in her eyes seems to fade away. Then, suddenly eager, she asks: 'Did you find anything out?'

'Yes,' I say.

And then I tell her the whole story.

When I'm done she doesn't say anything. She just nods to herself. As if nothing surprises her.

'So that's how it was,' she says eventually.

The silence around us is full of sounds.

'How is he?' she asks suddenly.

'Who?'

'Michael. How is he?'

'He's fine. He came to Oslo with me, but he didn't want to . . . intrude.'

'He's with me. In his own way.'

'I'll tell him you said as much.'

'Always in his own way,' she continues, looking up at the flowers.

'There's something else,' I say.

'Yes?'

'You and MacMullin . . .' I prompt, urging her to say it.

'Yes,' she whispers. It's as if she's dulling the pain by speaking softly. 'MacMullin and I. In Oxford.' Her eyes look at me with tenderness. 'He's such a handsome man, like you, such a handsome man.'

I glance over at the clock, following the second hand's arduous struggle against the inner workings.

'How did my father die, Grethe?'

She closes her eyes. 'It was so meaningless.'

'But how?'

'He was jealous, of your mother and Trygve.'

'So he knew about that? Him, too?'

'He never got over watching your mother fall in love with Trygve.'

'I can understand that.'

'But it was so silly. It didn't need to mean anything, not in the long run. She would have come back to him. But he couldn't handle watching his wife give herself to someone else.'

'But what happened?'

'It's none of my business. Or yours.'

'But you know?'

She sighs.

'Please, Grethe. What happened?'

'Don't pester me with this now, Little Bjørn.'

'Please.'

'Ask your stepfather, Little Bjørn. He knows.'

'Did he kill my father?'

'No.'

'Does my mother know what happened?'

'No.'

'But how . . .'

'No more questions.'

'Why won't you tell me this?'

'Because it's best this way.'

'Best?'

'For you.'

'How is this best?'

Her eyes are dull, lifeless. 'You don't want to know.'

'Please?'

She twiddles her fingers on top of the covers, a frail, fragile motion.

'Trust me. You don't want to know.'

'I do.'

'Oh, all right, all right.' She sighs.

She waits for a while before proceeding. 'I suppose you're

aware of everything that was going on between your mother and Trygve . . .'

I look down, as if I'm ashamed of my mother, which I am. 'I knew about it even back then,' I say.

'They cared about each other.'

'Strange how everyone cares about everyone else.'

'That's what happens.'

'And then my dad was in the way.'

'As is always the case when two people find each other when one of them already belongs to someone else.'

'And so they killed him?'

I'm surprised at how blasé I'm able to make this question sound.

She glances over at me.

I persist: 'Were they both in on it? Was it just the professor, or was my mother in on it, too?'

She clenches her teeth. 'No,' she says so softly that she's practically whispering, 'it wasn't like that.'

'Then who did it?'

'No one killed your father.'

'But . . .'

'Could you just calm down about that? None of them killed Birger.'

'So it was an accident?'

'No.'

'I don't understand.'

'Think about it, Little Bjørn.'

I think, but it doesn't help.

Then a membrane within her breaks. A tear runs down her cheek.

'Trygve was the one who was supposed to die that day, not Birger.'

'What?'

'Now do you get it?' she asks. Her voice is irritable.

'Trygve was supposed to die.'

I'm trying to collect my thoughts, trying to understand what's floating just beneath the surface.

'Do you understand what I'm saying?'

I raise my shoulders. 'No . . .' I say.

'Birger was the one who did something to the abseil anchor, so that Trygve would fall.'

She turns away, not ready to look me in the eye, as if the whole thing were her fault.

'Trygve was the one who was supposed to die that day,' she says again, tersely, coldly. 'Right before you guys left, Birger told me that he was planning to . . .' She pauses. '. . . do something to the abseil anchor. I don't know what. So that it would . . . But I never thought he would really . . . I certainly never thought . . . never, never in a million years.' She turns towards me, searching for my hand with her own. 'Your father was trying to kill Trygve. And then something went wrong.'

We sit there holding hands for a long time. I have no words, just isolated images: the dull grey rock, the rope coiled up at the base of the cliff, my mother's shrieks, the heap of clothes at the bottom of the cliff face, the blood, the tree trunk against my back, the bark scraping the back of my neck as I collapsed.

I wonder whether my mother and the professor have known this for all these years.

Grethe dozes off. I go out into the corridor and flop down on a chair just outside her door. My thoughts are all tangled up.

On the wall across from me, between two doors, I count fifteen tiles up and a hundred and forty across. Twenty-one hundred grey tiles. Someone has amassed a little herbarium of jumbled flower stalks on a wheeled aluminium trolley.

I go back in to see Grethe again a little later. Her eyes have slid shut again. She's resting peacefully.

'Grethe?'

Invisible threads tug at her eyelids. They fight their way open. 'I'm a tough old bird,' she says.

'You had a child.'

She looks at me with her eyes half closed. The look in them undergoes a sudden transformation.

'I met her,' I say.

Grethe stares at the ceiling.

'She's doing well. Diane. A lovely young woman,' I say.

Her smile comes from deep within. 'The most beautiful little girl in the world.' Her voice is so frail, so weak. Her smile loses its strength. She sighs deeply. 'I wasn't the mother she needed.' A low moan slips out through her lips. 'I didn't have it in me. Michael . . . it was different for him. I thought it was best like that, for her to stay . . . with him. For her never to find out . . . about me.'

She coughs painfully. She wants to say something. I shush her. Her lips move. She tells me something without using her voice.

'I'll stay with you,' I say softly.

'So tired,' she whispers.

I stroke her hand. She whimpers and looks at me. She tries to say something, but her body doesn't cooperate. She keeps coughing, but even her coughing lacks strength. Her breathing is shallow and laboured.

She tries to push herself up on to her elbows, but flops back down.

'Rest,' I whisper, stroking her forehead. It's cold and sweaty.

An hour passes . . .

*

I hold her hand. She drifts in and out of sleep. Every once in a while she looks up at me.

Hesitantly I set her hand back on the covers and go down to the cafeteria, where I eat a sandwich that was wrapped in cellophane and tastes like it. When I come back, Grethe's hand is exactly where I left it. I pick it up and give it a squeeze. I feel her trying to squeeze back.

We sit like this for a long time. Gradually her breathing becomes so quiet that I can't hear it. The sounds from the hallway filter in to where we are: quiet footsteps, subdued laughter, a child whining. One nurse calls to another.

Grethe's hand is limp in mine. I squeeze it. She's not up to squeezing back. We could have sat like this for hours. If it hadn't been for the machine. Some wires sticking up out of her hospital pyjamas are connected to a monitor with buttons and windows and glowing numbers. The machine starts beeping. At the same time, a strip of paper with two lines of curving ink ticks out of the machine. A shudder runs through Grethe. She opens her eyes wide and gasps.

I stroke her hand.

A nurse comes in, then a doctor.

I release her hand. It falls down on to the covers. As I stand up, I step backwards, knocking the chair over. It hits the floor with a clatter. I take a step to the side to let the doctor in.

First he turns off the machine. The beeping fades away. The silence is deafening. He presses his fingertips against her throat and nods to the nurse. He gently unbuttons her hospital pyjamas and presses the stethoscope to her chest.

'Aren't you going to do something?' I ask.

'It's best this way,' the doctor says.

The nurse gently rubs my upper arm. 'Are you her son?'

The doctor closes Grethe's eyes.

Outside, through the window, I see a man balancing on some scaffolding.

'Sort of,' I say.

No one says anything.

'She's in a better place now,' the nurse says, and gives my arm a little squeeze.

I look at Grethe.

'Would you like to be alone with her?' the nurse asks.

'Alone?'

'Before we prepare her and wheel her down?'

'Uh, I don't know . . .'

'If you'd like a little time to yourselves . . .'

'That won't be necessary.'

'We can just step out for a few minutes.'

'That's nice of you, but there's no need.'

'Just say the word.'

'Thank you, that's very kind, but it's really not necessary.'

They leave anyway to let me be alone with her.

I try to find harmony, warmth, a peaceful calm in her face, but she just looks dead.

I leave the room without looking back. As I leave the hospital, a gentle, drizzly rain begins.

2

We sit outside the fence of plastic orange netting, staring out of Bolla's windscreen. The rain trickles and drips. The tents have all been put away. Most of the equipment is still there, locked away in the shipping container. The wind sweeps over the field, whipping veils of rain with it. The strips of plastic tied to the tops of the marker stakes are fluttering like pennant flags. The wind has blown my director's chair over against the bird cherry bush. No one bothered to put it away in the container.

I picture the excavation site full of activity, the professor standing under the sheet, Moshe and Ian circling around the excavation pit like bloodthirsty mosquitoes.

When Professor Llyleworth disappeared, the work stopped. Now I'm sure everyone is wondering what will happen before the bulldozer pushes the piles of topsoil back into the pits.

I turn to Michael MacMullin. 'She asked for you,' I say.

He looks straight ahead. He's touched, his eyes are misty.

'It was so long ago,' he says. His words aren't meant for me. 'Another life, another time. It will be my turn soon. Maybe I'll see her again.'

His face is old, like parchment, but filled with a boyish gleam, an impatient eagerness. He looks younger than ever, as if his awareness of how close he is to his objective has made some inner light bulb turn on and shine through that thin layer of skin.

Something inside me trembles.

'Who are you?' I ask.

At first he is quiet. Then he says: 'You must have some idea, since you ask.'

The silence vibrates between us.

He rubs his palms together. 'You're not a stupid boy.'

Incredulous, I say: 'I know who you are. I've figured it out.'

'You have?'

'You're not just a member of the Council, are you?' I say.

He laughs stiffly.

I don't take my eyes off him. He straightens out his fingers. His nails are manicured. On his left hand, for the first time, I see a signet ring with an enormous opal.

I whistle quietly to myself. '*You're* the Grand Master,' I say.

He opens his mouth to say something. His cheeks flush.

'I am? Bjørn, you must understand. There are only twelve people in the whole world who know the identity of the Grand Master. Twelve people.'

'And you're the Grand Master!'

'You know that I can't answer that question,' he says.

'It wasn't a question.'

'Anyway . . .'

'Holy cow.' I chuckle. 'You're the Grand Master.'

'Can we go and get the shrine now?' he asks.

I need a moment to collect myself. It's unbelievable. I scrutinise him, for a long time – the esoteric features, his warm, gentle eyes.

'That's what Diane meant,' I say quietly. 'She's your only child.'

He looks at me.

'Shall we go and get the shrine?' he asks again.

'We don't need to go anywhere.'

He gives me a puzzled look.

'It's here.'

Confused: 'Here?' He gazes out into the rain.

'Would you like to see the octagon?'

'The shrine is here?'

'Follow me.'

We step out of the car, into the rain. I slip through a gap in the plastic orange fencing labelled DO NOT ENTER and hold it open for MacMullin. The motion causes a cascade of water droplets to drip off the plastic.

I stop next to the pit. MacMullin looks down at the octagonal foundation wall.

He simply says, 'The octagon.' An air of reverence has come over him.

The rain has washed the soil away from the ends of the rocks that are protruding from the muddy dirt.

'The octagon,' I repeat.

He's impatient: 'Can we go and get the shrine now?'

I hop down into the pit, squat down and start digging.

Only then does he work it out.

He starts to laugh, at first softly, then loudly, resound-ingly.

And while he laughs, as his laughter rolls and tumbles over the trenches and patchwork grid, through the rain showers, I dig the shrine out of my hiding place, exactly the same place where we had found it, the last place they would look.

The dirt squelches as I pull the bag containing the shrine out of the mud that surrounds it. I cautiously turn and hand the shrine to Michael MacMullin. The smell of dirt and rain around us is pungent and timeless.

3

I weave my gossamer of memories with a shaky hand.

Outside the window in the garden at my grandmother's house the leaves cling to the branches of the oak, as if they don't realise that autumn will be coming for them soon.

That evening a long time ago when I told Grethe that I was in love with her and she rejected me so tenderly and kindly that for a long time after that I felt as if she was hiding her deeper feelings for me, I slunk home through Oslo in a drizzle, from her flat in Frogner to my little student place in Grünerløkken. I was soaked. I still remember what she said when I left. She sat with me, holding my hand in hers and stroking it tenderly, like a mother wanting to comfort her son.

Nothing ever ends, she said, it just continues in a different way.

*

The men in the red Range Rover left along with MacMullin. They were standing there waiting when I parked Bolla in front of my grandmother's place. They're probably never far away.

Before he left, MacMullin squeezed my hand and told me I'd done the right thing.

That was the last time I saw him.

Once the Range Rover had driven up the country road and its red tail-lights had disappeared behind the foliage, I let myself in and walked up the creaking stairs to my childhood room.

Of course they had been in here.

Like invisible spirits, they searched the house from basement to attic, without leaving a trace. They removed Diane's things a long time ago, but they weren't infallible. Her four silk ropes are still dangling limply from the bedposts. Maybe they thought they were mine. And drew their own conclusions.

4

I push my desk over to the window and pull out my journal. The raindrops wind and trickle their way down the steamy windowpane. Through the threads of water the fjord looks like a quiet river – glistening and cold behind the leafless branches of the bushes.

My skin glows and tingles.

I think. I write. The words dissolve into nothingness – words about events that sort of never happened and people who never lived, fleeting, ephemeral, like words in a book you read long ago and then forgot once it was back on the bookshelf.

5

And that's how the story ended, or it could have ended that way. But when you come right down to it, nothing ever ends. Everything just continues in another way. Where does a circle begin or end?

After MacMullin took the shrine away with him into the silence, I stayed at the country house to, well, for lack of a better explanation, collect my thoughts. In the days that followed, I waited for an ending that never came. Every night I hoped that someone would come and knock on the door – Diane, MacMullin, Llyleworth, Peter ... or that someone would call. But nothing happened.

After a week I shut off the water, gave up on my expectations and went home to Oslo.

Slowly and obediently I returned to my old existence.

Every morning I strolled over to the Storo stop to catch the tram downtown. In my office I fulfilled my professional responsibilities with a lethargic, indifferent sense of duty. Every once in a while someone would ask me what had really happened the previous summer at Værne Monastery, but I brushed them aside with world-weary explanations.

Some evenings, when the darkness of a Norwegian winter became too oppressive, Diane would appear before me as a whisper of tastes and scents and longing. Occasionally I would pick up the phone and dial all but the last digit of her phone number. As I grew bolder, I would let it ring a couple times before hanging up. One Saturday morning I even waited until she picked up. I just wanted to wish her a happy new year. But it wasn't Diane. She was probably tied up, probably to the bedposts. I hung up before the sleep-slurred man managed to ask who I was or what I wanted.

Some time in January I lost touch with reality. I don't

remember exactly when or how it happened, but I didn't show up for work several days in a row. The professor and my mother found me sitting in a chair in the living room in my flat. An ambulance took me to the clinic. It was like coming home. At the clinic you don't have to pretend, don't have to act as if the sun is shining and that everything will be better tomorrow. As if there isn't a vast, treacherous, dull-blue mountain rising into the mist between you and the sun-filled valley where you could have lived like a cheerful hobbit in a grove of trees by the babbling brook. In the clinic you can throw yourself into the stormy sea and let yourself sink. And stay down there for as long as you want. In the diving bell of your life. After months of waiting and brooding, I was convinced that they'd tricked me. I found gaps in their explanations, flaws in their logic, glaring holes in their answers. I imagined that I had been the victim of a meticulously planned and well-choreographed hoax and that I'd played the part of the gullible, self-righteous inspector with such aplomb that my name had already been engraved on to the base of an Oscar. *Thank you, thank you . . . First of all I'd like to thank my mother and father . . .* I could picture them all laughing at me. Even when I pressed my hands to my ears and rocked back and forth, I heard their piercing, hysterical laughter. *Time machines!* Llyleworth and Arntzen would bellow in unison. *Flying saucers!* sobbed Anthony Lucas Winthrop, Jr. *Biblical manuscripts!* hooted Peter Levi. *Jesus conspiracies!* laughed MacMullin. *Merovingian treasure!* snorted Diane and my mother. And then they would slap their thighs and fall over backwards, laughing. One time, fuming with rage, I called SIS and demanded to talk to MacMullin. Of course he wasn't in. '*MacWho?*' In vain I tried to track down his phone number in Rennes-le-Château, where no one seemed to have heard of him. I called the Schimmer Institute several times, but never managed to fight my way past the switchboard's intricate maze of polite deflection.

Gradually my anger and indignation faded away. Fine, they tricked me, so what. Big deal. At least I'd given them a heck of a fight. When you got right down to it, it's not as if it was going to make any big difference to the well-being of humanity if, after eight hundred years in the dirt, the shrine wound up in the hands of scoundrels instead of a sterile glass display case in a sleepy museum on Frederik Street. It was thanks to MacMullin that it had turned up in the first place. Without him the earth would have hidden it for another eight hundred years. He deserved the secret in the shrine. Even if it's the elixir of immortality.

They declared me healthy and sent me home from the clinic in May. My mother came and picked me up in her Mercedes and saw me all the way up to the tenth floor.

In late June I headed back down to the country house by the water, this time on holiday. I passed Værne Monastery on my way down. Everything had been cleaned up. The farmer had levelled out our dirt piles and planted more grain. Only the pit around the octagon was cordoned off with plastic orange netting. The cultural heritage officials are still contemplating what they're going to do with the historic site.

When I unlocked the door to the summer house, it was as if the scent of Diane's perfume struck me. I stood there bewitched, my hand on the doorknob. I half expected to hear her voice saying, '*Hi, honey, you're late,*' accompanied by a wet kiss on the cheek. But when I closed my eyes and sniffed, it just smelled stuffy and dusty.

I quietly moseyed from room to room, opening the curtains, brushing dead flies off the windowsills and opening the windows a little. I struggled for a while to turn the water on again after the winter.

Then I let the fact that I was on holiday sink through me,

heavy and sluggish and warm. Sunny days and sultry nights alternated in a harmonious tedium.

I'm sitting out in the sun on the patio in khaki shorts and sandals. The radio is rattling off the temperature of various swimming sites. They're all quite warm. Bolærne Island looks as if it's hovering in the haze in the distance. Straight across the fjord, the towns of Horten and Åsgårdstrand form messy dots on the strip of blue coastline. I feel a profound peace. I had got myself a cold beer and opened it with a screwdriver. A few teenagers are hooting and hollering from the diving board mounted down on the smooth slabs of rock that form the shore. A girl shrieks as she falls into the water. A boy dives after her. I lazily wave away a wasp that's showing a little too much interest in my pilsner. Two terns are ducking and bobbing into the wind.

On impulse I drag myself out of my chair and go down to the garden gate to check the mailbox. Tucked in between some junk mail and a faded flier from the village of Fuglevik, I find a large manila envelope. I don't even want to know how long it's been in there. There's no return address on the envelope, but it was postmarked in France.

Like a sleepwalker, I bring the envelope up to my childhood room. I clip the little string with a pair of nail scissors and dump the contents out on to my desk:

A short letter, a newspaper clipping and a photograph.

The letter is handwritten. The handwriting is gnarled, ornate:

Rennes-le-Château, 14 July

Dear Mr B. Beltø,

You don't know me, but my name is Marcel Avignon and I'm a retired country doctor here in Rennes-le-

405

Château. I'm writing to you now at the urging of a mutual friend, Michael MacMullin, who provided me with your name and summer address. It pains me to tell you that Grandseigneur MacMullin died last night. He passed away following a brief and, fortunately, pain-free illness. He passed away at 4.30 this morning. Along with his beloved daughter, Diane, who had spent the night at his bedside, I was with him during his final hours. One of the last things he did was to instruct me regarding what I should write to you and what I should enclose. Furthermore he said that you (and now I'm forced to quote as best I can given my failing memory), 'as the tough nut he is, will do exactly what he so pleases with the information'. For my own part, I must permit myself to add that he said these words with such affection that it was clear to me that you were a most cherished friend. It is therefore a great honour and pleasure for me to perform the small service that Mr MacMullin asked of me, namely to send you a newspaper clipping and a photograph. He believed you would understand how they fit together. I hope you do, because to be truthful, I can't help you. Finally, let me offer my condolences, as I know the loss of your friend will pain you as it has me. If I can be of any further assistance, please do not hesitate to contact me.

    Sincerely,
    M. Avignon

The photograph is in black and white, showing fragments of an ancient manuscript on a white matte glass surface that's lit from below. A hand wearing a latex glove is gently brushing away invisible dust.

It's a chaotic arrangement of papyrus flakes, a puzzle waiting to be assembled.

The letters are unintelligible. The handwriting is consistent, straight.

There's a moist tingle in my eyes.

A manuscript . . .

Even though I can't read the alphabet or extract any meaning whatsoever from the foreign letters, I sit there studying them. I don't know for how long, but when I snap out of it – winded, bent over my desk with my journal open next to the picture and the newspaper clipping – it's almost eleven.

The clipping is from a newspaper called *La Dépêche du Midi* from Toulouse:

Priests protest restoration of Lelieu Church

BÉZIERS. The Béziers police took local demonstrators including two priests into custody yesterday for illegally demonstrating outside Lelieu Church, also known to locals as the Repos-du-Christ.

The disued church 1 km west of Béziers sold last month for 3 million euros to an undisclosed London-based firm that is now having the site archaeologically excavated. *La Dépêche du Midi* has obtained information suggesting that Béziers officials approved the eyebrow-raising purchase under pressure from the French government. Jean Bovary, one of the two priests arrested yesterday, who also chairs the board of trustees of the recently formed Preserve Lelieu Trust, repeatedly shouted 'Desecration!' during his arrest.

Graham Llyleworth, a well-known professor of archaeology heading up the excavation of the site, says the secret buyer has 'a genuine desire to restore the church to its former splendour'. Critics have vehemently protested about the project, which will necessitate dismantling and rebuilding the church structure stone by stone.

Critics also contend that the way the archaeologists working on the site have handled the controversy has not allayed fears. The excavation team have erected a 3m-high fence around the site, they are using night-time floodlights, and they have hired their own security guards to patrol the area and keep curious onlookers at a distance. Llyleworth commented generally that 'any archaeological project must be cordoned off from the public to some degree'.

According to local legend, Lelieu Church was built over a mountain cave where an unknown saint is alleg-edly buried. Speaking after his release on bail, Bovary said the church is one of the oldest in the Pyrenees and probably in France.

'The Romanesque parts of the church as it stands today were completed in 1198,' Bovary said. 'However, we can date late-classical parts of the church structure to AD 350, specifically the section we refer to as the East Wing as well as the yard where ruins of old foun-dations are visible. According to local tradition there was an early Christian sanctuary on the site even before that.'

Bovary fears archaeologists will try to excavate all the way down to the sepulchre that legend says is sealed in the rock below the altar. 'Let the dead rest in peace!' he says.

Llyleworth denies that his team are searching for any purported sepulchral monument. 'We have no knowledge of a tomb or other sepulchre under the church,' he says. 'If there should turn out to be one, we would of course respect the dignity of any saint interred here.'

I stare thoughtfully at the letter, the newspaper clipping and the photograph of the papyrus manuscript. I think about Diane and Grethe, about Michael MacMullin, about the desert monastery, about what's hidden under the church at Béziers.

I gaze out of the window and embers of curiosity and anticipation flare up within me. There are mysteries out there somewhere, questions.

In the living room below, the inner workings in the old grandfather clock rattle. The clock ticks and runs, but never tells the right time. It lives on its own time and is content with that. It suddenly begins cheerfully chiming away. It's 11.13: *ding dong!*

Something inside me starts tingling, a stubborn urge, to know, to understand.

My pen scrapes against the paper – a tapestry of words and memories – but there's always room for more. Nothing ever ends. I shut my journal impatiently. The story isn't over. I just need to find out what happens next.

Acknowledgements

No book is created without other books.

Værne Monastery, the ancient Johannite residence – with its archaeological riddles and its mysticism – can be found in Norway to this day if you drive through Moss and continue south towards Fuglevik. I found the information about Værne Monastery and the Johannites' more-than-three-hundred-year-long stay in Norway in the books *Gårder og slekter i Rygge* [Farms, Estates and Genealogies of Rygge Municipality] by Ingeborg Flood (Rygge Sparebank, 1957) and *Bygdehistorien i Rygge* [History of the Village of Rygge] until 1800 by Lauritz Opstad and Erling Johansen (Rygge Sparebank, 1957), among other sources.

If you are captivated by the mysteries about Bérenger Saunière and Rennes-le-Château, I refer you to *The Holy Blood and the Holy Grail* (1982) by Michael Baigent, Richard Leigh and Henry Lincoln. Although I've drawn on many of their contentious hypotheses, I've only scratched the surface of their tangle of religious conspiracy theories.

For more thorough analyses of the historical versus the religious figure of Jesus, I recommend Jacob Jervell's thin but informative book *Den historiske Jesus og Mannen som ble Messias* [The Historical Jesus and the Man Who Became the Messiah] by Karl Olav Sandnes and Oskar Skarsaune.

Thanks to Tom Koch of WBGH public broadcasting. I am indebted to their documentary *From Jesus to Christ*.

The Q manuscript exists as a hypothesis. Scholars at the Institute for Antiquity and Christianity in California have reconstructed the Q manuscript – word by word, verse by verse.

The Gospel of Thomas was translated into Norwegian after the first Norwegian edition of this novel was released.

Like the characters that gambol through the pages of this book, SIS and the Schimmer Institute exist only in my and your imagination.

I would like to thank all the patient experts and institutions that helped me by providing information, opinions, suggestions and corrections: the University of Oslo, the Royal Norwegian Office of Cultural Heritage, the British Museum and CERN (the European particle physics lab). I want to thank my editor at Aschehoug, Øyvind Pharo, and Knut Lindh, Olav Njaastad, Ida Dypvik and, as always, Åse Myhrvold Egeland for having read the manuscript and providing invaluable contributions. Thanks to Jon Gangdal, Sebjørg J. Halvorsen and Anne Weider Aasen. In addition to giving *Sirkelens ende* [Circle's End] a very nice public review in the midst of all the fuss about the *Da Vinci Code*, Bjørn Are Davidsen assisted me by being a thrilling creative sparring partner for my theological interpretations. Thanks to journalist Kaja Korsvold at *Aftenposten*, who pulled *Sirkelens ende* out of the dusty bookshelves. Thanks to my agent, Johan Almqvist at Aschehoug Agency, and to Øyvind Hagen at Bazar, who both contributed to launching the book internationally. And to Øyvind Pharo, Even Råkil, Alexander Opsal and the others at my Norwegian publishing house, Aschehoug, who brought a forgotten three-year-old book back for a new life with fresh enthusiasm.

None of the books or experts I used as sources or consultants is responsible for the flights of fancy and countless poetic liberties I took.

My most profound thanks to Åse, Jorunn, Vegard and Astrid . . . for the time.

Tom Egeland

Bibliography

Anyone wishing to delve into the theological-historical questions in the novel – and questions tied to the Da Vinci Code – has a fount of books to choose from. You can find them at your local bookshop or from an online bookshop. Here is a small selection:

Mannen som ble Messias [The Man who Became the Messiah] (Karl Olav Sandnes and Oskar Skarsaune), Norsk Kristelig Studieråd/NRK/IKO

Apokryfe evangelier [Apocryphal Gospels] (ed.: Halvor Moxnes and Einar Thomassen), Verdens hellige tekster [Holy Texts of the World], De norske bokklubbene [Norwegian Book Clubs]

Jesus. Bibelens fire evangelier [Jesus. The Bible's Four Gospels] (ed.: Jacob Jervell), Verdens hellige tekster [Holy Texts of the World], De norske bokklubbene [Norwegian Book Clubs]

Gnostiske skrifter [Gnostic Writings] (ed.: Ingvild Sælid Gilhus and Einar Thomassen), Verdens hellige tekster [Holy Texts of the World], De norske bokklubbene [Norwegian Book Clubs]

Den historiske Jesus [The Historical Jesus] (Jacob Jervell), Land og kirke

Thomasevangeliet [The Gospel of Thomas] (Svein Woje and Kari Klepp), Borglund forlag

Jesus døde ikke på korset. Urevangeliet Q. [Jesus Didn't Die on the Cross. Q, the Original Gospel] (Svein Woje and Kari Klepp), Borglund forlag

Da Vinci-koden. [The Da Vinci Code] (Dan Brown), Bazar forlag

The Da Vinci Hoax (Carl Olson and Sandra Miesel), Ignatius Press

The Holy Blood and the Holy Grail (Michael Baigent, Richard Leigh and Henry Lincoln), Dell (will be released soon in Norwegian, Bazar forlag)

The Dead Sea Scrolls Deception (Baigent/Leigh), Simon & Schuster

The Messianic Legacy (Baigent/Leigh/Lincoln), Dell

Hidden Gospels (Philip Jenkins), Oxford University Press

Jesus and the Victory of God: Christian Origins and the Question of God (N. T. Wright), Augsburg Fortress Publishers

The Contemporary Quest for Jesus (N. T. Wright), Augsburg Fortress Publishers

From Jesus to Christ: The Origins of the New Testament Images of Jesus (Paula Fredriksen), Yale University Press

Marginal Jew: Rethinking the Historical Jesus (Joseph Meier), Anchor Bible

The Templar Revelation (Lynn Picknett and Clive Prince), Touchstone

The Trial of the Templars (Malcom Barber), Cambridge University Press

Several websites that shed light on the topics in the novel:

www.bibelen.no

www.katolsk.no

Gospel of Thomas: www.thomasevangeliet.no

Gospel of Thomas: http://dromsmia.no/tomas.htm

Claremont Graduate University: www.cgu.edu

School of Religion at CGU: http://religion.cgu.edu

Ancient Biblical Manuscript Centre: www.abmc.org

Claremont School of Theology: www.cst.edu

Society of Biblical Literature: www.sbl-site.org

American Schools of Oriental Research: www.asor.org

The Oriental Institute of the University of Chicago: www.oi.uchicago.edu

ArchNet, WWW Virtual Library: http://archnet.asu.edu/archnet

Duke Papyrus Archive: http://scriptorium.lib.duke.edu/papyrus

Journal of Religion and Society: www.creighton.edu/JRS

Crisler Biblical Institute: www.crislerinstitute.com

Jesus Studies: www.jesusstudies.net

About Matthew, Mark and Luke: http://www.mindspring.com/~scarlson/synopt/faq.htm